He Shall Thunder in the Sky

Elizabeth Peters

HE SHALL THUNDER IN THE SKY

AN AMELIA PEABODY MYSTERY

Thorndike Press • Chivers Press
Thorndike, Maine USA   Bath, England

This Large Print edition is published by Thorndike Press, USA and by Chivers Press, England.

Published in the U.S. by arrangement with William Morrow, an imprint of HarperCollins Publishers, Inc.

Published in the U.K. by arrangement with the author.

U.S. Hardcover 0-7862-2827-X (Thorndike Basic Edition)
U.S. Softcover 0-7862-2828-8
U.K. Hardcover 0-7540-1498-3 (Windsor Large Print)

The text of this Large Print edition is unabridged.
Other aspects of the book may vary from the original edition.

Set in 16 pt. Plantin by Warren Doersam.

Printed in the United States on permanent paper.

British Library Cataloguing-in-Publication Data available.

Library of Congress Cataloging-in-Publication Data:

Peters, Elizabeth.
    He shall thunder in the sky : an Amelia Peabody mystery / Elizabeth Peters.
        p. cm.
    ISBN: 0-7862-2827-X (lg. print : hc : alk. paper)
    ISBN: 0-7862-2828-8 (lg. print : sc : alk. paper)
    1. Peabody, Amelia (Fictitious character) — Fiction.
2. Women archaeologists — Fiction. 3. Egyptologists — Fiction. 4. Egypt — Fiction. 5. Large type books. I. Title.
PS3563.E747 H38 2000b
    813'.54—dc21
                                          00-056819

To my daughter, Beth, with love

Then Re-Harakhte said:
Let Set be given unto me, to dwell with me and be my son. He shall thunder in the sky and be feared.

— Chester Beatty Papyrus
The Judging of Horus and Set

Editor's Foreword

The Editor is pleased to present the result of many months of arduous endeavor. Sorting through the motley collection that constitutes the Emerson Papers was no easy task. As before, the Editor has used the contemporary diary of Mrs. Emerson as the primary narrative, inserting letters and selections from Manuscript H at the appropriate points, and eliminating passages from the latter source that added no new information or insights to Mrs. Emerson's account. It was a demanding project and the Editor, wearied by her labors and emotionally wrung out, trusts that it will be received with the proper appreciation.

Information concerning the Middle East theater in World War I before Gallipoli is sparse. Military historians have been concerned, primarily and understandably, with the ghastly campaigns on the Western Front. Being only too familiar with Mrs. Emerson's prejudices and selective memory, the Editor was surprised to discover, after painstaking research, that her account agrees in all important particulars with the known facts. Facts hitherto unknown add, the Editor believes, a new and startling chapter to the history of the Great War. She sees no reason to suppress them now, since they explain, among other things, the curtailment of archaeological activity on the part of the Emersons during those years. As the Reader will discover, they had other things on their minds.

Acknowledgments

To George W. Johnson, who graciously supplied me with hard-to-find information about
World War I weaponry, uniforms and other
military details. If I put the wrong bullet in
the wrong gun, it is my own fault. And as always to Kristen, my invaluable and
long-suffering assistant, who, in addition to
innumerable other contributions, listens to
me complain and encourages me to perse-
vere.

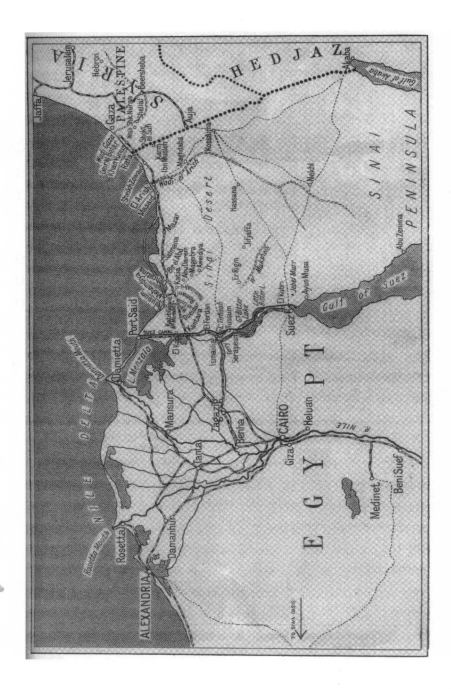

Prologue

The wind flung the snow against the windows of the coach, where it stuck in icy curtains. The boy's breath formed pale clouds in the darkness of the interior. No foot warmer or lap robe had been supplied, and his threadbare, outgrown overcoat was not much protection against the cold. He felt sorry for the horses, slipping and laboring through the drifts. He'd have pitied the coachman, too, perched on the open box, if the man hadn't been such a sneering swine. One of her creatures, like the other servants, as hard-hearted and selfish as their mistress. The chilly night was no colder than the welcome he anticipated. If his father hadn't died . . . A lot of things had changed in the past six months.

The coach jolted to a stop. He opened the window and looked out. Through the swirls of snow he saw the lighted panes of the lodge. Old Jenkins was in no hurry to open the gates. He wouldn't dare delay too long, though, or she would hear of it. Finally the door of the lodge opened and a man shambled out. It wasn't Jenkins. She must have dismissed him, as she had often threatened to do. The lodge keeper and the coachman exchanged

11

insults as the former unbarred the gates and pushed them open, straining against the weight of the snow. The coachman cracked his whip, and the tired horses started to move.

The boy was about to close the window when he saw them, shapes of moving darkness that gradually took on human form. One was that of a woman, her face hidden by a bonnet, her long skirts dragging. She leaned heavily on her companion. He was not much taller than she, but he moved with a man's strength, supporting her swaying form. As the coach approached, without slackening speed or changing direction, he pulled her out of its path, and the carriage lamps illumined his face. It would have been hard to tell his age; snow blurred the pale features that were twisted into a demonic grimace. His eyes met those of the staring occupant of the coach; then he pursed his lips and spat.

"Wait!" The boy put his head out the window, blinking snowflakes off his lashes. "Confound it, Thomas — stop! You — come back. . . ."

The vehicle lurched, throwing him to the floor. Raging, he scrambled up and thumped on the closed aperture. Either Thomas did not hear him or — more likely — he ignored the shouted orders. A few minutes later the vehicle stopped in front of the house. He jumped out and ran up the steps, breathless with anger and haste. The door was locked. He had to swing the heavy knocker several times before it opened. The butler's face was unfamiliar. So she'd got rid of poor old William too. He had been with the family for fifty years. . . .

The entrance hall was semicircular, in the classical style — marble columns and marble floor, shell-shaped niches in the curved walls. While his father lived, the alabaster urns in the niches had been filled with holly and pine branches at this season. Now they were empty, the pure white of walls and floor unrelieved. In the door to the drawing room his mother stood waiting.

She wore her widow's weeds well. Black suited her fair hair and ice-blue eyes. The soft, lightless fabric fell in graceful folds to her feet. Unmoving, her hands clasped at her waist, she looked at him with unconcealed distaste.

"Take off your wet things at once," she said sharply. "You are covered with snow. How did you get —"

For once he dared interrupt. "Tell Thomas he must follow my orders! He refused to stop and let me speak with them — a woman, and a boy with her . . ." His breath caught. The change in her expression was slight, but like all young, hunted animals, he had learned to recognize the movements of the enemy. "But — you know, don't you? They were here.

13

You saw them."

She inclined her head.

"And you sent them away — on such a night? She was very frail — ill, perhaps —"

"She always had a tendency toward consumption."

He stared at her. "You know her?"

"She was my dearest friend, close as a sister. Until she became your father's mistress."

The words were as brutal and calculated as a blow. The color drained from the boy's face.

"I would have spared you that shame," she went on, watching him.

"Shame?" He found his voice. "You speak to me of shame, after driving her away into the storm? She must have been desperate, or she would not have come to you."

"Yes." A thin smile curved her lips. "He had been sending them money. It stopped when he died, of course. I don't know where he got it."

"Nor do I." He tried to emulate her calm, but could not. He was only fourteen, and their temperaments were as different as ice and fire. "You kept a close hand on the purse strings."

"He squandered my dowry within a year. The rest, thanks to my father's foresight, was mine."

He ran to the door, flung it open, and rushed out. The butler, who had been watching, coughed. "Your ladyship wishes . . . ?"

"Send two of the footmen after him. They are to take him to his room and lock him in, and bring the key to me."

1

I found it lying on the floor of the corridor that led to our sleeping chambers. I was standing there, holding it between my fingertips, when Ramses came out of his room. When he saw what I had in my hand his heavy dark eyebrows lifted, but he waited for me to speak first.

"Another white feather," I said. "Yours, I presume?"

"Yes, thank you." He plucked it from my fingers. "It must have fallen from my pocket when I took out my handkerchief. I will put it with the others."

Except for his impeccably accented English and a certain indefinable air about his bearing (I always say no one slouches quite as elegantly as an Englishman), an observer might have taken my son for one of the Egyptians among whom he had spent most of his life. He had the same wavy black hair and thick lashes, the same bronzed skin. In other ways he bore a strong resemblance to his father, who had emerged from our room in time to hear the foregoing exchange. Like Ramses, he had changed to his working costume of wrinkled flannels and collarless shirt, and as they stood side by side they looked more like elder and younger brother than father and son. Emerson's tall, broad-shouldered frame was as trim as that of Ramses, and the streak of white hair at each temple emphasized the gleam of his raven locks.

At the moment the resemblance between them was obscured by the difference in their expressions. Emerson's sapphire-blue orbs blazed; his son's black eyes were half-veiled by lowered lids. Emerson's brows were drawn together, Ramses's were raised; Ramses's lips were tightly compressed, while Emerson's had drawn back to display his large square teeth.

"Curse it," he shouted. "Who had the confounded audacity to accuse you of cowardice? I hope you punched him on the jaw!"

"I could hardly have done that, since the kind donor was a lady," Ramses replied, tucking the white feather carefully into his shirt pocket.

"Who?" I demanded.

"What does it matter? It is not the first I have received, nor will it be the last."

Since the outbreak of war in August, a good many fowl had been denuded of their plumage by patriotic ladies who presented these symbols of cowardice to young men not in uniform. Patriotism is not a quality I despise, but in my humble opinion it is despicable to shame someone into facing dangers from which one is exempt by reason of gender, age, or physical disability. Two of my nephews and the sons of many of our friends were on their way to France. I would not have held them back, but neither would I have had it on my conscience that I had urged them to go.

I had not been obliged to face that painful choice with my son.

We had sailed for Egypt in October, since my dear Emerson (the greatest Egyptologist of this or any other age) would not have allowed anyone, much less the Kaiser, to interfere with his annual excavations. It was not a retreat from peril; in fact, we might soon be in greater danger than those who remained in England. That the Ottoman Empire would eventually enter the war on the side of Germany and Austria-Hungary no one of intelligence doubted. For years the Kaiser had courted the Sultan, lending him vast amounts of money and building railroads and bridges through Syria and Palestine. Even the German-financed archaeological expeditions in the area were believed to have an ulterior motive. Archaeology offers excellent cover for spying and subversion, and moralists were fond of pointing out that the flag of imperial Germany flew over the site of Megiddo, the biblical Armageddon.

Turkey's entry into the war came on November 5, and it was followed by the formal annexation of Egypt by Britain; the Veiled Protectorate had become a protectorate in reality. The Turks controlled Palestine, and between Palestine and Egypt lay the Sinai and the Suez Canal, Britain's lifeline to the east. The capture of the Canal would deal Britain a mortal blow. An invasion of Egypt would surely follow, for the Ottoman Empire had never forgiven or forgotten the loss of its former province. And to the west of Egypt the warlike Senussi tribesmen, armed and trained by Turkey, presented a growing threat to British-occupied Egypt.

By December Cairo was under martial law, the press censored, public assemblages (of Egyptians) forbidden, the Khedive deposed in favor of his more compliant uncle, the nascent nationalist movement suppressed and its leaders sent into exile or prison. These regrettable measures were justified, at least in the eyes of those who enforced them, by the increasing probability of an attack on the Canal. I could understand why nerves in Cairo were somewhat strained, but that was no excuse, in my opinion, for rude behavior to my son.

"It is not fair," I exclaimed. "I have not seen the young English officials in Cairo rushing off to volunteer. Why has public opinion concentrated on you?"

Ramses shrugged. His foster sister had

once compared his countenance to that of a pharaonic statue because of the regularity of his features and their habitual impassivity. At this moment they looked even stonier than usual.

"I have been rather too prone to express in public what I feel about this senseless, wasteful war. It's probably because I was not properly brought up," he added seriously. "You never taught me that the young should defer to their elders."

"I tried," I assured him.

Emerson fingered the dimple (or cleft, as he prefers to call it) in his chin, as was his habit when deep in thought or somewhat perturbed. "I understand your reluctance to shoot at poor fellows whose only crime is that they have been conscripted by their leaders; but — er — is it true that you refused to join the staff of the new Military Intelligence Department?"

"Ah," said Ramses thoughtfully. "So that bit of information is now public property? No wonder so many charming ladies have recently added to my collection of feathers. Yes, sir, I did refuse. Would you like me to justify my decision?"

"No," Emerson muttered.

"Mother?"

"Er — no, it is not necessary."

"I am greatly obliged to you," said Ramses. "There are still several hours of daylight left, and I want to get out to the site. Are you coming, sir?"

"Go ahead," Emerson said. "I'll wait for your mother."

"And you?" Ramses looked down at the large brindled feline who had followed him out of his room.

Like all our cats, Seshat had been named after an Egyptian divinity, in this case (appropriately enough) the patroness of writing; like most of them, she bore a strong resemblance to her ancestress Bastet and to the tawny, large-eared animals portrayed in ancient Egyptian paintings. With a few exceptions, our cats were inclined to concentrate their affections on a single individual. Seshat favored Ramses, and kept a close eye on his comings and goings. On this occasion she sat down in a decided manner and stared back at him.

"Very well," Ramses said. "I will see you later, then."

He might have been addressing me or the cat, or both. I stepped aside, and he proceeded on his way.

Emerson followed me to our room, and kicked the door shut. After attending a luncheon party at Shepheard's we had returned to the house to change, but while my husband and son proceeded with this activity I was delayed by a tedious and unnecessary discussion with the cook, who was going through another of his periodic crises des nerves. (At least that is what he would have called it had he been a French chef instead of a turbaned Egyptian.)

I turned round and Emerson began unbuttoning my frock. I have never taken a maid with me to Egypt; they are more trouble than they are worth, always complaining and falling ill and requiring my medical attention. My ordinary working costume is as comfortable and easy to assume as that of a man, which it rather resembles, for I long ago gave up skirts in favor of trousers and stout boots. The only occasions on which I require assistance are those for which I assume traditional female garb, and Emerson is always more than happy to oblige me.

Neither of us spoke until he had completed the task. I could tell by his movements that he was not in a proper state of mind for the sort of distraction that frequently followed this activity. After hanging the garment neatly on a hook, I said, "Very well, Emerson, out with it. What is the trouble?"

"How can you ask? This damned war has ruined everything. Do you remember the old days? Abdullah supervising the excavations as only he could do, the children working happily and obediently under our direction, Walter and Evelyn joining us every few years . . . Abdullah is gone now, and my brother and his wife are in England, and two of their sons are in France, and our children are . . . Well, hmph. It will never be the same again."

"Things" never are the same. Time passes; death takes the worthy and unworthy alike, and (on a less morbid note), children grow up. (I did not say this to Emerson, since he was in no fit state of mind for philosophical reflection.) Two of the children to whom Emerson referred, though not related to us by blood, had become as dear to us as our own. Their backgrounds were, to say the least, unusual. David, now a fully qualified artist and Egyptologist, was the grandson of our dear departed reis Abdullah. A few years earlier he had espoused Emerson's niece Lia, thereby scandalizing the snobs who considered Egyptians a lower breed. Even now Lia awaited the birth of their first child, but its father was not with her in England or with us; because of his involvement with the movement for Egyptian independence, he had been interned in India, where he would have to remain until the war was over. His absence was keenly felt by us all, especially by Ramses, whose confidant and closest friend he had been, but — I reminded myself — at least he was out of harm's way, and we had not given up hope of winning his release.

Our foster daughter Nefret had an even stranger history. The orphaned daughter of an intrepid but foolhardy English explorer, she had passed the first thirteen years of her life in a remote oasis in the western desert. The beliefs and customs of ancient Egypt had lingered in that isolated spot, where Nefret had been High Priestess of Isis. Not surprisingly, she had had some difficulty adjusting to the customs of the modern world after we brought her back to England with us. She had succeeded — for the most part — since she was as intelligent as she was beautiful, and, I believe I may say, as devoted to us as we were to her. She was also a very wealthy young woman, having inherited a large fortune from her paternal grandfather. From the beginning she and David and Ramses had been comrades and co-conspirators in every variety of mischief. David's marriage had only strengthened the bonds, for Lia and Nefret were as close as sisters.

It was Nefret's sudden, ill-advised marriage that had destroyed all happiness. The tragedy that ended that marriage had brought on a complete breakdown from which she had only recently recovered.

She *had* recovered, though; she had completed her interrupted medical studies and was with us again. Look for the silver lining, I told myself, and attempted to persuade Emerson to do the same.

"Now, Emerson, you are exaggerating," I exclaimed. "I miss Abdullah as much as you do, but the war had nothing to do with that, and Selim is performing splendidly as reis. As for the children, they were constantly in trouble or in danger, and it is a wonder my hair did not turn snow-white from worrying about them."

"True," Emerson admitted. "If you are fishing for compliments, my dear, I will admit you bore up under the strain as few women could. Not a wrinkle, not a touch of gray in that jetty-black hair . . ." He moved toward me, and for a moment I thought affection would triumph over morbidity; but then his expression changed, and he said thoughtfully, "I have been meaning to ask you about that. I understand there is a certain coloring material —"

"Don't let us get off the subject, Emerson." Glancing at my dressing table, I made certain the little bottle was not in sight before I went on. "Look on the bright side! David is safe, and he will join us again after . . . afterwards. And we have Nefret back, thank heaven."

"She isn't the same," Emerson groaned. "What is wrong with the girl?"

"She is not a girl, she is a full-grown woman," I replied. "And it was you, as her legal guardian, who insisted she had the right to control her fortune and make her own decisions."

"Guardian be damned," said Emerson gruffly. "I am her father, Amelia — not legally, perhaps, but in every way that matters."

I went to him and put my arms around him. "She loves you dearly, Emerson."

"Then why can't she call me . . . She never has, you know."

"You are determined to be miserable, aren't you?"

"Certainly not," Emerson growled. "Ramses is not himself either. You women don't understand these things. It isn't pleasant for a fellow to be accused of cowardice."

"No one who knows Ramses could possibly believe that of him," I retorted. "You aren't suggesting, I hope, that he enlist in order to prove his critics wrong? That is just the sort of thing men do, but he has better sense, and I thought you —"

"Don't be absurd," Emerson shouted. My dear Emerson is never more handsome than when he is in one of his little tempers. His blue eyes blazed with sapphirine fire, his lean brown cheeks were becomingly flushed, and his quickened breathing produced a distracting play of muscle across his broad chest. I gazed admiringly upon him; and after a moment his stiff pose relaxed and a sheepish smile curved his well-shaped lips.

"Trying to stir me up, were you, my dear? Well, you succeeded. You know as well as I do that not even a moronic military officer would waste Ramses's talents in the trenches. He looks like an Egyptian, he talks Arabic like an Egyptian — curse it, he even thinks like one! He speaks half a dozen languages, including German and Turkish, with native fluency, he is skilled at the art of disguise, he knows the Middle East as few men do . . ."

"Yes," I said with a sigh. "He is a perfect candidate for military intelligence. Why wouldn't he accept Newcombe's offer?"

"You should have asked him."

"I didn't dare. The nickname you gave him all those years ago has proved to be appropriate. I doubt if the family of Ramses the Great would have had the audacity to question him, either."

"I certainly didn't," Emerson admitted. "But I have certain doubts about the new Department myself. Newcombe and Lawrence and Leonard Woolley were the ones who carried out that survey of the Sinai a few years ago; it was an open secret that their purpose was military as well as archaeological. The maps they are making will certainly be useful, but what the Department really wants is to stir up an Arab revolt against the Turks in Palestine. One school of thought believes that we can best defend the Canal by attacking the Turkish supply lines, with the assistance of Arab guerrillas."

"How do you know that?"

Emerson's eyes shifted. "Would you like me to lace your boots, Amelia?"

"No, thank you, I would like you to answer my question. Curse it, Emerson, I saw you deep in conversation with General Maxwell at the luncheon; if he asked you to be a spy —"

"No, he did not!" Emerson shouted.

I realized that quite inadvertently I must have hit a tender spot. Despite the reverberant voice that had (together with his command of invective) won him the admiring appellation of Father of Curses, he had a certain hangdog look. I took his hand in mine. "What is it, my dear?"

Emerson's broad shoulders slumped. "He asked me to take the post of Adviser on Native Affairs."

He gave the word "native" a particularly sardonic inflection. Knowing how he despised the condescension of British officials toward their Egyptian subjects, I did not comment on this, but pressed on toward a firmer understanding of his malaise.

"That is very flattering, my dear."

"Flattering be damned! He thinks I am only fit to sit in an office and give advice to pompous young fools who won't listen to it anyhow. He thinks I am too old to take an active part in this war."

"Oh, my dear, that is not true!" I threw my arms around his waist and kissed him on the chin. I had to stand on tiptoe to reach that part of his anatomy; Emerson is over six feet tall and I am considerably shorter. "You are the strongest, bravest, cleverest —"

"Don't overdo it, Peabody," said Emerson.

His use of my maiden name, which had become a term of affection and approbation, assured me that he was in a better humor. A little flattery never hurts, especially when, as in the present case, it was the simple truth.

I laid my head against his shoulder. "You may think me selfish and cowardly, Emerson, but I would rather you were safe in some boring office, not taking desperate chances as you would prefer, and as, of course, you could. Did you accept?"

"Well, damn it, I had to, didn't I? It will interfere with my excavations . . . but one must do what one can, eh?"

"Yes, my darling."

Emerson gave me such a hearty squeeze, my ribs creaked. "I am going to work now. Are you coming?"

"No, I think not. I will wait for Nefret and perhaps have a little chat with her."

Emerson departed, and after assuming a comfortable garment I went up to the roof, where I had arranged tables and chairs, potted plants and adjustable screens, to create an informal open-air parlor.

From the rooftop one could see (on a clear day) for miles in all directions: on the east, the river and the sprawling suburbs of Cairo, framed by the pale limestone of the Mokattam Hills; to the west, beyond the cultivated land, the limitless stretch of the desert, and, at eventide, a sky ablaze with ever-changing but always brilliant sunsets. My favorite view was southerly. In the near distance rose the triangular silhouettes of the pyramids of Giza, where we would be working that year. The house was conveniently located on the West Bank, only a few miles from our excavations and directly across the river from Cairo. It was not as commodious or well designed as our earlier abode near Giza, but that house was not one to which any of us cared to return. It held too many unhappy memories. I tried, as is my habit, to keep them at bay, but Emerson's gloomy remarks had affected me more than I had admitted to him. The war had certainly cast a shadow over our lives, but some of our troubles went farther back — back to that frightful spring two years ago.

Only two years. It seemed longer; or rather, it seemed as if a dark, deep abyss separated us from the halcyon days that had preceded the disaster. Admittedly, they had not been devoid of the criminal distractions that frequently interrupt our archaeological work, but we had become accustomed to that sort of thing and in every other way we had good cause to rejoice. David and Lia had just been married; Ramses was with us again after some months of absence; and Nefret divided her time between the excavation and the clinic she had started for the fallen women of

Cairo. There had been a radiance about her that year. . . .

Then it had happened, as sudden and unexpected as a bolt of lightning from a clear sky. Emerson and I had come home one morning to find the old man waiting, a woman and a small child with him. The woman, herself pitiably young, was a prostitute, the old man one of the city's most infamous procurers. The sight of that child's face, with its unmistakable resemblance to my own, was shock enough; a greater shock followed, when the little creature ran toward Ramses, holding out her arms and calling him Father.

The effect on Nefret had been much worse. In the clinic she had seen firsthand the abuses inflicted on the women of the Red Blind district, and her attempts to assist the unhappy female victims of the loathsome trade had taken on the dimensions of a crusade. Always hot-tempered and impetuous, she had leaped to the inevitable conclusion and fled the house in a passion of revulsion with her foster brother.

I knew, of course, that the inevitable conclusion was incorrect. Not that Ramses had never strayed from the paths of moral rectitude. He had toddled into trouble as soon as he could walk, and the catalog of his misdemeanors lengthened as he matured. I did not doubt his relationships with various female persons were not always of the nature I would approve. The evidence against him was strong. But I had known my son for over twenty strenuous years, and I knew he was incapable of committing that particular crime — for crime it was, in the moral if not the legal sense.

It had not taken us long to ferret out the identity of the child's real father — my nephew Percy. I had never had a high opinion of my brothers and their offspring; this discovery, and Percy's contemptible attempt to pass the blame on to Ramses, had resulted in a complete rift. Unfortunately, we were unable to avoid Percy altogether; he had joined the Egyptian Army and was stationed in Cairo. However, I had at least the satisfaction of cutting him whenever we chanced to meet. He cared nothing for his little daughter, and it would have been impossible for us to abandon her. Sennia had been part of our family ever since. She was now five years of age, a distraction and a delight, as Ramses called her. We had left her in England with the younger Emersons this year, since Lia, mourning the absence of husband and brothers, was even more in need of distraction than we. Emerson missed her very much. The only positive aspect of the arrangement (I was still trying to look on the bright side) was that Nefret's surly, spoiled cat, Horus, had stayed with Sennia. I cannot truthfully say that any of us, except possibly Nefret, missed Horus.

Before she learned the truth about Sennia's parentage, Nefret had married. It came as a considerable surprise to me; I had known of Geoffrey's attachment to her, but had not suspected she cared for him. It was a disaster in every sense of the word, for within a few weeks she had lost not only her husband, but the small seed of life that would one day have been their child.

Ramses had accepted her apologies with his usual equanimity, and outwardly, at least, they were on perfectly good terms; but every now and then I sensed a certain tension between them. I wondered if he had ever completely forgiven her for doubting him. My son had always been something of an enigma to me, and although his attachment to little Sennia, and hers to him, displayed a side of his nature I had not previously suspected, he still kept his feelings too much to himself.

This was not the first time he and Nefret had been together since the tragedy; ours is an affectionate family, and we try to meet for holidays, anniversaries, and special occasions. The latest such occasion had been the engagement of Emerson's nephew Johnny to Alice Curtin. Ramses had come back from Germany, where he had been studying Egyptian philology with Professor Erman, for that. Of all his cousins he had a special affection for Johnny, which was somewhat surprising, considering how different their temperaments were: Ramses sober and self-contained, Johnny always making little jokes. They were usually rather bad jokes, but Johnny's laughter was so infectious one could not help joining in.

Was he able to make jokes now, I wondered, in a muddy trench in France? He and his twin Willy were together; some comfort, perhaps, for the boys themselves, but an additional source of anguish for their parents.

Hearing the tap of heels, I turned to see Nefret coming toward me. She was as beautiful as ever, though the past years had added maturity to a countenance that had once been as glowing and carefree as that of a child. She had changed into her working costume of trousers and boots; her shirt was open at the throat and her red-gold hair had been twisted into a knot at the back of her neck.

"Fatima told me you were here," Nefret explained, taking a chair. "Why aren't you at Giza with the Professor and Ramses?"

"I didn't feel like it today."

"But my dear Aunt Amelia! You have been waiting all your life to get at those pyramids. Is something wrong?"

"It is all Emerson's fault," I explained. "He was going on and on about the war and how it has changed our lives; by the time I finished cheering him up I felt as if I had given him my

34

entire store of optimism and had none left for myself."

"I know what you mean. But you mustn't be sad. Things could be worse."

"People only say that when 'things' are already very bad," I grumbled. "You look as if you could stand a dose of optimism yourself. Is that a spot of dried blood on your neck?"

"Where?" Her hand flew to her throat.

"Just under your ear. You were at the hospital?"

She sat back with a sigh. "There is no deceiving you, is there? I thought I'd got myself cleaned up. Yes; I stopped by after the luncheon, just as they brought in a woman who was hemorrhaging. She had tried to abort herself."

"Did you save her?"

"I think so. This time."

Nefret had a large fortune and an even larger heart; the small clinic she had originally founded had been replaced by a women's hospital. The biggest difficulty was in finding female physicians to staff it, for naturally no Moslem woman, respectable or otherwise, would allow a man to examine her.

"Where was Dr. Sophia?" I asked.

"There, as she always is. But I'm the only surgeon on the staff, Aunt Amelia — the only female surgeon in Egypt, so far as I know. I'd rather not talk about it anymore, if you don't mind. It's your turn. Nothing particular has happened, has it? Any news from Aunt Evelyn?"

"No. But we can assume that they are all perfectly miserable too." She laughed and squeezed my hand, and I added, "Ramses was given another white feather today."

"He'll have enough for a pillow soon," said Ramses's foster sister heartlessly. "Surely that isn't what is bothering you. There is something more, Aunt Amelia. Tell me."

Her eyes, blue as forget-me-nots, held mine. I gave myself a little mental shake. "Nothing more, my dear, really. Enough of this! Shall we ask Fatima to bring tea?"

"I am going to wash my neck first," said Nefret, with a grimace. "We may as well wait for the Professor and Ramses. Do you think they will be long?"

"I hope not. We are dining out tonight. I ought to have reminded Emerson, but what with one thing and another, I forgot."

"Two social engagements in one day?" Nefret grinned. "He will roar."

"It was his suggestion."

"The *Professor* suggested dining out? With whom is your appointment, if I may ask?"

"Mr. Thomas Russell, the Assistant Commissioner of Police."

"Ah." Nefret's eyes narrowed. "Then it isn't a simple social engagement. The Professor is on someone's trail. What is it this time, the theft of antiquities, forgery of antiquities, illegal dealing in antiquities? Or — oh, don't tell me it's the Master Criminal again!"

"You sound as if you hope it were."

"I'd love to meet Sethos," Nefret said dreamily. "I know, Aunt Amelia, he's a thief and a swindler and a villain, but you must admit he is frightfully romantic. And his hopeless passion for you —"

"That is very silly," I said severely. "I don't expect ever to see Sethos again."

"You say that every time — just before he appears out of nowhere, in time to rescue you from some horrible danger."

She was teasing me, and I knew better than to respond with the acrimony the mention of Sethos always inspired. He had indeed come to my assistance on several occasions; he did profess a deep attachment to my humble self; he had never pressed his attentions. . . . Well, hardly ever. The fact remained that he had been for many years our most formidable adversary, controlling the illegal-antiquities game and robbing museums, collectors and archaeologists with indiscriminate skill. Though we had sometimes foiled his schemes, truth compels me to admit that more often we had not. I had encountered him a number of times, under conditions that might reasonably be described as close, but not even I could have described his true appearance. His eyes were of an ambiguous shade between gray and brown, and his skill at the art of disguise enabled him to alter their color and almost every other physical characteristic.

"For pity's sake, don't mention him to Emerson!" I exclaimed. "You know how he feels about Sethos. There is no reason whatever to suppose he is in Egypt."

"Cairo is crawling with spies," Nefret said. She leaned forward, clasping her hands. She was in dead earnest now. "The authorities claim all enemy aliens have been deported or interned, but the most dangerous of them, the professional foreign agents, will have eluded arrest because they aren't suspected of being foreigners. Sethos is a master of disguise who has spent many years in Egypt. Wouldn't a man like that be irresistibly drawn to espionage, his talents for sale to the highest bidder?"

"No," I said. "Sethos is an Englishman. He would not —"

"You don't know for certain that he is English. And even if he is, he would not be the first or the last to betray his country."

"Really, Nefret, I refuse to go on with this ridiculous discussion!"

"I apologize. I didn't mean to make you angry."

"I am not angry! Why should I be —" I broke off. Fatima had come up with the tea tray. I motioned to her to put it on the table.

"There's no use pretending this is a normal season for us, Aunt Amelia," Nefret said quietly. "How can it be, with a war going on, and the Canal less than a hundred miles from Cairo? Sometimes I find myself looking at people I've known for years, and wondering if they are wearing masks — playing a part of some kind."

"Nonsense, my dear," I said firmly. "You are letting war nerves get the better of you. As for Emerson, I assure you he is exactly what he seems. He cannot conceal his feelings from me."

"Hmmm," said Nefret. "All the same, I think I will join you this evening, if I may."

When she proposed the scheme later, Emerson agreed so readily that Nefret was visibly cast down — reasoning, I suppose, that he would not have allowed her to come if he was "up to something." She decided to come anyhow. Ramses declined. He said he had other plans, but might join us later if we were dining at Shepheard's.

From Manuscript H

Ramses made a point of arriving early at the Club so that he could not be refused a table. The committee would have loved an excuse to bar him altogether, but he had carefully avoided committing the unforgivable sins, such as cheating at cards.

From his vantage point in an obscure corner he watched the dining room fill up. Half the men were in uniform, the drab khaki of the British Army outshone and outnumbered by the gaudy red and gold of the British-led Egyptian Army. They were all officers; enlisted men weren't allowed in the Turf Club. Neither were Egyptians of any rank or position.

He had almost finished his meal before the table next to his was occupied by a party of four — two middle-aged officials escorting two ladies. One of the ladies was Mrs. Pettigrew, who had presented him with his latest white feather. She and her husband always reminded him of Tweedledum and Tweedledee; as some married couples do, they had come to resemble one another to an alarming degree. Both were short and stout and red-faced. Ramses rose with a polite bow, and was not at all surprised when Mrs. Pettigrew cut him dead. As soon as they were all seated they put their heads together and began a low-voiced conversation, glancing occasionally in his direction.

Ramses didn't doubt he was the subject of the conversation. Pettigrew was one of the most pompous asses in the Ministry of Public Works and one of the loudest patriots in Cairo. The other man was Ewan Hamilton, an engineer who had come to Egypt to advise on the Canal defenses. A quiet, inoffensive man by all accounts, his only affectation was the kilt (Hamilton tartan, Ramses assumed) he often wore. That night he was resplendent in formal Scottish dress: a bottle-green velvet jacket with silver buttons, lace at his chin and cuffs. And, Ramses speculated, a skean dhu in his sock? Gray tarnished the once-blazing red of his hair and mustache, and he squinted in a way that suggested he ought to be wearing spectacles.

Perhaps he had left them off in order to impress the handsome woman with him. Mrs. Fortescue had been in Cairo less than a month, but she was already something of a belle, if a widow could be called that. Gossip spread like wildfire in Anglo-Egyptian society; it was said that her husband had perished gallantly at the head of his regiment during one of the grisly August campaigns that had strewn the fields of France with dead. Meeting Ramses's speculative, shamelessly curious gaze, she allowed her discreetly carmined lips to curve in a faint smile.

As if to emphasize their disapproval of Ramses, the Pettigrews were extremely gracious to another group of diners. All three were in uniform; two were Egyptian Army, the other was a junior official of the Finance Ministry and a member of the hastily organized local militia known derisively as Pharaoh's Foot. They met daily to parade solemnly up and down on the grounds of the

41

Club, carrying fly whisks and sticks because there were not enough rifles for them. The situation looked promising. Ramses sat back and eavesdropped unabashedly.

Once the Pettigrews had finished dissecting his history and character, their voices rose to normal pitch — quite piercing, in the case of Mrs. Pettigrew. She talked about everything under the sun, including the private sins of most members of the foreign community. Inevitably the conversation turned to the war. The younger woman expressed concern over the possibility of a Turkish attack, and Mrs. Pettigrew boomed out a hearty reassurance.

"Nonsense, my dear! Not a chance of it! Everyone knows what wretched cowards the Arabs are — except, of course, when they are led by white officers —"

"Such as General von Kressenstein," said Ramses, pitching his voice loud enough to be heard over her strident tones. "One of Germany's finest military strategists. He is, I believe, adviser to the Syrian Army?"

Pettigrew snorted and Hamilton gave him a hard look, but neither spoke. The response came from the adjoining table. Simmons, the Finance fire-eater, flushed angrily and snapped,

"They'll never get an army across the Sinai. It's a desert, you know; there's no water."

His smirk vanished when Ramses said, humbly but clearly, "Except in the old Roman wells and cisterns. The rains were unusually heavy last season. The wells are overflowing. Do you suppose the Turks don't know that?"

"If they didn't, people like you would tell them." Simmons stood up and stuck out his chin — what there was of it. "Why they allow rotten traitors in this Club —"

"I was just trying to be helpful," Ramses protested. "The lady was asking about the Turks."

One of his friends caught the irate member of Pharaoh's Foot by the arm. "One mustn't bore the ladies with military talk, Simmons. What do you say we go to the bar?"

Simmons had already had a few brandies. He glowered at Ramses as his friends led him away; Ramses waited a few minutes before following. He bowed politely to each of the four at the next table, and was magnificently ignored by three of them. Mrs. Fortescue's response was discreet but unmistakable — a flash of dark eyes and a faint smile.

The hall was crowded. After ordering a whiskey Ramses retired to a corner near a potted palm and located his quarry. Simmons was such easy prey, it was a shame to take advantage of him, but he did appear to be suitably worked up; he was gesticulating and ranting to a small group that included his

43

friends and a third officer who was even better known to Ramses.

Whenever he saw his cousin Percy, he was reminded of a story he had read, about a man who had struck an infernal bargain that allowed him to retain his youthful good looks despite a life of vice and crime. Instead, those sins marked the face of the portrait he kept concealed in his library, until it became that of a monster. Percy was average in every way — medium height and build, hair and mustache medium brown, features pleasant if unremarkable. Only a biased observer would have said that his eyes were a little too close together and his lips were too small, girlishly pink and pursed in the heavy frame of his jaw. Ramses would have been the first to admit he was not unbiased. There was no man on earth he hated more than he did Percy.

Ramses had prepared several provocative speeches, but it wasn't necessary to employ any of them. His glass was still half full when Simmons detached himself from his friends and strode up to Ramses, squaring his narrow shoulders.

"A word with you," he snapped.

Ramses took out his watch. "I am due at Shepheard's at half past ten."

"It won't take long," Simmons said, trying to sneer. "Come outside."

"Oh, I see. Very well, if you insist."

He hadn't intended matters to go this far,

44

but there was no way of retreating now.

Unlike the Gezira Sporting Club, with its polo field and golf course and English-style gardens, the Turf Club was planted unattractively on one of the busiest streets in Cairo, with a Coptic school on one side and a Jewish synagogue on the other. In search of privacy, Ramses proceeded toward the rear of the clubhouse. The night air was cool and sweet and the moon was nearing the full, but there were dark areas, shaded by shrubbery. Ramses headed for one of them. He had not looked back; when he did so, he saw that Simmons's two friends were with him.

"How very unsporting," he said critically. "Or have you two come to cheer Simmons on?"

"It's not unsporting to thrash a cowardly cad," said Simmons. "Everyone knows you don't fight like a gentleman."

"That might be called an oxymoron," Ramses said. "Oh — sorry. Bad form to use long words. Look it up when you get home."

The poor devil didn't know how to fight, like a gentleman or otherwise. He came at Ramses with his arms flailing and his chin irresistibly outthrust. Ramses knocked him down and turned to meet the rush of the others. He winded one of them with an elbow in the ribs and kicked the second in the knee, just above his elegant polished boot — and then damned himself for a fool as Simmons, thrashing ineptly around on the ground, abandoned the last shreds of the old school tie and landed a lucky blow that doubled Ramses up. Before he could get his breath back the other two were on him again. One was limping and the other was whooping, but he hadn't damaged them any more than he could help. He regretted this kindly impulse as they twisted his arms behind him and turned him to face Simmons.

"You might at least allow me to remove my coat," he said breathlessly. "If it's torn my mother will never let me hear the end of it."

Simmons was a dark, panting shape in the shadows. Ramses shifted his balance and waited for Simmons to move a step closer, but Simmons wasn't about to make the same mistake twice. He raised his arm. Ramses ducked his head and closed his eyes. He wasn't quick enough to avoid the blow altogether; it cut across his cheek and jaw like a line of fire.

"That's enough!"

The hands that gripped him let go. Reaching out blindly for some other means of support, he caught hold of a tree limb and steadied himself before he opened his eyes.

Percy was standing between Ramses and Simmons, holding Simmons by the arm. Unexpected, that, Ramses thought; it would have been more in character for Percy to pitch in. The odds were the kind he liked, three or four to one.

Then he saw the other man, his black-and-white evening clothes blending with the play of light and shadow, and recognized Lord Edward Cecil, the Financial Adviser, and Simmons's chief. Cecil's aristocratic features were rigid with disgust. He raked his subordinate with a scornful eye and then spoke to Percy.

"Thank you for warning me about this, Captain. I don't doubt your cousin appreciates it too."

"My cousin is entitled to his opinion, Lord Edward." Percy drew himself up. "I do not agree with it, but I respect it — and him."

"Indeed?" Cecil drawled. "Your sentiments do you credit, Captain. Simmons, report to my office first thing tomorrow. You gentlemen —" his narrowed eyes inspected the flowers of the Egyptian Army, now wilting visibly — "will give me your names and the name of your commanding officer before you leave the club. Come with me."

"Do you need medical attention, Ramses?" Percy asked solicitously.

"No."

As he followed Cecil and the others at a discreet distance, Ramses knew he had lost another round to his cousin. There was no doubt in his mind that Percy had prodded Simmons and the others into that "ungentlemanly" act. He was good at insinuating ideas

47

into people's heads; the poor fools probably didn't realize even now that they had been manipulated into punishing someone Percy hated but was afraid to tackle himself.

Ramses went round the clubhouse and stopped at the front entrance, wondering whether to go in. A glance at his watch informed him it was getting on for half past ten, and he decided he'd made a sufficient spectacle of himself already.

He let the doorman get him a cab. Recognizing him, the driver laid his whip aside and greeted him enthusiastically. None of the Emersons allowed the horses to be whipped, but the size of the tip made up for that inconvenience. "What happened to you, Brother of Curses?" he inquired, employing Ramses's Arabic soubriquet.

Ramses put him off with an explanation that was extremely improper and obviously false, and got into the cab. He was still thinking about Percy.

They had despised one another since their childhood days, but Ramses hadn't realized how dangerous Percy could be until he'd tried to do his cousin a favor.

It only went to prove the truth of his father's cynical statement: no good deed ever goes unpunished. Wandering aimlessly through Palestine, Percy had been taken prisoner and held for ransom by one of the bandits who infested the area. When Ramses went into the camp to get him out, he found his cousin comfortably ensconced in Zaal's best guest room, well supplied with brandy and other comforts and waiting complacently to be ransomed.

He hadn't recognized Ramses in his Bedouin disguise, and after watching Percy snivel and grovel and resist escape with the hysteria of a virgin fighting for her virtue, Ramses had realized it would be wiser not to enlighten him as to the identity of his rescuer. Percy had found out, though. Ramses had not underestimated his resentment, but he had not anticipated the malevolent fertility of Percy's imagination. Accusing Ramses of fathering his carelessly begotten and callously abandoned child had been a masterstroke.

Yet tonight Percy had defended him, physically and verbally. Spouting high-minded sentiments in front of Lord Edward Cecil was designed to raise that influential official's opinion of Captain Percival Peabody, but there must be something more to it than that — something underhanded and unpleasant, if he knew Percy. What the devil was he planning now?

I looked forward with considerable curiosity to our meeting with Mr. Russell. I had known him for some years and esteemed him highly, in spite of his underhanded attempts to make Ramses into a policeman. Not that I have anything against policemen, but I did not consider it a suitable career for my son. Emerson had nothing against policemen either, but he was not fond of social encounters, and, like Nefret, I suspected he had an ulterior motive in proposing we dine with Russell.

Russell was waiting for us in the Moorish Hall when we arrived. His sandy eyebrows went up at the sight of Nefret, and when Emerson said breezily, "Hope you don't mind our bringing Miss Forth," I realized that the invitation had been Russell's, not Emerson's.

Nefret realized it at the same time, and gave me a conspiratorial smile as she offered Russell her gloved hand. Emerson never paid the least attention to social conventions, and Russell had no choice but to appear pleased.

"Why, uh, yes, Professor — that is, I am delighted, of course, to see — uh — Miss — uh — Forth."

His confusion was understandable. Nefret had resumed her maiden name after the death of her husband, and Cairo society had found this hard to accept. They found a good many of Nefret's acts hard to accept.

We went at once to the dining salon and the table Mr. Russell had reserved. I thought he appeared a trifle uncomfortable, and my suspicions as to his reason for asking us to dine were confirmed. He wanted something from us. Assistance, perhaps, in rounding up some of the more dangerous foreign agents in Cairo? Glancing round the room, I began to wonder if I too was beginning to succumb to war nerves. Officers and officials, matrons and maidens — all people I had known for years — suddenly looked sly and duplicitous. Were any of them in the pay of the enemy?

At any rate, I told myself firmly, none of them was Sethos.

Emerson has never been one to beat around the bush. He waited only until after we had ordered before he remarked, "Well, Russell, what's on your mind, eh? If you want me to persuade Ramses to join the CID, you are wasting your time. His mother won't hear of it."

"Neither will he," Russell said with a wry smile. "There's no use trying to deceive you, Professor, so if the ladies will excuse us for talking business —"

"I would rather you talked business than nonsense, Mr. Russell," I said with some asperity.

"You are right, ma'am. I should know better."

He sampled the wine the waiter had poured into his glass and nodded approval. While our glasses were being filled, his eyes focused on Nefret, and a frown wrinkled his forehead. She was the picture of a proper young lady — pretty and innocent and harmless. The low-cut bodice of her gown bared her white throat; gems twinkled on her breast and in the red-gold hair that crowned her small head. One would never have supposed that those slender hands were more accustomed to hold a scalpel than a fan, or that she could fend off an attacker more effectively than most men.

She knew what Russell was thinking, and met his doubtful gaze squarely.

"A number of people in Cairo will tell you I am no lady, Mr. Russell. You needn't mince words with me. It's Ramses, isn't it? What's he done now?"

"Nothing that I know of, except make himself thoroughly disliked," Russell said. "Oh, the devil with — excuse me, Miss Forth."

She laughed at him, and his stern face relaxed into a sheepish grin. "As I was about to say — I may as well be honest with all of you. Yes, I did approach Ramses. I believe there is not an intelligence organization in Egypt, military or civilian, that has not tried to get him! I had no more luck than the others. But he could be of particular value to me in capturing that fellow Wardani. You all know who he is, I presume."

Emerson nodded. "The leader of the Young Egypt Party, and the only one of the nationalists who is still at large. You managed to round up all the others — including my niece's husband, David Todros."

"I don't blame you for resenting that,"

Russell said quietly. "But it had to be done. We daren't take chances with that lot, Professor. They believe their hope of independence lies in the defeat of Britain, and they will collaborate with our enemies in order to bring it about."

"But what can they do?" Nefret asked. "They are scattered and imprisoned."

"So long as Wardani is on the loose, they can do a great deal of damage." Russell leaned forward. "He is their leader, intelligent, charismatic and fanatical; he has already gathered new lieutenants to replace the ones we arrested. You know the Sultan has declared a jihad, a holy war, against unbelievers. The mass of the fellahin are apathetic or afraid, but if Wardani can stir up the students and intellectuals, we may find ourselves fighting a guerrilla war here in Cairo while the Turks attack the Canal. Wardani is the key. Without him, the movement will collapse. I want him. And I think you can help me to get him."

Emerson had been calmly eating his soup. "Excellent," he remarked. "Shepheard's always does a superb potage; à la duchesse."

"Are you trying to annoy me, Professor?" Russell asked.

"Why, no," said Emerson. "But I'm not going to help you find Wardani either."

Russell was not easily roused to anger. He studied Emerson thoughtfully. "You are in

53

sympathy with his aims? Yes, well, that doesn't surprise me. But even you must admit, Professor, that this is not the right time. After the war —"

Emerson cut him off. My husband *is* easily roused to anger. His blue eyes were blazing. "Is that going to be your approach? Be patient, be good little children, and if you behave yourselves until the war is won, we will give you your freedom? And you want *me* to make the offer because I have a certain reputation for integrity in this country? I won't make a promise I cannot keep, Russell, and I know for a fact you, and the present Government, would not keep that one." Refreshed and relieved by this outburst, he picked up his fork and cut into the fish that had replaced his bowl of soup. "Anyhow, I don't know where he is," he added.

"But you do," Nefret said suddenly. "Don't you, Mr. Russell? That's why you asked the Professor to join you this evening — you've located Wardani's hideout, and you are planning to close in on him tonight, but you're afraid he will get away from you, as he has always done before, and so you want . . . What the devil do you want from us?"

"I don't want anything from *you,* Miss Forth." Russell took out his handkerchief and mopped his perspiring forehead. "Except to remain here, and enjoy your dinner, and stay out of this!"

"She cannot dine alone, it would not be proper," I remarked, draining my glass of wine. "Shall we go now?"

Emerson, eating heartily but neatly, had almost finished his fish. He popped the last morsel into his mouth and made inquiring noises.

"Don't talk with your mouth full, Emerson. I do not suggest you carry out Mr. Russell's insulting proposal, but an opportunity to talk with Mr. Wardani is not to be missed. We may be able to negotiate with him. Anything that would avoid bloodshed — including his — is worth the effort."

Emerson swallowed. "Just what I was about to say, Peabody."

He rose and held my chair for me. I brushed a few crumbs off my bodice and stood up.

Russell's eyes had a glazed look. In a quiet, conversational voice he remarked, "I don't quite know how I lost control of this situation. For the love of heaven, Professor and Mrs. Emerson, order — persuade — ask Miss Forth to stay here!"

"Nefret is the only one of us who has met Mr. Wardani," I explained. "And he is more likely to listen to an attractive young lady than to us. Nefret, you have dropped your gloves again."

Russell, moving like an automaton,

reached under the table and retrieved Nefret's gloves.

"Let us make certain we understand one another, Russell," Emerson said. "I agree to accompany you in order that I may speak with Mr. Wardani and attempt to convince him he ought to turn himself in — for his own good. I will make no promises and I will brook no interference from you. Is that clear?"

Russell looked him straight in the eye. "Yes, sir."

I had not anticipated this particular development, but I had thought something of interest might ensue, so I had come prepared. As I watched a bemused Assistant Commissioner of Police help Nefret on with her cloak, I realized she had done the same. Like my outer garment, hers was dark and plain, with no glitter of jet or crystal beads, but with a deep hood that covered her hair. I doubted she was armed, for the long knife she favored would have been difficult to conceal on her person. Her skirt was straight and rather narrow, and layers of petticoats were no longer in fashion.

My own "arsenal," as Emerson terms it, was limited by the same consideration. However, my little pistol fit neatly into my bag and my parasol (crimson to match my frock) had a stout steel shaft. Not many ladies carried parasols to an evening party, but people had become accustomed to my having one always with me; it was considered an amusing eccentricity, I believe.

"I will drive us to our destination," Emerson announced, as we left the hotel. "Fortunately I brought the motorcar."

Unfortunately he had. Emerson drives like a madman and he will allow no one else to drive him. I did not express my misgivings, for I felt certain Mr. Russell would express his. After a long look at the vehicle, which was very large and very yellow, he shook his head.

"Everyone in Cairo knows that car, Professor. We want to be unobtrusive. I have a closed carriage waiting. But I wish the ladies would not —"

Nefret had already jumped into the cab. Russell sighed. He got up onto the box next to the driver and Emerson politely handed me in.

After circling the Ezbekieh Gardens the cab passed the Opera House and turned into the Muski. The hour was early for Cairo; the streets were brightly lighted and full of traffic, from camels to motorcars. The excitement that had filled me at the prospect of action began to fade. This section of Cairo was boringly bright and modern. We might have been in Bond Street or the Champs Élysée.

"We are heading toward the Khan el Khalili," I reported, peering out the window.

But we never reached it. The cab turned south, into a narrower street, and passed the Hotel du Nil before coming to a stop. Russell jumped down off the box and came to the door.

"We had best go on foot from here," he said softly. "It isn't far. Just down there."

I inspected the street he indicated. It appeared to be a cul de sac, only a few hundred yards long, but it was nothing like the enticingly foul areas of the Old City into which I had often ventured in search of criminals. The lighted windows of several good-sized houses shone through the dark.

"Your fugitive appears to be overly confident," I said disapprovingly. "If I hoped to elude the police I would go to earth in a less respectable neighborhood."

"On the other hand," said Emerson, taking my arm and leading me on, "they aren't as likely to look for him in a respectable neighborhood. Russell, are you sure your informant was correct?"

"No," the gentleman replied curtly. "That is why I asked you to come with me. It's the third house — that one. Ask the doorkeeper to announce you."

"And then what?" Emerson inquired. "Upon hearing our names Wardani will rush into the room and welcome us with open arms?"

"I'm sure you will think of something, Professor. If you don't, Mrs. Emerson will."

"Hmph," said Emerson.

Russell struck a match and examined his watch. "It is a quarter past ten. I'll give you half an hour."

"Hmph," Emerson repeated. "Nefret, take my other arm."

Russell withdrew into a patch of shadow and we proceeded toward the door he had indicated. The houses were fairly close together, surrounded by trees and flowering plants. "What is he going to do if we don't come out within thirty minutes?" Nefret asked in a low voice.

"Well, my dear, he would not have implied he would rush to our rescue if his men weren't already in position," Emerson replied placidly. "They are well-trained, aren't they? I've only spotted two of them."

Nefret would have stopped in her tracks if Emerson had not pulled her along. "It's a trap," she gasped. "He's using us —"

"To distract Wardani while the police break in. Certainly. What did you expect?"

Raising the heavy iron ring that served as a knocker, he beat a thunderous tattoo upon the door.

"He lied to us," Nefret muttered. "The bastard!"

"Language, Nefret," I said.

"I beg your pardon, Aunt Amelia. But he is!"

"Just a good policeman, my dear," said Emerson. He knocked again.

"What are you going to do, Professor?"

"I'll think of something. If I don't, your Aunt Amelia will."

The door swung open.

"Salaam aleikhum," said Emerson to the servant who stood on the threshold. "Announce us, if you please. Professor Emerson, Mrs. Emerson, and Miss Forth."

The whites of the man's eyes gleamed as he rolled them from Emerson to me, to Nefret. He was young, with a scanty beard and thick spectacles, and he appeared to be struck dumb and motionless by our appearance. With a muffled oath Emerson picked him up and carried him, his feet kicking feebly, into the hall.

"Close the door, Peabody," he ordered. "Be quick about it. We may not have much time."

Naturally I obeyed at once. The small room was lit by a hanging lamp. It was of copper, pierced in an intricate design, and gave little light. A carved chest against one wall and a handsome Oriental rug were the only furnishings. At the far end a flight of narrow uncarpeted stairs led up to a landing blocked by a wooden screen.

Emerson sat the servant down on the chest and went to the foot of the stairs. "Wardani!" he bellowed. "Emerson here! Come out of your hole, we must talk."

If the fugitive was anywhere within a fifty-yard radius, he must have heard. There was no immediate reaction from Wardani, if he was there, but the young servant sprang up, drew a knife from his robe, and flew at Emerson. Nefret lifted her skirts in a ladylike manner and kicked the knife from his hand. The youth was certainly persistent; I had to whack him across the shins with my parasol before he fell down.

"Thank you, my dears," said Emerson, who had not looked round. "That settles that. He's here, all right. Upstairs?"

He had just set foot upon the first stair when two things happened. A police whistle sounded, shrill enough to penetrate even the closed door, and from behind the screen at the top of the stairs a man appeared. He wore European clothing except for low slippers of Egyptian style, and his black head was uncovered. I could not make out his features clearly; the light was poor and the dark blur of a beard covered the lower part of his face; but had I entertained any doubt as to his identity, it would have been dispelled when he vanished as suddenly as he had appeared.

Fists and feet beat on the door. Amid the shouts of the attackers I made out the voice of Thomas Russell, demanding that the door be opened at once. Emerson said, "Hell and damnation!" and thundered up the stairs, taking them three at a time. Skirts raised to her knees, Nefret bounded up after him. I followed her, hampered to some extent by the parasol, which prevented me from getting a firm grip on my skirts. As I reached the top of the stairs I heard the door give way. Whirling round, I brandished my parasol and shouted, "Stop where you are!"

Somewhat to my surprise, they did. Russell was in the lead. The small room seemed to be filled with uniforms, and I noted, more or less in passing, that the young man who had admitted us had had the good sense to make himself scarce.

"What the devil do you mean by this, Mrs. Emerson?" Russell demanded.

I did not reply, since the answer was obvious. I glanced over my shoulder.

Straight ahead a corridor lined with doors led to the back of the villa. There was an open window at the far end; before it stood the man we had followed, facing Nefret and Emerson, who had stopped halfway along the passage.

"Is that him?" Emerson demanded ungrammatically.

There was no answer from Nefret. Emerson said, "Must be. Sorry about this, Wardani. I had hoped to talk with you, but Russell had other ideas. Another time, eh? We'll hold them off while you get away. Watch out below, there may be others in the garden."

Wardani stood quite still for a moment, his frame appearing abnormally tall and slender against the moonlit opening. Then he stepped onto the sill and swung himself out into the night.

Emerson hurried to the window. Putting out his head, he shouted, "Down there! He's gone that way!" Shouts and a loud thrashing in the shrubbery followed, and several shots rang out. One must have struck the wall near the window, for Emerson ducked back inside, swearing. After milling about in confusion, the policemen who were inside the house ran out of it, led by Russell.

I descended the stairs and went to the door, which they had left open. There appeared to be a great deal of activity going on at the back of the villa, but the street was dark and quiet. Cairenes were not inclined to interfere in other people's affairs now that the city was under virtual military occupation.

After a short interval I was joined by Emerson and Nefret.

"Where did he go?" I asked.

Emerson brushed plaster dust off his sleeve. "Onto the roof. He's an agile rascal. We may as well go back to the cab. I'll wager he's got well away by now."

Mr. Russell was quick to arrive at the same conclusion. We had not been waiting long before he joined us.

63

"Eluded you, did he?" Emerson inquired. "Tsk, tsk."

"Thanks to you."

"I was of less assistance than I had hoped to be. Confound you, Russell, if you had given me five minutes more I might have been able to win his trust."

"Five minutes?" Russell repeated doubtfully.

"It would have taken Mrs. Emerson even less time. Oh, but what's the use? If you are coming with us, get in. I want to go home."

We spoke very little on the way back to the hotel. I was preoccupied with an odd idea. I had caught only a glimpse of the silhouetted figure, but for a moment I had had an eerie sense of déjà vu, as when one sees the unformed features of an infant take on a sudden and fleeting resemblance to a parent or grandparent.

Nefret had put the idea into my head. I told myself it was absurd, and yet . . . Had I not sworn that I would know Sethos at any time, in any disguise?

The carriage drew up in front of Shepheard's. Russell got down from the box and opened the door for us.

"It's still early," he said pleasantly. "Will you do me the honor of joining me in a liqueur or a glass of brandy, to prove there are no hard feelings?"

"Bah," said Emerson. But he said no more.

We made our way through the throng of flower vendors and beggars, dragomen and peddlers who surrounded the steps; and as we mounted those steps I beheld a familiar form advancing to meet us.

"Good evening, Mother," he said. "Good evening, Nefret. Good evening —"

"Ramses," I exclaimed. "What have you done now?"

It might have been more accurate to ask what someone had done to him. He had made an attempt to tidy himself, but the raised weal across his cheek was still oozing blood and the surrounding flesh was bruised and swollen.

Russell stepped back. "I must ask to be excused. Good night, Mrs. Emerson — Miss Forth — Professor."

"Snubbed again," said Ramses. "Nefret?" He offered her his arm.

"Your coat is torn," I exclaimed.

Ramses glanced at his shoulder, where a line of white showed against the black of his coat. "Damn. Excuse me, Mother. It's only a ripped seam, I believe. May we sit down before you continue your lecture?"

Nefret had not said a word. She put her hand on his arm and let him lead her to a table.

In the bright lights of the terrace I got a good look at my companions. Emerson's cravat was wildly askew — he always tugged at it when he was exasperated — and he had not got all the plaster dust off his coat. Nefret's hair was coming down, and there was a long rent in my skirt. I tucked the folds modestly about my limbs.

"Dear me," said Ramses, inspecting us. "Have you been fighting again?"

"I might reasonably ask the same of you," said his father.

"A slight accident. I've been waiting a good half hour or more," said Ramses accusingly. "The concierge informed me you had left the hotel, but since the motorcar was still here I assumed you would be back sooner or later. Might one inquire —"

"No, not yet," said Emerson. "Was it here at Shepheard's that you had your — er — accident?"

"No, sir. It was at the Club. I dined there before coming on to meet you." His lips closed tight, but Emerson continued to fix him with that cold blue stare, and after a moment he said reluctantly, "I got into a little argument."

"With whom?" his father inquired.

"Father —"

"With whom?"

"A chap named Simmons. I don't think you know him. And — well — Cartwright and Jenkins. Egyptian Army."

"Only three? Good Gad, Ramses, I had thought better of you."

"They didn't fight like gentlemen," Ramses said.

The corners of his mouth turned up a trifle. Ramses's sense of humor is decidedly odd; it is not always easy for me to ascertain whether he is attempting to be humorous.

"Are you attempting to be humorous?" I inquired.

"Yes, he is," Nefret said, before Ramses could reply. "But he is not succeeding."

Ramses caught the eye of the waiter, who hurried to him, ignoring the urgent demands of other patrons. Being snubbed by the Anglo-Egyptian community has only raised Ramses in the opinions of native Cairenes, most of whom admire him almost as much as they do his father.

"Would you like a whiskey and soda, Mother?" he asked.

"No, thank you."

"Nefret? Father? I will have one, if you don't mind."

I did mind, for I suspected he had already had more than was good for him. Catching Emerson's eye, I remained silent.

Nefret did not. "Were you drunk tonight?" she demanded.

"Not very. Where did you go with Russell?"

Emerson told him, in some detail.

"Ah," said Ramses. "So that was what he wanted. I suspected as much."

"He told us you had refused to help him find Wardani," Emerson said. "Ramses, I know you rather like the rascal —"

"My personal feelings are irrelevant." Ramses finished his whiskey. "I don't give a damn what Wardani does so long as David is not involved, and I won't use any influence I may have with Wardani to betray him to Russell."

"The Professor felt the same," Nefret said quietly. "He only wanted to talk to the man. We tried to warn him —"

"How kind. I wonder if he knows that." He turned in his chair, looking for the waiter.

"It is time we went home," I said. "I am rather tired. Ramses? Please?"

"Yes, Mother, of course."

I let Emerson go ahead with Nefret, and asked Ramses to give me his arm. "When we get home I will rub some of Kadija's ointment onto your face," I said. "Is it very painful?"

"No. As you have so often remarked, the medicinal effects of good whiskey —"

"Ramses, what happened? That looks like the mark of a riding crop or whip."

"It was one of those fashionable little swagger sticks, I think," Ramses said. He opened the door and helped me into the tonneau.

"Three of them against one," I mused, for I now had a clear idea of what had occurred. "Contemptible! Perhaps they will be too ashamed of themselves to mention the incident."

"Everyone who was at the Club knows of it, I expect," Ramses said.

I sighed. "And everyone in Cairo will know of it tomorrow."

"No doubt," Ramses agreed, with — I could not help thinking — a certain relish.

I had never known Ramses to drink more than he ought, or allow himself to be drawn into a vulgar brawl. Something was preying on his mind, but unless he chose to confide in me there was nothing I could do to help him.

2

One might have supposed that with a war going on, people would have better things to do than engage in idle gossip, but within a few days the news of Ramses's latest escapade was all over Cairo. I was informed of the impertinent interest of others in our affairs by Madame Villiers, whose expressions of concern served as an excuse for her real motive (malicious curiosity) in ringing me up. As the mother of a plain, unmarried daughter, Madame could not afford to alienate the mother of an eligible unmarried son, though I could have told her Celestine's chances were on the order of a million to one. I did not tell her, nor did I correct her version of the story, which was wildly inaccurate.

Not quite as inaccurate as I had first supposed, however. One of the things she told me roused my curiosity to such an extent that I decided I must question Ramses about it.

We were all together on our roof terrace, taking tea and occupied in various ways: Emerson muttering over his notebook, Nefret reading the *Egyptian Gazette*, and Ramses doing nothing at all except stroking the cat that lay beside him on the settee. He was his usual self, uncommunicative and out-wardly composed, though for a while his face had presented an unattractive piebald ap-pearance — one cheek smooth and brown, the other greasily green and bristly. Like love and a cold, the use of Kadija's miraculous ointment could not be concealed. From her Nubian foremothers she had inherited the recipe to whose efficacy we had all become converts, though not even Nefret had been able to determine what the effective ingredi-ents might be. It had had its usual effect; the swelling and bruising were gone, and only a thin red line marked his lean cheek.

"Is it true that Percy was present when you were attacked the other evening at the Club?" I inquired.

Nefret lowered the newspaper, Emerson looked up, and Seshat let out a hiss of protest.

"I beg your pardon," said Ramses, ad-dressing the cat. "May I ask, Mother, who told you that?"

"Madame Villiers. She usually gets her facts wrong, but there would seem to be no reason for her to repeat such a story unless there was a germ of truth in it."

"He was present," Ramses said, and said no more.

"Good Gad, Ramses, must we use thumb-screws?" his father demanded hotly. "Why didn't you tell us? By heaven, he's gone too far this time; I will —"

"No, sir, you won't. Percy was not one of my antagonists. In fact, it was he who brought Lord Edward Cecil onto the scene in time to — er — rescue me."

"Hmph," said Emerson. "What do you suppose he's up to now?"

"Trying to worm his way back into our good graces, I suppose," I said with a sniff. "Madame said that on several occasions he has spoken up in Ramses's defense when someone accused him of cowardice. *She* said *Percy* said that his cousin was one of the bravest men he had ever known."

Ramses became very still. After a moment he said, "I wonder what put that extraordinary notion into his head."

"What is extraordinary is the source," Emerson said gruffly. "The statement itself is true. Sometimes it requires more courage to take an unpopular stand than to engage in heroics."

Ramses blinked. This, together with a slight nod at his father, was the only sign of emotion he allowed himself. "Never mind Percy, I cannot imagine why any of us should care what he thinks of me or says about me. Is there anything of interest in the *Gazette*, Nefret?"

She had been staring at her clasped hands, frowning as if she had discovered a blemish or a broken fingernail. "What? Oh, the newspaper. I was looking for a report about Mr. Russell's failed raid, but there is only a brief paragraph saying that Wardani is still at large and offering a reward for information leading to his capture."

"How much?" Ramses inquired.

"Fifty English pounds. Not enough to tempt you, is it?"

Ramses gave her a long level look. "Wardani would consider it insultingly low."

"It is a large amount to an Egyptian."

"Not large enough for the risk involved," Ramses replied. "Wardani's people are fanatics; some of them would slit a traitor's throat as readily as they would kill a flea. You ought not have expected the censors would allow any report of the incident. Wardani pulled off another daring escape and made Russell look like an incompetent ass. I don't doubt that all Cairo knows of it, however."

Nefret appeared to be watching the cat. Seshat had rolled onto her back and Ramses's long fingers were gently rubbing her stomach. "Is press censorship really that strict?" she asked.

"We are at war, my dear," Ramses replied in an exaggerated public-school drawl. "We can allow nothing to appear in print that might give aid and comfort to the enemy." He added in his normal tones, "You had better not pass on any personal confidences to Lia when you write her. The post will also be read and censored, quite possibly by an officer who is an acquaintance of yours."

Nefret's brow furrowed. "Who?"

"I've no idea. But you do know most of them, don't you?"

"That would be an unacceptable violation of the fundamental rights of free English persons," I exclaimed. "The rights for which we are fighting, the basic —"

"Yes, Mother. All the same, it will be done."

"Nefret does not know anything that could give aid and comfort to the enemy," I insisted. "However . . . Nefret, you didn't tell Lia about our encounter with Wardani, did you?"

"I haven't mentioned anything that might worry her," Nefret said. "Which leaves me with very little to write about! The primary topic of conversation in Cairo is the probability of an attack on the Canal, and I am certainly not going to tell her that."

"Damned war," said Emerson. "I don't know why you insist on talking about it."

"I was not talking about the war, but about Mr. Wardani," I reminded him. "If there were only some way we could manage to talk with him! I feel certain I could convince him that for his own good and the good of Egypt he ought to modify his strategy. It would be criminal to throw away his life for what is at present a hopeless cause; he has the potential to become a great leader, the Simón Bolívar or Abraham Lincoln of Egypt!"

The line between Nefret's brows disappeared, and she emitted one of her musical, low-pitched laughs. "I'm sorry," she sputtered. "I had a sudden image of Aunt Amelia knocking Mr. Wardani over the head with her parasol and holding him prisoner in one of our guest rooms, where she can lecture him daily. With tea and cucumber sandwiches, of course."

"Enjoy your little joke, Nefret," I said. "All I want to do is talk with him. I am reckoned to have fair powers of persuasion, you know. Is there nothing you can do, Ramses? You have your own peculiar methods of finding people — you tracked Wardani down once before, if I remember correctly."

Ramses leaned back against the cushions and lit a cigarette. "That was entirely different, Mother. He knew I wouldn't have done anything to betray him so long as David was involved. Now he has no reason to trust me, and a hunted fugitive is inclined to strike first and apologize afterward."

"Quite right," Emerson ejaculated. "I cannot imagine what you were thinking of, Peabody, to suggest such a thing. Ramses, I strictly forbid . . . uh . . . I earnestly request that you will make no attempt to find Wardani. If he didn't cut your throat, one of his fanatical followers would."

"Yes, sir," said Ramses.

From Manuscript H

They met just after nightfall, in a coffee shop in the Tumbakiyeh, the tobacco warehouse district. Massive doors, iron-hinged and nail-studded, closed the buildings where the tumbak was stored; but much of the area was falling into decay, the spacious khans abandoned, the homes of the old merchant princes partitioned into tenements.

There were four of them, sitting cross-legged around a low table in a back room separated from the coffee shop itself by a closed door and a heavy curtain. A single oil lamp on the table illumined the oblong board on which the popular game called mankaleh was played, but none of them, not even the players, was paying much attention to the distribution of the pebbles. Conversation was sparse, and a listener might have been struck by the fact that names were not used.

Finally a large gray-bearded man, dressed like a Bedouin in khafiya and caftan, muttered, "This is a stupid place to meet and a dangerous time. It is too early. The streets are full of people, the shops are lighted —"

"The Inglizi are drinking at their clubs and hotels, and others are at the evening meal." The speaker was a man in his early twenties, heavily built for an Egyptian, but with the unmistakable scholar's squint. "You are new to our group, my friend; do not question the

76

wisdom of our leader. One is less conspicuous in a crowd at sunset than in a deserted street at midnight."

The older man grunted. "He is late."

The two who had not yet spoken exchanged glances. Both were clad like members of the poorer class, in a single outer garment of blue linen and turbans of coarse white cotton, but there was something of the student about them too. A pair of thick spectacles magnified the eyes of one man; he kept poking nervously at the folds of his turban, as if he were unaccustomed to wearing that article of dress. The other youth was tall and graceful, his smooth cheeks rounded, his eyes fringed with thick dark lashes. His zaboot was open from the neck nearly to the waist; on the sleek brown skin of his chest lay an ornament more commonly worn by women, a small silver case containing a selection from the Koran. It was he who responded to the Bedouin. "He comes when he chooses. Make your move."

A few minutes later the curtain at the door was swept aside and a man entered. He wore European clothing — tweed coat and trousers, kid gloves, and a broad-brimmed hat that shadowed the upper part of his face but exposed a prominent aquiline nose and clean-shaven chin. The gray-bearded man sprang up, his hand on his knife. The others stared and started, and the handsome youth clapped his hand to his chest.

"So you appreciate my little joke. Convincing, is it?"

The voice was Wardani's, the swagger with which he approached the table, the wolfish grin. He swept off his hat and bowed ironically to the Bedouin. "Salaam aleikhum. Don't be so quick to go for the knife. There is nothing illegal about this little gathering. We are only five."

The bespectacled student let out a string of pious oaths and wiped his sweating palms on his skirt. "You have shaved your beard!"

"How observant." They continued to stare, and Wardani said impatiently, "A false beard is easily assumed. This widens the range of disguises available to me — not only a clean-shaven chin but a variety of facial decorations. I learned a number of such tricks from David, who had learned them from *his* friend."

"But — but you look exactly like *him!*"

"No," Wardani said. "Take a closer look." He stooped so that the single lamp shone on his face. "At a distance I resemble the notorious Brother of Demons closely enough to pass unmolested by a police officer, but you, my band of heroes, should not be so easily deceived — or intimidated."

"I see the difference now, of course," one of them said.

A chorus of embarrassed murmurs seconded the statement. "He would intimidate me if he walked into this room," the bespectacled student admitted. "They say he has friends in every street in Cairo, that he talks with afreets and the ghosts of the dead . . . Pure superstition, of course," he added hastily.

"Of course," Wardani said. He straightened and remained standing, looking down at the others.

The handsome boy cleared his throat. "Superstition, no doubt; but he is an enemy, and dangerous. The same is true of his family. Emerson Effendi and the Sitt Hakim were with Russell the other night. Perhaps we should take steps to render them harmless."

"Steps?" Wardani's voice was very soft. With a sudden movement he swept the game from the table. The aged wood of the board split when it struck the floor, and pebbles rattled and rolled. Wardani planted both hands on the table. "You presume on your position, I believe. You are my chosen aides, for the present, but you do not give the orders. You take them — from me."

"I did not mean —"

"You have the brains of a louse. Leave them strictly alone, do you understand? All of them! There is one true thing in the lies they tell about the Father of Curses. When his anger is aroused he is more dangerous than a wounded lion. He is not our friend, but he is no pawn of Thomas Russell's either. Touch his wife or his daughter and he will hunt you down without mercy. And there is another thing." Wardani lowered his voice to a menacing whisper. "They are friends of my friend. I could not look him in the face again if I had allowed any one of them to be harmed."

The silence was complete. Not a chair creaked, not a breath was drawn. Wardani studied the downcast faces of his allies, and his upper lip drew back in a smile.

"So that is settled. Now to business, eh?"

Only two of them took part in the conversation — Wardani and the gray-bearded man. Finally the latter said, in answer to a question from Wardani, "Two hundred, to start. With a hundred rounds of ammunition for each. More later, if you can find the men to use them."

"Hmmm." Wardani scratched his chin. "How many others have you approached with this enticing offer?"

"None."

"You lie."

The other man rose and reached for his knife. "You dare call me a liar?"

"Sit down," Wardani said contemptuously. "You made the same offer to Nuri al-Sa'id and to that scented sodomite el-Gharbi. Sa'id will sell the weapons to the highest bidder, and el-Gharbi will laugh himself sick and ship the guns to the Senussi. Do you think his women and his pretty boys will shoot at the British troops, who are their best customers? No!" He brought his fist down on the table, and fixed a furious glare on the Bedouin. "Be quiet and listen to me. I am the best and only hope of your masters, and I am willing to discuss the matter with them. With them, not with middlemen and underlings! You will inform your German friends that they have forty-eight hours to arrange a meeting. And don't tell me that is not time enough; do you suppose I am unaware of the fact that they have agents here in the city? If you do as I ask, I won't tell them about the others. Make your shady little arrangements and collect your dirty little baksheesh from them. Well?"

Graybeard was quivering with rage and frustration. He called Wardani a vile name and strode toward the door.

"The back way, you son of an Englishman," Wardani said.

The narrow panel at the back of the room looked like a door for an animal, not a man; the Bedouin had to bend his knees and bow his head to get through, which did not improve his temper. "I will kill you one day," he promised.

"Better men than you have tried," said Wardani. "In the meantime — the Khan el Khalili, the shop of Aslimi Aziz, at this same

81

hour the day after tomorrow. Someone will be there."

"You?"

"One never knows."

The only one who dared speak was the man with the squint. He waited until the door had closed behind the Arab.

"Was that wise, Kamil? He won't come back."

"But yes, my friend." Wardani now spoke French. "He will have to come back because his German masters will insist. They are clever persons, these Germans; they know I wield more power in Cairo than any other man, and that I hate the British as much as they do. I gave him a way out — a way to hide his dishonor and make his profit. That is how one deals with Turks."

"Turk?" The dark eyes widened. "He is an Arab and a brother."

Wardani gave his young friend a kindly look and shook his head. "You need to apply yourself to the study of languages, my dear. The accent was unmistakable. Well, we've been here long enough; we meet again two days from now."

"But you, sir," the tall youth ventured. "Have you found a safe hiding place? How can we reach you if there is need?"

"You cannot. Merde alors, if you are unable to keep out of trouble for two days, you need a nursemaid, not a leader."

He replaced his hat and went to the curtained entrance. Before he drew the hanging back, he turned and grinned at the others. "Ramses Emerson Effendi does not crawl through holes, but that is your way out, friends. One or two at a time."

He went through the front room and into the street, walking with long strides but without haste. After passing the convent mosque of Beybars he turned off the Gamalieh into a narrow lane and broke into a run. Many of the old houses that abutted on the lane had fallen into ruin, but a few were still occupied; a lantern by one door cast a feeble light. Pausing in front of a recessed doorway, Wardani bent his knees and sprang, catching hold of the top of the lintel and drawing himself up onto a carved ledge eight feet above the ground. An unnecessary precaution, perhaps, but he had not remained alive until now by neglecting unnecessary precautions.

He did not have to wait long. The form that picked its way cautiously along the littered alley was unmistakable. Farouk was six inches taller than any of the others, and vain as a peacock; the shawl he had wrapped round his head and face was of fine muslin, and the light glinted off the silver ornament on his breast.

Perched on the ledge, Wardani waited until his pursuer had passed out of sight around a curve in the winding lane. Then he waited a little longer before stripping off coat, waistcoat, and stiff collar and rolling them and the hat into an anonymous bundle. Shortly thereafter a stoop-shouldered, ragged old man shuffled out of the lane and proceeded along the Gamalieh. He stopped at the stall of a bean seller and counted out coins in exchange for a bowl of fuul medemes. Leaning against the wall, he ate without really tasting the food. He was thinking hard.

He'd feared Farouk would be trouble. Despite his pretty face, he was several years older than the others, and a new recruit, and Wardani hadn't missed the flash of anger in the black eyes when he forbade action against the Emersons. There was only one reason he could think of why Farouk would follow him, and it wasn't concern for his safety.

That was all he needed, an ambitious rival. He wondered how much longer he could keep this up. Just long enough, inshallah — long enough to get his hands on those weapons. . . . He returned the empty bowl to the merchant with a murmured blessing and shambled off.

From Letter Collection B

Dearest Lia,

Delighted to hear "the worst is over" and that you are eating properly again. I apologize for the euphemism, I know you despise them as much as I do, but I don't want to shock the censor! I'm sure Sennia is tempting you with jam and biscuits and other good things, and I hope you are stuffing them down! She is a comfort to you, I know, and I am so glad. Greatly as we miss her, she is far better off with you.

We miss all of you too. That is a very flat expression of a very heartfelt sentiment, darling. I can't confide in anyone as I do in you, and letters aren't suitable for certain kinds of news. After all, we wouldn't want to shock the censor.

It is wonderful that you finally heard from David, even if the letter was brief and stiff. His letters are certainly *being read by the military, so you mustn't expect him to pour his heart out. At least he is safe; that is the most important thing. The Professor hasn't given up hope of gaining his release — if not immediately, at least before the baby comes. The dear man has been badgering Important Personages in Cairo, from General Maxwell on down. That he should take time from his beloved excavations to pursue this should prove, if proof were needed, how much he cares for David.*

We haven't got inside the tomb yet. You know the Professor; every square inch of sand has to be sifted first. The entrance . . .

(The editor has omitted the following description, since it is repeated by Mrs. Emerson.)

Excavation is, essentially, an act of destruction. To clear a site, tomb, temple or tell down to the lowest level means that all the upper levels are gone forever. For this reason it is absolutely essential to keep detailed records of what has been removed. My distinguished spouse was one of the first to establish the principles of modern excavation: precise measurements, accurate copies of all inscriptions and reliefs, innumerable photographs, and the thorough sifting of the debris. I could not quarrel with Emerson's high standards, but I must admit that there were times when I wished he would stop fussing and get on with the job. I had made the mistake of saying something of the sort when we began digging that season. Emerson had rounded on me with bared teeth and an impressive scowl.

"You, of all people, ought to know better! As soon as a monument is exposed it begins to deteriorate. Remember what happened to the mastabas Lepsius found sixty years ago. Many of the reliefs he copied have now disappeared, worn away by weather or vandalized by thieves, nor are the copies as accurate as one would wish. I will not uncover the walls of this tomb until I have taken all possible means to protect them, or go on to the next mastaba until Ramses has recorded every damned scratch on every damned wall! And furthermore —"

I informed him that he had made his point.

One morning a few days after the conversation on the rooftop I had allowed the others to go on before me, since I had to speak to Fatima about various domestic matters. I had completed this little chore and was in my room, checking my pockets and my belt to make certain I had with me all the useful implements I always carry, when there was a knock on the door.

"Come in," I said, as I continued the inventory. Pistol and knife, canteen, bottle of brandy, candle and matches in a waterproof box . . . "Oh, it is you, Kadija."

"May I speak to you, Sitt Hakim?"

"Certainly. Just one moment while I make certain I have everything. Notebook and pencil, needle and thread, compass, scissors, first-aid kit. . . ."

Her large dark face broke into a smile as she watched me. For some reason my accoutrements, as I called them, were a source of considerable amusement to my acquaintances. They were also a source of considerable aggravation to Emerson, despite (or perhaps because of) the fact that on numerous occasions one or another of them had proved our salvation.

"There," I said, hooking to my belt a coil of stout cord (useful for tying up captured enemies). "What can I do for you, Kadija?"

The members of our dear Abdullah's extended family were friends as well as loyal workers, some of them on the dig, some at the house. Since Abdullah's grandson had married our niece, one might say they were also related to us in some degree or other, though the precise relationships were sometimes difficult to define. Abdullah had been married at least four times and several of the other men had more than one wife; nieces, nephews, and cousins of varying degrees formed a large and closely knit clan.

Kadija, the wife of Abdullah's nephew Daoud, was a very large woman, taciturn, modest, and strong as a man. Painstakingly and formally she inquired about each member of the family in turn, including the ones she had seen within the past hours. It took her a while to get to Ramses.

"He had a difference of opinion with someone," I explained.

"A difference of opinion," Kadija repeated slowly. "It looked to me, Sitt Hakim, as if more than words were exchanged. Is he in trouble of some kind? What can we do to help?"

"I don't know, Kadija. You know how he is; he keeps his own counsel and does not confide even in his father. If David were here . . ." I broke off with a sigh.

"If only he were." Kadija sighed too.

"Yes." I realized I was about to sigh again, and stopped myself. Really, my own thoughts were gloomy enough without Kadija adding to them! I gave myself a little shake and said briskly, "There is no use wishing things were other than they are, Kadija. Cheer up!"

"Yes, Sitt Hakim." But she was not finished. She cleared her throat. "It is Nur Misur, Sitt."

"Nefret?" Curse it, I thought, I might have known. She and Nefret were very close; all the rest had been leading up to this. "What about her?"

"She would be angry if she knew I had told you."

Now thoroughly alarmed — for it was not in Kadija's nature to tell tales — I said, "And I will be angry if there is something wrong with Nefret and you do not tell me. Is she ill? Or — oh, dear! — involved with some unsuitable male person?"

I could tell by the look on her broad, honest face, that my last surmise was the right one. People are always surprised when I hit on the truth; it is not magic, as some of the Egyptians secretly believe, but my profound understanding of human nature.

I had to wring it out of Kadija, but I am good at doing that. When she finally mentioned a name, I was thunderstruck.

"My nephew Percy? Impossible! She despises him. How do you know?"

"I may be wrong," Kadija muttered. "I hope, Sitt, that I am. It was a closed carriage waiting, on the other side of the road; she was going to the hospital, walking to the tram station, and when she came out of the house a man's face appeared at the window of the carriage, and he called her name, and she crossed the road and stood talking to him. Oh, Sitt, I am ashamed — I do not spy, I only happened to go to the door —"

"I am glad you did, Kadija. You didn't hear what they said, I suppose."

"No. They did not talk long. Then she turned and walked away, and the carriage passed her and went on."

"You are not certain it was Captain Peabody?"

"I could not swear an oath. But it looked like him. I had to tell you, Sitt, he is an evil man, but if she learned I had betrayed her —"

"I won't tell her. Nor ask you to spy on her. I will take care of *that* myself. Don't breathe a word of this to anyone else, Kadija. You did the right thing. You can leave it to me now."

"Yes, Sitt." Her face cleared. "You will know what to do."

I didn't, though. After Kadija had taken her departure I tried to get my thoughts in order. Not for a moment did I doubt Kadija's word, or her assessment of Percy. He had been a sly, unprincipled child and he had become a cunning, unprincipled man. He had proposed marriage to Nefret several times in

90

the past. Perhaps he had not given up hope of winning her — her fortune, rather, since in my opinion he was incapable of honorable affection. She would have to meet him on the sly, since he would not dare come openly to the house. . . .

Oh, no, I thought, my imagination is running away with me. It is not possible. Nefret was passionate, hot-tempered and in some ways extremely innocent; it would not be the first time she had fallen in love with the wrong man, but surely she knew Percy's character too well to succumb to his advances. The callous abandonment of the child he had fathered was only one of his many despicable acts. Nefret knew of that. She knew Percy had done his best to encourage the false assumption that Ramses was responsible. Kadija must have been mistaken. Perhaps the man had been a tourist, asking directions.

I could not confront Nefret directly, but I knew I would never be at peace until I was certain. I would have to watch her and find out for myself.

Spy on her, you mean, my conscience corrected me. I winced at the word, but did not flinch from the duty. If spying was necessary, spy I would. The worst of it was I could not count on anyone else, not even my dear Emerson, for help. Emerson has a forthright manner of dealing with annoyances, and

Percy annoyed him a great deal. Punching Percy's face and pitching him into the Nile would not improve matters. As for Ramses . . . I shuddered at the thought of his finding out. Neither of them must know. It was up to me, as usual.

However, as I guided my amiable steed along the road to the pyramids, a strange foreboding came over me. It was not so strange, in fact, for I often have them. I knew what had caused this one. I had been thinking about it ever since the night we saw Wardani.

Was Sethos in Cairo, up to his old tricks? I did not — could not — believe he would turn traitor, but the situation was ideal for the kind of skulduggery at which he excelled. Excavations had been cancelled, many archaeological sites were inadequately guarded or not guarded at all, the Services des Antiquités was in disorder with Maspero gone and his successor still in France engaged in war work, the police occupied with civil unrest. What an opportunity for a master thief! And with Sethos's skill in the art of disguise he could assume any identity he chose. A series of wild surmises passed through my mind: Wardani? General Maxwell?

Percy?

As Emerson might have said, that idea was too bizarre even for my excellent imagination. I burst out laughing, and turned to happier thoughts. I never approached the pyramids without a thrill passing through me.

To excavate in the cemeteries of Giza was the culmination of a lifetime's dream, but sadness shadowed my pleasure, for we would not have been given permission to do so had not the stroke of a pen transformed friends into enemies and made former colleagues personae non gratae in the country where they had labored so long and effectively. Mr. Reisner, who held the concession for a large part of the Giza necropolis, was an American and would soon begin his winter season, but the German group under Herr Professor Junker would not return until the war was over.

It had been Junker himself who asked Emerson to deputize for him.

They say the war will be over by Christmas, [he had written]. *But they are wrong. God alone knows when this horror will end, and how. Some might condemn me for being concerned about antiquities when so many lives are at hazard, but you, old friend, will understand; and you are one of the few men whom I trust to protect the monuments and carry out the work as I would do. I pray with all my heart that despite the strife between our two peoples the friendship between us will endure and that everyone in our field of science may be guided by the ancient maxim: in omnibus caritas.*

This touching epistle brought tears to my eyes. How sad it was that the violent passions of men could destroy reason, affection, and scientific accomplishment! Emerson himself had been deeply moved by Junker's letter, though he concealed his emotion by cursing everybody he could think of, beginning with the Kaiser and ending with certain members of the British community in Cairo, in whose minds charity had little place. With the permission of the Antiquities Department he had taken up the torch thrown him by Junker, and I must admit that my own regrets were tempered by delight at finally coming to grips with a site where I had always yearned to excavate.

Tourists who visit Giza today cannot possibly imagine what a splendid sight it was four thousand years ago: the sides of the pyramids covered with a smooth coating of white limestone, their summits crowned with gold, their temples bright with painted columns; the mighty Sphinx with his nose and beard intact and his headcloth striped in red and gold; and, surrounding each pyramid, rank upon rank of low structures whose sides also gleamed with the soft luster of limestone. They were the tombs of princes and officials of the royal house, furnished with chapels and statues and funerary equipment that would nourish the soul of the man or woman whose body lay in the burial chamber, at the bottom of a deep shaft cut through the super-structure.

One could only hope that immortality did not depend on the survival of the objects that had filled these tombs, or on the physical remains of their owners. Gone, all gone, alas, centuries before — the ornaments and jars of oil and boxes of fine linen into the hoards of tomb robbers, the bodies of the dead ripped apart in the search for valuables. Over the millennia, later tombs had been added, around and beside and sometimes on top of the Old Kingdom monuments, and the entire area had been buried by drifted sand; roofing stones had fallen, and walls had collapsed. Making sense of the resultant jumble was not at all easy, even for an experienced excavator, and before he could begin to do so he had to remove the accumulated debris of centuries, some of it several meters deep.

Junker had located the walls of the tomb the previous year, but the sand had drifted over it again. Emerson had caused the soil to be removed to the top of the walls, and the men had begun clearing the interior. Some excavators simply discarded this fill without examining it, but that was not Emerson's way. After discovering that the interior walls were covered with remarkably well-preserved painted reliefs, he had insisted on erecting a temporary roof over the chamber. Rainstorms are not unknown in Cairo, and even blowing sand could damage the fragile paint.

I guided my steed past the carriages and camels and cabs and throngs of tourists toward the site where we were working, but I could not resist casting frequent glances at the towering slopes of the Great Pyramid. I am particularly attracted to pyramids. It was delightful to be working in such proximity to the mightiest of them all and know that, for the time being and in a limited sense, it was mine! I had no great hope of exploring it in the immediate future, however. Emerson meant to concentrate on the private tombs. Anyhow, the pyramid was a major tourist attraction, and it would have been difficult to work there in peace. Our own excavations were so close to the south side, we were always having to shoo wandering visitors away.

From Manuscript H

Every time Ramses entered the tomb he felt a pang of sympathy for the German archaeologist who had been forced to leave it. Removing the fill and erecting the shelter had taken a long time, but the first chamber of what appeared to be a large complex tomb had now been emptied, and he had begun copying the reliefs. The painted carvings along the west wall showed the prince Sekhemankhor and his wife Hatnub seated before an offering table loaded with foodstuffs and flowers. The inscriptions identified the pair, but so far they had not found a reference to the king whose son Sekhemankhor claimed to be.

Ramses was working alone that afternoon, inspecting the wall to ascertain how much of the relief had been damaged and whether restoration was possible. His thoughts were not the best of company these days, so when Selim came looking for him his response was ungracious.

"Well? What do you want?"

"It is an emergency," said Selim. He often spoke English with Ramses, trying to improve his command of the language, and his voice lingered lovingly on the long word. "I think you had better come."

Ramses straightened. "Why me? Can't you deal with it?"

"It is not that sort of emergency." The light was poor; they had been using reflectors, since the supply of electric batteries was limited and his father would not permit candles or torches; but he saw Selim's teeth gleam in the black of his beard. He was obviously amused about something, and determined to share it with his friend.

They emerged from the tomb into the mellow light of late afternoon, and Ramses heard voices. The bass and baritone bellows of the men mingled with the excited cries of children, and over them all rose and fell a series of penetrating sounds like the whistle of a locomotive. Egyptians enjoyed a good argument and did it at the top of their lungs, but the loudest voice sounded like that of a woman. He quickened his pace.

Straight ahead rose the southern face of Egypt's mightiest pyramid. The crowd had gathered around the base. They were all Egyptians except for a few foreigners, obviously tourists. One of the foreign females was doing the screaming.

Ramses raised his voice in a peremptory demand for silence and information. The men came trotting toward him, all yelling and gesticulating. Selim, just behind him, raised an arm and pointed. "Up there, Ramses. Do you see?"

Ramses shaded his eyes and looked up. The sun was low in the western sky and its slanting rays turned the pyramid's slope to gold. Several dark shapes stood out against the glowing stone.

Climbing the Great Pyramid was a popular tourist sport. The layers of stones formed a kind of staircase, but since most of the stones were almost three feet high, the climb was too arduous for the majority of visitors without the help of several Egyptians, hauling from above and sometimes pushing from below. Occasionally a timid adventurer balked when he was only partway up, and had to be hauled ignominiously down by his assistants. Perhaps that was what had happened, but he couldn't understand why Selim had dragged him away from his work to enjoy the discomfiture of some unfortunate man . . . No, not a man. Squinting, he realized the motionless form was female.

She was a good half way up, two hundred feet from the ground, sitting bolt upright on one of the stones, with her feet sticking straight out. He couldn't make out details at this distance — only a bare dark head and a slender body clad in a light-colored frock of European style. Not far away, but not too close either, were two men in the long robes of the Egyptians.

He turned to Sheikh Hassan, the nominal chief of the guides who infested Giza. "What is going on?" he demanded. "Why don't they bring her down?"

"She won't let them." Hassan's round face broke into a grin. "She calls them bad names, Brother of Demons, and strikes them with her hand when they try to take hold of her."

"She slapped them?" Ramses was tempted to laugh. The situation was too serious for that, however. The wretched female must have become hysterical, and if the guides took hold of her against her will, her struggles could result in injury to her and charges of assault — or worse — against them. No proof of malicious intent would be needed, only her word. He swore in Arabic, and added irritably, "Can someone stop that woman yelling? Who is she?"

The woman in question pulled away from the arms that held her and ran toward Ramses. "Why are you standing there?" she demanded. "You are English, aren't you? Go and get her. Save the child!"

"Calm yourself, madam," Ramses said. "Are you her mother?"

He knew she wasn't, though. She might have had "governess" printed across her forehead. The ones he had met fell into two categories: the timid and wispy and the loud and dictatorial. This woman was of the second type. She glared at him from under her unplucked eyebrows and rubbed her prominent nose with a gloved hand.

"Well, sir? As an English gentleman —"

"English, at any rate," said Ramses. He was tempted to point out that his nationality did not qualify him to tackle the job, which any Egyptian could do better, but he knew there was no sense arguing with a frantic female. He detached the large hand that gripped his arm and pushed her into the reluctant grasp of Selim. "Yes, ma'am, I'll go after her."

And if she tries to slap me, he thought, I'll slap back. A sovereign cure for hysteria, his mother always claimed. What the deuce was wrong with the damned fool governess, allowing a child to attempt such a dangerous feat? Either she was incompetent or the kid was unmanageable.

Like a certain unmanageable boy whose competent mother hadn't been able to prevent him from attempting equally dangerous feats. As he started up, he remembered the first time he had climbed the pyramid alone. He had been ten years old, and he'd come close to breaking his neck several times. His mother seldom employed corporal punishment, but she had spanked him soundly after that escapade. Perhaps he was in no position to be critical of adventurous children.

Pulling himself from step to step, he looked up only often enough to orient himself. He'd climbed all four sides of the Great Pyramid at various times, but he wasn't fool enough to take unnecessary chances. Some of the stones had crumbled at the edges, some were broken, and they were of different heights. Nor did he raise his eyes when a voice from above hailed him.

"O Brother of Demons! We came with her, we did what she said. Then she sat down and would not move, and she struck at us when we tried to help her. Will you speak for us? Will you tell them we did our best? Will you —"

"Make certain you are paid?" Ramses stepped onto the same level as the speaker. He was a wiry little man, his long robe tucked up to expose bony shanks, his feet bare. He and his wife inhabited a hut in Giza Village with several goats, a few chickens, and two children. Two others had died before they were a year old.

Ramses reached in his pocket and pulled out a handful of coins. "Here. Go down now, I can manage her better alone."

Blessings showered him as the two guides began the descent. He made certain his expression was stern before he turned to face the object of the emergency. He'd formed a picture of her in his mind. She'd be eleven or twelve, with scabs on her knees and elbows, freckles on her nose, a stubborn chin.

He had been right about the chin. There was a scattering of freckles too. His guess about her age was verified by her hideous and impractical garments. The dress looked like a female version of the sailor suits his mother had forced on him when he was too young to fight back; the knotted tie hung like a limp blue rag from the base of her throat. The skirt reached just below her knees, and the legs that stuck out at a defiant angle were encased in thick black stockings. He could only begin to wonder what she was wearing underneath — several layers of woollies, if his understanding of the governess mentality was accurate. Mouse-brown hair hung in damp tangles down her back, and her rounded cheeks were wet with perspiration. Her eyes were her most attractive feature, the irises a soft shade of hazel. He put their penetrating stare down to terror, and decided she needed reassurance, not a scolding.

He sat down next to her. "What happened to your hat?" he asked casually.

She continued to stare, so he tried another approach. "My name is Emerson."

"No, it's not."

"That is odd," he said, shaking his head. "To think that for over twenty years I have been mistaken about my own name. I must have a word with my mother."

Either she had no sense of humor or she was in no mood for jokes. "It's your father's name. That's what people call him. I've heard about him. I've heard about you too. They call you Ramses."

"Among other things." That got a faint smile. He smiled back at her and went on, "You mustn't believe all you hear. I'm not so bad when you get to know me."

"I didn't know you looked like this," she said softly.

The stare was beginning to bother him. "Has my nose turned blue?" he asked. "Or — horns? Are they sprouting?"

"Oh." The color flooded into her face. "I've been rude. I apologize."

"No need. But perhaps we should continue this conversation in more comfortable surroundings. Are you ready to go down now?" He stood up and held out his hand.

She pressed herself farther back against the stone. "My hat," she said in a strangled voice.

"What about it?"

"It fell off." Her slender throat contracted as she swallowed. "The strap must have broken. It fell . . . it bounced. . . ."

He looked down. One couldn't blame her for losing her nerve. The angle of the slope was approximately fifty degrees, and she was two hundred feet up. Watching the pith helmet bounce from step to step to step, and picture one's body doing the same thing, must have been terrifying.

"The trick is never to look down," he said easily. "Suppose you keep your back turned. I'll go first and lift you from one level to the next. Do you think you could trust me to do that?"

She inspected him from head to foot and back, and then nodded. "You're pretty strong, aren't you?"

"Strong enough to manage a little thing like you. Come on now. No, don't close your eyes; that does make one giddy. Just keep looking straight ahead."

She gave him her hand and let him raise her to her feet.

He went slowly at first, till her taut muscles relaxed and she yielded trustingly to his grasp. She didn't weigh anything at all. He could span her waist with his hands. They were still some distance from the bottom when she laughed and looked up at him over her shoulder. "It's like flying," she said gleefully. "I'm not afraid now."

"Good. Hang on, we're almost there."

"I wish we weren't. Miss Nordstrom is going to be horrid to me."

"Serves you right. It was a silly thing to do."

"I'm glad I did it, though."

A crowd had clustered round the base of the structure. The upturned faces were ovals of coffee-brown and umber and sunburned red. One of them was a particularly handsome shade of mahogany. His mother must have sent his father to fetch him home; he'd lost track of the time, as usual.

He dropped from the last step to the ground and swung her down. When he would have set her on her feet she fell back against him and clung to his arm.

"My ankle! Oh, it hurts!"

Since she seemed about to collapse, Ramses picked her up and turned to receive the applause of the audience. The English and Americans cheered, the Egyptians yelled, and his father pushed through the spectators.

Emerson's expression was one of affable approval; it broadened into a smile as he looked at the girl. "All right, are you, my dear?" he inquired. "Well done, Ramses.

Present me to the young lady, if you please."

"I fear I neglected to ask her name," Ramses said. Now that she was safely down he was beginning to be annoyed with the "young lady." There wasn't a damned thing wrong with her foot; she was trying to look pathetic in the hope of staving off the expected and well-deserved scolding. To give the governess credit, she appeared to be more relieved than angry.

"It was my fault, sir," said the girl. "I was so frightened and he was so kind . . . My name is Melinda Hamilton."

"A pleasure," said Emerson, bowing. "My name —"

"Oh, I know who you are, sir. Everyone knows Professor Emerson. And his son."

"Most kind," said Emerson. "Are you going to put her down, Ramses?"

"I'm afraid I hurt my foot, sir," said the young person winsomely.

"Hurt your foot, eh? You had better come to our house and let Mrs. Emerson have a look. I'll take her, Ramses. You can bring Miss — er — um — with you on Risha."

Damned if I will, Ramses thought, as his erstwhile charge slipped gracefully from his arms into those of his father. His splendid Arabian stallion would make nothing of the extra weight, but Miss Nordstrom would probably accuse him of trying to ravish her if he hauled her up onto the saddle and rode off with her into the sunset or any other direction.

Emerson strode away, carrying the girl as easily as if she had been a doll and talking cheerfully about tea and cakes and the Sitt Hakim, his wife, who had a sovereign remedy for sprained ankles, and their house, and their pets. Did she like cats? Ah, then she must meet Seshat.

Ramses stood watching them, nagged by the obscure and irrational sense of guilt that always filled him when he saw his father with a child. Neither of his parents had ever reproached him for failing to present them with grandchildren; he had believed they didn't much care until Sennia had entered their lives. He still wasn't certain how his mother felt, but his father's attachment to the little girl was deep and moving. Ramses missed her too, but for a number of reasons he was glad Sennia was safe in England.

He located the carriage Miss Nordstrom had hired and told the driver to bring the lady to their house. Then he mounted Risha and headed for home, wondering what his mother would make of his father's latest pet.

I have become quite accustomed to having the members of my family bring strays of all species home with them. Nefret is the worst offender, for she is constantly adopting wounded or orphaned animals, but they are

107

less trouble than wounded or orphaned humans. When Emerson strode into the sitting room carrying a small human of the female gender, a familiar sense of foreboding filled me. Men have a number of annoying qualities, but over the years women — especially young women — have given me considerable trouble. Most of them fall in love with my husband or my son, or both.

Emerson deposited the young person in a chair. "This is Miss Melinda Hamilton, Peabody. She hurt her foot climbing the Great Pyramid, so I brought her to you."

Miss Hamilton did not appear to be in pain. She returned my clinical stare with a broad smile. A gap between her two front teeth and a sprinkling of freckles gave her a look of childish innocence, but I judged her to be in her early teens. She had not yet put up her hair or lengthened her frock. The former was windblown and tangled, the latter dusty and torn. She was not wearing a hat.

"You are not an orphan, are you?" I asked.

"Peabody!" Emerson exclaimed.

"As a matter of fact, I am," said the young person coolly.

"I beg your pardon," I said, recovering myself. "I was endeavoring, rather clumsily, I confess, to ascertain whether some anxious person is looking all over Giza for you. Surely you did not go there alone."

"No, ma'am, of course not. My governess

was with me. The Professor just picked me up and brought me here. He is so kind." She gave Emerson an admiring look.

"Yes," I said. "He is also thoughtless. Emerson, what have you done with the governess?"

"Ramses is bringing her. Is tea ready? I am sure our guest is tired and thirsty."

He was reminding me of my manners — something he seldom gets a chance to do — so I rang for Fatima and asked her to bring tea. I then knelt before the girl and removed her shoe and stocking. She protested, but of course I paid no attention.

"There is no swelling," I announced, inspecting a small, dusty bare ankle. "Oh — I am sorry, Miss Melinda! Did I hurt you?"

Her involuntary movement had not been caused by pain. She had turned toward the door. "My friends call me Molly," she said.

"Ah, there you are, Ramses," said his father. "What have you done with the governess?"

"And what have you done with your pith helmet?" I inquired. Like his father, Ramses is always losing his hats. He passed his hand over his tumbled hair, trying to smooth it back. He ignored my question, probably because he did not know the answer, and replied to his father.

"She will be here shortly. I passed the carriage a few minutes ago."

"Hurry and clean up," I ordered. "You look even more unkempt than usual. What have you been doing with yourself?"

"Rescuing me," said Miss Molly. "Please don't scold him. He was splendid!"

Ramses vanished, in that noiseless fashion of his, and I said, "I thought it was the Professor who rescued you."

"No, no," said Emerson. "It was Ramses who brought her down from the pyramid. She'd hurt her foot, you see, and —"

"And lost my head." The girl smiled sheepishly. "I was afraid to go up or down. I made a perfect fool of myself. Mrs. Emerson, you have been so kind — may I ask another favor? Would it be possible for me to bathe my face and hands and tidy myself a bit?"

It was a reasonable request, and one I ought to have anticipated. Before I could respond, however, there was another interruption, in the form of a large female clad in black, who rushed at the girl and showered her with mingled reproaches and queries. No question of *her* identity, I thought. I hushed the woman and directed them to one of the guest chambers. Emerson's offer to carry Miss Molly was rejected in no uncertain terms by Miss Nordstrom, who glowered at him as if she suspected him of evil designs on her charge. She led the girl away, supporting her.

When they returned, the rest of us were

gathered round the tea table, including Nefret, who had spent the afternoon at the hospital.

"Here they are," I said. "I have just been telling Miss Forth about your adventure. Nefret, may I present Miss Nordstrom and Miss Melinda Hamilton."

Waving aside Emerson's offer of assistance, the governess lowered her charge into a chair. The child's appearance was greatly improved. Her hair had been tied back from her forehead with a white ribbon, and her face shone pink from scrubbing. Her shoe and stocking had been replaced. Of course, I thought, a woman like Miss Nordstrom would consider it improper to bare any portion of the lower anatomy in the presence of a man.

"Is that wise?" I inquired, indicating the shod foot. "A tight boot will be painful if her foot swells. Perhaps you would like Miss Forth to have a look at it. She is a physician."

"Not necessary," said Miss Nordstrom, looking at Nefret with shocked surprise.

Nefret smiled. She was accustomed to having people react to that announcement with disbelief or disapproval. "I would be happy to."

When the offer was again rejected she did not persist. A cup of tea removed the governess's ill humor. She began to apologize for inconveniencing us.

"Think nothing of it," I said. "You are newcomers to Cairo, I believe? How do you like it?"

"Not at all," said Miss Nordstrom bluntly. "I have never seen so many beggars and so much dirt. The guides are impertinent. And none of the wretches speak English! I was against our coming, but Major Hamilton was determined to have his niece with him, and duty brought him here. Are you acquainted with him?"

"I have heard his name," Emerson said. "With the Corps of Engineers, is he?"

"He was called in to consult on the defenses of the Canal and reports directly to General Maxwell," Miss Nordstrom corrected. She was obviously proud of her employer; she went on to tell us in tedious detail about his past triumphs and present importance.

Miss Molly was unimpressed. More — she was bored. She brightened, however, when the only missing member of the family sauntered in, tail swinging. Seshat went straight to Ramses, who held out his hand.

"So you finally woke up?" he inquired. "Good of you to join us."

"Oh, it's beautiful," Miss Molly exclaimed. "Is it yours, Ramses?"

"Molly!" Miss Nordstrom exclaimed. "You are being familiar!"

"That's all right," Ramses said, with a reassuring smile at the girl. "This is Seshat, Molly. She, not it, if you don't mind."

Seshat condescended to be introduced and have her back stroked — once. She then returned to Ramses. Seeing Molly's face fall, Nefret said, "Are you fond of animals? Perhaps you would like to visit my menagerie."

Miss Nordstrom declined the invitation, and since I found the woman very tedious, I went off with Nefret and Miss Molly. The poor little thing perked up as soon as we were out of the room.

"Miss Nordstrom is rather strict," I said sympathetically.

"Oh, Nordie means well. It's just that she won't let me do anything interesting. This is the best time I've had since we got here."

"What do you usually do for entertainment?" Nefret asked.

Molly gave a little skip. "Do my lessons and take drives around the city while Nordie reads out of Baedeker. Sometimes we have people to tea. Children, I mean. I'm not out yet, so I'm not allowed to associate with young ladies. And the children are so young!"

Nefret laughed. "How old are you?"

"Seventeen." She looked from Nefret to me and back to Nefret, and realized that little fabrication was not going to be believed. "Well . . . I will be sixteen in a few months."

"Fifteen?" Nefret inquired; her brows were arched and a dimple trembled at the corner of her mouth. "Are you sure you don't mean fourteen — or thirteen — or —"

"Almost thirteen." Molly admitted defeat with a scowl at Nefret.

She forgot her grievance when Nefret showed her round the "menagerie." Narmer, the unattractive yellow mongrel whom Nefret persisted in calling a watchdog, greeted us with his customary howls and bounds, and had to be shut in the shed to keep him from jumping at everyone. Miss Molly did not care much for him (neither did I), but a litter of puppies brought her to her knees, and as the little creatures crawled over her she raised a face shining with pleasure. "They're so sweet. I do wish I could have one."

"We'll ask your uncle, shall we?" Nefret suggested. "I'm always looking for good homes for my strays."

"He'll say it's up to Nordie, and she'll say no. She thinks animals are dirty and make too much trouble."

She was still playing with the puppies when Ramses joined us. "Enjoying yourself?" he asked, smiling down at her. "I'm sorry to interrupt, but Miss Nordstrom sent me to fetch you. She is anxious to get you home."

"That dreary hotel isn't home." But she removed the puppies from her lap and held out her arms to Ramses. "It still hurts. Will you carry me?"

"There's no swelling," said Nefret, running experienced fingers round the small foot. "I think it would be better for you to walk it off. Here, let me help you up."

She left Miss Molly little choice, lifting her to her feet and taking firm hold of her arm.

"Are you really a doctor?" the girl asked.

"Yes."

"Is it very hard, to be a doctor?"

"Very," Nefret said rather grimly.

Miss Nordstrom was pacing impatiently up and down the room, so we saw them to their waiting cab and parted with mutual expressions of goodwill.

"Why did you leave me alone with that dreadful woman?" Emerson demanded.

"Sssh! Wait until they are farther away before you begin insulting her," I said.

"Well, I don't care if she hears. She's awfully hard on the child, you know. By her own admission she never takes her anywhere. Can you believe it, Peabody — this was their first visit to Giza, and they haven't even been to Sakkara or Abu Roash!"

"A cruel deprivation indeed," I said, laughing. "Not everyone is interested in ancient sites, Emerson."

"She would be if she had the chance," Emerson declared. "She asked me all sorts of questions when I was bringing her here. Why don't you write to her uncle, Peabody, and ask if she can visit us from time to time."

115

"You'll have to have Miss Nordstrom too."

"Damnation. I suppose that's so." Emerson brooded. "Ah, well. We might ask her and her uncle for Christmas dinner, eh? She's a bright, cheerful little thing, and she seemed to enjoy our company, don't you think?"

"Oh, yes," Nefret said. "No question about that."

From Letter Collection B

Dearest Lia,

You have every right to reproach me for being a poor correspondent. Life is so dull and quiet here, there is very little to write about. Not that I wouldn't talk for hours if you were here! We can always find things to talk about, can't we? Never mind, the war can't last much longer, and then we will all be together again, with a little newcomer to train up in archaeology! The Professor is moping a bit; he would never admit it, since he hates to be thought sentimental, but I think he is lonesome for Sennia. You know how he loves children. Something rather amusing happened yesterday; he came home from the dig with a new pet — a young English girl who had got herself marooned halfway up the Great Pyramid. She had panicked, as people sometimes do, and wouldn't let her guides help her, so someone sent for Ramses. He brought her down safely, but she claimed she had hurt her

116

foot and the Professor insisted she come to the house to have it looked after. She was accompanied by an extremely formidable governess, who snatched her away as soon as was decently possible. But I'm afraid we haven't seen the last of her.

Why do I say "afraid?" Well, my dear, you know the effect Ramses has on females of all ages, especially when he lets his guard down, as he does with children, and gives them a real smile instead of that quirk of the lips that is his usual expression of mild amusement or pleasure. He has quite a devastating smile — or so I have been told, by various bemused women. This one isn't a woman, she's only twelve, but what female could resist being rescued by a handsome, sun-bronzed, athletic young man? There wasn't a thing wrong with her ankle. I hope she isn't going to be trouble.

3

"Music," Ramses remarked, "is one of the most effective tools of the warmonger."

This sententious observation was overheard by all at the railing of Shepheard's terrace, where we stood watching the military band marching past on its way to the bandstand in the Ezbekieh Gardens. Today the musicians had halted in front of the hotel, marking time and (one would suppose) catching their breaths before launching into the next selection. The brilliant crimson-and-white uniforms made a gaudy show, and sunlight struck dazzlingly off the polished brass of trumpets and trombones and tubas.

I caught the eye of Nefret, who was on Ramses's other side. Her lips parted, but like myself she was not quick enough to head him off. Leaning on the rail, Ramses continued, in the same carrying voice, "Stirring marches confuse rational thought by appealing directly to the emotions. Plato was quite correct to forbid certain types of music in his ideal society. The Lydian mode —"

A blast of drums and brasses drowned him out as the band burst into "Rule, Britannia."

The loyal watchers attempted to join in, with only moderate success; as the Reader may know, the verse has a series of rapid arpeggios that are very difficult to render clearly. What the singers lacked in musicality they made up for in enthusiasm; faces glowed with patriotic fervor, eyes shone, and as soprano tremolo and baritone rumble mingled in the stirring words of the chorus: "Britons never, never, never will be slaves!" I felt my own pulse quicken.

The onlookers formed a cross-section of Anglo-Egyptian society, the ladies in filmy afternoon frocks and huge hats, the gentlemen in uniform or well-cut lounge suits. Down below, waiting for the street to be cleared so they could go about their affairs, were spectators of quite a different sort. Some wore fezzes and European-style suits, others long robes and turbans; but their faces bore similar expressions — sullen, resentful, watching. A conspicuous exception was an individual directly across the street; his well-bred countenance was tanned to a handsome brown and he was half a head taller than those around him. He was not wearing a fez, a turban, or a hat. I waved at him, but he was talking animatedly to a man who stood next to him and did not see me.

"There is your father at last," I said to Ramses. "Whom is he conversing with?"

The band had moved on, and it was now

possible to make oneself heard without shouting. Ramses turned, his elbow on the rail. "Where? Oh. That's Philippides, the head of the political CID."

I studied the fellow's plump, smiling face with new interest. I had not met him, but I had heard a number of unpleasant stories about him. His superior, Harvey Pasha, had made him responsible for rounding up enemy aliens, and it was said he had acquired a small fortune from people he threatened with deportation. The guilty parties paid him to overlook their transgressions and the innocent parties paid him to be left in peace. He terrorized a good part of Cairo, and his shrewish wife terrorized him.

"Why on earth would your father spend time with a man like that?" I demanded.

"I've no idea," said Ramses. "Unless he hopes Philippides will use his influence on David's behalf. Shall we go back to our table? Father will join us when he chooses, I suppose."

In point of fact, I was surprised Emerson had condescended to join us at all. He disliked taking tea at Shepheard's, claiming that the only people who went there were frivolous society persons and tedious tourists. In this he was correct. However, in justice to myself, I must explain that my reasons for this particular outing were not frivolous.

Spying on Nefret without appearing to do

so had driven me to expedients that were cursed difficult to arrange, much less explain. I could not insist on accompanying her wherever she went, or demand verification of her movements; and on the one occasion when I attempted to follow her disguised in a robe and veil I had borrowed from Fatima, the inconvenient garb handicapped me to such an extent that Nefret reached the station and hopped onto a departing tram while I was attempting to disentangle my veil from a thornbush.

Considering alternatives, I concluded that the best plan would be to fill our calendar with engagements that involved the entire family. The approach of the Yuletide season, with its attendant festivities, made this procedure feasible, and today's excursion was one of that sort.

My other motive was one I was reluctant to admit even to myself. After all, what had we to do with spies? Rounding the rascals up was the responsibility of the police and the military. Yet the seed of suspicion Nefret had sowed in my mind had found sustenance there; whenever I stamped upon it with the boot of reason, it sent up another green shoot. If Sethos was in Cairo, we were the only ones who stood a chance of tracking him down — the only ones who were familiar with his methods, who had met him face-to . . . well, to several of his many faces.

Now I wondered if the same notion had occurred to Emerson. Jealousy, unwarranted but intense, as well as professional dislike, burned within him; nothing would give him greater satisfaction than to bring the Master Criminal to justice. Was he at this very moment on the trail of Sethos? Why else would he stoop to amiable converse with a man like Philippides?

I fully intended to ask him, but I did not suppose he would admit the truth. Good Gad, I thought, if I am forced to spy on Emerson as well as on Nefret, I will find myself fully occupied.

When he joined us a few minutes later, his noble brow was furrowed and his white teeth were bared in what was probably not a smile. Instead of greeting us properly, he flung himself into a chair and demanded, "What have you done now, Ramses?"

"Done?" Ramses repeated, raising his eyebrows. "I?"

"I have just been informed," said Emerson, beckoning the waiter, "by that consummate ass Pettigrew, that you were making seditious remarks while the band played patriotic airs."

"I was talking about Plato," said Ramses.

"Good Gad," said his father, in some bewilderment. "Why?"

Ramses explained — at greater length, in my opinion, than was strictly necessary. Having warmed to his theme, he developed it further. "We will soon be seeing a resurgence of sentimental ballads that present a romanticized version of death and battle. The soldier boy dreaming of his dear old mother, the sweetheart smiling bravely as she sends her lover off to war —"

"Stop it," Nefret snapped.

"I am sorry," said Ramses, "if you find my remarks offensive."

"Deliberately provocative, rather. People are listening."

"If they take umbrage at a philosophical discussion —"

"Both of you, stop it," I exclaimed.

Spots of pink marked Nefret's smooth cheeks, and Ramses's lips were pressed tightly together. I was forced to agree with Nefret. Ramses had almost given up his old habit of pontificating at length on subjects designed to annoy the hearer (usually his mother); this relapse was, I thought, deliberate.

The terrace of Shepheard's hotel had been a popular rendezvous for decades. It was even more crowded than usual that afternoon. All the first class hotels were filled to bursting. The War Office had taken over part of the Savoy; Imperial and British troops were pouring into the city. Yet, except for the greater number of uniforms, Shepheard's looked much the same as it had always done — white cloths and fine china on the tables, waiters running back and forth with trays of food and drink, elegantly dressed ladies and stout gentlemen in snowy linen. Thus far the war had done very little to change the habits of the Anglo-Egyptian community; its members amused themselves in much the same fashion as they would have done in England: the women paying social calls and gossiping, the men patronizing their clubs — and gossiping. Another form of amusement, between persons of opposite genders, was perhaps the inevitable consequence of boredom and limited social contacts. I believe I need say no more.

I glanced at my lapel watch. "She is late."

At this innocuous remark Emerson broke off in the middle of a sentence and turned a formidable frown on me.

"She? Who? Curse it, Peabody, have you invited some fluttery female to join us? I would never have agreed to come here if I had suspected —"

"Ah, there she is."

She was very handsome in a mature, rather Latin, style, with very red lips and very dark hair, and although she wore the black decreed for recent widows, it was extremely fashionable mourning. Chiffon and point d'esprit filled in the waist opening, and her hat was heaped with black satin bows and jet buckles.

The man whose arm she held was also a

124

newcomer to Cairo. He looked familiar; I stared rather sharply until I realized that the narrow black mustache and the eyeglass through which he was inspecting the lady reminded me of a sinister Russian I had once known. He was not the only man with her; she was virtually surrounded by admirers civilian and military, upon whom she smiled with practiced impartiality.

"Is that her?" Emerson demanded. "I hope you didn't invite the whole lot of them as well."

"No." I raised my parasol and waved. This caught the lady's eye; with a little gesture of apology she began to detach herself from her followers. I went on, "She is a Mrs. Fortescue, the widow of a gentleman who perished heroically in France recently. I received a letter from her enclosing an introduction from mutual friends — you remember the Witherspoons, Emerson?"

From Emerson's expression I could tell he did remember the Witherspoons and was about to express his opinion of them. He was forestalled by Ramses, who had been studying the lady with interest. "Why should she write you, Mother? Is she interested in archaeology?"

"So she claimed. I saw no harm in extending the hand of friendship to one who has suffered such a bitter loss."

"She does not appear to be suffering at the

moment," said Nefret.

Her brother gave her a sardonic look, and I said, "Hush, here she comes."

She had shed all her admirers but one, a fresh-faced officer who looked no more than eighteen. Introductions ensued; since the youth, a Lieutenant Pinckney, continued to hover, watching the lady with doglike devotion, I felt obliged to ask him to join us. Emerson and Ramses resumed their chairs, and Mrs. Fortescue began to apologize for her tardiness.

"Everyone is so kind," she murmured. "It is impossible to dismiss well-wishers, you know. I hope I have not kept you waiting long. I have so looked forward to this meeting!"

"Hmph," said Emerson, who is easily bored and who does not believe in beating around the bush. "My wife tells me you are interested in Egyptology."

From the way her black eyes examined his clean-cut features and firm mouth, I suspected Egyptology was not her only interest. However, her reply indicated that she had at least some superficial knowledge of the subject, and Emerson at once launched into a description of the Giza mastabas.

Knowing he would monopolize the conversation as long as she tolerated it, I turned to the young subaltern, who appeared somewhat crestfallen by the lady's desertion. My motherly questions soon cheered him up, and he was happy to tell me all about his family in Nottingham. He had arrived in Egypt only a week before, and although he would rather have been in France, he had hopes of seeing action before long.

"Not that Johnny Turk is much of a challenge," he added with a boyish laugh and a reassuring glance at Nefret, who had been studying him fixedly, her chin in her hand. "You ladies haven't a thing to worry about. He'll never make it across the Canal."

"We aren't at all worried," Nefret said, with a smile that made the boy blush.

"Nor should you be. There are some splendid chaps here, you know, real first-raters. I was talking to one the other night at the Club; didn't realize it at the time, he's not the sort who would put himself forward, but one of the other chaps told me afterward he was an expert on the Arab situation; had spent months in Palestine before the war, and actually let himself be taken prisoner by a renegade Arab and his band of ruffians so he could scout out their position. Then he broke out of the place, leaving a number of the scoundrels dead or wounded. But I expect you know the story, don't you?"

In his enthusiasm he talked himself breathless. When he stopped, no one replied for a moment. Nefret's eyes were downcast and she was no longer smiling. Ramses had also been listening. His expression was so bland I felt a strong chill of foreboding.

"It seems," he drawled, "that it is known to a good many people. Would that fellow standing by the stairs be the hero of whom you speak?"

Nefret's head turned as if on a spring. I had not seen Percy either. Obviously Ramses had. He missed very little.

"Why, yes, that's the chap." Young Pinckney's ingenuous countenance brightened. "Do you know him?"

"Slightly."

Percy was half-turned, conversing with another officer. I did not doubt he was aware of us, however. Without intending to, I put my hand on Ramses's arm. He smiled faintly.

"It's all right, you know, Mother."

Feeling a little foolish, I removed my hand. "What is he doing in khaki, instead of that flamboyant Egyptian Army uniform? Red tabs, too, I see; has he been reassigned?"

"Red tabs mean the staff, don't they?" Nefret asked.

"That's right," said Pinckney. "He's on the General's staff. It was jolly decent of him to talk to a chap like me," he added wistfully.

With so many eyes fixed on him, it was inevitable that Percy should turn. He hesitated for a moment, and then bowed — a generalized bow, directed at all of us, including the delighted Lieutenant Pinckney — before descending the steps.

I did not think I could endure listening to any more encomiums about Percy, so I attempted to join in the conversation between Emerson and Mrs. Fortescue. However, she was not interested in conversing with *me*.

"I had no idea it was so late!" she exclaimed, rising. "I must rush off. May I count on seeing you — all of you — again soon? You promised, you know, that you would show me your tomb."

She offered her hand to Emerson, who had risen with her. He blinked at her. "Did I? Ah. Delighted, of course. Arrange it with Mrs. Emerson."

She had a pleasant word for each of us, and — I could not help noticing — a particularly warm smile for Ramses. Some women like to collect all the personable males in their vicinity. However, when Mr. Pinckney would have accompanied her, she dismissed him firmly but politely, and as she undulated toward the door of the hotel I saw she had another one waiting! He ogled her through his monocle before taking her arm in a possessive fashion and leading her into the hotel.

"Who is that fellow?" I demanded.

Pinckney scowled. "A bally Frenchman. Count something or other. Don't know what the lady sees in him."

"The title, perhaps," Nefret suggested.

"D'you think so?" The boy stared at her, and then said with a worldly air, "Some ladies are like that, I suppose. Well, I mustn't intrude any longer. Dashed kind of you to have me. Er — if I happen to be at the pyramids one day, perhaps I might . . . er . . ."

He hadn't quite the courage to finish the question, but Nefret nodded encouragingly, and he left looking quite happy again.

"Shame on you," I said to Nefret.

"He's young and lonely," she replied calmly. "Mrs. Fortescue is far too experienced for a boy like that. I will find a nice girl his own age for him."

"What the devil was that story he was telling you about Percy?" Emerson demanded. He has no patience with gossip or young lovers.

"The same old story," Ramses replied. "What is particularly amusing is that everyone believes Percy is too modest to speak of it, despite the fact that he published a book describing his daring escape."

"But it's a bloody lie from start to finish," Emerson expostulated.

"And getting better all the time," Ramses said. "Now he's claiming he allowed himself to be caught and that he had to fight his way out."

It had taken us far longer than it ought to have done to learn the truth about that particular chapter of Percy's wretched little book.

Ramses had not spoken of it, and I had never bothered to peruse the volume; the few excerpts Nefret had read aloud were quite enough for me. It was Emerson who forced himself to plow through Percy's turgid prose — driven, according to Emerson, by mounting disbelief and indignation. When he reached the part of the book that described Percy's courageous escape and his rescue of the young Arab prince who had been his fellow prisoner, my intelligent spouse's suspicions had been aroused, and, in his usual forthright manner, he had confronted Ramses with them.

"It was you, wasn't it? It couldn't have been Prince Feisal, he'd never be damned fool enough to take such a risk. And don't try to tell me Percy was the hero of the occasion because I wouldn't believe it if I had the word direct from God and all his prophets! He couldn't escape from a biscuit tin, much less rescue someone else."

Thus challenged, Ramses had had no choice but to confess, and correct Percy's version. He had also admitted, under considerable pressure, that the truth was known to David and Lia and Nefret. "I asked them not to speak of it," he had added, raising his voice to be heard over Emerson's grumbles. "And I would rather you didn't mention it again, not even to them."

He had been so emphatic about it that we

had no choice but to accede to his wishes. Now Emerson cleared his throat. "Ramses, it is up to you, of course, but don't you think you ought to let the true story be known?"

"What would be the point? No one would believe me, anyhow. Not now."

Emerson leaned back in his chair and studied his son's impassive countenance thoughtfully. "I understand why you did not choose to make the facts public. It does you credit, though in my opinion one can sometimes carry noblesse oblige too damned far. However, given the fact that Percy's military career seems to have been based on that series of lies, some individuals might feel an obligation to expose him. He could do a great deal of damage if he were entrusted with duties he is incapable of carrying out."

"He'll take care to avoid such duties," Ramses said. "He's good at that sort of thing. Father, what were you talking about with Philippides?"

The change of subject was so abrupt as to make it evident Ramses had no intention of discussing the matter further. I glanced at Nefret, whose failure to offer her opinion had been decidedly unusual. Her eyes were fixed on her teacup, and I thought her cheeks were a trifle flushed.

"Who?" Emerson looked shifty. "Oh, that bastard. I just happened to find myself standing next to him, so I took advantage of the opportunity to put in a good word for David. Philippides has a great deal of influence with his chief; if he recommended that David be released —"

"It's out of his hands now," Ramses said. "David's connection with Wardani was well known, and it would take a direct order from the War Office to get him out."

"It never hurts to try," said Emerson. "I was mingling with the crowd, taking the temper of the community —"

"What nonsense!" I exclaimed.

"Not at all, Mother," Ramses said. "What is the temper of the community, Father?"

"Sour, surly, resentful —"

"Naturally," I said.

"You didn't allow me to finish, Peabody. There is something uglier than resentment in the air. The enforcement of martial law has not ended anti-British sentiment, it has only driven it underground. Those blind idiots in the Government refuse to see it, but mark my words, this city is a powder keg waiting to be —"

The next word was drowned out by a loud explosion, rather as if an unseen accomplice had provided dramatic confirmation of Emerson's speech. Some little distance down the street I saw a cloud of dust and smoke billow up, accompanied by screams, shouts, the rattle of falling debris, and the frantic braying of a donkey.

Ramses vaulted the rail, landing lightly on the pavement ten feet below. Emerson was only a few seconds behind him, but being somewhat heavier, he dropped straight down onto the Montenegrin doorkeeper and had to pick himself up before following Ramses toward the scene of destruction. Several officers, who had descended the steps in the normal fashion, ran after them. Other people had converged on the spot, forming a shoving, struggling, shouting barricade of bodies.

"Let us not proceed precipitately," I said to Nefret, neatly blocking her attempt to get round the table and past me.

"Someone may be hurt!"

"If you go rushing into that melee, it will be you. Stay with me."

Taking her arm in one hand and my parasol in the other, I pushed through the agitated ladies who huddled together at the top of the stairs. The street was a scene of utter chaos. Vehicular and four-footed traffic had halted; some vehicles were trying to turn and retreat, others attempted to press forward. People were running in all directions, away from and toward the spot. The fleeing forms were almost all Egyptians; I fended a wild-eyed flower vendor off with a shrewd thrust of my parasol, and drew Nefret out of the path of a portly turbaned individual who spat at us as he trotted past.

By the time we reached the scene the crowd

had dispersed. Ramses and Emerson remained, along with several officers, including Percy. The Egyptians had vanished, except for two prisoners who struggled in the grip of their captors, and a third man who lay crumpled on the ground. Standing over him was a tall, rangy fellow wearing the uniform of an Australian regiment.

"Excuse me," Nefret said. The Australian moved automatically out of her way, but when she knelt beside the fallen man he reached for her, exclaiming, "Ma'am — miss — here, miss, you can't do that!"

Ramses put out a casual hand, and the young man's arm flew up into the air.

"Keep your hands off the lady," Percy ordered. "She is a qualified physician, and a member of one of this city's most distinguished families."

"Oh? Oh." The young man rubbed his arm. Colonials are not so easily intimidated, however; looking from Ramses to Percy, he said, "If she's a friend of yours, *you* get her away from here. This is no place for a lady." He transferred his critical stare to me. "Any lady. Is this one a friend of yours too?"

Percy squared his shoulders. "I would claim that honor if I dared. You may go, Sergeant; you are not needed."

Reminded thus of their relative ranks, the young man snapped off a crisp salute and backed away.

"What's the damage, Nefret?" Emerson inquired, studiously ignoring Percy.

"Broken arm, ribs, possible concussion." She looked up. The brim of her flower-trimmed hat framed her prettily flushed face. The flush was due to anger, as she proceeded to demonstrate. "How many of you *gentlemen* kicked him after he was down?"

"It was necessary to subdue the fellow," Percy said quietly. "He was about to throw a second grenade onto the terrace of Shepheard's."

"Dear me," I said. "What happened to it?"

Too late, I remembered I had sworn never to speak to Percy again. With a smile that showed me *he* had not forgotten, he removed his hand carefully from his pocket.

"Here. Don't worry, Aunt Amelia, I got it away from him before he had removed the pin."

Nefret refused to leave her patient until an ambulance arrived. He was still unconscious when they put him into it. By that time the police were on the scene and the soldiers had dispersed. Percy had been the first to leave, without speaking to any of us again.

Emerson helped Nefret to her feet. Her pretty frock was in a deplorable state; Cairo streets are covered with a number of noxious substances, of which dust is the least offensive. Ramses inspected her critically and suggested we take her straight home.

136

"Shall I drive, Father?"

Emerson said no, of course, so the young people got in the tonneau and I took my place beside my husband. At my request he drove more slowly than usual, so that we could converse.

"Did Percy really snatch a live grenade from the hand of a terrorist?" I inquired.

"Don't know," said Emerson, pounding on the horn. A bicylist wobbled frantically out of our way and Emerson went on, "When I arrived, a pleasant little skirmish was already in process. Ramses — who was slightly in advance of me — and Percy were fending off the presumed anarchist and a mob of his supporters armed with sticks and bricks. Most of them dropped their weapons and scampered off when our reinforcement arrived, although, . . ." Emerson coughed modestly.

"The scampering began as soon as they recognized you," I suggested. "Well, my dear, that is not surprising. What is surprising is that the leader had grenades, and the others only sticks and stones."

"I don't believe the others were involved," Emerson said. "They pitched in out of sympathy when they saw an Egyptian attacked by soldiers. It was a singularly amateurish attempt; the first grenade only blew a hole in the pavement and wounded a donkey." He turned his head and shouted, "Did you recognize the fellow, Ramses?"

"No, sir. Sir — that cab —"

Emerson yanked at the brake. "Nor did I. He looked like a harmless tradesman. A more important question is where he obtained modern weapons."

"The police will undoubtedly wring the answer from him," I said grimly.

"Don't be melodramatic, Peabody. This isn't the Egypt we once knew; even in the provinces the kurbash has been outlawed and torture forbidden."

Emerson swerved wildly around a camel. Camels do not yield the right of way to anyone, even Emerson. I clutched at my hat and uttered a mild remonstrance.

"It was the fault of the camel," said Emerson. "All right back there, Nefret?"

"Yes, Professor."

It was the only sentence either of the children had uttered, nor did they speak during the rest of the drive. Emerson said only one thing more. "All the same, Peabody, someone had better find out how that fellow laid his hands on those grenades. Where there are two, there may be more."

From Manuscript H

I must be getting old, Ramses thought. It's becoming more difficult to remember, from one encounter to the next, precisely who I'm supposed to be.

A glance in the long mirror next to the divan where he sat reassured him: gray hair, lined face, fez, a flashy stickpin, and hands loaded with rings. There were a lot of mirrors in the room, not to mention beaded hangings, soft cushions, and furniture so heavily gilded it glowed even in the dim light. In the distance, muffled by the heavy velvet hangings over windows and doors, he heard women's voices raised in laughter, and the thump of music. The air was close and hot and heavy with a musky perfume.

Invisible hands drew the hangings aside and a figure entered. It was draped in filmy white fabric that fluttered as it waddled toward him. Ramses remained seated. The precise etiquette would have been difficult to determine, but whatever else el-Gharbi might be, he was not a woman. He was, however, in absolute control of the brothels in el Was'a.

The huge figure settled itself onto the divan next to Ramses, who wrinkled his nose involuntarily as a wave of patchouli wafted round him. El-Gharbi didn't miss much. His round black face broadened in amusement.

"My perfume offends you? It is very rare and expensive."

"Tastes differ," said Ramses, in his own voice. El-Gharbi knew who he was. The disguise was only a precaution, in case he was seen entering the place.

139

He waited with the patience he had acquired through long experience in Egypt while the formal litanies of greeting were exchanged. May God grant you a good evening; how is your health? God bless you; and finally a courteous and conventional, My house is your house.

"Beiti beitak, Brother of Demons. I never thought I would have the honor of entertaining you here."

"You know I didn't come here for entertainment," Ramses said. "If I had the power to do so I'd put you out of business."

Gargantuan laughter shook the divan. "I admire an honest man. Your sentiments, and those of the other members of your family, are well known to me. But my dear young friend, putting me out of business would only worsen the conditions to which you object. I am a humane employer."

Ramses couldn't deny it. Why were moral questions so often cloudy, with no clear-cut right and wrong? The right thing, the only right thing, would be the complete elimination of the filthy trade; but given the fact that it existed and probably always would, the unfortunates, male and female, who plied it were better off with el-Gharbi than they had been with some of his perverted predecessors. "Better than some," Ramses admitted grudgingly.

"Such as my former rival Kalaan." The big

man pursed his reddened lips and shook his head. "A disgusting sadist. I owe his removal to you, and I acknowledge the debt. That is why you came, wasn't it, to ask a favor? I presume it concerns your cousin. We haven't seen as much of him lately, though he does drop by now and then."

"His habits are no concern of mine," Ramses said. "I came about another matter. You have heard, I suppose, about the incident outside Shepheard's this afternoon?"

"Incident! A pretty word! All Cairo knows of it. You aren't suggesting I had a hand in that? My business is love, not war."

"Another pretty word for an ugly business. Where did he get the grenades? Who were his confederates?"

"Since he died before he could speak, we will never know the answer. The other men denied complicity; it is believed they will soon be released."

"Died? When? He was alive when they took him to hospital."

"Less than an hour ago. Have I told you something you did not know?"

"You haven't told me what I want to know."

El-Gharbi sat like a grotesque statue, his eyes hooded. "He did not get the weapons from me. Certain . . . merchandise sometimes passes through my hands. I sell it in other markets. A man does not scatter poison in his

141

own garden. I tell you this much because, to be honest, my dear, I don't want you coming round and stirring up trouble. Not that it isn't a pleasure just to look at you," he added, simpering.

Ramses laughed. "Most kind. Where did he get them, then?"

"Well, dear boy, we all know there are German and Turkish agents in Cairo. However, I do not believe they would make use of a nobody like that fellow. So, that leaves only one likely source. It is not necessary to mention his name. I do not know his present whereabouts. He does not approve of me." El-Gharbi folded his fat, ringed hands and sighed soulfully.

"He wouldn't, no. Can I believe you?"

"In the matter of War — of his present whereabouts, yes. Frankly, I hope you catch him. Patriotism is a nuisance; it stirs up trouble. I don't want trouble. It interferes with business."

"I do believe that. Well . . ." Ramses uncrossed his legs, preparatory to rising.

"Wait. Don't you want to know about your cousin?"

"What makes you suppose I would ask about him?"

"Two reasons. Either you wish revenge for his part in that . . . unfortunate affair a few years ago, or you have forgiven him for it and hope to save him from my vile influence."

With a rich, oily chuckle, he offered the box of cigarettes. "It is said in the city that he is trying to get back in the good graces of you and your family."

Ramses selected a cigarette and took his time lighting it while he considered this remarkable speech. He felt as if he were engaged in a verbal chess game with someone whose skill was far beyond his own. How much did el-Gharbi know about that "unfortunate affair?" The girl Percy had abused and got with child had not been one of his stable, but the identity of Sennia's father was probably known to every prostitute and procurer in the Red Blind District. The rest of the story, and Percy's part in it, was not common knowledge. And yet el-Gharbi had spoken of revenge . . .

Ramses looked up to meet a pair of hard brown eyes, the lashes darkened, the lids outlined with kohl. "Don't be deceived," the procurer said, his lips barely moving. "When he is drunk on brandy, he boasts of what he did. Are you aware that your first meeting with the child was no accident? That it was he who arranged it — who taught her to call you Father — who paid Kalaan to bring her and her mother to your house in order to shame you before your parents and the woman you loved? Ah. I see you are aware of that. But do you know that he had told a certain honorable gentleman

143

who also loved the lady of what he planned to do? It was because of your cousin that the gentleman was waiting for her when she fled the house that day; he comforted her, confirmed the lies that had been told about you, and persuaded her to marry him with the promise that he would make *no demands* on her and would set her free if and when she wished. He had made her believe he was ill and might not live many months. An unconvincing story, to be sure, but I am told she is impetuous by nature."

"We will not speak of her."

El-Gharbi clapped his ringed hands over his painted mouth, like a child who has talked out of turn. His eyes were bright with malicious amusement. "So finally I have told you something you did not know. Why does he hate you so much?"

Ramses shook his head. El-Gharbi's latest disclosure had left him stunned; he was afraid to speak for fear he would say more than he ought.

"Very well," the procurer said. "You walk among naked daggers, Brother of Demons. Be on your guard. Your cousin has even fewer scruples than I."

He clapped his hands. The draperies covering the door were drawn aside by a servant. The interview was over. Ramses got to his feet. "Thank you for the warning. I can't help wondering . . ."

"Why I take the trouble to warn you? Because I hope you will spare *me* trouble. And because you are honest and young and very beautiful."

Ramses raised shaggy gray eyebrows and the grotesque figure shook with silent laughter. "These eyes of mine see below the surface, Brother of Demons. Now go with Musa; he will show you to a less public entrance than the one you used. I trust your discretion as you must trust mine. Allah yisallimak. You will need his protection, I think."

Ramses followed the silent servant along the dimly lit passages. His brain felt numbed as he struggled to assimilate the information el-Gharbi had flung at him like a series of missiles. For years he had agonized over that hasty marriage of Nefret's, dismissing his suspicions of Percy's involvement as wishful thinking and wounded vanity, and, worse than vanity, the fear that she had given herself to him that night out of pity, after he had finally betrayed his love and his need of her. Nefret did nothing by halves; affection and compassion and the wholehearted generosity that was so much a part of her would have produced a convincing imitation of ardor, even to a man who had not wanted her as desperately as he had done.

But el-Gharbi's disclosure had to be true, it had come straight from Percy himself. Unless the procurer was lying, for some obscure reason of his own. . . .

True or false, the story had been told him for a reason, and he doubted el-Gharbi's motives were altruistic.

Could it be true, though? He knew Nefret too well to doubt that it might have happened that way. Five minutes before they came downstairs that morning, she had been in his arms, returning his kisses. Then to be faced with the diabolically constructed web of evidence that branded him guilty of a crime she held to be worse than murder . . . He could remember only too well the sickening, breath-stopping effect of that accusation on himself, innocent though he knew himself to be.

And he had let her go. He'd had other responsibilities — the child, his parents, the imminent danger to the child's mother — but he had reacted as irrationally as Nefret had done, and for the same very childish and very human reasons: hurt and anger and a sense of betrayal. They had both behaved like love-struck lunatics, but it would have come out all right in the end, if Percy hadn't taken a hand.

What had el-Gharbi tried to tell him about Percy?

He handed the servant a few coins and slipped out into the alley behind the brothel. Gradually his steps slowed until he was standing stock-still. A single phrase had lodged in his mind. ". . . he would make no demands on her. . . ."

No demands *of any kind?* Was it possible? It would explain so many things. Losing the baby had been the final blow that had broken her spirit. If that brief, miserable marriage had not been consummated — if she had discovered, too late, that she was carrying his child — if she still loved him, and believed her lack of faith in him had destroyed his love for her . . .

A flood of pity and tenderness and remorse filled him. I'll make it up to her, he thought. If it's true. If she'll let me. If it's not too late.

First, though, there was the other business.

The Yuletide season was fast approaching, but I was unable to work up much in the way of Christmas spirit. Small wonder, with the family scattered, and rumors of Turkish troops approaching the Sinai, and the casualty lists from the Western Front appallingly high. When I thought of those two handsome sensitive lads, whom I loved so dearly, in the mud of the trenches facing death, my spirits sank. It was even harder for their parents, of course, and for the girl to whom Johnny was engaged. What agonies she must be suffering!

However, I am never one to shirk my duty, and in my opinion the general gloom made it all the more imperative to celebrate the season and enjoy the company of those friends

147

who were still with us. There were, alas, fewer than in other years. M. Maspero had retired as head of the Antiquities Department; he had been ailing for some time, and the wounding of his son Jean earlier that autumn had been a bitter blow to him. The young man, a fine scholar in his own right, was now back in the trenches. Howard Carter had remained in Luxor for the winter; his patron, Lord Carnarvon, had been awarded the firman for the Valley of the Kings after Mr. Theodore Davis gave it up. Howard did not agree with Davis that there were no more royal tombs in the Valley. He was itching to get at it.

Our closest friends, Katherine and Cyrus Vandergelt, were working nearby, at Abusir. Katherine would need comforting too; her son had been among the first to enlist. Bertie had been slightly wounded at Mons, but was now back in action.

So I sent out my invitations and accepted others. Emerson complained of taking time away from his work, as he always did, and when I inquired whether he would care to attend a costume ball at Shepheard's, his indignation reached such a pitch I was obliged to close the door of my study, where the conversation was taking place.

"Good Gad, Peabody, have you forgotten what happened when last we attended a masked ball? Had I not arrived in the proverbial nick of time, you would have been carried off by a particularly unpleasant villain whom you took for me! Nobody knows who anybody is in those costumes," Emerson continued, abandoning syntax in the extremity of his passion.

He looked so handsome, his sapphirine eyes blazing, his teeth bared, the cleft in his chin quivering, that I could not resist teasing him a bit. "Now, Emerson, you know you enjoy wearing disguises. Especially beards! It is most unlikely that any such thing could happen again. Anyhow, I had a more revealing costume in mind for you. You have such well-shaped lower limbs, I thought a Roman centurion or a kilted Scot, or perhaps a pharaoh —"

"Wearing nothing but a short skirt and a beaded collar?" Emerson glowered. "And you in one of those transparent pleated robes, as Nefertiti? See here, Peabody . . . Oh. You are joking, aren't you?"

"Yes, my dear," I said, laughing. "We needn't attend if you don't want to, the affair is several weeks off. You had better run along now; I will just finish these notes before I join you."

Believing the discussion was at an end, I turned back to the desk and picked up my pen.

"I would like to see you as Nefertiti, though." Emerson came to stand behind me,

149

his hand on my shoulder.

"Now, Emerson, you know I do not resemble that elegant lady in the slightest. I am too — my dear, what are you doing?"

In fact, I knew very well what he was doing. Raising me to my feet, he drew me into a close embrace. "I would rather have you than Nefertiti, Cleopatra, or Helen of Troy," he murmured against my cheek.

"Now?" I exclaimed.

"Why not?"

"Well, for one thing, it is eight o'clock in the morning, and for another, they are waiting for you at Giza, and . . . and . . ."

"Let them wait," said Emerson.

It was like the old days, when Emerson's tempestuous affection was wont to display itself in places and under circumstances some might consider inappropriate. I had never been able to deny him then; I was unable to deny him now. When he left me I was in a much improved state of mind. Humming under my breath, I returned to my study to finish my letters.

Not until the euphoria of the encounter had begun to subside did I begin to harbor certain suspicions. Emerson's demonstrations of affection are often spontaneous and always overwhelming. He knows very well how they affect me, and he is not above employing them for purposes of distraction.

Putting down my pen, I reconsidered our

150

conversation. Had there not been something unusual about his willingness to incur delay? As a rule he was impatient to get to the site, nagging the rest of us to hurry. We had talked about costumes and disguises, and now that I thought about it he had had a somewhat shifty look when I mentioned beards. . . . Curse the man, I thought, he is up to something! His disclaimers notwithstanding, I knew he yearned to play some part in the war effort. He sympathized with Ramses's pacifist sentiments, but did not entirely share them, and I suspected that what he really wanted was a chance to prowl the streets of Cairo in disguise, looking for spies and exposing foreign agents. I had no strong objections, so long as he did not try to prevent me from doing it too.

At Emerson's request I had written to Major Hamilton inviting him and his niece to tea. The following afternoon I was in receipt of a brief communication from him. Nefret was reading her own messages; the one she was presently perusing appeared to contain something of particular interest.

We were on the roof terrace waiting for the others to return from the dig. For the past several days I had been the one to sort through the messages and letters that had arrived in our absence. Naturally I would never have opened a letter addressed to Nefret; I only wanted to know whether Percy would have the audacity to correspond with her. Thus far she had received no communication that aroused suspicion, but today she had got to the post basket on the hall table before me.

"Not bad news, I hope?" I inquired, seeing a frown wrinkle the smooth surface of her brow.

"What?" She looked up with a start. "Oh. No, nothing of the sort. Only an invitation I shan't accept. Is there anything of interest in your letters?"

"I have heard from Major Hamilton — you know, the uncle of the young lady who was here the other day. It is a rather curious communication. What do you think?"

I handed her the letter, thinking it might inspire her to return the compliment. It did not. She folded her own letter and slipped it into her skirt pocket before taking the paper from my hand. As she read it her lips pursed in a silent whistle.

"Curious? Rude, rather. The terms in which he declines your invitation make it clear he doesn't care to make our acquaintance, and has no intention of allowing his niece to visit us. He doesn't say why."

"I think I can hazard a guess."

Nefret looked at me in surprise. "I didn't think you knew."

"Knew what?"

She looked as if she were sorry she had spoken, but my unblinking gaze silently demanded a response. "About Ramses having cut the Major out with Mrs. Fortescue."

"What a vulgar way of putting it. Do you mean that Ramses and that woman are — er — associating? She is old enough to be his mother. What about her other admirer — that French count?"

Nefret's delicate lips curled. "I detest this sort of gossip, but I do wish you would speak to Ramses. The Major probably won't do anything except snub him, but the Count has threatened to call him out."

"Challenge him, you mean? How absurd."

"Not to the Count. He is quite a gallant, in the European style. Kisses hands, clicks heels."

"You know him?"

"Slightly. Oh, well, I daresay nothing will come of it. There is another reason why the Major might not care to improve his acquaintance with us. What responsible guardian would allow a young girl to associate with a man who is not only a pacifist and a coward, but a notorious seducer of women?"

"Nefret!"

"I'm sorry, Aunt Amelia! But that's what they say about him, you know. They know the stories are all lies, and yet they continue to repeat them, and there's not a damned thing we can do about it!"

"They will be forgotten eventually," I said,

wishing I could believe it.

The angry color faded from her cheeks, and she smiled and shook her head. "He does bring it on himself, in a way. One can hardly blame the child for being swept off her feet."

"Literally as well as figuratively, I believe," I said. "My dear Nefret, he didn't bring this on himself; once appealed to, he had to rescue the child."

"It's not what he does, it's the *way* he does it!"

I couldn't help laughing. "I know what you mean. Well, my dear, he won't do it again — at least not to Miss Hamilton. The Major's letter, though discourteous, relieves me of a responsibility I am happy to avoid. Emerson will be disappointed, though."

When Emerson turned up he was accompanied by Cyrus and Katherine Vandergelt, who were to dine and attend the opera with us that evening. I deduced that they had come in their car, since both wore appropriate motoring costumes. Cyrus was something of a dandy; his dust coat was of fine white linen and his cap had attached goggles, now pushed up out of the way. Katherine began the task of unwinding the veils in which she was swathed, and after greeting me affectionately, Cyrus explained, "We stopped at Giza to collect Emerson."

"And a good thing, too, or he would still be there," I said. "Where is Anna? You didn't leave her at home alone, I hope. She has, I believe, a tendency to brood. That is unhealthy. Perhaps she should spend more time with us. We will keep her busy and cheerful."

"You are an incurable busybody, Amelia," said my husband, settling himself comfortably in a chair and picking up the little pile of messages. "What makes you suppose Katherine needs your advice on how to manage her daughter?"

"Amelia's advice is always welcome," Katherine said with an affectionate smile. She looked as if she could use a little cheering-up too. Her plump cheeks were thinner and there was more gray in her hair now than there had been only a year earlier.

"We left Anna with Ramses," she went on. "He hadn't quite finished, and she decided to stay and keep him company."

"We will not wait tea for them, then," I declared. "Emerson, will you call down to Fatima and tell her we are ready?"

There was no response from Emerson, who had tossed most of the letters onto the floor, in his impetuous fashion, and was staring fixedly at one of them. I had to repeat his name rather loudly before he looked up.

"What are you shouting at me for?" he asked.

"Never mind, Professor, I'll tell her," Nefret said, rising.

"Tell who what?" Emerson demanded.

"Both questions are now irrelevant," I said. "Really, Emerson, it is very rude of you to read the post when we have guests present. What is that letter that absorbs you so?"

Silently Emerson handed it to me.

"Oh, the note from Major Hamilton," I said. "You are not going to lose your temper over it, I hope."

"I am in no danger of losing my temper," my husband retorted, transferring his piercing stare to me. "Can you think of any reason why I should?"

"Well, my dear, it is a rather brusque communication, and I know you were looking forward to seeing —"

"Bah," said Emerson. "I don't want to discuss it, Peabody. Where is — ah, there you are, Fatima. Good. I want my tea."

Fatima and her young assistant were arranging the tea things when a lithe brindled form landed on the parapet, so suddenly that Cyrus started.

"Holy Jehoshaphat," he ejaculated. "How did she get up here? Not by way of the stairs, or I'd have seen her coming."

Seshat gave him a critical look and began washing her face. "She climbs like a lizard and flies through the air like a bird," I said, laughing. "It is quite uncanny to see her soar from one balcony to another eight feet distant. Our cats have always been clever creatures, but we've never had one as agile as this."

The appearance of Seshat anticipated by less than a minute the arrival of Ramses; either she had seen him coming, from some vantage point atop the house, or the uncanny instincts of a feline had warned her of his approach. Anna was with him.

Katherine's daughter by her first, unhappy marriage, was now in her early twenties. She was, truth compels me to admit, a rather plain young woman. She did not at all resemble her mother, who was pleasantly rounded where Anna was not, and whose green eyes and gray-streaked dark hair gave her the look of a cynical tabby cat. Anna's eyes were a faded brown, her cheeks thin and sallow; she scorned the use of cosmetics and preferred severe, tailored garments that did nothing to flatter her figure. She had never appeared interested in a member of the opposite sex, except for one extremely embarrassing period during which she had taken a fancy to Ramses. He had not taken a fancy to her, so it was a relief when she got over it.

It seemed to me that there was a certain coolness in her manner toward him that day. After greeting us she sat down on the settee next to Nefret and began questioning her about the hospital.

"I have decided I want to train for a nurse," she explained.

"You are welcome to visit anytime," Nefret said slowly. "But we do not have the facilities for such training. If you are serious —"

"I am. One must do whatever one can, mustn't one?"

"You could receive better training in England," Nefret said. "I can give you several references."

"There must be something I can do here!"

"Some of the ladies have formed committees," I remarked. "They meet to drink tea and wind bandages."

"That is better than doing nothing," Anna declared. She directed a glance at Ramses, who appeared not to notice. Ah, I thought; so that is the trouble. Her brother, to whom she was devoted, was in France. I did hope she was not going to add to Rames's collection of feathers. Open contempt would be even more awkward than expressions of unwelcome affection.

We had been able to obtain a box for the opera season that year, since many of the former patrons had left the country — voluntarily, or after they had been expelled as enemy aliens. The performance that night was *Aida*, one of Emerson's particular favorites, since the music is very loud and the renditions of Egyptian costume and scenery give him an opportunity to criticize them.

There was not room for all of us in a single vehicle, so Nefret went with us and Ramses accompanied the Vandergelts. I had, much against his will, persuaded Emerson to let Selim drive us that evening. The Reader can have no idea of how I looked forward to NOT being driven by Emerson. He was looking particularly handsome in white tie, which was de rigeur for box holders.

"I do wish Ramses would have the courtesy to tell us of his plans in advance," I said, taking Emerson's hat from him so he would not sit on it or let it fly out the window. "I was under the impression he was going with us until he turned up in ordinary evening kit instead of white tie."

"What difference does it make?" Emerson demanded.

"Where is he going?"

"I did not have the impertinence to inquire, my dear. He is a grown man and is not obliged to give us an account of his activities."

"Hmph," I said. "Nefret, I don't suppose you —"

"No," said Nefret. "Perhaps I ought to have mentioned earlier that I won't be coming home with you."

"Have you and Ramses something planned?"

"As I told you, I have no idea what his plans are, except that they do not include me."

"Where are you — ouch!"

159

Emerson removed his elbow from my ribs and began talking very loudly about Wagner.

When the Vandergelts joined us in our box, Katherine said — in answer to my question — that they had left Ramses off at the Savoy. That was not one of his usual haunts; he must plan to meet someone, or call for someone who was staying there.

Speculation could get me no further, so I abandoned the question for the time being.

The Opera House had been built by the Khedive Ismail as part of his modernization of Cairo in preparation for the visit of the Empress Eugénie to open the Suez Canal in 1869. Rumor had it that Ismail was madly in love with the French empress; he had built for her not only an elaborate palace but a bridge by which she could reach it, and a road to Giza so that she could visit the pyramids in comfort. The Opera House was lavish with gilt and crimson velvet hangings and gold brocade. Ismail had commissioned *Aida* for the grand opening, but Verdi didn't get around to finishing it for another two years, so the Khedive and the Empress had to settle for *Rigoletto*. Several boxes had been designed for the ladies of Ismail's harem; screened off from the view of the audience, they were now reserved for Moslem ladies.

Katherine and I at once took out our opera glasses and looked to see who was there, with whom they had come, and what they were wearing. I do not apologize for this activity, which Emerson took pleasure in deriding. At worst it is harmless; at best, it is informative. The grandiose khedival box was occupied that evening by none other than General Maxwell. Since the declaration of war and the institution of martial law, he was the supreme power in Egypt, and his box was full of officers and officials who had come to pay their compliments (i.e., flatter the great man in the hope of gaining favor). I was not surprised to see Percy among them.

Even as we scrutinized we were being scrutinized. The General was not immune to this form of polite social intercouse; seeing my eyes fixed on his box, he acknowledged me with a gracious salutation. I nodded and smiled — full into the teeth of Percy, who had the audacity to pretend the greeting was meant for him. Displaying the said teeth in a complacent smile, he bowed. I cut him as ostentatiously as was possible, and was annoyed to see Anna respond with a wave of her hand. She had met him, I recollected, on an earlier occasion, while our relations with Percy were still relatively civil.

I interposed my person between her and Percy and scanned the audience below. Mrs. Fortescue was present, her escort that evening a staff officer with whom I was not acquainted. I asked Katherine to point out Major Hamilton.

"I don't see him," was the reply. "Why are you curious about the gentleman?"

"I told you about his niece's little adventure on the pyramid," I replied.

"Oh, yes. He hasn't called on you to express his thanks?"

"Quite the contrary. He has written informing me he will not allow the child to associate with us."

"Good gracious! Why would he do that?"

"Don't be tactful, Katherine, not with me. I can only suppose that he has heard some of the vicious gossip about Ramses."

Anna had been an interested listener. In her gruff boyish voice she remarked, "Are you referring to his pacifist sentiments or his reputation with women, Mrs. Emerson?"

"I see no reason why we should discuss either slander," Katherine said sharply.

Anna's sallow cheeks reddened. "He is a pacifist. It is not slanderous to call him that."

This exchange caught Nefret's attention. "I wouldn't call Ramses a pacifist," she said judiciously. "He is perfectly willing to fight if he believes it to be necessary. He's damned good at it too."

"Nefret," I murmured.

"I beg your pardon," said Nefret. "Just trying to set the record straight. Have you joined one of the bandage-rolling committees, Anna?"

Her disdainful tone made Anna stiffen angrily. "I want to do something more . . . more difficult, more useful."

"Do you?" Nefret propped her chin on her hand and smiled sweetly at the other young woman. "Come round to the hospital tomorrow, then. We can use another pair of hands."

"But I wouldn't be nursing soldiers."

"No. Only women who have been abused in another sort of war — the longest-lasting war in history. A war that won't be won quickly or easily."

"I'm sorry for them, of course," Anna muttered. "But —"

"But you see yourself gently wiping the perspiration from the brows of handsome young officers who have suffered genteel wounds in the arm or shoulder. I think," Nefret said, "it would do you good to meet some of the women who come to us, and hear their stories, and see their injuries. It will give you a taste of what war is really like. Are you game?"

Anna bit her lip, but no young woman of spirit could have resisted that challenge. "Yes," she said defiantly. "I'll show you I'm not as frivolous as you think me. I will come tomorrow and do any job you ask me to do, and I'll stick it out until you dismiss me."

"Agreed."

I caught Katherine's eye. I expected her to object, but she only smiled slightly and picked up her opera glasses. "Ah — there is Major Hamilton, Amelia. Third row center, reddish-gray hair, green velvet coat."

"Dear me, how picturesque," I said, identifying the individual in question without difficulty because of the unusual color of his hair. "Is he wearing a kilt, do you think?"

"Presumably. It goes with the coat."

Since my readers are of course familiar with the opera, I will not describe the performance in detail. When the curtain fell, accompanied by the thunderous crash that sealed the doomed lovers forever in their living tomb, we all joined in the applause except for Emerson, who began fidgeting. If he had his way, he would bolt for the exit the moment the last note of music died. I consider this discourteous and unpatriotic, so I always make him sit through the curtain calls and "God Save the King."

Cyrus suggested we stop somewhere for a bite of supper, but the hour was late and I knew Emerson would be up before dawn, so we said good night to the Vandergelts and got into our motorcar.

"You can let me off at the Semiramis, Selim," said Nefret.

I said, "With whom are you having supper, Nefret?"

I expected a poke in the ribs from Emerson. Instead he cleared his throat noisily and muttered, "You need not answer that,

Nefret. Er — unless you choose."

"It is not a secret," Nefret said. "Lord Edward Cecil and Mrs. Fitz, and some of their set. You know Mrs. Canley Tupper, I believe?"

I did. Like the others in that "set," including Lord Edward, she was frivolous and silly, but not vicious.

"And," said Nefret, "Major Ewan Hamilton may join us."

I found it impossible to sleep that night, though Emerson slumbered sweetly and sonorously at my side. Nefret had not returned by the time we retired, nor had Ramses. Where were they and what were they doing — and with whom? I turned from one unsatisfactory position to another, but it was worry, not physical discomfort, that affected me. In some ways the children had been less trouble when they were young. At least I had had the right to control their actions and question them about their plans. Not that they always obeyed my orders or answered truthfully. . . .

The intruder's noiseless entrance gave me no warning. It was on the bed, advancing slowly and inexorably toward my head, before I was aware of its presence. A heavy weight settled onto my chest and something cold and wet touched my cheek.

"What is it?" I whispered. "How did you get in here?"

There was no audible response, only a harder pressure against my face. When I moved, the weight lifted from me and the shadowy form disappeared. I got out of bed without, as I believed, waking Emerson. Delaying only long enough to assume dressing gown and slippers, I went to the door. The cat was already there. As soon as I opened the door, she slipped out.

A lamp had been left burning on a table in the hall. I snatched it up. Seshat led me along the hall, looking back now and then to make sure I was following.

The only way she could have entered our room was through the window. One of her favorite promenades was along the balconies that ran under the first-floor windows. As I had expected, she stopped in front of Ramses's door and stared up at me.

I knocked softly on the door. There was no response. I tried the door.

It was locked.

Well, I had expected that. Ramses had always been insistent on maintaining his privacy, and of course he had every right to it.

I had taken the precaution, some days earlier, of finding a key that fitted Ramses's door. I had one for Nefret's door too. I had not felt it necessary to mention this expedient to the persons concerned, because they would almost certainly have found other security measures which would not have been so easy to circumvent. Naturally I would never have dreamed of using the keys except in cases of dire emergency. Clearly this was such a case.

I unlocked the door and flung it open. This is my customary procedure when I anticipate discovering an unauthorized intruder, but I admit the bang of the door against the wall does often startle people other than the intruder. It produced a muffled oath from Emerson, of whose approach I had not been aware. Hastening to my side, he put his hand on my arm.

"Peabody, what the devil are you —"

The sentence ended in a catch of breath.

There was enough light from the windows giving onto the balcony to show the motionless shape in the bed, covered to the chin by sheet and blanket, and the dark head on the pillow. Another form lay facedown on the floor between the bed and the window. It appeared to be that of a peasant, for the feet were bare and the dark blue gibbeh was threadbare and torn.

I gave Emerson the lamp and ran to kneel beside the fallen man.

"Ramses! What has happened? Are you hurt?"

There was no answer, which more or less settled the matter. As I tugged at my son's limp body, Emerson put the lamp on a nearby table. "I'll fetch a doctor."

167

"No," I said sharply. I had managed to turn Ramses onto his back. My peremptory grasp had pulled the robe apart, baring his chest and the bloodstained cloth wound clumsily round his upper arm and shoulder. It must have been cut or torn from his shirt, since that garment was in fragmentary condition. His only other article of clothing, aside from the belt that held his knife, was a pair of knee-length cotton drawers, completing the costume of an Egyptian of the poorer classes.

"No," Ramses echoed. His eyes had opened and he was trying to sit up. I caught hold of him and pulled him down onto my lap. Ramses muttered something under his breath, and Seshat growled.

"No?" Emerson's brows drew together. "I see. Your medical kit, Peabody?"

"Close the door behind you," I said. "And for the love of God don't wake any of the servants!"

I drew Ramses's knife from its sheath and began to cut away the crude bandage. He lay still, watching me with an understandable air of apprehension. The knife was very large and very sharp.

"Goodness, what a mess you've made of this," I said.

"I was in something of a hurry."

I paused for a moment in what was admittedly a delicate operation, and looked more closely at his face. When I ran my fingertip along his jaw it encountered several slightly sticky patches. "What happened to the beard and the turban, and the other elements of your disguise?"

"I don't remember. I was in the water at one time. . . ." He stiffened as I slid the point of the knife under the next layer of cloth, and then he said, "How did you find out?"

"That you have been engaged in some sort of secret service work? Not from any slip on your part, if that is what is worrying you. I knew you would not shirk your duty, however dangerous and distasteful it might be."

The corners of Ramses's lips tightened. He turned his head away. "I'm sorry," I said. "I am trying not to hurt you."

"You didn't hurt me. But you will have to, you know. I daren't risk allowing a doctor to treat what is obviously a bullet wound."

"These injuries were not made by a bullet," I said, flinching as another fold of cloth parted, to display a row of ragged gashes just above his collarbone.

Ramses squinted, trying to see down the length of his nose and chin. "Not those, no," he said.

"Curse it," I muttered, cutting away the last of the cloth. There was unfortunately no doubt about the nature of the bloody hole in his upper arm. "Where were you tonight?"

"I was supposed to have been at the bar at Shepheard's. The habitués only snub people

169

they dislike, they don't shoot at them."

"You might have been attacked on your way home, by a thief."

"You know better than —" His breath caught painfully, and Seshat put a peremptory paw on my hand. Her claws were out just enough to prick the skin.

"Sorry," I said — to the cat.

"It's all right," said Ramses — to the cat. "That story won't wash, Mother."

"No," I admitted. "Cairo thieves don't carry firearms. The only people who do . . . Are you telling me you were shot by a policeman or a soldier? Why, for heaven's sake?"

Before I could pursue my inquiries Emerson came back carrying my medical kit and, I was pleased to note, wearing his trousers. Between us we got Ramses out of his filthy garments and into bed, removing from it the heaped-up pillows and black wig. Emerson filled a basin with water from the jug, and I began cleaning the injuries.

"Could be worse," Emerson announced, though his grave look belied his optimistic words. "How far away were you when the shot was fired?"

"As far as I could get," said Ramses, with a faint grin. "It was pure bad luck that —"

He broke off, sinking his teeth into his lower lip as the alcohol-soaked cloth touched one of the ragged cuts, and I said sharply, "Stop trying to be heroic. Ramses, I don't

170

like the look of this. The bullet has gone straight through the fleshy part of your arm, but it must have scraped another surface immediately afterward. You appear to have been struck by several fragments of stone. One is rather deeply imbedded. If Nefret is not already on her way home we can send for her. I would rather leave this to her."

"No, Mother! Nefret mustn't know of this."

"Surely you don't think she would betray your secret!" I exclaimed with equal vehemence. "Nefret?"

"Mother, will you please try to get it into your head . . . I'm sorry! But this isn't one of our usual family encounters with criminals. Do you suppose I don't trust you and Father? I wouldn't have told you either. I wasn't allowed. This job is part of a larger game. The Great Game, some call it. . . . What an ironic name for a business that demands deceit, assassination, murder, and betrayal of every principle we've been taught is right! Well, I won't kill except in self-defense, no matter what they say, but I swore to follow the other rules of the game, and the most important of them is that without permission from my superiors I *cannot* involve anyone else! The more you know, the greater the danger to you. I shouldn't have come home tonight, I should have gone —"

He stopped with a sharp catch of breath,

and Emerson, who had been watching him with furrowed brows, put a hand on his perspiring forehead.

"It's all right, my boy, don't talk anymore. I understand."

"Thank you, Father. I suppose it was Seshat who gave me away?"

"Yes," I said. "Thank God she did! But how do you plan to explain to Nefret why you are bedridden tomorrow?"

Ramses's lips set in a stubborn line. "I'll be at the dig tomorrow as usual. No, Mother, please don't argue, I haven't the energy to explain. Can't you just take my word *for once* that this is necessary, and get on with it?"

He fainted eventually, but not as soon as I would have liked.

4

After I had extracted the last fragment of stone I handed it to Emerson, who wiped it off with a bit of gauze and examined it intently. "No clue there, it's just a bit of ordinary limestone. Where was he tonight?"

"He wouldn't tell me."

"We'll have to get it out of him somehow," Emerson said. "But not now. Shall I do that, my dear?"

"No, I can manage. Lift his arm — gently, if you please."

By the time I finished bandaging the injuries, Ramses had regained consciousness. "The novocaine will wear off before long," I said. "Would you rather have laudanum or some of Nefret's morphine? I think I can get the needle into a vein."

"No, thank you," Ramses said, feebly but decidedly.

"You must have something for pain."

"Brandy will do."

I doubted it very much, but I could hardly pinch his nose and pour the laudanum down his throat. I prepared the brandy and Emerson helped him to sit up. He had just taken the glass in his hand when I heard footsteps in the hall outside.

"Hell and damnation!" I ejaculated, for I knew those light, quick steps. "Emerson, did you lock the —"

The haste with which he sprinted for the door made it evident that he had neglected to do so. Emerson can move like a panther when it is required, but this time he was too slow. However, he managed to get behind the door as it was flung open.

Nefret stood in the doorway. In the light from the corridor her form glimmered like that of a fairy princess, the gems in her hair and on her arms sparkling, the chiffon skirts of her gown surrounding her like mist. I had just presence of mind enough to kick the ugly evidence of our activities under the bed. The smell of blood and antiseptic was overcome by a strong reek of brandy. Ramses had slid down so that the sheet covered him clear to his chin, except for the arm that held the glass. Half the contents had spilled onto the sheet.

"How kind of you to drop in," he said, with a curl of his lip. "You missed Mother's lecture on the evils of drink, but you're just in time to hold the basin while I throw up."

She stood so still that not even the gems on her hands twinkled. Then she turned and vanished from sight.

Not until we had heard her door close did any of us move. Emerson shut Ramses's door and turned the key. Ramses tipped the rest of the brandy down his throat and let his head fall back against the pillow. "Thank you, Mother," he said. "There's no need for you to stay. Go to bed."

I ignored the suggestion, as he must have known I would. Indicating the basin and the stained cloths that filled it, I said, "Dispose of this, Emerson — I leave it to you to find a safe hiding place. Then make the rounds and —"

"Yes, my dear, you need not spell it out." His hand brushed my hair.

No sooner had the door closed behind him than Ramses's eyes opened. "I still hate this bloody war, you know," he said indistinctly.

"Then why are you doing this?"

His head moved restlessly on the pillow. "It isn't always easy to distinguish right from wrong, is it? More often the choice is between better and worse . . . and sometimes . . . sometimes the line between them is as thin as a hair. One must make a choice, though. One can't wash one's hands and let others take the risks . . . including the risk of being wrong. There's always better . . . and worse. . . . I'm not making much sense, am I?"

"It makes excellent sense to me," I said gently. "But you need to rest. Can't you sleep?"

"I'm trying." He was silent for a moment. Then he said, "You used to sing me to sleep.

When I was small. Do you remember?"

"I remember." I had to clear my throat before I went on. "I always suspected you pretended to sleep so you wouldn't have to listen to me sing. It is not one of my greatest talents."

"I liked it."

His hand lay on the bed, palm up, like that of a beggar asking for alms. When I took it his fingers closed around mine. My throat was so tight I thought I could not speak, much less sing, but the iron control I have cultivated over the years came to my aid; my voice was steady, if not melodious.

"There were three ra'ens sat on a tree
Down a down, hey down a down . . ."

There are ten interminable verses to this old ballad, which is not, as persons unfamiliar with it might suppose, a pretty little ditty about birds. As soon as he was old enough to express an opinion on the subject, Ramses had informed me that he found lullabies boring, and had demanded stronger stuff. This attitude was, perhaps, not unnatural in a child who had been brought up with mummies; but I would be the first to admit that Ramses was not a normal child.

His lips curved slightly as he listened, and his eyes closed; by the time I got to the verse where the dead knight's lover "lifts his bloody

176

head," his breathing had slowed and deepened.

I bent over him and brushed the damp curls away from his brow. I had been in error; he was not quite asleep. His heavy lids lifted.

"I was a bloodthirsty little beast, wasn't I?"

"No," I said unsteadily. "No! You never harmed a living creature, not even a mouse or a beetle. You put yourself constantly at risk in order to keep them from being hurt, by cats or hunters or cruel owners. That is what you are doing now, isn't it? Risking yourself to keep people . . ." It was no use, I could not go on. He squeezed my hand and smiled at me.

"Don't worry, Mother. It's all right, you know."

The tears I had held back burst from my eyes, and I wept as I had not wept since the day Abdullah died. Dropping to my knees, I pressed my face into the covers in an attempt to muffle my sobs. He patted me clumsily on my bowed head, and that made me cry harder.

When I had stopped crying I raised my head and saw that he was asleep at last. Shadows softened the prominent features and the strong outline of jaw and chin; with the cat curled up next to him on the pillow he looked like the boy he had been, not so very many years before.

I was sitting by the bed when the key turned in the lock and Emerson slipped in.

"All quiet," he whispered. "No sign of any-one about."

"Good."

He crossed the room and stood behind me, his hands on my shoulders. "Were you cry-ing?"

"A little. Rather a lot, in fact. I don't know that I can bear this, Emerson. I suppose I ought to be accustomed to it, after living with you all these years, but he courts peril even more recklessly than you did. Why must he take such risks?"

"Would you have him any other way?"

"Yes! I would have him behave sensibly — take care — avoid danger —"

"Be someone other than himself, in short. We cannot change his nature, my dear, even if we would; so let us apply ourselves to think-ing how we can help him. What did you put in the brandy?"

"Veronal. Emerson, he cannot get out of bed tomorrow, much less work in the tomb."

"I know. I am going to find David."

"David." I rubbed my aching eyes. "Yes, of course. David is here, isn't he? That's how Ramses managed to be in two different places tonight. David was at Shepheard's and Ramses was . . . I apologize, Emerson, I am a trifle slow. What role has he been playing?"

"Think it through, my dear." He squeezed my shoulders. "You have been under some-thing of a strain, but I don't doubt your quick wits will reach the same conclusion mine have reached. I mustn't stay, if I am to get David back here before morning."

"Do you know where he is?"

"I think so. I will be as quick as I can. Try to rest a little."

He tilted my head back and kissed me. As he walked to the door there was a spring in his step I had not seen for weeks, and when he turned and smiled at me I beheld the Emerson I knew and loved, eyes alight, shoulders squared, tall frame vibrant with resolve. My dear Emerson was himself again, intoxicated by danger, spurred on by the need for action!

The night wore on. I sat quietly, resting my head against the back of the chair, but sleep was impossible. It was like Emerson to throw out that amiable challenge, so that I would tax my wits instead of fretting. And of course, once I got my mind to work on the problem, the answer was obvious.

The business in which Ramses was presently engaged had been worked out long in advance, and with the cooperation of someone high in the Government. It would take a man like Kitchener himself to authorize and arrange the deception, sending another man to India in place of David. I had wondered why he had been imprisoned there instead of in Malta, where the other nationalists were interned; now I understood. No one who knew David could be allowed to meet the impostor. There are secret methods of communication into and out of the most tightly guarded prison, and if ever the word got back to Cairo that David was not where he was supposed to be, interested parties might wonder where he *really* was.

Interested parties, of whom there were, alas, only too many, might also wonder whether Ramses's outspoken opposition to the war was a cover for the sort of clandestine activities for which he was particularly well suited. If he was playing another role, the only way in which he could disarm suspicion was to have David take his part at strategic intervals. Knowing Ramses, I did not doubt his loathing of the war was utterly sincere, but it had also been part of the plan. He had made himself so thoroughly unpopular, few people would associate with him — or, as the case might be, with David.

Emerson had been correct; the answer was obvious. If one man could be secretly removed from exile, another could be secretly sent into it. The militant nationalist for whom the British authorities were searching was not Kamil el-Wardani, but my son — and that was why Thomas Russell had taken the unusual step of inviting us to accompany him on his futile raid, and why Wardani had got away so handily. The raid had been meant to fail. Its sole purpose had been to supply unimpeachable witnesses who could testify that Wardani was elsewhere while Ramses made a spectacle of himself at the Club; and the reason for the substitution must have to do with what Russell had said that night. Something about fighting a guerrilla war in Cairo while the Turks attacked the Canal . . . Wardani the key . . . without him, the movement would collapse.

I had reached this point in my train of thought when a faint rustling sound brought me bolt upright. A quick glance at Ramses assured me that he had not stirred. The sound had not been that of the bedclothes. It was . . . it must have been . . .

Springing to my feet, I felt under the mattress and found Ramses's knife where he had asked me to place it. I hurried to the window and slipped through the curtains, in time to see a dark form swing itself over the stone balustrade of the small balcony. It saw me. It spoke.

"Aunt Amelia, don't! It's me!"

My first impulse was to throw my arms around him, but I was sensible enough to draw him into the room before I did so. It was as well he had spoken; even in the light I would not have recognized the bearded ruffian whose scarred face was set in a permanent sneer. The scar ran up under the patch that covered one eye, but the other eye was David's, soft and brown and shining with tears of emotion. He returned my embrace

181

with such hearty goodwill that his beard scraped painfully across my cheek.

"Oh, David, my dear boy, it is so good to see you! Where is Emerson?"

"Coming through the house in the usual way. We thought it better for me not to risk that."

"You ought not have risked coming here at all," said a critical voice from the bed.

The key turned in the lock and Emerson slipped into the room. "Whew," he remarked. "That was close. Fatima will be stirring soon. Peabody, put the knife down. What the devil do you think you are doing?"

"Defending her young," said David, with a horrible, distorted grin. "She was about to fly at me when I identified myself."

"You ought not be here," Ramses insisted. Obviously I had not given him quite enough of the sleeping medication. His eyes were half-closed, but the extremity of his annoyance enabled him to articulate.

"We haven't time to argue," Emerson said coolly. "David, hurry and change, and get rid of that beard, and — do whatever else you need to do."

"Don't worry," David said, peeling off his beard and turning toward the washbasin in the corner of the room. "I've played Ramses often enough lately to fool most people. But you'll have to keep Nefret away from me. She knows both of us too well to be deceived. I need more light, Aunt Amelia."

I picked up the lamp and went to him. After rummaging in a nearby cupboard he removed several bottles and boxes and studied his face in the small shaving mirror.

"May I be allowed to say a word?" inquired Ramses, still prone and still thoroughly exasperated.

"No," said his father. "David and I have it worked out. Peabody, you will tell Fatima that Ramses is in the middle of some filthy experiment, and that she is not to allow anyone in the room. It won't be the first time. I depend on you to make sure he is supplied with everything he needs before we leave the house this morning. Now get out of here so David can change his clothing."

I put the lamp down on a table. David had wiped off the scar and removed the invisible tape that had pulled his mouth out of shape. He saw me staring and gave me a sidelong smile. "The resemblance needn't be that exact, Aunt Amelia. They know Ramses is here and they know I'm not, so they will see him, not me. It will be all right — if I can get out of the house without encountering Nefret."

"Later . . . on the dig . . ." I began.

"Precisely," said Ramses. "David cannot possibly carry this off. If we were working at a larger site, such as Zawaiet, he might be able to stay at a distance, but we've only cleared one room of the tomb, and I've been —"

"We will have to extend the area of our operations, that is all," said Emerson coolly. "Leave it to me."

"But, Father —"

"Leave it to me, I said." Emerson fingered the cleft in his chin. "If I understand the situation correctly, the important thing is that you must be seen today behaving normally and with no sign of injury."

Ramses stared at his father. "How much do you know?"

"Explanations will have to wait. There is no time now. Am I right?"

"Yes, sir." The lines of strain (and temper) that marked his face smoothed out. Emerson has that effect on people; the very sight of him, blue eyes steady and stalwart frame poised for action, would have been reassuring even to one who did not know him as well as did his son.

"In fact," Ramses went on, "it would be helpful if David could put on a brief but very public demonstration of strength and fitness at some point."

"Any suggestions?" David added a few millimeters of false hair to his eyebrows.

"You can rescue me," I said. "I will persuade my horse to run away with me, or fall into a tomb shaft, or perhaps —"

"Control yourself, Peabody," said my husband in alarm.

Laughing, David turned from the mirror

and gave me a quick hug.

Our performance at breakfast resembled some energetic children's game — a combination of musical chairs and hide-and-seek. Mercifully Nefret was not yet down; I cannot imagine what we would have done if she had been at table, since I scuttled in and out with baskets of food and pitchers of water, while David and Emerson pretended to eat twice as much as they actually consumed and David sat hunched over his plate speaking only in monosyllables and Emerson distracted Fatima by breaking various bits of crockery (not an uncommon occurrence, I might add). My rapid comings and goings reduced Ramses to speechlessness (which *was* an uncommon occurrence). After I had made certain he had everything he needed I ordered him to go to sleep, left Seshat on guard, and locked his door before I went downstairs. Shortly after I took my place at the table Nefret came in.

"Where is everyone?" she asked.

I put my spoon down and looked more closely at her. Her cheeks were pale and her eyes circled by violet shadows.

"My dear girl, are you ill? Or was it one of your bad dreams? I thought you had got over them."

"Bad dreams," Nefret repeated. "No, Aunt Amelia, I haven't got over them."

"If you could come to an understanding of what causes them —"

"I know what causes them, and there is nothing I can do about it. Don't badger me, Aunt Amelia. I am perfectly well. Where is — where are the Professor and Ramses?"

"Gone on to the dig."

"How is he this morning?"

"Ramses? Just as usual. A trifle out of sorts, perhaps."

"Just as usual," Nefret murmured.

"Promise me you won't lecture him, my dear. I have spoken with him myself, and any further criticism, especially from you —"

"I've no intention of lecturing him." Nefret pushed her untouched food away. "Shall we go?"

"I haven't finished yet. And you should eat something." Emerson obviously had some scheme in mind for getting David out of the way, and since I did not know what it was I wanted to give him plenty of time.

"Did you have a pleasant evening?" I asked, reaching for the marmalade.

A line of annoyance appeared between Nefret's arched brows, but she began to nibble at her egg. "It was rather boring."

"So you came home early."

"It wasn't very early, was it?" She hesitated for a moment, and then said, "Why don't you just ask me straight out, Aunt Amelia? I saw a light under Ramses's door and felt the need of intelligent conversation after a tedious evening with 'the Best People.' "

"So I assumed," I said. "There was no need for you to explain."

"I'm sorry." She pushed a loosened lock of hair away from her forehead. "I didn't get much sleep last night."

Not only you, I thought, and went on eating my toast. Nefret gave herself a little shake. "As a matter of fact, I did meet one interesting person," she said, looking and sounding much brighter. "None other than Major Hamilton, who wrote that rude letter to you."

"Is he one of the 'Best People'?" I inquired somewhat sardonically.

"Not really. He's older than the others and less given to silly jokes — that's how they spend their free time, you know, ragging one another and everyone else. Perhaps," said Nefret, "that is why he talked mostly to me. He's really quite charming, in a solemn sort of way."

"Oh, dear," I said. "Nefret, you didn't —"

"Flirt with him? Of course I did. But I didn't get very far," Nefret admitted with a grin. "He behaved rather like an indulgent uncle. I kept expecting him to pat me on the head and tell me I'd had quite enough champagne. We spent most of the time talking about Miss Hamilton. Nothing could have been more proper!"

187

"What did he say about her?"

"Oh, that she was bored and that he didn't know quite what to do with her. He's childless; his wife died many years ago and he has been faithful to her memory ever since. So I asked him why he wouldn't let Molly come to see us."

"In those precise words?" I exclaimed.

"Yes, why not? He hemmed and hawed and mumbled about not wanting her to make a nuisance of herself, so I assured him we wouldn't let her, and invited them to come to us for Christmas. I hope you don't mind."

"Well," I said, somewhat dazed by this unexpected information, "well, no. But —"

"He accepted with pleasure. I really don't want any more to eat, Aunt Amelia. Are you ready to go?"

I could delay her no longer, and I confess my heart was beating a trifle more quickly than usual as we approached the Great Pyramid. There were already a good number of tourists assembled. The majority were gathered at the north face, where the entrance was located, but others had spread out all round the structure, and as we rode to the south side I heard Emerson bellowing at a small group who had approached our tomb. Some visitors appeared to be under the impression that we were part of the tourist attractions of Giza.

"Impertinent idiots," he remarked, as they scattered, squawking indignantly.

I dismounted and handed the reins to Selim. Had there been, among those vacuous visitors, one who had come our way for a more sinister purpose than curiosity?

"Where is Ramses?" Nefret asked. "Inside?"

"No," Emerson said. "I received disquieting news this morning, my dears." He hurried on before she could ask how he had received it. "It seems someone has been digging illicitly at Zawaiet el 'Aryan. I sent Ramses there to see what damage has been done. He stopped here only long enough to pick up a few supplies."

Zawaiet was the site a few miles south where we had worked for several years — one of the most boring sites in Egypt, I would once have said, until we came across the Third Dynasty royal burial. Strictly speaking, it was a reburial, of objects rescued from an ancient tomb robbery, but the find was unique and some of the objects were rare and beautiful. Fragile, as well; it had taken us an entire season to preserve and remove them. Many of the private tombs surrounding the royal pyramid had not been excavated, and although it was not part of our concession, Emerson felt a proprietorial interest in the site.

"Goodness gracious, how distressing," I exclaimed. "Perhaps I ought to go after him and see what I can do to help."

"You may as well," said Emerson casually. "Selim can help Nefret with the photography. Er — try not to let anyone shoot at you or abduct you by force, Peabody."

"My dear, what a tease you are," I said, laughing merrily.

As I rode along the well-known southward path over the plateau, I was filled with relief and with admiration for Emerson's cleverness. The excuse was valid, the explanation sufficient. A good number of people, including our own men, had seen "Ramses" astride Risha, looking his normal self; he could spend most of the day away without arousing suspicion, and when he returned . . . Perhaps Emerson had already worked that out with David. If he had not, I had a few ideas of my own.

Since I was in no hurry I let the horse set its own pace. It was still early, the air cool and fresh. The sun had lifted over the Mokattam Hills and sparkled on the river, which lay below the desert plateau on my left. The fertile land bordering the water was green with new crops. From my vantage point above the cultivation I could see traffic passing along the road below — fellahin going to work in their fields and shops, and tourists on their way to Sakkara and the other sites south of Giza. Part of me yearned to descend and follow that road back to the house, but I dared not risk it; I could not get to Ramses without being seen by Fatima or one of the others.

Zawaiet is only a short distance from Giza; it was not long before I saw the tumbled mound that had once been a pyramid (though not a very good one.) David had been looking out for me. He came hurrying to meet me, and I slowed my steed to a walk so that we could exchange a few words without being overheard by the small group of Egyptians waiting near the pyramid. They must be local villagers, hoping for employment.

As David approached I wondered how two men could look so much alike as he and Ramses, and yet look so different! He was wearing Ramses's clothes, and his pith helmet shadowed his face, and their outlines were almost identical — long legs and narrow waists and broad shoulders — but I could have told one from the other just by the way they moved.

"A few of the local lads turned up," David explained.

"I suppose one ought to have expected that. They are always anxious for work, and extremely curious."

"It's all to the good, really. More unobservant and uncritical witnesses."

"What are you going to do with them?"

David grinned. "Start them clearing away sand. There's plenty of it. Perhaps you'd care to interrogate them about the illicit digging while I stalk about scribbling notes and looking enigmatic."

"Was there illicit digging?"

"There always is."

There always was. Under my expert questioning, one of the villagers broke down and admitted he and a few friends had found and cleared a small mastaba over the past summer. I demanded he show me the place and made a great fuss about it, though if he had not lied to me (which was entirely possible), the tomb was not likely to have contained anything of value, being one of the smaller and poorer variety. We had found very little ourselves, even in the larger tombs.

I was forced to wait until midday, when the men went off to eat and rest, before I could have a private conversation with David. There was no shelter, not even a patch of shade, so I put up my useful parasol and we made ourselves as comfortable as we could with our backs up against the pyramid, and got out the sandwiches and tea David had brought with him.

"Now," I said. "Tell me everything."

"That's rather a tall order, Aunt Amelia."

"Take all the time you like."

"How much has Ramses told you?"

"Nothing. He was too ill. Now, see here, David, I fully intend to get it out of you, and if Ramses does not like it, that is too damned — er — too bad."

He choked on the tea he was drinking. I

patted him on the back. "I am glad to see you, even under these circumstances," I said affectionately. "I presume Ramses has kept you informed about our loved ones back in England. Lia is doing splendidly."

"No, she's not." He bowed his head, and I saw there were lines in his face that had not been there before. "She's lonely and worried and frightened — and so am I, for her. I should be with her."

"I know, my dear. Perhaps you can be soon."

"I hope so. A few more weeks will tell the tale. By then we will have succeeded or failed."

"That is a relief," I said, trying not to think about the second alternative. "Now, David, start at the beginning."

David hesitated, looked at me, and sighed. "Oh, well, I've never been able to keep anything from you, have I? Ramses has been playing the role of a certain person —"

"Kamil el-Wardani? Aha, I thought I must be right. But why?"

"The Germans and the Turks are hoping to provoke an uprising in Cairo, to coincide with their attack on the Canal. If any man could bring such a thing off, it is Wardani. They approached him first last April. Oh, yes, they knew war was imminent, and they knew Turkey would come in; there was a secret treaty signed in early August. They think ahead, these Germans. I got wind of the plan from Wardani himself, so of course I told Ramses."

"It must have been difficult, betraying the confidence of a friend." I added quickly, "You were absolutely right to do so, of course."

"Ramses is more than my friend. He is my brother. And there were other reasons. For all his rhetorical bombast, Wardani was not a believer in violent revolution when I joined the movement. He had changed. He kept talking about blood being necessary to water the tree of liberty. . . . It made me sick to hear him. A revolt could not have succeeded, but before it was put down, hundreds, perhaps thousands, of deluded patriots and innocent bystanders would have been slaughtered. I want independence for my country, Aunt Amelia, but not at that price."

I had long admired David's strength of character; now, as I studied his thin brown face and sensitive but resolute lips, I was so moved I took his hand and gave it a little squeeze. "My dear," I said. "You learned of Lia's expectations, so greatly desired by you both, in September. You could have withdrawn from the scheme then. No one would have blamed you."

"Ramses urged me to do so. We had quite an argument about it, in fact. He didn't give in until I threatened to tell Lia the whole story and ask her to make the decision. He knew she'd insist I stand by him. He's walking a tightrope, Aunt Amelia; there's a river filled with crocodiles under it, and vultures hovering overhead, and now it looks as if somebody is sawing at the rope."

"Poetic but uninformative, my dear," I said uneasily. "Precisely who is after him?"

"Everybody. Except for the few people who are in on the secret, every police officer in Cairo is trying to arrest Wardani. The Germans and the Turks are using him for their own ends; they'd do away with him in an instant if they thought he was playing a double game. Then there are the hotheads in the movement itself. He has to keep them inactive without arousing their suspicions. If they believed he had softened toward the British they would — they would find another leader."

"Kill him, you mean."

"They would call it an execution. And of course if they ever learned his real identity, that would be the end of him."

"And of you. David," I cried, "it is insane for you and Ramses to take these risks! You said yourself that Wardani is the only man who could lead a successful revolt. Let it be known that he has been captured. His followers will be left leaderless and ineffectual, Ramses will be safe, and you can sail at once for England, and Lia. A pardon or amnesty can be arranged —"

"That is what will happen eventually. But it can't be done just yet."

"Why not?"

"The enemy has begun supplying Wardani with arms — rifles, pistols, grenades, possibly machine guns. We must hang on until we get those weapons into our hands, and find out how and by whom they are being brought into Cairo."

I caught my breath. "Of course! I ought to have realized."

"Well, yes, you ought," David said, with an affectionate smile. "Without arms there can't be a revolution, only a few hysterical students preaching jihad, and Ramses is doing his best to prevent even that. He doesn't like seeing people hurt, you know."

"I know."

"If we act too soon, the Turks will find other supply routes and other recipients. Ramses thinks that one of his own lieutenants is trying to supplant him, and Farouk is not the only ambitious revolutionary in Cairo. The first delivery — two hundred rifles and the ammunition to go with them — was supposed to take place last night."

"And Ramses was there?"

"Yes, ma'am. At least I assume he was. You see, Ramses took Mrs. Fortescue to dinner at Shepheard's last night. The idea was . . . I told him it wouldn't work, but he . . ." David gave me a sidelong look from under his lashes. "I don't think I had better tell you this part."

"I think you *had* better."

"Well, he had to leave at eleven in order to be at the rendezvous. Obviously I couldn't take his place with Mrs. Fortescue. A substitution at such close quarters . . . er. So the idea was that he would offend the lady by making — er — rude advances, so she would storm out and leave him — me, that is — to sulk silently but visibly in the bar. Unfortunately she . . ."

"Was not offended? David, how can you laugh when the situation is so desperate? Confound it, I believe you and Ramses actually enjoy these machinations!"

David got himself under control. "I'm sorry, Aunt Amelia. I suppose in a way we do. The situation is so damned — excuse me — deuced desperate, we have to find what humor we can in it. Someday you must get him to tell you about the time he turned up at a meeting disguised as himself."

"With that gang of cutthroats? He didn't!"

"Oh, yes, he did. Gave them a lecture on the art of disguise while he was about it."

"I do not know what is the matter with that boy! So how did he get away from her? You need not go into detail," I added quickly.

"You'll have to ask him. He was late meeting me and in a hurry, and in no mood to answer questions." The glint in David's dark eyes reminded me that, for all his admirable qualities, David was, after all, a man.

"Hmmm," I said. "It is probable then, that he reached the rendezvous unscathed. Dear me, this is confusing! Did the individual who shot him believe he was shooting at Wardani or at Ramses?"

David pushed his hat back and wiped his perspiring forehead with the back of his hand — a good touch, that, I thought approvingly. Ramses never has a handkerchief.

"That's the question, isn't it? Apparently Ramses fears the latter may be the case, or rather, that the fellow suspected Wardani was . . . shall we say, not himself? The truth about Wardani's present whereabouts is a closely guarded secret, but no secret is one hundred percent secure. If word got out that Wardani was interned in India, people wouldn't wonder for long who had taken his place. Ramses's talents are too well known. That's why I have appeared in public as Ramses on several occasions when Wardani was conspicuously elsewhere."

"And on at least one occasion you appeared as Wardani while Ramses was conspicuously elsewhere. Really," I said, in considerable chagrin, "I cannot imagine how I could have been so easily fooled!"

"You had never met Wardani," David said consolingly.

"That is true. I did sense something out of the way — something oddly familiar about him. My instincts were correct, as usual, but I was misled by — er — well, that is now irrelevant. One of these days I will give myself the pleasure of a little conversation with Thomas Russell. He has been laughing up his sleeve at me the whole time!"

"I assure you, Aunt Amelia, he's not laughing now. I was supposed to have reported to him early this morning, after I had heard from Ramses. He must be badly worried."

"You must have been worried too, when Ramses failed to meet you."

"I was beginning to be when the Professor turned up — scaring me half out of my wits, I might add! Ramses and I always try to meet after these exchanges, if only to bring one another up-to-date; there was one time, I remember, when I had to pretend to be drunk and incoherent in order to avoid a conversation with Mr. Woolley. Lawrence was with him, and I was afraid one of them would demand an explanation next time they saw him."

"By the time this is over, no respectable person in Cairo will be speaking to Ramses," I said with a heartfelt sigh. "Do not mistake me, David; if nothing worse than that happens I will be heartily grateful. So he was supposed to have gone to you last night before returning to the house?"

David nodded. His arms rested on his raised knees and his lashes, long and thick like those of my son, veiled his eyes. "I doubt he was in condition to think very clearly. He must have headed blindly for home."

"Yes." I took out my handkerchief and dabbed at my eyes. "Good gracious, there is a great deal of sand blowing about today. Well, David, it looks as if we must play this same game again tomorrow. The following day is Christmas Eve; Ramses should be on the mend by then, and we can have a quiet few days at home. All of us except you, my dear. Oh, I wish . . ."

"So do I."

"Don't kiss me, Ramses never does," I said, sniffing.

He kissed me anyhow. "Now," he said, "have you given any thought as to how I am going to put on a show for the general populace this afternoon without Nefret getting a close look at me?"

"It is going to be horribly difficult, but that isn't the only reason I wish Nefret could be told. David, he won't see a doctor, and I did the best I could, but I am not qualified to treat injuries like those, and she is, and she would never —"

"Aunt Amelia." He took my hand. "I knew this was going to come up. In fact, I had meant to raise the subject myself if you didn't. Ramses told me he was afraid he had failed to convince you that she mustn't know the truth. There are two excellent reasons why that is impossible. One is a simple matter of arithmetic: the more people who know a secret, the greater the chance that someone will inadvertently let it slip. The other reason is a little more complicated. I don't know that I can make you understand, but I have to try.

"You see, there's a bizarre sort of gentleman's code in this strange business of espionage. It applies only to gentlemen, of course." His finely cut lips tightened. "The poor devils who take most of the risks aren't included in the bargain. But the men who run the show keep hands off the families and friends of their counterparts on the other side. They have to, or risk retaliation in kind. If Ramses and I were suspected, they wouldn't use you to get at us, but if it were known that you, or the Professor, or Nefret, or anyone else, were taking an active part in the business, you'd be fair game. That's why he didn't want you to find out, and that is why Nefret mustn't find out. Good God, Aunt Amelia, you know how she is! Do you suppose she wouldn't insist on taking a hand if she thought we were in danger?"

"She would, of course," I murmured.

"I know you're worried about him," David said gently. "So am I. And he's worried about you. He'd never have brought you into it if he'd had a choice, and he's feeling horribly guilty for endangering you and the Professor. Don't make it harder for him."

I have always said that timing is all-important in these matters. When we returned to Giza the sun was low enough to cast useful shadows; the tourists had begun to disperse, but there were still a number of people ready to turn and stare. As well they might! Draped dramatically across the saddle and supported by David's arms, my loosened hair streaming out in the wind, I rested my head against his shoulder and said, under my breath, "This is a cursed uncomfortable position, David. Let us not linger any longer than is absolutely necessary."

"Sssh!" He was trying not to laugh.

Trailed by a curious throng, Risha picked his way through the tumbled sand and debris till we were close to our tomb. David pulled him up in a flamboyant and completely unnecessary rearing stop, and Emerson came running toward us.

"What has happened?" he shouted at the top of his lungs. "Peabody, my dear —"

"I am perfectly all right, Emerson," I shouted back. "A little fall, that is all, but you know how Ramses is, he insisted on carrying me back. Let me down, Ramses."

I wriggled a bit. Risha turned his aristocratic head and gave me a critical look, and

David gripped me more firmly. Unfortunately the movement resulted in my parasol, slung beside the saddle, jabbing painfully into my anatomy. I let out a shriek.

"Take her straight on home," Emerson cried loudly. "We will follow."

"Just in time," I muttered, while we withdrew as fast as safety permitted. "Nefret had just come out of the tomb; she got only a glimpse of us. David, did you happen to notice the woman to whom Emerson was talking when we arrived?"

David shifted me into a less uncomfortable position. "Mrs. Fortescue," he said. "Had she been invited to visit the dig?"

"We had spoken of it, but I had not got round to issuing a particular invitation. An odd coincidence, is it not, that she happened to drop by today?"

As soon as I entered the house I told Fatima to prepare a very extensive tea, which got her out of the way. David and I then hurried to Ramses's room. When I saw that the bed was unoccupied, my heart sank down into my boots. Then Ramses stepped out from behind the door. He was fully dressed, straight as a lance, and several shades paler than usual.

"Goodness, what a fright you gave me!" I exclaimed. "Get back into bed at once. And take off your shirt, I want to dress the wounds. You had no business —"

"I wanted to be certain it was you. How did it go?"

"All right, I think." David examined him critically. "You're a trifle off-color."

"Am I?" He went to the mirror.

I watched as he uncorked a bottle and applied a thin layer of liquid to his face. He must have been in and out of bed several times; not only was he clean-shaven but he had set up a peculiar-looking apparatus on his desk — tubes and coils and glass vessels of various sizes. From it wafted a horrible smell.

"Where is Seshat?" I inquired. "I told her to make sure you stayed in bed."

Ramses returned the little bottle to the cupboard and closed the door. "What did you expect her to do, knock me down and sit on me? She went out the window when she heard you coming. She'd been here all day."

"What went wrong last night?" David asked.

"Later." Ramses sat down, rather heavily, on the side of the bed. "Where are the others?"

"On their way," I said. "Ramses, I insist you allow me —"

"Get on with it, then, while David tells me what I did today."

So I got on with it, and David summarized the events of the day. The account served to distract Ramses from the unpleasant things I was doing to him. He was rather white

204

around the mouth by the time I finished, but he laughed when David described our arrival at Giza.

"I wish I could have seen you. Your idea, Mother?"

"Yes. I would have preferred to do something more flamboyant, but I was afraid to risk it. You may be sure Nefret would have been first on the spot, burning to tend to me, and then she would have got a close look at David."

Ramses nodded approval. "Good thinking. And you say Mrs. Fortescue just happened to be there?"

"Do you suspect her?" I asked.

"It did occur to me," said my son, glancing at David, "that her — uh — affability the evening we dined together might have been prompted by something other than — er . . ."

"So, she was affable, was she?" I remarked.

"So David told you about that, did he?" remarked Ramses, in the same tone. "I thought so. I don't know how you do it, but he babbles like a brook whenever you get him to yourself. I would not have referred to it had I not felt it necessary to clear up certain misapprehensions you both seem to harbor. I do not suspect the lady any more than I suspect all other newcomers without official credentials, but the fact remains that she did her best to detain me when I was on my way to an important meeting. Difficult as it may be for you and David to believe, she may not have been swept off her feet by — er . . ."

"Now, now, don't get excited," I said soothingly. "Without wishing in any way to contradict your appraisal of your personal attractions, I believe it is entirely possible that her motives for calling on us had nothing to do with you. Perhaps it is your father she's after."

David and Ramses exchanged glances. "If you don't mind, Mother," said my son, "I would rather not continue this line of speculation. David, you'll probably have to take my place again tomorrow, so you had better stay here tonight. Lock the door after we leave."

David nodded. "We need to talk."

"That, too."

"Ramses," I said. "You —"

"Please, Mother, don't argue! There's no time now. David can't take my place at dinner, not with Nefret and Fatima there. We'll talk later. A council of war, as you used to say."

I told Fatima we would take tea in the sitting room that evening. It was not a room we often used for informal family gatherings, since it was too spacious to be cozy and somewhat gloomy because of the small, high windows. However, it would spare Ramses the stairs to the roof; not much help, but the best I could do.

I made haste in bathing and changing, but the others were already there when I entered the parlor.

"Where is Mrs. Fortescue?" I asked. "Didn't you ask her to come to tea?"

"If that inquiry is addressed to me," said Emerson, with great emphasis, "the answer is, no, why the devil should I have done? She turned up this afternoon without warning and without an invitation, and expected me to drop what I was doing and show her every cursed pyramid at Giza. I was trying to think of a way to get rid of her when you saved me the trouble."

"She asked where Ramses was," Nefret said.

He had taken a chair some little distance from the sofa where she was sitting, and I observed he was now wearing a light tweed coat, which served to conceal the rather lumpy bandages. "How nice," he murmured. "Which of her admirers was with her, the Count or the Major?"

"Neither," Emerson said. "It was that young Pinkerton."

"Pinckney," Nefret corrected.

"Ah," said Ramses. "I didn't see him."

"He was inside the tomb, with me. I was showing him the reliefs."

"Hmmm," said Ramses.

Nefret glared at him, or tried to; her prettily arched brows were incapable of looking menacing. "If you are implying —"

"I'm not implying anything," Ramses said.

He was, of course. I had had the same thought. Mr. Pinckney might have brought the lady along as camouflage for his romantic designs on Nefret. Or she might have brought him along as camouflage for her designs on Emerson. Or . . .

Good Gad, I thought, this is even more complicated than our usual encounters with crime. The only thing of which I was certain was that neither Pinckney nor Mrs. Fortescue was Sethos.

Nefret subjected Ramses to another glare, and then turned to me. "The Professor assured me you were not seriously injured, Aunt Amelia, but I would like to have a look at you. What happened?"

"It was all a great fuss about nothing, my dear," I replied, seating myself next to her on the sofa. "I took a little tumble into a tomb and twisted my arm."

"This arm?" Before I could stop her she grasped my hand and pushed my sleeve up. "I don't see anything. Does it hurt when I do this?"

"No," I said truthfully.

"Or this? Hmmm. Well, it appears there is no break or sprain."

"The greatest damage was to another portion of her anatomy," said Ramses. "She landed on her . . . that is, in a sitting position."

As he had no doubt expected, my look of chagrin put an end to Nefret's questions.

"Never mind," I said, with a little cough. "Have you asked Fatima to serve tea, Nefret?"

"Yes, it should be here shortly. I wanted to get an early start, since I am dining out this evening."

"Dining out," I repeated. "Have you told Fatima?"

"Yes."

"You look very nice. Is that a new frock?"

"I haven't worn it before. Do you like it?"

"Not very much," said Ramses, before I could reply. "Is that the latest in evening dress? You look like a lamp shade."

She did, rather. The long overtunic had been stiffened at the bottom so that it stood out around the slim black skirt in a perfect circle. I could tell by Emerson's expression that he was of the same opinion, but he was wise enough to remain silent.

"It's a Poiret," Nefret said indignantly. "Really, men have no sense of fashion, have they, Aunt Amelia?"

"A very pretty lamp shade," Ramses amended.

"I refuse to discuss fashions," Emerson grumbled. "Peabody, what did you think of the situation at Zawaiet? Ramses has just informed me that the local bandits have been wreaking havoc with the place."

"I wouldn't go that far," I said.

"Nor would I," said Ramses. "However, I think — with your permission, Father — I will spend at least one more day there, if for no other reason than to establish the presumption that we are keeping an eye on the place. Also, the pit tomb the men uncovered today should be cleared. I doubt there's much there, but I want to make certain nothing has been overlooked."

Fatima came in with the tea tray and I busied myself preparing the genial beverage — lemon for Nefret, milk and three teaspoons of sugar for Emerson. Ramses declined in favor of whiskey, which he mixed himself.

Nefret's announcement had come as a considerable relief. If she was out of the house we could retire early, to Ramses's room. I wanted to get him back into bed and I was determined to hold that council of war. There were so many unanswered questions boiling round in my head, I felt as if it would burst. Nor were Ramses and David the only ones I intended to interrogate. My own husband, my devoted spouse, had obviously kept me in the dark about certain of his own activities.

As for Nefret, I could only hope she was not dining with Percy or some other individual of whom I would not approve. There wasn't much I could do about it; a direct inquiry might or might not produce a truthful answer.

She had entered with seeming interest into the discussion about Zawaiet el 'Aryan. "You won't be needing me to take photographs, then?" she asked.

"I see no reason for it," Emerson answered. "In fact, I hope Ramses can finish at Zawaiet tomorrow or the next day. The cursed place isn't our responsibility, after all; it is still part of Reisner's concession."

"Perhaps I ought to notify him of what has been going on," Ramses suggested.

"He is in the Sudan," Emerson said. "It can wait."

"Very well." Ramses got up and went to the table, where he poured another whiskey. Nefret's eyes followed him, but she made no comment.

"I suppose, Peabody," said my husband, "you will insist we leave off work Christmas and Boxing Day."

"Now my dear, you know I never insist. However, respect for the traditions of the faith that is our common heritage —"

"Confounded religion," said Emerson predictably.

"We haven't even done anything about a Christmas tree," Nefret said. "Perhaps, Aunt Amelia, you would rather not go to the trouble this year."

"It is difficult to get in the proper frame of mind," I admitted. "But for that very reason it is all the more important, in my opinion, that we should make an effort."

"Whatever you say." Nefret returned her cup to its saucer and stood up. "I'll help you with the decorations, of course. Palm branches and poinsettias —"

"Mistletoe?" Ramses inquired softly.

She had started for the door. She stopped, but did not turn. "Not this year."

There seemed to be a certain tension in the air, though I could not understand why — unless it was the fact that her first and last attempt to supply that unattractive vegetable had been the Christmas before her ill-fated marriage. "It doesn't hold up well in this climate," I said. "The last time we had it, the berries turned black and fell off onto people's heads."

"Yes. I must go now," Nefret said. "I won't be late."

"With whom are you —"

She quickened her step and got out the door before I could finish the question.

None of us did justice to Mahmoud's excellent dinner. I could see that Ramses had to force each bite down, and my own appetite was not at its best. After we had finished, Emerson told Fatima we would have coffee in his study, since we intended to work that evening. Taking the heavy tray from her hands — a kindness he often performed — he told her to go to bed.

We had arranged a signal with David —

two soft taps, a louder knock, and three more soft taps. Of course I could have unlocked the door with my own key, but I saw no reason to let its existence be known. My harmless little subterfuge was in vain; Ramses's first question, once we were safely inside his room, was, "How did you get in last night, Mother? I had locked the door before I left the house."

"She had a spare key, of course," said Emerson, while I was trying to think of a way of evading the question. "You might have known she would. Now then, my boy, lie down and rest."

He put the tray on a table and David offered Ramses a supporting arm. Ramses waved it away. "I'm all right. David, we'll get you something to eat after Fatima has gone to bed. Where —"

"Oh, for pity's sake!" I exclaimed irritably. "At least sit down, if you won't lie down, and stop trying to distract me. I have a great many questions for all of you."

"I'm sure you do," Ramses said. He lowered himself carefully into an armchair. "Where is — ah, there you are."

This remark was directed at the cat, who entered the room by way of the window. After giving his boots a thorough inspection she jumped onto the arm of the chair and settled down, paws folded under her chest.

"She's been keeping watch on the balcony," David said seriously. "But she must have thought I looked hungry, because she brought me a nice fat rat about an hour ago."

I glanced involuntarily round the room, and David laughed. "Don't worry, Aunt Amelia, I got rid of it. Tactfully, of course. Where is Nefret?"

"Gone out for the evening. I only wish to goodness I knew where, and with whom." The boys exchanged glances, and I said, "Do you know?"

"No," Ramses said.

"Leave that for now," Emerson ordered. He had poured coffee for us; David brought a cup to me and one to Ramses, and Emerson went on, "David has told me — and you too, I presume, Peabody — about the scheme to supply arms to Wardani's revolutionaries. There is no need to emphasize the seriousness of the matter. Your plan to prevent it was well worked out. What I want to know is: first, how many more deliveries are planned; second, how much progress have you made in discovering how the weapons are brought into Cairo; and third, what went wrong last night."

"Well reasoned, Emerson," I said approvingly. "I would only add —"

"Excuse me, Mother, but I think that is quite enough to start with," Ramses said. "To take Father's questions in order: There are two more deliveries scheduled, but I haven't yet been informed of the dates. By the end of January we will have stockpiled over a thousand rifles and a hundred Luger pistols, with ample ammunition for both. The Lugers are the 08 model, with an eight-shot magazine."

"Good Lord," Emerson muttered. "Yes, but how many of your — er — Wardani's rag-tag army knows how to use a firearm?"

"It doesn't require much practice to throw a grenade into a crowd," David said soberly. "And some of the rank and file are former army."

"As for your second question," Ramses went on, "unfortunately the answer is: not much. Last night's delivery point was east of the city, in an abandoned village on the outskirts of Kubbeh. The fellow in charge is a Turk who is approximately as trustworthy as a pariah dog, so I made a point of checking the inventory. He didn't like it, but there wasn't much he could do about it except call me rude names."

"Was it he who shot you?" Emerson asked.

"I don't know. It may have been. Farouk — one of my lieutenants — is another candidate. He's an ambitious little rascal. It happened just after I left them; they were supposed to take the weapons on to Cairo. . . ." He picked up his cup. The coffee spilled over, and he quickly replaced it in the saucer. Emerson took his pipe from his mouth.

"Do you want to rest awhile? This can wait."

"No, it can't." Ramses rubbed his eyes. "David needs to know this, and so do you. In case . . ."

"David, there is a bottle of brandy in that cupboard," I said. "Go on, Ramses."

"Yes, all right. Where had I got to?"

He sounded drowsy and bewildered, like a lost child. I couldn't stand it any longer.

"Never mind," I said. "Get into bed."

"But I haven't told you —"

"It can wait." I took the glass from David and held it to Ramses's lips. "Drink a little."

He revived enough to study me suspiciously from under his lashes. "What did you put in it?"

"Nothing. But if you are not asleep within ten minutes I will take steps. David, can you get his boots off?"

I began unbuttoning his shirt. He shied back and pushed at my hand, to no avail. I have had a good many years practice dealing with stubborn male persons. "All right, Mother, all right! I will do as you ask, providing you stop that at once."

"I am not leaving this room until you are in bed."

He scowled at me. I was pleased to see him feeling more alert, so I said graciously, "I will turn my back. How's that?"

"The best I can get, obviously," muttered

Ramses. "There's one more thing. The weapons are cached in one of the abandoned tobacco warehouses. At least that's where they are supposed to be. David knows which one. Someone should go round there to make certain. Someone has to tell Russell about —"

"Certainly, my boy." Emerson tapped out his pipe and rose. "Here, let me help you."

"I don't need —"

"There you are," said Emerson cheerfully. "Nicely tucked up, eh?"

I turned round. Ramses snatched at the sheet, which Emerson was trying to tuck in. They had got his clothes off, anyhow. I decided not to inquire further.

"You had better get some rest too, David," I said. "We will carry out the same procedure tomorrow. I will be here at . . . Oh, dear, I almost forgot. You haven't had any supper. I will just slip down —"

"I'll do it," said Emerson. "Back in a minute, boys. Peabody, off to bed with you."

"One last question —"

"I thought you wanted him to rest."

"I do. But —"

"Not another word!" Emerson picked me up and started for the door. Just before it closed behind us I heard a muffled laugh from David, and a comment from Ramses which I could not quite make out.

I waited until we had reached our room be-

217

fore I spoke. "Very well, Emerson, you have had your way."

"Not yet," said Emerson. "But I will get David a bite of food first. Don't stir from this spot, Peabody."

He put me down on the bed and slipped out before I could object.

He was not gone long, but I had ample time to consider what I meant to say, and I was ready for him when he returned. "Do not suppose, my dear Emerson, that you can distract me in the manner you obviously intend. You have avoided my questions thus far, but —"

"My darling girl, we have not had a moment to —"

"Endearments now!" I cried, pushing his hand away.

"And why the devil not?" Emerson's blue eyes snapped. "Curse it, Peabody —"

"And leave off interrupting me!"

"Damnation!" Emerson shouted.

"Don't bellow! Someone will hear you."

Emerson sat down on the edge of the bed and seized me by the shoulders. A formidable scowl distorted the face that was now only six inches from mine. He was breathing heavily, and I must confess that rising ire had caused my own respiration to quicken.

After a moment his thunderous brows drew apart and his narrowed eyes resumed their usual look of sapphirine affability.

"There is nothing unusual in our shouting at one another," he remarked. "May I assist you with your buttons and bootlaces, my dear?"

"If you continue to converse as you do so."

"Fair enough. What is your first question?"

"How did you know where to find David?"

He took my foot in his hand. Emerson's little explosions of temper always relieve him; he was smiling as he unlaced my boots with the delicacy of touch he always demonstrates with antiquities and with me. "Do you remember the house in Maadi?"

"What house? Oh — you mean the one where Ramses took little Sennia and her mother after he got them away from that vile procurer?"

"Until the bastard tracked them down," Emerson said grimly, starting on the other boot. "I went there one day with Ramses; we hoped Rashida might have returned to the only refuge she knew — a doomed hope, as you know. Ramses admitted that he and David had used the place before, during the years when they were roaming round the suks in various disguises. I thought it likely they would use it again, since it is an excellent hideout; the old woman who owns it is half blind and slightly senile."

By this time Emerson had proceeded with his other suggestion, and I felt a pleasant lethargy seize my limbs. I opened my mouth to speak, but found myself yawning instead.

"Close your eyes," Emerson said softly, doing it for me. His fingers moved from my eyelids to my cheek. "You didn't get a wink of sleep last night, and tomorrow will be another busy day. There. That's right. Good night, my love."

Through the veils of sleep Emerson's gentle hands had wrapped round me I was conscious of a vague sense of irritability. His explanation had been reasonable, so far as it went, but . . . I was too weary to continue the discussion. Of all the questions that still vexed me, one of the most inconsequential pursued me into slumber. How the devil had Ramses got away from Mrs. Fortescue?

5

From Manuscript H

He'd been as rude as he could manage and rougher than he liked. Most women would have taken offense at his frequent glances at his watch during dinner, but she appeared not to notice. After they had dined he led her straight to the most secluded alcove in the Moorish Hall. He expected at least a token protest, but she moved at once into his arms, and when he kissed her she kissed him back with a force that made his teeth ache. Further familiarities aroused an even more ardent response, and he began to wonder how far he would have to go before she remembered where they were and what sort of woman she was supposed to be. Nefret would have broken his arm if he'd handled her so cavalierly.

Nefret. The memory of that night, the only night they had been together, was imprinted in every cell of his body, so much a part of him that he couldn't touch another woman without thinking of her. His caresses became even more mechanical, but they had a result he had not anticipated; she brought her lips close to his ear and suggested they retire to her room at the Savoy.

He took out his watch. It was later than he'd thought, and annoyance, at himself and at her, provoked him into direct insult. "Damn! I beg your pardon, madam, but I am late for an appointment with another lady. I will let you know when I am free."

He made his escape, collected his hat and coat from the attendant, and slipped out the side door. Another story to go the rounds of society gossip, he supposed; she wouldn't be able to keep it to herself, but she would certainly revise it to make him appear even more of a boor. Attempted rape in the Moorish Hall? There were a number of people in Cairo who would believe it.

David was waiting for him in a part of the hotel grounds no guest ever saw, between a reeking heap of refuse and a stack of bricks designed for some repair job that had never been begun. A sickly acacia tree shadowed the area and provided convenient limbs on which to hang objects temporarily. "You're late," he whispered. "What happened? I told you —"

"Shut up and hold this." A rat ran across the top of the bricks.

"Has she left the hotel?"

"I don't know. I hope so. Watch out for her."

They made the exchange of clothing as they spoke. Ramses had simplified his cumbersome evening garb as much as possible; his shirt had attached collar and cuffs, and buttons instead of links. Under it he wore the loose shirt and drawers of a peasant. David handed over his robe and knife belt and sandals. Forcing his stockinged feet into Ramses's shoes, he grumbled, "Couldn't you buy evening pumps one size larger? I'm getting blisters."

"You should have mentioned it before. Here, take my coat and hat. I'll see you later." He pulled a woolen scarf from his coat pocket and wound it round his face and throat.

"Good luck."

"And to you. Take care." They clasped hands briefly but warmly, and Ramses slid away into the darkness.

His demand to be put in touch with the man running operations in Cairo had been rejected. He'd thought it was worth a try, but he hadn't really expected they would agree. They didn't trust Wardani any more than Wardani would have trusted them. It had been the Turk who turned up at Aslimi's, with the information about the time and place of the first delivery.

Being late, he risked taking a cab for part of the distance. After the driver had let him off near the station at Demerdash he proceeded on foot, running when he could do so without attracting attention. It took less than half an hour to cover the two miles, and another five minutes to assume the rest of his disguise. He'd done it so often he didn't even need a mirror: beard and mustache, a neatly wound turban, a few lines and patches of shadow rubbed round his eyes.

The village was off the main road; it had been abandoned for years, and like many villages in Egypt, it had been built of stone vandalized from ancient ruins. Segments of remaining walls stood up like jagged teeth around the roofless house that had been designated as the rendezvous.

The others were already there. He could hear low voices and the sounds of movement. He'd hoped to arrive in time to spot the wagon, which might have given him a clue as to where it had come from. Too late now. Damn Mrs. Fortescue.

His own men welcomed him with unconcealed relief. Farouk was particularly effusive, clasping him in a close embrace and inquiring solicitously after his health. Ramses shrugged him off and turned to exchange brief, insincere greetings with the Turk. The big man was obviously in a hurry to be gone. Urged on by his low-voiced curses, Wardani's men had almost finished unloading the wagon into the smaller donkey carts they had brought. Ramses climbed into the wagon and began unwrapping one of the long cloth-wrapped bundles.

"Here! What are you doing? There is no time for —"

"There is time. Why the hurry? Did you run into trouble with one of the camel patrols?"

"There was no trouble. I know how to avoid it."

It was a less informative reply than Ramses had hoped for, but he did not pursue the matter. The bundle contained ten rifles. He freed one from the wrappings and examined it. It was one of the Turkish models that had been used in the 1912 War, and it appeared to be in good condition. He passed it into the eager hands of Bashir. How the poor fools loved to play soldier! Bashir probably didn't know which end to point.

"Ten in each. Two hundred in all. Where's the ammunition?"

The Turk kept up a monotonous undercurrent of cursing as Ramses checked the other bundles and located the boxes of ammunition and grenades. There was another, larger box.

"Pistols?" Ramses pried the top off with the blade of his knife.

"A bonus," said the Turk. He spat. "Are you satisfied now?"

"I wouldn't want to detain you," Ramses said politely. "When do we meet again, and where?"

"You will be notified." The Turk climbed

onto the seat of the wagon and picked up the reins. The mule team started to move.

Turning, Ramses was annoyed to see that his enthusiastic followers were passing round the pistols and trying to insert the clips. "How does it go?" Asad asked.

"In the grip. Like this." It would be Farouk, Ramses thought. The others followed his lead, much more clumsily, and Ramses snapped, "Put those back and close the box. By the life of the Prophet, I would be better off with a bunch of el-Gharbi's girls! Can I trust you to cover the loads and get moving? You've a long way to go and a lot to do before morning."

"You aren't coming with us?" Asad asked. A vagrant ray of moonlight shone off his eyeglasses as he turned to his leader.

"I go my way alone, as always. But I will know whether you carry out your orders. Maas salameh."

He could still hear the creak of the wagon wheels and he too had a lot to do before morning.

He hadn't gone more than fifty yards before there was a shout: "Who's there?" or "Who's that?" Ramses stopped and looked round. Not a sign of anyone. Had the damned fools got the wind up over a wandering dog or jackal? He started back, intending to put the fear of God into them before they roused the whole neighborhood. When the first shot was fired he didn't bother to take cover, but when a second and third followed, they came close enough to remind him that there were several people around who didn't like him much. Discretion being the better part of valor, he turned tail and ran.

He'd waited a little too long. The impact of the bullet spun him sideways and knocked him to the ground. He managed to roll into a convenient depression beside a wall and lay there, unable to move and expecting at any moment to see a shadowy form looking down at him and the dark glint of light on the barrel of a gun.

As the seconds passed, so did the numbness in his arm and shoulder. He drew his knife and then froze as footsteps approached his hiding place and an agitated voice called his name. He couldn't tell which one of them it was; the voice was as high-pitched as a girl's. Another, equally agitated voice answered. "Farouk! Come back, we must hurry."

"There was someone in that grove of trees — with a gun! I fired back —"

"You missed, then. No one is there now."

"But I tell you, I saw *him* fall. If he is dead, or wounded —"

"He would wish us to go on." The speaker had come closer. It was Asad, sounding frightfully noble and pompous, but, thank God, sensible enough to follow orders.

"Hurry, I say. Someone may have heard the shots."

Someone almost certainly did, Ramses thought, fighting the waves of faintness that came and went. He had to stop the bleeding and get the hell out of there, but he dared not move while Farouk was nearby. Farouk might or might not be telling the truth when he claimed some unknown party had fired first; in either case, Ramses knew he couldn't risk being in the tender care of Wardani's followers. Under close scrutiny there were a dozen ways in which he might betray himself.

Finally the footsteps moved away. He slashed and tore at the fabric of his shirt and bound the uneven strips around his arm. The pain was rather bad by then, but he was able to pull himself to his feet.

The rest of the journey was a blank, broken by brief intervals of consciousness; he must have kept moving, though, because whenever he became aware of his surroundings he was farther along — on the railroad platform at Kurreh, slumped in a third-class carriage, and finally, facedown in an irrigation ditch. That woke him, and he crawled up the muddy bank and examined his surroundings. He had crossed the bridge — he couldn't remember how — and was on the west bank, less than a mile from the house. Still on hands and knees, he wiped the mud from his face and tried to think. He'd meant to head for

Maadi, where David was waiting for him. No hope of getting there now, he'd be lucky to make it home.

The cool water had revived him a little, and he managed to stay on his feet for the remainder of the distance. He covered the last few yards in a staggering run and leaned against the wall wondering how in God's name he was going to get up to his room. The trellis with its climbing vine was as good as a ladder when he was in fit condition, but just now it looked as long and as steep as the Grand Gallery in the Great Pyramid.

A soft sound from above made him look up. Poised on the edge of the balcony was Seshat. She stared at him for a moment, and then jumped onto the mass of entwined stems and descended, as surefooted as if she were on level ground. He had never known a cat who could do that; they were first-rate climbers, but once they got up they didn't seem to know how to come down. Even his beloved Bastet . . .

Teeth and claws sank into his bare ankle, and the pain jarred him back to full awareness. Having got his attention, Sheshat put her large head against his foot and shoved.

One foot at a time, he thought hazily. Right.

She climbed with him, muttering discontentedly and pushing at him when he stopped. Finally he hauled himself over the edge of the balcony and fell to hands and knees. Another shove from Seshat got him to his feet; he hung on to the window frame and looked into the room. It was dark and quiet, just as he'd left it; no trouble there, anyhow, thank God for small blessings. The bed looked as if it were a mile away. He couldn't think beyond that — reaching the bed, lying down. He took three faltering steps and fell.

When he came back to his senses he saw his mother bending over him, and his father, standing by. The cat was out of the bag now, or soon would be. He didn't know whether to be glad or sorry.

My frame of mind was considerably improved next day. David had gone off to Zawaiet alone and Emerson took Nefret with him to Giza, so I was able to spend a little time with Ramses. When I removed the bandages I saw that someone, probably David, had smeared Kadija's green salve all over the area. Whether it was that, or the mercury and zinc-cyanide paste I had applied, or Ramses's own recuperative powers, the infection I had feared had not occurred. He was still fussing about Thomas Russell, however, so I told him to stop worrying; that I would deal with the matter. He appeared somewhat alarmed at the prospect.

"I won't scold him," I promised. "But if you were to give me a few more details . . ."

He really had no choice but to do so. By the time I left him I had obtained answers to most of my remaining questions, and as I proceeded along the Giza Road I pondered the information.

After hearing his account of what had happened at the rendezvous and afterwards, I understood why he had been so insistent about carrying out his normal activities. The would-be assassin might have been the Turk, or Wardani's ambitious lieutenant, or an unknown third party; whoever he was, and whatever his motive, he was probably aware of the fact that "Wardani" had suffered an injury of some sort. Ramses had also admitted, upon interrogation, that he had reason to believe his masquerade was suspected. He refused to elaborate, claiming it was more a sense of uneasiness than a specific fact — "like one of your famous forebodings, Mother."

I could not quarrel with that, for I knew how significant such feelings could be. There were a number of ways in which the truth about Wardani's whereabouts might have come out. The peculiar nature of Anglo-Egyptian officialdom had become even more complicated after the formal annexation of the country. Kitchener had been replaced by Sir Henry MacMahon, with the new title of High Commissioner; General Sir John Maxwell was the Commander of the

Army; the Cairo Police force was still under the command of Harvey Pasha, with Russell as his assistant and Philippides, the unsavory Levantine, as director of the political CID; the new intelligence department was headed by Gilbert Clayton, who was also the Cairo representative of the Sirdar of the Sudan; under Clayton was Mr. Newcombe and his little group of Oxbridge intellectuals, which included Leonard Woolley and Mr. Lawrence. At the beginning Ramses had dealt only with Russell, whose intelligence and integrity he trusted, as he did not trust some of the others; but it had been necessary to involve higher authorities in order to carry out the supposed deportation of David and the secret imprisonment of Wardani. In theory the only persons who knew of the impersonation were Kitchener himself, MacMahon, General Maxwell, and Thomas Russell.

I didn't believe it. Unnamed personages in the War Office in London must have been informed; General Maxwell might have confided in certain members of his staff and in Clayton. Men believe women are hopeless gossips, but women *know* men are. The poor creatures are worse than women in some ways, because they cannot admit to themselves that they are gossiping, or doubt the discretion of the individuals in whom they confide. "Strictly in confidence, old boy, just between you and me . . ."

Yes, the word would spread, in private offices and in the clubs, and, if I may be permitted a slight vulgarity, in the boudoir. I did not doubt there were agents of the Central Powers in Cairo; some might have penetrated the police and the intelligence departments. The longer the boys continued their perilous task, the greater the danger that the truth would reach the ears of the enemy. It might already have done so.

The effect of this depressing conclusion was to inspire me with even greater determination. When I reached Giza, I found the others hard at work. I stopped for a moment to gloat over the painted reliefs, for they were really lovely. However, I would be the first to admit that my primary interest lay in the burial chamber, or chambers. There were two of them connected with the mastaba; we had located the tops of the deep shafts that led down to them, but Emerson did not intend to dig them out until after he had finished with the mastaba itself. The outer chamber, or chapel, had been cleared, but the doorway leading to a second room was still blocked with debris.

Nefret was at the wall, electric torch in hand, comparing the drawings Ramses had made from her photographs with the originals and emending them when she found errors. This would certainly lead to an argument, for Ramses did not accept correction graciously and Nefret was not the most tactful of critics. An involuntary sigh escaped my lips when I thought of the days when David had been our copyist; no one had his touch, and even Ramses deferred to him when there was a disagreement. How foolish and how petty of me to regret such minor losses, I thought, and offered up a silent little prayer. Only let them finish their dangerous job alive and unharmed, and I would ask nothing more of the Power that guides our lives. Not until next season, anyhow.

"Where is Emerson?" I asked.

Selim, holding a reflector that cast additional light, only shook his head. Nefret glanced round. "He said he wanted to consult the records at Harvard Camp."

"What about?"

"He did not condescend to inform me," said Nefret. "Ramses has gone to Zawaiet. Daoud went with the Professor. Aunt Amelia, may I be excused for a few hours this afternoon? I want to go into Cairo to do some shopping."

"You had better ask Emerson."

"He said to ask you."

She looked and sounded rather sulky. Rapidly I weighed the advantages and disadvantages of acceding to her request. If she was out of the way when David returned, the transfer of identities would be much easier, but I did not really believe she wanted to shop. Could I follow her without being observed? Could I insist on accompanying her? Maternal affection exerted a powerful pull; I yearned to be with my son, caring for him, making certain he did precisely what I wanted him to do, which he would not unless I made him. And what of Emerson? It was not like him to absent himself from his work. Was he really consulting the records of Mr. Reisner, or had he gone off on some absurd errand of his own? Ramses had said Russell must be informed. . . .

These conflicting and confusing ideas passed through my mind with the rapidity that marks my cogitations. There was, I believe, scarcely a pause before I replied.

"I have a few purchases to make too. I will go with you."

"If you like."

I could always change my mind after I had conferred with Emerson.

He did not return for over an hour. I had given up all pretense of accomplishing any useful work, and was outside, watching for him.

"What the devil are you doing, Peabody?" he exclaimed. "Gawking at the pyramid again? You should be sifting debris."

The black scowl that accompanied his grumble did not disturb me for a moment. He was only trying to distract me.

"I will not allow you to distract me, Emer-

235

son," I informed him. "Where have you been?"

"I wanted to consult —"

"No, you didn't."

One of the men emerged from the tomb entrance carrying a basket. I drew Emerson aside. "Where did you go?"

"Back to the house. I wanted to use the telephone."

"To ring Russ—"

He clapped a hand over my mouth — or, to be precise, the entire lower half of my face. Emerson has very large hands. I peeled his fingers off.

"Really, Emerson, was that wise? I had intended to speak to him this afternoon, in private."

"I thought you would." Emerson removed his pith helmet, dropped it onto the ground, and ran his hand through his hair. "That is why I determined to anticipate you. Don't worry, I gave nothing away."

"You must have had to go through various secretaries and sergeants and —"

"I disguised my voice," Emerson said, with great satisfaction.

"Not a Russian accent, Emerson!"

Emerson wrapped a muscular arm round my waist and squeezed. "Never you mind, Peabody. The point is, I got through to him and was able to reassure him on certain points. So for God's sake don't go marching into his office this afternoon. Were you planning to accompany Nefret to Cairo or go alone?"

"I was going with her. I may yet. Only . . ."

"Only what?"

"While you were at the house, did you happen to look in on Ramses?"

Emerson's face took on an expression of elaborate unconcern. "I thought so long as I was there, I might as well. He was sleeping."

"Oh. Are you certain he —"

"Yes." Emerson squeezed my ribs again. "Peabody, not even you can be in two places at once. Get back to your rubbish heap."

"Two places! Three or four, rather. Zawaiet, the tomb here, the house —"

"The suk with Nefret. Go with her, my dear, and keep her out of the way so we won't have to repeat the wearying maneuvers we executed yesterday."

"Will David be there when we come back? I would like to see him once more."

"Don't talk as if you were planning to bid him a final farewell," Emerson growled. "We'll put an end to this business soon, I promise you. As for tonight, I told him to go straight back to the house from Zawaiet; he won't leave until after dark, so you will see him then. Run along now."

Several slightly interesting objects turned up in the fill that was being removed from the second chamber. The bits of bone and mummy wrappings and wooden fragments indicated that there had been a later burial above the mastaba. By the Twenty-Second Dynasty — to which period I tentatively assigned this secondary interment — the mastabas of Giza had been deserted for over a thousand years, and the sand must have lain deep upon their ruins. It had not been much of a burial, and even it showed signs of having been robbed.

Emerson dismissed Nefret and me shortly after 2 P.M. and we returned to the house to change. I chattered loudly and cheerfully with Nefret as we walked along the corridor to our sleeping chambers. There was no sound from behind Ramses's closed door.

"What sort of experiment is he doing?" Nefret asked.

"I believe he is hoping to develop a preservative that will protect wall paintings without darkening or damaging them." I hurried her past. "It smells horrid, but then most of his experiments do."

I had hoped for an opportunity to peek in on him before we left, but I had not quite finished dressing before Nefret joined me to ask if I would button her up the back. Several of the younger women of Abdullah's family would have been delighted to take on the position of lady's maid, but like myself, Nefret scorned such idle attentions. So I obliged, and she did the same for me, and we went down together, to find Daoud waiting for us.

"The Father of Curses said I should go with you," he explained, his large, honest face beaming. "To guard you from harm."

We could not have had a more formidable escort. Daoud was even taller than my tall husband, and correspondingly broad. He was no longer a young man, but most of his bulk was solid muscle. He would have liked nothing better than to fight a dozen men in our defense.

Smiling, Nefret took his arm. "We are only going to the Khan el Khalili, Daoud. I'm afraid nothing of interest will occur."

Normally shy and taciturn, Daoud was quite a conversationalist when he was with us. He demanded news of his absent friends, particularly Lia, to whom he was devoted. "She should be here," he declared, his brow furrowing. "Where you and Kadija and Fatima and the Sitt Hakim could care for her."

I had earned my name of Lady Doctor in my early days in Egypt, when physicians were few and far between; some of our devoted men still preferred my attentions even to those of Nefret, who was far better qualified than I. Modestly I disclaimed any skill in obstetrics, adding, "She felt too unwell to risk the sea voyage, Daoud, and travel now would be unwise. She will have the best possible care, you may be certain."

When we reached the Khan el Khalili we left the carriage and proceeded on foot through the tortuous lanes, with Daoud so close on our heels, I felt as if we were being followed by a moving mountain. Nefret was in a merry mood, laughing and chattering; at several places — a goldsmith's, a seller of fine fabrics — she made me go on with Daoud and wait at a distance. I assumed she wanted to surprise me with a gift, so I amiably agreed.

"The Professor is always difficult," she declared, after she had made a number of purchases. "I know! Let's see if Aslimi has any interesting antiquities."

"Huh," said Daoud. "Stolen antiquities, you mean? Aslimi deals with thieves and tomb robbers."

"All the more reason to rescue the objects from him," Nefret said.

The setting sun cast slanting streaks of gold through the matting that roofed the narrow lanes. We passed the area devoted to dyers and fullers and finally reached Aslimi's shop. It was larger than some of the others, which consisted only of a tiny cubicle with a mastaba bench where the customer sat while the proprietor showed him the merchandise. When we entered the showroom it appeared to be deserted. Nefret went to a shelf on which a row of painted pots was displayed and began examining them.

"You won't find anything here except fakes," I said. "Aslimi keeps his better objects hidden. Where is the rascal?"

The curtain at the back of the room was drawn aside; but the man who came through it was not Aslimi. He was tall and young and quite handsome, and when he spoke, it was in excellent English.

"You honor my poor establishment, noble ladies. What can I show you?"

"I had not heard that Aslimi had sold his shop," I said, studying him curiously.

The young man's teeth flashed in a smile. "I spoke amiss, honored lady, taking you for a stranger. My cousin Aslimi is ill. I am managing the business for him until he recovers."

I doubted very much that he had been unaware of my identity. He had been watching us through the curtain for some time before he emerged, and we were known to everyone in Cairo. Certainly the combination of myself, Nefret, and Daoud was unmistakable.

"I am sorry to hear of his illness," I said politely. "What is the matter with him?"

The youth placed his hands — smooth, long-fingered hands, adorned with several rings — on his flat stomach. "There is much pain when he eats. You are the Sitt Hakim — I know you now. You can tell me, no doubt, what medicines will relieve him."

"Not without examining him," I said dryly. "Nefret?"

She had turned, one of the pots in her hand. "Knowing Aslimi, it could be an ulcer. His nerves have always been bad."

"Ah." The young man straightened, throwing his shoulders back, and gave her a melting smile. Nefret had that effect on men, and this one obviously did not have a low opinion of himself. "What should we do for him, then?"

"Bland diet," said Nefret. "No highly spiced foods, or liquids. It can't hurt him, anyhow," she added, glancing at me. "He should see a proper doctor, Mr. — what is your name?"

"Said al-Beitum, at your service. You are most gracious. Now, what can I show you? That pot is a forgery — as you know."

"And not a very good one." Nefret returned the object to the shelf. "Have you anything that might please the high standards of the Father of Curses?"

"Or the Brother of Demons?" Said grinned. "So quaint, these names — but suitable. Like yours, Nur Misur."

"You did know us," I said.

"Who does not? It is your holiday season, yes? You look for gifts for those you love. Be seated; I will give you tea and show you my finest things."

Another decidedly possessive pronoun, I

242

thought, settling onto the stool he indicated. Was this fellow Aslimi's designated heir? I had never seen him before.

He knew something of antiquities, for the objects he produced from the back room were of good quality — and probably obtained illegally. In the end Nefret purchased several items: a string of carnelian beads, a heart scarab of serpentine framed in gold, and a fragment of carved and painted relief that showed a running gazelle. Listening to Said bargain ineffectively and without much interest, I thought Aslimi would not be long in business if his cousin continued to manage the shop. He shook hands with us in the European style before we took our departure and stood in the doorway watching as we walked away.

"Well!" I said.

"Quite," said Nefret.

"Have you more purchases to make?"

"No. Let's go home."

I waited until we were in the carriage before I resumed the conversation. "What did you think of Aslimi's manager?"

"He's a pretty creature, isn't he?"

Daoud grumbled protestingly, and Nefret laughed. "I assure you, Daoud, I don't fancy him in the least."

"Fancy?" Daoud repeated blankly.

"Never mind. What did you think? Had you ever seen him before?"

"No. But," Daoud said, "I do not know Aslimi's family. No doubt he has many cousins."

"This one is well educated," I said.

Nefret nodded. "And perhaps overly optimistic. Aslimi isn't dead yet. Now, Aunt Amelia, and you, Daoud, swear you won't tell anyone what I bought. I want to surprise them."

Our council of war that night was not as late as I had feared. Nefret retired early to her room, saying she had letters to write and presents to wrap. When we joined David, we found him at the mirror applying his makeup. The disguise was not the same one in which I had seen him before; he looked even more disgusting, but less formidable, in the rags of a beggar and a stringy gray beard. Ramses studied him critically.

"Your hands are too clean."

"I'll rub dirt into them when I'm outside. They won't be visible, you know, except when I hold one out and whine for baksheesh from Russell. He's become quite adept at palming the report."

He demonstrated, extending his hand. Half-concealed under his thumb, the small roll of paper was no larger than a cigarette.

"Is that how you do it?" I asked. "Most interesting. I will have to practice that myself. But David, must you go? I've hardly seen you, and Ramses should have at least one more day in bed. Can't this wait until tomorrow night?"

Both curly black heads moved in emphatic negation. Ramses said, "Our report to Russell has been too long delayed already. I ought to be going myself."

"Out of the question," David said. He picked up a strip of dirty cloth and wound it deftly into a turban. "You'll be flat on your back again if you don't go slowly for a few days. I could come here after I've seen Russell — take your place again tomorrow. . . ."

Again Ramses shook his head. "We've pushed our luck too far already. It is a miracle Fatima hasn't decided this room needs cleaning, or Nefret hasn't spotted you."

He had been pacing like a nervous cat, and when he brushed the hair back from his forehead I saw it was beaded with perspiration. "Sit down," I ordered.

Emerson took his pipe from his mouth. "Yes, sit down. And you, Peabody, stop fussing. David must go, there is no question of that, and you are only delaying him. I'll see to it that Ramses does not exert himself unduly tomorrow."

"I must be outside the Club before midnight, Aunt Amelia," David explained. "That is when Russell will leave, and he can't very well hang about waiting for me."

"And afterwards you will investigate the warehouse?"

"No," said Ramses. "We agreed at the outset that David was to stay far, far away from Wardani's old haunts and Wardani's people. Russell is supposed to have been keeping the warehouse under surveillance. I hope to God he has! With me out of the way, one of the lads might decide to assert his authority and move the damned things elsewhere."

"They don't know you are out of the way," Emerson said calmly. "Do they?"

"No," Ramses admitted. "Not for certain. Not yet."

"Then stop worrying. David, you had better be off. Er — take care of yourself, my boy."

He wrung David's hand with such fervor the lad winced even as he smiled. "Yes, sir, I will. Good-bye, Aunt Amelia."

"A bientôt," I corrected.

We embraced, and Ramses said, "I'll see you in three days' time, David."

"Or four," I said.

"Three," said Ramses.

"I'll be there," David said hastily. "Both nights."

Seshat followed him to the balcony. I heard a faint, fading rustle of foliage, and after a few moments the cat returned.

"Bed now," I said, rising.

Ramses rolled his eyes heavenward.

Dear Lia,

I'm sorry Sylvia Gorst's letter upset you. She is an empty-headed, vicious gossip, and you ought to know better than to believe anything she says. If I had known she was writing you, I would have had a few words with her. In fact, I will have them next time I see her.

How could you possibly have given any credence to that story about Ramses fighting a duel with Mr. Simmons? I admit Ramses is not popular in Cairo society these days. The Anglo-Egyptian community is war-mad to the point of jingoism, and you know Ramses's views about the war. He's even collected white feathers from a few obsessed old ladies. But a duel? It's pure Prisoner of Zenda, *my dear.*

As for my new admirers, as Sylvia calls them, I cannot imagine why she should have singled out Count de Sevigny and Major Hamilton; you would laugh if you met them, because neither is your (or my) idea of a romantic suitor. I find the Count's pretensions quite amusing; he stalks about like a stage villain, swirling his black cape and ogling women through his monocle.

Yes, Lia dear, including me. I ran into him at an evening party a few days ago and he favored me with his undivided attentions; told me all about his château in Provence, and his vineyard, and his devoted family retainers. He's been married three times, but is now, he assured me as he ogled, a lonely, wealthy widower.

I asked about his wives, hoping that would put him off, but he made use of the inquiry to pay me extravagant compliments.

"They were all beautiful, and naturellement of the highest birth. Though none, mademoiselle, was as lovely as you." He was so moved the glass fell from his eye. He caught it quite deftly and went on pensively, "I have never married a lady of your coloring. Celeste was a brunette, Aline had black hair — her mother, vous comprenez, was a Spanish noblewoman, and Marie was blonde — a silvery blonde, with blue eyes, but ah! ma chère mademoiselle, your eyes are larger and deeper and bluer and . . ."

He was beginning to run out of adjectives, so I interrupted. "And all three died? How tragic for you, monsieur."

"Le bon Dieu took them from me." He bowed his head, giving me an excellent view of a suspiciously shiny black head of hair. "Celeste was thrown from her horse, Aline succumbed to a wasting fever, and poor Marie . . . but I cannot speak of her, it was too painful."

That gives you a taste of the Count, I hope. I don't believe in his wives or his château or *his protestations of admiration, but he is very entertaining, and he does know something about Egyptology.*

The Major isn't entertaining, but he is a nice old fellow. Old, my dear — at least fifty! He's taken a fancy to me, I think, but his interest is purely paternal. He is the uncle of the child I told you about, and I was curious to meet him.

Sylvia's other "bit of news" is really the limit. I have NOT been "seeing" Percy, as she puts it. Oh, certainly, I've seen him; one can hardly avoid doing so, since he is now on the General's staff and quite popular with his brother officers and the ladies. I have even spoken with him once or twice. I would appreciate it if you would not pass on that bit of gossip to the family. It would only cause trouble. And don't lecture me, please. I know what I'm doing.

Our holiday celebrations were happier than I had expected, possibly because I had not expected very much. But there was cause for rejoicing in that we had pulled off our deception without being detected, and that Ramses was making a good recovery. I believe I may claim that my medical skills were at least partially responsible, though his own strong constitution may have helped.

At Emerson's request, he had spent most of the day before Christmas writing up his report on Zawaiet. It was based on the notes David and I had taken and on a certain amount of what I would term logical extrapolation. The rest of us put in a half day's work at our mastaba; to have done otherwise would have been a suspicious deviation from the norm. When we gathered round the tree on Christmas Eve, only the concerned eye of a parent would have noticed any difference in Ramses's appearance; his lean face was a little thinner and the movements of his left arm were carefully controlled, but his color was good and his appetite at dinner had been excellent.

The inadequacies of the little acacia tree had been disguised by Nefret's decorations; candles glowed softly and charming ornaments of baked clay and tin filled in the empty spaces. David had made those ornaments; for years now they had been part of our holiday tradition. The sight of them dampened my spirits for a moment; I hated to think of him passing the holiday alone in that wretched hovel in Maadi, only a few miles away. At least I had pressed upon him a parcel of food and a nice warm knitted scarf, made by my own hands. My friend Helen McIntosh had shown me how to do it, and I found, as she had claimed, that it actually assisted in ratiocination, since the process soon became mechanical and did not require one's attention. I had made the scarf for Ramses, but he assured me he did not at all mind relinquishing it to his friend.

After all the gifts had been unwrapped, and I had put on the elegant tea gown that had been Nefret's present, and Ramses had pretended to be delighted by the dozen white handkerchiefs I had given him, Emerson rose from his chair.

"One more," he said, beaming at me. "Close your eyes, Peabody, and hold out your hands."

He had not attempted to wrap the thing; it would have made a cumbersome parcel. As soon as it came to rest on my outstretched palms I knew what it was.

"Why, Emerson, how nice!" I exclaimed. "Another parasol. I can always use an extra, and this one —"

"Is more than it appears," said my husband. "Watch closely."

Seizing the handle, he gave it a twist and a pull. This time my exclamation of pleasure was louder and more enthusiastic.

"A sword umbrella! Oh, Emerson, I have always wanted one! How does it work?"

He demonstrated again, and I rose to my feet, kicking the elegant lace flounces of my gown aside. "En garde!" I cried, brandishing the weapon.

Nefret laughed. "Professor, that was sweet of you."

"Hmmm," said Ramses. "Mother, watch

out for the candles."

"I may need a few lessons," I admitted. "Ramses, would you show me —"

"What, now?" His eyebrows tilted till they formed a perfect obtuse angle.

"I cannot wait to begin!" I cried, bending my knees and thrusting.

Emerson hastily moved aside — an unnecessary precaution, since the blade had not come within a foot of him. "I am glad you like it, Peabody, but you had better learn how to use it before you go lunging at people."

Ramses was trying not to laugh. "I beg your pardon, Mother," he gasped. "It's just that I've never fenced with an opponent armed with an umbrella, whose head barely reaches my chin."

"I see no reason why that should be a difficulty. Do you, Nefret?"

She was watching Ramses, who had dropped into a chair, helpless with laughter. She started when I addressed her.

"What? Well, Aunt Amelia, I'm sure you can persuade him. Not with that umbrella, though; it looks frightfully sharp."

"Quite," said Emerson, who looked as if he was having second thoughts. "You'll need proper foils, with blunted tips. And masks, and plastrons and —"

That set Ramses off again. I could not understand why he was so amused, but I was pleased to have cheered him up. As David had said, it was necessary to find what enjoyment we could in an otherwise dismal situation.

After Ramses had calmed down, he condescended to show me how to salute my opponent and place my feet and arms. He stood well behind me, even though I had, of course, sheathed the blade, and for some reason he found it necessary to read me a little lecture.

"Now, Mother, promise me that if you encounter someone armed with a saber or sword, you won't whip that thing out and rush at him."

"Quite," said Emerson emphatically. "He'd have you impaled like a butterfly before you got within reach. That is the trouble with deadly weapons; they make people — some people! — overly confident."

"What should I do, then?" I inquired, lunging.

"Run," said Ramses, helping me up from the floor.

After we had parted for the night and Emerson and I were alone in our room I thanked him again, with gestures as well as words. "I don't know any other man who would have given his wife such a lovely gift, Emerson."

"I don't know any other woman who would have been so thrilled about a sword," said Emerson.

Afterwards, Emerson immediately dropped off to sleep. I could not follow suit. I was remembering my son's face, alight with laughter, and wishing I could see that look more often. I thought again of David and the peril he faced because of love and loyalty. I consigned Thomas Russell to the nethermost pits of Hades for putting my boys in such danger — and then, since it was the season of peace and goodwill, I forgave the scoundrel. He was only doing his job.

Abdullah was also in my thoughts. I dreamed of him from time to time; they were strange dreams, unlike the usual vague vaporings of the unconscious mind, for they were distinct and consistent. In them I saw my old friend as a man still in his prime, his face unlined, his black hair and beard untouched by gray. The setting of the dreams was always the same: the clifftop behind Deir el Bahri at Luxor, where we had so often stopped to rest for a moment after climbing the steep path to the top of the plateau. In one such vision he had warned me of storms ahead — had told me I would need all my courage to pass through them, but in the end . . . "The clouds will blow away," he had said. "And the falcon will fly through the portal of the dawn." He frequently employed such irritating parables, and refused to explain them even when I pressed him. There was no doubt about the stormclouds he had mentioned; even now they hung heavy over half the world. The rest of it sounded hopeful, but when I was in a discouraged state of mind I needed more than elegant literary metaphors to cheer me. I could have used his reassurance now. But I did not dream of Abdullah that night.

Dawn light was bright in the sky when I woke. There was a great deal to be done, since we were expecting the Vandergelts for dinner and holding an open house afterwards. However, I could not resist trying out my new parasol, and I was lunging and parrying with considerable skill (having seen Mr. James O'Neill in the film of *The Count of Monte Cristo*) when a comment from Emerson made me stumble and almost lose my balance. After a short discussion and a longer digression of another nature, he consented to give me a few lessons if Ramses would not. He had studied fencing some years before, but had not kept it up, having found that his bare hands were almost as effective in subduing an attacker.

"I'm not certain Ramses can bring himself to do it," he remarked. "A gentleman does not find it easy to attack a lady, especially if the lady is his mother. He is in considerable awe of you, my dear."

"He certainly didn't sound as if he were in awe of me last night," I remarked, buttoning my combinations.

Still recumbent, his hands behind his head, Emerson watched me with sleepy appreciation. "It was good to see him laugh so heart-ily."

"Yes. Emerson —"

"I know what you are thinking, my dear, but dismiss those worries for today at least." He got out of bed and went to the washbasin. "Fatima has put rose petals in the water again," he grumbled, trying to sieve them out with his fingers. "As I was saying, the situation is temporarily under control. Russell has been informed of what transpired and will keep the warehouse under surveillance."

"I still think we ought to have invited him to our open house. We might have found an opportunity for a little chat."

Emerson deposited a handful of dripping petals onto the table and reached for his shaving tackle. "No, my dear. The fewer contacts between him and Ramses, the better."

We had only the family for dinner that year, including Cyrus and Katherine, who were as close as family. They had brought gifts for us, so we had another round of opening presents. It was difficult to find appropriate gifts for Cyrus and Katherine, since they were wealthier than we and lacked for nothing, but I had found a few trinkets that seemed to please them, and Cyrus exclaimed with pleasure over the little painting of the gazelle Nefret had given him.

"Looks like Eighteenth Dynasty," he declared. "Where did you find it, if I may ask?"

"One of the damned antiquities dealers, no doubt," Emerson grumbled. "Like the cursed heart scarab she gave me. Not that I don't appreciate the thought," he added quickly.

Nefret only laughed. She had heard Emerson's views on buying from dealers too often to be discomposed by them. "It was from Aslimi, as a matter of fact. He had several nice things."

"I don't suppose you bothered to ask the rascal where he obtained them," Emerson muttered.

"I would have done if he had been there, though I doubt he'd have confessed."

Ramses, who had been examining the painted scrap appreciatively, looked up. "He wasn't there?"

"He's ill. The Professor would probably say it serves him right." Nefret chuckled. "The new manager is much handsomer than Aslimi, and not nearly as skilled at bargaining."

She made quite an entertaining little tale of our visit. Cyrus declared his intention of visiting the inept manager as soon as possible, and Katherine demanded a description of the beautiful young man. The only one who contributed nothing to the conversation was Ramses.

The table made a brave show, sparkling with crystal and aglow with candles, but as I looked upon the sadly diminished group I seemed to see the ghostly forms of those who had formerly been with us: the austere features of Junker, whose formal demeanor concealed the warmest heart in the world; the beaming face of Karl von Bork, mustaches bristling; Rex Engelbach and Guy Brunton, who had exchanged their trowels for rifles; and those who were dearest of all — Evelyn and Walter, David and Lia. Fortunately Cyrus had brought several bottles of his favorite champagne, and after we had toasted absent friends and a quick conclusion to the hostilities and everything else Cyrus could think of, our spirits rose. Even Anna smiled on us all. She was looking quite attractive that day, in a rose-pink muslin frock whose ruffles flattered her boyish frame, and I saw, with surprise, that she had put color on her lips and cheeks.

She had been at the hospital every day since Nefret had challenged her that night at the opera, and according to Nefret she had performed a good deal better than anyone had expected.

"I haven't made it easy for her," Nefret admitted. "She hasn't any nursing skills, of course, so she's doing all the filthy jobs — emptying bedpans and changing sheets and picking maggots out of wounds. The first day she threw up three times and I didn't expect to see her again, but she was there bright and early next morning. I'm beginning to admire the girl, Aunt Amelia. I've given her a few little hints about her appearance, and she has taken them more graciously than I expected."

We had only a brief interlude between the conclusion of the meal and the arrival of our guests. One of the first to arrive was young Lieutenant Pinckney, who made a beeline for Nefret and drew her aside. Mrs. Fortescue attempted to do the same with Emerson, but I was able to forestall her, keeping Emerson with me as I greeted additional guests. Her cavaliers must have all deserted her, since she came alone. There was no doubt in my mind that her cheeks and lips owed their brilliant color to art rather than nature, but she looked very handsome in black lace, with a mantilla-like scarf draping her head.

Many of the men — too many, alas — were in khaki. Among these were Mr. Lawrence and Leonard Woolley. Remembering what David had told me about his "drunken" encounter with them, I watched with some trepidation as they entered into conversation with Ramses, but the few words I overheard indicated that they were talking amiably of archaeological matters. I observed with some amusement that Mr. Lawrence had unconsciously risen onto his toes as he spoke to Ramses; his diminutive size and ruffled fair hair made him look like a child addressing his mentor.

I had been looking forward to making the acquaintance of Major Hamilton, but when his niece arrived she was accompanied only by her formidable governess.

"The Major asked me to convey his profound apologies," the latter explained. "A sudden emergency necessitated his departure for the Canal last evening."

"I am so sorry," I replied. "It is sad, is it not, that the celebrations of the birth of the Prince of Peace should be interrupted by preparations for war."

Emerson gave me a look that expressed his opinion of this sentiment, which was, I admit, somewhat trite. Miss Nordstrom appeared quite struck by it, however.

Miss Molly did not even hear it. Attired in the white muslin considered suitable for young girls, with a huge white bow atop her head, she delayed only long enough to thank us for asking her before darting away.

They were among the last to come, and after I had introduced Miss Nordstrom to Katherine and Anna, I felt I deserved a respite. As any proper hostess must do, I glanced round the room to make certain no one was alone and neglected. Everyone appeared to be having a good time; Miss Molly had detached Ramses from Woolley and Lawrence, and Mrs. Fortescue was talking with Cyrus, who responded to her smiles and flirtatious glances with obvious enjoyment.

He had always been "an admirer in the most respectful way of female loveliness," but I knew his interest was purely aesthetic. He was absolutely devoted to his wife, and if he appeared to be in danger of forgetting it, Katherine would certainly remind him.

Turning to my husband, I found him staring into space with a singularly blank expression. I had to speak to him twice before he responded.

"I beg your pardon, Peabody?"

"I invited you to join me in a cup of tea, my dear. What has put you in such a brown study?"

"Nothing of importance. Where is Nefret? I don't see her or that young officer. Have they gone into the garden?"

"She does not require to be chaperoned, my dear. If the young man forgets himself, which I consider to be unlikely, she will put him in his place."

"True," Emerson agreed. "I will not take tea; I want to talk to Woolley about the Egyptian material he found at Carchemish."

After a while someone — it was Mr. Pinckney — asked if we might not have a little informal dance, but his ingenuous face fell when Nefret went to the pianoforte.

"We do not have a gramophone," I explained. "Emerson hates them and I confess I find those scratchy records a poor substitute for the real thing."

"Oh," said Mr. Pinckney. "I say, that's a bit hard on Miss Forth, isn't it? I wouldn't have suggested it if I had realized she couldn't dance."

He was overheard by Miss Nordstrom, who must have had quite a lot of Cyrus's champagne, for she beamed sentimentally at the young man and offered to take Nefret's place. Mr. Pinckney seized her hand and squeezed it. "I say," he exclaimed. "I say, that is good of you, Miss — er — mmm."

So Mr. Pinckney got his dance. As is usual at my parties, there were more gentlemen than ladies present, so he had to share Nefret. Miss Nordstrom played with a panache I would not have expected from such a proper female, but her repertoire was more or less limited to the classics — polkas, mazurkas, and waltzes. Even Mr. Pinckney did not dare inquire whether she could play ragtime; but after a further glass of champagne, urged on her by Cyrus, she burst into a particularly rollicking polka, and Pinckney (who had also refreshed himself between dances) swung Nefret exuberantly round the room and ended by lifting her off her feet and spinning her in a circle.

Emerson glowered at the young fellow like a papa in a stage melodrama, but Nefret laughed and the others applauded. Miss Molly's treble rose over the other voices. "Play it again, Nordie!" She ran to Ramses and held up her arms. "Spin me round like that, please! I know you can, you lifted me all the way down the pyramid. Please?"

Miss Nordstrom had already begun the encore. I heard Katherine say, "Now, Cyrus, don't try that with me!"

You may well believe, Reader, that the anxiety of a mother had not been entirely assuaged. I started toward Ramses with some confused notion of interfering, but he caught my eye and shook his head.

They were, unfortunately, the center of attention. She was so tiny and he was so tall, they made a comical and rather touching picture; her head was tilted back and her round, freckled face shone with childish laughter as he guided her steps. It was his right arm that circled her waist and turned her, but a prickle of anxiety ran through me as I saw how hard she clung to his other hand. The dance neared its end; the corners of his mouth tightened as he caught her up and swung her round, not once but several times. After he had set her on her feet, she caught hold of his sleeve. "That was wonderful," she gasped. "Do it again!"

"You must give the Professor a turn," said Nefret, drawing the child away from Ramses. "He waltzes beautifully."

"Yes, quite," said Emerson. "A waltz, if you please, Miss — er — Nordstrom."

I went to Ramses, who was leaning against

the back of the sofa. "Come upstairs," I said in a low voice.

"Just hold my arm up," Ramses said, adding, with a breath of laughter, "There aren't many women of whom I could ask that. I'll be all right in a minute."

He had put his other arm round my waist and since there was no reasonable alternative I supported his hand and followed his steps.

"Is it bleeding?"

"It's all right, I tell you."

"Did you have to do that?"

"I think so. Don't you agree?"

"Curse it," I muttered.

"It is not necessary for you to lead, Mother."

I put an end to the dancing after that. Nefret took Miss Nordstrom's place at the piano and we finished the evening, as we always did, with the dear familiar carols. Mr. Pinckney insisted on turning pages for Nefret, leaning so close his breath stirred the loosened hair that curled round her cheek. Mrs. Fortescue was the surprise of the evening. Her rich contralto voice had obviously been trained, and I observed she had unconsciously taken on the pose of a concert singer, hands folded lightly at her waist, shoulders back. But when I praised her singing and asked if she would give us a solo she shook her head in feigned modesty.

"I had a few lessons in my youth," she murmured. "But I would much rather join in with the rest of you — so like family, so appropriate to the season."

Few lessons indeed, I thought, though of course I did not press her. She had sung professionally at some time. There was nothing wrong with that, of course, nor any reason why that fact should cast doubt on her story. All the same, I decided I wanted to know more about Mrs. Fortescue.

I have never been more relieved to see a party end. Katherine and Cyrus always stayed after the rest, and for once I begrudged these dear old friends their time with us. At least we were all able to sit down and put our feet up and admit we were tired. Emerson had his coat off before the door had closed on the last of the other guests. Tie and waistcoat soon followed, and so did the top button of his shirt — clean off, for Emerson's forceful manner of removing his clothing has a devastating effect on buttons. I picked this one up from the floor.

"Whiskey, my dear?" Emerson inquired.

"I believe I will, now that you mention it." I lowered myself into an armchair.

Emerson and I and Ramses were the only ones who indulged. Cyrus declared he and the others would finish the champagne, of which there was not a great deal left. It had certainly had an interesting effect. A good many tongues had been loosened; several people had forgotten if only briefly, to keep their masks in place.

"What a wonderful party," Anna murmured. The champagne had affected her as well; she looked almost pretty, the severity of her features softened by a smile.

"I am glad you enjoyed yourself," I said somewhat absently.

"Oh, I did. It was a bittersweet pleasure in some ways, though; all those fine young men in uniform, destined before long to face —"

"Not tonight, Anna," Katherine said sharply.

"If it is Mr. Pinckney you are thinking of, he isn't going anywhere for a while," Nefret said, giving the other girl's hand a friendly pat. "He told me tonight he has been seconded to the staff as a courier. He's so thrilled! It means he can ride one of those motorbicycles."

Anna blushed and denied any particular interest in any particular individual. "I would love to learn to drive one of them, though," she declared. "There is no reason why a woman cannot do it as well as a man, is there?"

She stuck out her chin and looked challengingly at Ramses, who replied, "It is not much more difficult than riding a bicycle."

"I'm surprised you have not got one."

"They make too much noise and emit a vile stench." Ramses shifted position slightly, leaning back in his chair and folding his hands. "Perhaps you can persuade Pinckney to give you a ride in the sidecar. You won't like it, though."

I let my attention wander. Katherine looked tired, I thought, and reproached myself for not spending more time with her. She needed distraction. It was cursed difficult to carry on our normal lives, though.

Cyrus had also observed his wife's weariness and soon declared they must go. Before leaving he repeated his invitation to Emerson to visit his excavations at Abusir.

"I've come across something that might interest you," he said, stroking his goatee.

Emerson's abstracted expression sharpened. Archaeology can distract him from almost anything. "What?" he demanded.

"You'll have to see for yourself." Cyrus grinned. "Why don't you all come by one day? Stay for dinner."

We said we would, though without committing ourselves to a particular date, and they took their departure. Nefret declared her intention of retiring at once, and I said we would do the same, so Fatima and her crew could get to work cleaning up.

I was fairly itching to discuss the evening's developments with Emerson, and even more anxious to learn what damage Ramses's reckless performance had done to him. That it had done some damage I did not doubt; his feet were a trifle unsteady as he mounted the stairs. Nefret noticed too; she gave him a quick, frowning glance, but did not remark upon what she probably took to be intoxication. He had had quite a number of glasses of champagne; however, most of it had gone into one of my potted plants. I had noticed it was looking sickly.

We gave Nefret time to settle down before we went to his room, where we found him sitting on the edge of the bed. As I suspected, the wound had reopened. It had stopped bleeding, but the bandage was saturated and his shirtsleeve was not much better.

"Another shirt ruined," said Emerson, taking out his pipe.

"It must be a hereditary trait," I said grimly.

Ramses said, "Why didn't you tell me about your visit to Aslimi's shop?"

I came back with, "Why should I have done? Lean forward, if you can, you are getting blood on the pillowcase."

"For God's sake, Mother, this is important! I —" He broke off, bit his lip, and continued in a more moderate tone. "I beg your pardon. You didn't know. Aslimi is one of our people — Wardani's, I should say. He's a damned reluctant conspirator, but he's been involved from the beginning and his shop has been very useful. In technical terms it is what is called a drop. The messages we leave are concealed in objects that are picked up by apparently harmless purchasers."

"And the other way round?"

Ramses nodded. He was trying very hard not to swear or groan, and he waited until I had finished cleaning the wound before he ventured to open his mouth. "A buyer may examine several items before settling on one, or buy nothing at all. He can easily insert something into a jar or hollowed-out statue base without being seen by anyone except Aslimi — who puts that particular object aside until the proper person calls for it."

"This is not good news," Emerson said gravely. "What do you suppose has happened to the bastard?"

"The important question is not what has happened to Aslimi, but what is Farouk doing at the shop."

I began, "He said his name was —"

"He lied. It must be Farouk, the description fits, and Aslimi has no cousins named Said. Damnation!"

"There is nothing you can do about it now," I said uneasily. "Perhaps the explanation is perfectly innocent. If Aslimi fell ill, your — Wardani's — people could not allow a stranger to take over the management of the shop. Let us hope so, for things are complicated enough already. There, I have finished; you can unclench your teeth. I don't believe you have done much damage, but the incident was certainly unfortunate. Was it an accident?"

"It couldn't have been anything else," Ramses said slowly. "The child certainly acted in all innocence."

"With whom was she talking just before she ran to you?" I inquired.

"I didn't notice. It might have been Mrs. Fortescue. She is what you would call a highly suspicious character. I wonder if anyone has thought to check her story."

"She has been a professional singer," I said.

Neither of them questioned the assessment; I had not been the only one to observe the clues. Emerson grinned. "And we all know that singers are persons of doubtful virtue," he remarked. The grin faded into a scowl. "Pinckney is now attached to the staff. Woolley and Lawrence are members of the intelligence department. Several others have contacts with the military. There has been a leak of information, hasn't there? Someone is in the pay of the enemy."

Ramses said a bad word, apologized, and turned a critical stare on Emerson. "Is that an informed guess, Father?"

"A logical deduction," Emerson corrected. "You would not go to such lengths to maintain your masquerade if you didn't suspect there was a spy in our midst."

"We must assume there are several agents

of the Central Powers still at large," Ramses said. "One at least has had access to information that was known only to a few. There have been a number of leaks, some of them involving the Canal defenses."

"You've no idea who it might be?" Emerson asked.

"Russell suspects Philippides. He knows everything that is known to Harvey Pasha, which is why I won't . . . Mother, what do you think you are doing?"

"Pay no attention to me," I said, removing his shoe and starting to unlace the other one.

"How would the head of the local CID know about the Canal defenses?" Emerson inquired.

Ramses sighed. "The devil of it is that all these departments are interconnected in one way or another. They have to be, since their functions overlap, but that makes it damned difficult to trace the source. Philippides is in a particularly useful position; it is his responsibility to identify and remove enemy aliens. If he is as venal as rumor makes him out to be, the individual in question could be paying him to ensure his silence."

"You think there is a single individual in charge of operations here?" Emerson asked, his keen eyes fixed on Ramses's face.

"If it were our lot, I'd say no. We take a perverse pride in our famed British muddle. However, I give the Germans credit for better

271

organization. They've been planning this for years, while we scampered around arresting harmless radicals and arguing about whether or not to formalize our bizarre position with regard to Egypt. Their man has probably been here for years, leading a normal life and ready to act when he was needed. Wardani's little revolution is a side show — not a negligible part of the whole, but only one of several operations, including information gathering and subversion."

"Hmm," said Emerson. "If we could identify this fellow —"

"Yes, sir, that would be useful." Amusement warmed Ramses's black eyes for a moment, to be replaced by a look of consternation. "No, Father! Don't even think of it. We may get a lead to the man through our show, but tracking him down isn't my job or yours. Leave him to Maxwell and Clayton."

"Certainly, my boy, certainly. You had better get some rest now. Come along, Peabody."

"Can I get you anything more, Ramses?" I asked. "Whiskey and soda? A few drops of laudanum to help you sleep? A nice wet cloth to —"

"No, thank you, Mother. I don't need anything to help me sleep, and I don't want any whiskey, and I am quite capable of washing my own face and taking off my own clothes."

"Then I will leave you to it, on one condition."

"What's that?" Ramses asked warily.

"Promise me you will not go out tonight. I want your solemn word."

Ramses considered this. "Would you believe my solemn word? All right, Mother, don't scold; I was joking. I won't leave the house tonight. It's taking a chance, but I think I can safely wait another day or two."

"A chance of what?" I asked, looking down at him.

"Of my enthusiastic young friend Farouk convincing the others that Wardani is dead and that he is his logical successor. Even if it wasn't he who tried to kill me, he would be more than happy to take advantage of my presumed demise." His lips curved in a rather unpleasant smile. "I'm rather looking forward to seeing the lad's face fall when I turn up, suffering but steadfast, and worst of all, alive. Perhaps I should bare my wounds for the admiration of all. It's the sort of theatrical gesture Wardani would appreciate."

6

Emerson had been less than truthful when he said he did not expect us to work on Boxing Day. We did not go to Giza, but we spent most of the day catching up on paperwork. Few laymen realize how much of this is necessary, but as Emerson always says, the keeping of accurate records is as important as the excavation itself. I did not object, since it served to keep Ramses from exerting himself. I also managed to prevent him from going out that night. He put up an argument, but of course I prevailed, adding just a touch of veronal to his after-dinner coffee in order to make certain that after I had got him into bed he would stay there.

After breakfast the following morning I drew Emerson aside.

"Can't you invent some chore for Ramses to do here at home? I don't believe he ought to go into that dusty hot tomb today."

Emerson studied me curiously. "What's come over you lately, Peabody?"

"I don't know what you mean."

"You've turned into an absolute mother hen. You never fussed over him like this before, even when he was a child and getting into one grisly scrape after another. Now don't deny it; you keep trying to put him to bed and make him sit down and lie down and take his medicine. When he refused a second serving of oatmeal this morning I thought you were going to pick up a spoon and feed him yourself."

"Hmmm," I said. "Am I really doing that? How odd. I wonder why?"

"He is terrifyingly like you, you know."

"Like *me?* In what way, pray tell?"

"Brave as a lion, cunning as a cat, stubborn as a camel —"

"Really, Emerson!"

"Concealing the affectionate and vulnerable side of his nature under a shell as hard as a tortoise's," said Emerson poetically. "As you do, my love, with everyone except me. I understand, Peabody, but for God's sake control yourself. All he has to do today is sit quietly on a campstool and copy texts. It should be particularly restful after his other recent activities."

There was no denying that. However, the best-laid plans of mice and men, including Emerson, often go awry (I translate from the Scottish.) When we arrived at Giza, Selim was waiting for us. Our young reis has an open, candid face, and the splendid beard he had grown in order to inspire more respect from his men failed to conceal his emotions. One look at him was all Emerson needed.

"What has happened?" he demanded. "Has a wall collapsed? Anyone hurt?"

"No, Father of Curses." Selim wrung his hands. "It is worse than that! Someone has tried to rob the tomb."

With a vehement oath Emerson ran for the entrance. In his haste he did not duck his head far enough under the stone lintel; I heard a thud and a swear word before he vanished inside.

The rest of us followed. Selim was babbling, as he did when he was upset. "It is my fault. I ought to have posted a guard. But who would have supposed a robber would be so bold? Here, at the very foot of the Great Pyramid, with visitors and guards and. . . ."

Such boldness was surprising, but not unheard of. The illicit diggers who infest the ancient sites are extremely skilled and sly. Tombs like these were comparatively easy to vandalize once they had been uncovered; the fine reliefs were in great demand by collectors, and the wall surface consisted of separate blocks which could be removed one by one. In the process considerable damage was done to the plaster, but the robbers cared nothing for that, and apparently neither did the collectors. Archaeological fever temporarily replaced my other concerns, and I was in a state of profound professional agitation as I entered the dimly lit chamber.

A hasty glance round the room showed

first, Emerson, upright and rigid in the center of the floor; and second, the walls intact as they had been when I last saw them. The prince Sekhemankhor and his lady gazed with serene satisfaction at the offering table before them; the long ranks of servants carrying vessels and flowers, leading cattle and cutting grain were unmarred. A great gasp of relief issued from my throat. A great shout of fury issued from Emerson.

"What the devil do you mean by this, Selim? Nothing has been disturbed. Are you afflicted by dreams and visions, or . . ." His eyes narrowed. Seizing the young fellow by the collar, he pulled him close. "You haven't taken to hashish, have you?"

"No, Father of Curses." Selim looked hurt, but not especially worried. The men were all accustomed to Emerson's explosive temper. It was his low, measured tones they feared.

"You were too quick," Selim went on in an injured voice. "You did not let me explain. It is not this part of the tomb that has been entered. It is the burial shaft."

"Oh." Emerson released his grip. "Sorry. Show me."

As I have explained, the tombs of this period consist of one or more rooms aboveground that served the funerary cult of the deceased. The mummy and its grave goods lay at the bottom of a deep shaft cut down through the superstructure into the underlying rock. Lacking museums and tourists desirous of purchasing works of art, the ancient thieves stole only what they could use themselves or sell to their unsophisticated contemporaries — linen, oil, jewelry, and the like. Therefore (as the Reader has no doubt deduced) they went straight for the burial chamber. Of all the tomb shafts thus far excavated, only one unplundered burial had been found.

Could this be such another? Let him who will deny it, but that hope is foremost in the minds of all archaeologists. Amelia P. Emerson is not such a hypocrite. I wanted — primarily of course for my dear Emerson — an untouched burial, with its grave goods intact — collars of gold and faience, bracelets and amulets, an inscribed coffin, vessels of copper and stone — a burial even finer than the one Mr. Reisner had discovered two years earlier. There was cause for optimism. The knowledgeable tomb robbers of Giza had considered the shaft worth investigating.

It had been completely filled with sand. Emerson had intended to leave it till the last, since, as I have explained, there is seldom anything down there. The opening had been located, however, and it was there we went.

Someone had certainly been doing something. Where there had been only a dimple in the ground now gaped a hole some three feet deep. Stone lined it on all four sides and sand was scattered around the opening, the unmistakable signs of a hasty excavation.

Hands on hips, brows lowering, Emerson stared down into the hole and remarked forcibly, "Curse it!"

"Why do you say that, Emerson?" I inquired. "Surely this is a hopeful sign. The tomb robbers of Giza —"

"May already have found what they were looking for," Emerson said.

"So near the surface?" Ramses asked. He put out a hand to steady Nefret, who was teetering on the edge of the opening.

Emerson brightened. "Well, perhaps not. They may have been frightened away by a guard. I made it easy for the bastards, though, erecting that roof to hide them from passersby. Now I suppose we must clear the damned thing out before they have another go at it."

"One of us will stay here at night," Selim said.

"Hmph." Emerson fingered the cleft in his chin. "Good of you to offer, Selim, but I don't think that will be necessary. I will just have a few words with the head gaffir."

"Including the words 'tear out your liver?' " Nefret inquired. Her blue eyes sparkled and a rosy flush warmed her tanned cheeks. Ah yes, I thought fondly; archaeological fever runs strong in all of us. Perhaps this development would keep the child out of

279

mischief for a while.

Emerson gave her an affectionate smile. "I may just mention something of the sort. I want you and Ramses back in the tomb, Nefret; the sooner you finish photographing and copying the reliefs, the happier I will be. Selim can get the men started emptying the shaft. Stop them instantly if they come across any object whatever, and make certain . . ."

He went on for some time giving Selim unnecessary instructions; the young man had been trained by his father, the finest reis Egypt had ever known, and by Emerson himself. Selim's beard kept twitching, but I could not tell whether the movements of his lips were caused by repressed amusement or repressed impatience. He knew better than to interrupt, but when Emerson paused for breath, he said, "Yes, Father of Curses, it shall be done as you say."

I could have wished that morning that there were three of me: the archaeologist wanted to hover over Selim and his men, watching for artifacts; the detective (for I believe I have some modest claim to that title) would have preferred to keep a keen eye out for suspicious visitors; the mother yearned to watch over her impulsive offspring and prevent him from doing something foolish. It was as well the last identity won out. As I scrambled down the slope of sand toward the tomb entrance I heard voices raised in heated discussion. The voices were those of Ramses and Nefret, and they were arguing with all their old vivacity.

"Now what is going on?" I demanded, entering the chamber.

They were standing side by side before the wall. Nefret swung round and brandished the sheet of copying paper she held. The room was shadowed, but I could see the bright spots of temper on her cheeks.

"I told him there is absolutely no need to go over my emendations!"

"They are all wrong." Ramses sounded like a sulky child.

"No, they aren't. Aunt Amelia, just look here —"

"Mother, tell her —"

"Goodness gracious," I said. "I would have thought you two had got over that childish habit of bickering. Give me the copy, Nefret, and I will check it myself, while you get on with the photography."

Daoud, who had been standing by with one of the mirrors we used to light the interior, moved into position. Directed by his skilled hands, the patch of reflected sunlight centered and steadied on a section of the wall. The elaborately carved and painted shape was that of a door, through which the soul of the deceased could emerge to partake of offerings. The lintels and architrave bore the prince's name and titles, and a cylindrical shape over the false opening represented a rolled matting, which in a real door would have been lowered and raised as required. Archaeological fever momentarily overcame my other concerns; I sucked in my breath appreciatively.

"It is one of the finest false doors I have ever seen, and there is a surprising amount of paint remaining. A pity we cannot preserve it."

"What about the new preservative you've been working on?" Nefret inquired of her brother. "If its effectiveness is in proportion to its pervasive smell, it should work well. Every time I passed your door I held my breath."

Ramses's rigid features relaxed into a more affable expression. "Sorry about that. I have high hopes for the formula, but I don't want to try it out on something as fine as this. The real test is how it holds up over time, without darkening or destroying the paint."

She smiled back at him, her face softening. Pleased that I had brought about a temporary truce, I said briskly, "Back to work, eh?" and took the copy of the offering scene to the wall.

I had not been at it long, however, before I heard a shout from Emerson, who had not, after all, left the excavation of the shaft to Selim. The words were undistinguishable, but the tone was peremptory. Torn between fear — that the shaft had collapsed onto Emerson — and hope — that some object of interest had turned up — I ran out of the tomb.

Fear predominated when I failed to make out the impressive form of my husband among the men who clustered round the opening.

"What has happened?" I panted. "Where is Emerson?"

As I might have expected, he was in the shaft, which had now been emptied to a depth of almost six feet. The men made way for me and Daoud took hold of my arm to steady me as I peered down into the opening.

"What are you doing down there, Emerson?" I demanded.

Emerson looked up. "Kindly refrain from kicking sand into my eyes, Peabody. You had better come and see for yourself. Lower her down, Daoud."

Daoud took me firmly but respectfully by the waist and lowered me into the strong hands that were raised to receive me.

Emerson set me on my feet but continued to hold me close to him, remarking, "Don't move, just look. There."

I had not seen it from above, for it was not much different in color from the pale sand. "Good Gad!" I cried. "It is a sculptured head — the head of a king! Is the rest of it there?"

"The shoulders, at least." Emerson frowned. "As for the body, we will have to wait and see. It will take a while to get the sand out from around it and a support under it. All right, Peabody, up you go."

Daoud pulled me back to the surface. Ramses and Nefret were there; I told them of the discovery as Selim joined Emerson in the shaft. I knew my husband would trust no one else with the delicate work of extracting the statue. It had to be handled carefully for fear of breakage. Even stone — and this was limestone, a relatively soft material — might have cracked under the pressure of impacted sand.

Nefret was dancing with excitement, so I persuaded her to move back a few feet. "Which king is it?" she asked. "Could you tell?"

"Hardly, my dear. If there is an inscription naming the monarch it will be on the back or the base. From the style and the workmanship it appears to be Old Kingdom."

"You are certain it is a royal statue?" Ramses asked.

"Of that, yes, I am certain. It wears the Nemes Crown and there is a uraeus on the brow."

"Hummm," said my son.

"I hate it when you make enigmatic noises," Nefret exclaimed. "What is that supposed to mean?"

Ramses raised his eyebrows at her — an equally enigmatic and exasperating sort of commentary. Before she could respond, Emerson's head appeared. "Ramses!" he shouted.

"Sir?" Ramses hastened to him and gave him a hand up.

I could tell by Emerson's flushed face and glittering eyes that he had momentarily forgotten everything except the discovery. He began barking out orders and the men flew off in all directions.

When we stopped for luncheon we knew the find was even more remarkable than we had hoped. It was a seated statue, almost life-sized and in superb condition.

"It's Khafre," said Nefret, who had insisted on being lowered down to have a look for herself.

"What makes you think so?" I inquired.

"It looks like Ramses."

Rendered temporarily speechless by a mouthful of bread and cheese, her brother rolled his eyes in a silent but eloquent display of derision.

"There is a certain resemblance to the diorite statue of Khafre discovered by Mariette," I admitted. "Emerson, sit down and stop fidgeting! Have another cucumber sandwich."

Avoiding my attempt to catch hold of him, Emerson bounced up and directed a hail of invective at a group of people who had approached the shaft. There were four of them, fitted out in tourist style with blue goggles and green parasols; the men wore solar topees and the women quantities of veiling, and all of them were trying to get past Selim and Daoud, who stood guard.

Emerson's apoplectic countenance and carefully enunciated remarks sent them into rapid retreat.

"The curse of the working archaeologist," said my husband, resuming his seat. "I wonder how many other idiots will try to get a look."

"The news of such discoveries spreads quickly," I said, selecting another sandwich. "And everyone wants to be the first to see them. It is a basic trait of human nature, my dear. Have another cucumber —"

"You've eaten them all," said Emerson, inspecting the interiors of the remaining sandwiches.

My surmise had been correct; the news of our discovery did spread, and we were forced to station several of the men a little distance off to warn visitors away. By late afternoon even Emerson was forced to admit we could not get the statue out that day. The light was failing and it would have been foolish to go on.

Again Selim offered to stand guard. This time Emerson did not demur. "You and Daoud and six or seven others," he ordered.

"Is that enough, do you think?" I asked.

"With the addition of myself, it will be more than enough."

"Yes, yes," said Daoud, nodding vigorously. "No robber would dare rob the Father of Curses."

"Or Daoud, famous for his strength and justly feared by malefactors," said Ramses in his most flowery Arabic. "Nevertheless, I will join you tonight if you will permit me."

"And me," Nefret said eagerly.

"Certainly not," said Emerson, jarred out of his archaeological preoccupation by this offer.

"Professor, darling," Nefret began, raising cornflower-blue eyes to his.

"No, I said! I want those plates developed tonight. You can help her, Peabody, and bring our excavation diary up-to-date."

"Very well," I said.

"It is absolutely imperative that we —" Emerson broke off. "What did you say?"

"I said, very well. Now come along to the house and get your camping gear together. Selim, I will send food for you and the others back with the Professor and Ramses."

We had left the horses at Mena House, where there was proper stabling for them. As we walked along the road toward the hotel, I took Emerson's arm and let the children draw ahead.

"I know this is an exciting discovery, my dear, but pray do not allow it to blind you to other urgent matters."

"Exciting," Emerson repeated. "Hmmm, yes. What do you mean?"

"Emerson, for pity's sake! Have you forgotten that Ramses means to go tonight to meet that gang of murderers? I want you to keep him with you."

"I had not forgotten." Emerson put his hand over mine, where it rested on his sleeve. "And there is not a damned thing I can do to prevent him from going. David will be waiting for him, and David is at risk too. Matters have gone too far for either of them to withdraw from this business. I will dismiss him from guard duty later. Selim and the others will believe he has gone home."

From Manuscript H

His father's help made it much easier for him to absent himself without arousing suspicion. He had expected an argument with his mother, whose recent attack of protectiveness had surprised him as much as it secretly pleased him; however, she gave in after making a number of preposterous suggestions, which his father firmly vetoed. Not until later did it occur to Ramses that she hadn't been serious when she proposed those outrageous disguises. Surely not even his mother believed she could walk the streets of Cairo at that hour in burko and black robe, or prowl the alleys in a fez and a hastily hemmed galabeeyah!

The original meeting had been set for the previous night, at the same café where they had met the Turk. Obedient little rabbits that they were, they would almost certainly turn up again the following night. He went in through the back entrance this time, and would have had his throat slit by Farouk if he hadn't anticipated some such possibility. Looking down at the boy, who was sprawled on the floor rubbing his shin, he said pleasantly, "I take it you were not expecting me?"

The only one of the others who had moved was Asad. He was under the table. A chorus of sighs and murmured thanks to Allah broke out, and Asad got sheepishly to his feet.

"We didn't know what to think! Where have you been? Farouk said you had been shot, and we were afraid —"

"Farouk was right."

Shock replaced the relief on their faces. Ramses had been joking when he expressed his intention of displaying his injuries, but he was suddenly overcome by one of those melodramatic impulses that seemed to run in his family. Slowly, taking his time, he slipped his arm out of the sleeve of his robe, untied the cord at the neck of his shirt, and pulled it off his shoulder. Fatima's green ointment added a colorful note to the bruised flesh and unhealed gashes. Asad covered his mouth with his hand and looked sick.

"Which one of you fired the shot?" Ramses asked.

Farouk had started to get up. He sat down with a thud and held up his hands. "Why do you look at me? It was not I! I shot at the man who tried to kill you! He was hiding. He had a rifle. He . . ."

"Calm yourself," Ramses said irritably. He laced up his shirt and slid his arm back into his robe. "A fine revolutionary you make! If you tried to creep up on a sentry he'd hear you ten yards off, and then you'd probably kill the wrong man. The rest of you keep quiet. Did any of you see who the purported assassin was?"

"No." Asad twisted his thin, ink-stained hands. "We thought — the Turk? Don't be angry. We searched for him, and for you. And we brought the guns back. They are —"

"I know. Have you heard anything about the next delivery?"

"Yes." Asad nodded vigorously. "Farouk has been at Aslimi's shop —"

"I know. Whose brilliant idea was that?"

Asad looked guilty, but then he always did. The nom de guerre he had chosen meant "lion." It couldn't have been more inappropriate.

"Someone had to!" he quavered. "Aslimi has taken to his bed. It is his stomach. He has —"

"Pains after he eats," Ramses interrupted. "I know that too. Someone had to take his place, I grant you that. Why Farouk?"

"Why not?" Farouk demanded. "I know the business, the —"

"Be quiet. When is the delivery?"

"It is for a week from tomorrow — the same time — the ruined mosque south of the cemetery where Burckhardt's tomb is."

"I'll be there. And, Farouk —"

"Yes, sir?"

"Initiative is an admirable quality, but don't carry it too far."

"What do you mean?"

"I think you know what I mean. Don't be tempted to make your own arrangements with our temporary allies. They are using us for their own purpose, and that purpose is not ours. Do you suppose the Ottoman Empire would tolerate an independent Egypt?"

"But they promised," Bashir began.

"They lied," Ramses said curtly. "They always lie. If the Turks win, we will only exchange one set of rulers for another. If the British win, they will suppress a revolt without mercy, and most of us will die. Our best and only hope of achieving our goal is to use one side against the other. I know how to play that game. You don't. Have I made myself clear?"

Nods and murmurs of agreement indicated that he had convinced them. Not even

291

Farouk had the courage to ask him to elaborate. Ramses decided he had better go before someone did ask; he hadn't the faintest idea what he was talking about.

"You are leaving us?" Farouk scrambled to his feet. "Let us go with you, to make sure you are safe. You are our leader, we must protect you."

"From whom?" He smiled at the beautiful face that was gazing soulfully at him. The dark-fringed eyes fell, and Ramses said gently, "Do not follow me, Farouk. You aren't very good at that either."

He was in no mood for gymnastics that night, so he hoped the unsubtle hint would have the desired effect. The others would be suspicious of Farouk now — and serve him right, the little swine — but he made certain there was no one on his trail before he approached the tram station. Trains were infrequent at this hour, but he wasn't in the mood for a ten-mile hike either. Squatting on a hard bench in the odorous confines of a third-class carriage, he again considered alternate methods of transportation and again dismissed them. The motorbicycles made too much noise, and Risha was too conspicuous.

It took him almost an hour to reach Maadi. He approached the house from the back. It was unlighted, as were all the others in that huddle of lower-class dwellings — the remains of the old village, now surrounded and in part supplanted by elegant new villas. There were few streetlights even in the new section, and this area was pitch-black. He wouldn't have seen the motionless form, only slightly darker than the wall against which it stood, if he had not been looking for it.

David grasped his outstretched hand and then motioned toward the open window. "How did it go?"

"No trouble. I hope you didn't wait up for me last night."

They spoke in the low voices that were less carrying than whispers. Once they were inside the room, David said, "I was watching for you, but I didn't really suppose you'd be able to get away from Aunt Amelia. Was Farouk there tonight?"

"Mmmm. Innocent as a cherub and sticking to his story. The next delivery is Tuesday, the old mosque near Burckhardt's tomb. David, it has occurred to me, somewhat belatedly, that you had better find new quarters. If Father knows about this place, it may be known to others."

"A man came here yesterday. A stranger."

"Damnation! What did he look like?"

"I wasn't here. Mahira couldn't give me much of a description; the poor old girl is as blind as a mole and getting more senile by the day."

"That settles it. We're leaving now, tonight. You ought to have vacated the premises as soon as you heard."

"You wouldn't have known where I was."

"And you wanted to make certain there was no one lying in wait for me when I came? David, please do me the favor of trying not to get yourself killed on my account. I've enough on my conscience as it is."

"I'm doing my best." David put a hand on his shoulder. "Where shall I go?"

"I'll leave that to you. Some safe, flea-ridden hovel in Old Cairo or Boulaq, I suppose. God, I hate doing this to you."

"Not as much as I hate doing it." David had gathered his scanty possessions and was tying them into a bundle. "You know what I miss most? A proper bath. I dream of lying in that tub of Aunt Amelia's, with hot water up to my chin."

"Not the food? Mother wanted me to bring you a parcel of leftover turkey and plum pudding."

"Fatima's plum pudding?" David sighed wistfully. "Couldn't you have secreted a small slice under your shirt?"

"Yes, right. I'd have had rather a time explaining that, if it had tumbled onto the floor while I was kicking Farouk's feet out from under him."

David stopped halfway out the window and turned to stare at him. "I thought you said nothing happened."

"Nothing of importance. Go on, I'm getting edgy."

David took him across the river in the small boat they had acquired for that purpose. On the way Ramses explained what had happened with Farouk.

"Reasonable behavior, I suppose," David admitted, pulling at the oars. "They must have been rather worried."

"Yes. Farouk is the only one of the lot who has any fighting instincts. Poor old Asad was petrified. I hope I can get him out of this and talk some sense into him. He's a braver man than Farouk. He's afraid all the time, and yet he sticks."

And you're a braver man than I am, Ramses thought, watching his friend bend and straighten with the oars. If I had a wife who adored me and a child on the way, I wouldn't have risked myself in a stunt like this one.

For a few seconds the soft splash of water was the only thing that broke the silence. Then Ramses said thoughtfully, "Farouk made one little slip tonight. He claimed the man who fired first used a rifle. But the first shot wasn't from a rifle, it was from a pistol, like the ones that followed, and if Farouk was aiming at someone other than me, he was a damned poor shot. It's not absolute proof; but I think we had better gather Farouk into the loving arms of the law. I'll try to arrange a meeting with Russell. I know we aren't supposed to be seen together, but we'll have to risk it."

"Why?" David demanded. "Can't you tell me what you've got in mind and let me pass it on?"

"It's just as risky for you to meet with him as it is for me," Ramses said. "I'll tell you, though, in case I can't reach Russell, or in case . . . This is a perfect opportunity to get Farouk out of the way without involving me. If the police raided Aslimi's shop, I wouldn't have much trouble convincing my associates that Aslimi had finally cracked and confessed."

"Aslimi had better be put in protective custody, then."

"That's part of the plan, yes." Ramses laughed softly. "He'll probably be relieved as hell. When I see the Turk Tuesday, we will arrange an alternative drop."

The current carried them downstream, so that he was not far from Giza when they landed. They sat in silence for a time. It was a beautiful night, with a small crescent moon hanging in the net of stars, and good-byes were difficult when there was always a chance they would not meet again. "Just in case" was a phrase both of them had learned to hate.

"Is there anything else you should tell me?" David asked.

"I don't think so." David's very silence was

a demand. After a moment Ramses said, "All right, then. It's possible that Farouk was planted on us by the other side. That's what I would do if I weren't entirely confident of the reliability of my temporary allies. If this is the case and if he can be persuaded to talk, he could lead us to the man in charge of operations here in Cairo. You know what that would mean, don't you? We could put an end to this business within a few days."

David's breath caught. "It would be too much to hope for."

The pain and longing in his friend's voice stabbed Ramses with renewed guilt. He said roughly, "Don't hope. I've no proof, only what Mother would call a strong premonition. In any case, Farouk is dangerous, and the sooner we remove him, the safer for us. I'd better go before I fall asleep. Can you let me know where to find you? Our emergency method — use hieroglyphs, sign Carter's name, and hire a messenger to deliver it."

David steadied the boat as he climbed out. "I'll tell you on Tuesday."

Ramses slipped on the muddy bank, caught himself, and spun round to face his friend.

"Don't waste your breath," David said. "Do you suppose I'd let you go alone after what happened last time? I'll find a place to hide and be in concealment before sundown. No one will know I'm there. And I might just get a clue as to where your friend the Turk has come from."

"I can't stop you, can I?"

"Not in your present condition." David sounded amused. "I'll contact you somewhere along the homeward path. Look for a dancing girl in gauzy pantaloons."

After Nefret and I had developed the photographs I sent her to bed and retired to my own room. Needless to say, I was still lying sleepless in the dark, my door ajar, when I finally heard the sound I had been waiting for — not footsteps, for Ramses walked lightly as a cat, but the soft click of the latch when he opened the door of his room.

I was wearing my dressing gown but not my slippers. I do not believe I made any noise at all. However, when I approached Ramses's door he was waiting for me. Putting one hand over my mouth, he drew me into the room and shut the door.

"Stand still while I light a lamp," he whispered.

"How did you know I would —"

"Sssh."

He tossed the bundled-up robe and turban he had worn that night onto the bed. Seshat sniffed curiously at it. The smell was certainly pungent.

"I thought you might wait up for me," Ramses said softly. "Though I hoped you would not. Go back to bed, Mother. It's all right."

"David?"

"He was annoyed with me because I didn't bring the plum cake. You had better get some sleep. Father will have us up at dawn."

"I've been thinking about that house in Maadi. If your father knew its location —"

"David left the place tonight."

"Was that handsome young man — Farouk? — at the meeting?"

"Yes." He began unbuttoning his shirt. It was another hint, which I ignored.

"In my opinion, you ought to have the shop raided and Farouk taken into custody at once."

Ramses stared at me. His eyes were very wide and very dark. "There are times when you terrify me, Mother," he said, under his breath. "What put that idea into your head?"

"Logical ratiocination," I explained, pleased to have got his attention. "The enemy has no reason to trust Wardani. If they are sensible people, as the Germans are known to be, they would place a spy in the organization. Farouk's behavior has been highly suspicious. At the least, arresting him will remove a potential source of danger to you, and at best he might be persuaded to betray his employer, who is almost certainly —"

"Yes, Mother." Ramses sat down rather heavily on the side of the bed. "Believe it or not, I had come to the same conclusion."

"Good. Then all we need do is present the plan to Mr. Russell and insist he carry it out."

"Insist?" He rubbed his unshaven chin, and the corners of his mouth turned up. "I suppose you have also worked out a method of communicating with Russell?"

"Yes, indeed. I will arrange for us to see him tomorrow at Giza. Just leave it to me."

Ramses got slowly to his feet. Having undone the shirt buttons, he was not prepared to go further. He came to me and took me by the shoulders. "Very well, I will. Thank you. Please be careful."

"Certainly. Have you ever known me to take unnecessary chances?"

His lips parted in one of his rare, unguarded smiles. I thought for a moment he would kiss my cheek, but he did not. He gave my shoulders a little squeeze and turned me toward the door. "Good night, Mother."

With my mind now at ease, at least for the time being, I was able to sleep. It seemed to me my eyes had hardly closed before they opened again to see a familiar face in close proximity to mine.

"Ah," said Emerson in a satisfied voice. "You are awake."

He kissed me. I made wordless noises indicative of appreciation and approval, but Emerson soon left off kissing me and went to the washbasin.

"Up you get, my love. I have a feeling we will be deluged by curiosity seekers and I need you to fend them off with your parasol."

I said, "Ramses is home, safe and sound."

"I know. I looked in on him before I came here."

"You didn't wake him, did you?"

"He was already awake." Emerson finished splashing water all over the floor and the washstand and himself, and reached for a towel. "Hurry and dress. I want that statue out and in a safe place before dark."

I hastened to comply, for in fact I was not at all averse to playing the role of guard. It would give me an opportunity to inspect at close hand every visitor who approached. If ever there was an event to attract the interest of the Master Criminal, this was it — a new masterpiece of Egyptian art, not yet under lock and key. Surely, if he was in Cairo, he would be unable to resist the temptation to have a look at it. And as soon as I set eyes on him I would know him, whatever disguise he might assume.

I therefore took pains to collect all my weapons. When I strode into the dining room, parasol in hand, four pairs of eyes were focused on me.

"I could hear you jingling all the way down the hall," remarked Emerson, rising to hold a chair for me.

Ramses, who had also risen, looked me

over. "The mere sight of you bristling with weapons should deter any thief," he said. "I presume there are more of them in your pockets?"

"Only a pair of handcuffs, a stocking, which I will fill with sand, and my pistol," I replied. "That reminds me, Emerson; the release on my parasol has been sticking."

"Oh, Sitt." Fatima wrung her hands. "What is going to happen? Is there danger?"

"Nothing is going to happen," Nefret said firmly.

"Possibly not, but it is always best to be prepared." I smacked my egg with a spoon and lifted the top off. "Do you have your knife?"

Smiling, she pushed her coat back. The weapon was belted to her waist.

"Ramses?"

He had resumed his chair. "No. I feel certain Father and I can count on you two to protect us. Fatima, is there more bread?"

Fatima trotted off, shaking her head and murmuring to herself.

Emerson was not at all pleased to learn that I had invited Mr. Quibell to come by that morning. I had sent a messenger the night before, since I knew Emerson would not, but it was our obligation to inform the Antiquities Department of any major finds. With the new director still in France, Quibell was the highest-ranking Egyptologist presently in Cairo,

302

and of course he was also an old friend.

I pointed this out to Emerson, between bites and swallows.

"Who else did you invite?" he growled.

"Only General Maxwell."

Nefret choked on her coffee and Emerson appeared to be on the brink of an explosion. "He won't come," I said quickly. "He has far too many other things on his mind. It was only a courteous gesture."

"Good Gad." Emerson jumped up.

"And Mr. Woolley —"

"Stop! I don't want to hear any more. The whole damned city of Cairo will be converging on my tomb."

I had been certain that he would interrupt me before I finished the list. Catching Ramses's eye, I smiled and winked.

"Shall we go, then?" I suggested.

The sun was rising over the hills of the Eastern Desert when we mounted our horses. As usual, Emerson suggested we take the motorcar. As usual, I overruled him. Those early-morning rides were such a pleasant way to begin the day, with the fresh breeze caressing one's face and the sunlight spreading gently across the fields. My intelligent steed, one of Risha's offspring, knew the way as well as I, so I let the reins lie loose and fixed my eyes on the view — which I certainly could not have done had I been sitting beside Emerson in the car.

Early as we were, we had only just arrived at the tomb when our first visitor appeared. Visitors, I should say, for Quibell had brought his wife Annie along. She was a talented artist who had worked for Petrie at Sakkara. It was then she had met her future husband, and I well remembered the day when poor James had come staggering into our camp at Mazghuna requesting medicine for himself and "the young ladies." Mr. Petrie's people were always suffering from stomach trouble, owing to his peculiar dietary habits; the half-spoiled food he expected them to eat never bothered him in the slightest.

Emerson greeted his colleague with a grumble. James, who was quite accustomed to him, replied with a smile and hearty congratulations. Selim and Daoud lowered him down into the shaft while Emerson hovered over it like a gargoyle.

"Khafre, do you think?" James called up. "I don't see an inscription."

"There may be one on the base," Emerson replied. "As you see, we have not yet uncovered it. If you will get out of there, Quibell, we can proceed."

Annie declined to emulate her husband's example; her sensible short skirt and stout boots were suitable for hiking in the desert but not for being lowered into shafts. So we took her to the little rest place I had set up, arranging camp stools and tables and a few packing cases, in the cleared area in front of the tomb, and left the men to get on with it. She was impressed by the quality of the reliefs, and declared that the false door would make a splendid watercolor.

"Unfortunately we have no one who could do it," Ramses said.

"Yes; you must miss David. What a pity . . ." She did not finish the sentence.

"Tragedy, rather," I said. "Part of the greater tragedy that has overtaken the world. Ah, well, we must all do what we can, eh? But I believe I hear a party of confounded tourists approaching. If you will excuse me, Annie, I am on guard duty today and must not shirk my task."

By mid-morning, when we stopped for tea, I had driven away a good two dozen people, none of whom were known to me. Annie and James had left, after discussing the disposition of the statue with Emerson. James's suggestion, that it be taken directly to the Museum, had been rejected by Emerson with the scorn it deserved. "You will claim it in the end, no doubt, but until we make the final division of finds, it will be safer in my custody. The security measures at the Museum are perfectly wretched."

Soon after we returned to work, other visitors came, whom it was impossible to drive away. Clarence Fisher, who was about to be-

305

gin work in the West Cemetery field, dropped by to have a look; the High Commissioner, Sir Henry MacMahon, arrived, escorting some titled visitors who were aching to "see something dug up." They soon became bored with the slow, tedious process, but they were replaced by Woolley and Lawrence and several officers with archaeological leanings. Emerson sent Ramses up to entertain them (i.e., keep them out of his way) while he went on with the job. As courtesy demanded, I offered refreshment, which they were pleased to accept.

Bedrock was several meters below the unexcavated portion of the cemetery, so my little rest area was walled by sand on two sides. All of us (except Emerson) retired thither, and I poured tea.

"I trust our discovery has not lured you away from your duties," I remarked. "We are counting on you gentlemen to save us and the Canal from the Turks, you know."

My friendly touch of sarcasm was not lost on Woolley, who laughed good-naturedly. "Fortunately, Mrs. Emerson, your safety is not solely dependent on the likes of us. All we do is sit poring over maps. It is good to get away from the office for a while. I miss being in the field."

Lawrence was discussing Arabic dialects with Ramses, who — for a wonder — let him do most of the talking. One had to admire the young man's zeal, if not his appearance; he was not wearing a belt, and his uniform looked as if he had slept in it. I thought Ramses looked bored.

It was Nefret who first saw the newcomers. She nudged Ramses. "Brace yourself," she said.

"What for?" He looked in the direction she indicated, and jumped up in time to catch hold of the bundle of flying hair and skirts that came tumbling down the slope of sand beside him. Miss Molly brushed herself off and grinned broadly.

"Hullo!"

"Good morning," said Ramses. "Where is Miss Nordstrom?"

"Sick," said the young person with, I could not help suspect, some satisfaction. "At her stomach."

"Surely you did not come alone," I exclaimed.

"No, I came with them." She gestured. Peering down at us was a pair of faces, one surmounted by a solar topee, the other by a large hat and veil. "Their names are Mr. and Miss Poynter. I heard them tell Nordie they were coming out to see the statue, so I said we would come with them, but then Nordie got sick — at her stomach — so I came without her."

Trying not to grind my teeth, I indicated an easier descent to the Poynters and greeted them more politely than I would have done had they not accompanied the young person. When Miss Poynter removed her veil, displaying a countenance that consisted mostly of chin and teeth, she looked so pleased with herself I realized she must have made use of the child to gain an introduction. We had achieved a certain notoriety in Cairo and were known not to welcome strangers.

They settled down with every intention of remaining indefinitely and Miss Poynter began telling me all about her family connections and the swath she was cutting in Cairo society. Bored to distraction, I heard Miss Molly demanding that Ramses take her to see the statue, and his somewhat curt reply.

"As you see, we have other guests. You will have to wait."

How she got away unobserved I do not know; but several minutes later I tore my fascinated gaze away from Miss Poynter's teeth in order to acknowledge Woolley's farewells. "We've played truants long enough," he explained. "Thank you, Mrs. Emerson, for —"

"Where is she?" I exclaimed, rising. "Where has she gone?"

All of us except the Poynters immediately scattered in search of the girl. Knowing the reckless habits of young persons of a certain age, I was filled with apprehension; there were pitfalls and tomb shafts all over the area. We had been looking for several minutes be-

fore a shrill hail attracted our attention toward a dump area west of the street of tombs.
Ours was not the only expedition to pile sand
and rubble there; the mound was almost
twenty feet high. Atop it a small figure waved
triumphantly.

"She's up there," Lawrence said, shielding
his eyes. He chuckled. "Spoiled little devil."

Nefret looked anxious. "She could hurt
herself. Someone had better go after her."

"She's quite capable of getting down by
herself," said Ramses, folding his arms.

Nefret had removed her coat earlier. Slim
as a boy in trousers and flannel shirt, she began to mount the slope. She reached the top
without mishap and held out her hand to the
child. Miss Molly danced blithely away from
her. A shrill laugh floated down to us.

"Stop that, Molly!" I shouted at the top of
my lungs. "You are to come down at once, do
you hear?"

She heard. She stopped and looked down.
Nefret made a lunge for her, and then . . . I
could not see what happened; I only saw
Nefret lose her balance and fall. There was
nothing to stop her; followed by a long plume
of sand and broken stone, she rolled all the
way to the ground. The child's scream of
laughter changed to quite another sort of
scream.

I hastened at once to where my daughter
lay on her side in a tumble of loosened golden

hair and twisted limbs, but I was not the first to reach her. When I joined him Ramses had brushed the sand from her face. His fingers were stained with blood. "Your canteen," he said, and took it from me.

"Don't move her," I cautioned.

"No. Nefret?" He poured the water in a steady stream, bathing her eyes and mouth first. She stirred, murmuring, and Ramses said, "Lie still. You fell. Is anything broken?"

Woolley and Lawrence hurried up. "Shall I go for a doctor?" the latter inquired. "Bound to be one, in that gaggle of tourists."

"I am a doctor," Nefret said, without opening her eyes. "Is Molly all right?"

"She is coming down by herself, quite competently," I said, looking round.

She had selected a nice smooth slope of sand and was descending in a sitting position, and — to judge by her expression — quite enjoying herself. However, as soon as she reached the ground and saw Nefret, she began to cry out.

"I've killed her! It's my fault! Oh, I am sorry, I am sorry!"

She ran toward us and would have flung herself down on Nefret had not Ramses intercepted her. She clung to him, weeping bitterly. "I didn't mean to! Is she dead? I am sorry!"

"So you damned well should be," said Ramses. He shoved her away. "Woolley, take her back to the Poynters."

"Don't be unkind to the child." Cautiously Nefret stretched her limbs, one after the other, and sat up. A trickle of crimson laced her cheek, from a cut on her temple. "I'm not hurt, Molly. No bones broken, and no concussion," she added, giving me a shaky but reassuring smile.

Ramses bent and lifted her up into his arms. I thought she stiffened a little; then she rested her head against his shoulder and closed her eyes. He started back toward the tomb, but he had not gone more than a few steps when he was met by Emerson, who must have been told of the incident by one of the onlookers. My husband was in an extreme state of agitation and dishevelment. He snatched Nefret out of his son's grasp and pressed her to his broad breast.

"Good God! You should not have lifted her! She is bleeding — unconscious —"

"No, sir, I'm not unconscious," Nefret said out of the corner of her mouth. "But you are covered with sand, and it is getting in my eyes."

"Take her back to the shelter," I directed. "She is only a bit shaken up."

"She is bleeding, I tell you," Emerson shouted, squeezing her even more tightly. Both corners of her mouth were now pressed against his shirtfront, but I heard a stifled giggle and a murmur of reassurance.

"Head wounds always bleed copiously," I said. "Don't just stand there, Emerson, go on."

I then turned my attention to Molly. She looked so woebegone and guilty, my annoyance faded. After all, she had intended no harm, and no real harm had been done. I took her hand and led her toward the shelter. She went unresisting, head bowed and eyes downcast.

"It was an accident," she muttered. "I didn't mean —"

"You are becoming repetitive," I informed her. "If you regret your actions you can best show it by returning at once to Cairo with the Poynters."

The Poynters would have lingered, but I gave them no excuse to do so. Once they had departed, and Woolley and Lawrence had gone on their way, I bathed Nefret's head and was about to apply iodine to the cut when she requested I use alcohol instead.

"That rusty red clashes horribly with the color of my hair," she explained. "Thank you, Aunt Amelia, that will do nicely. Now shall we all get back to work?"

"You should return to the house and rest," Emerson said anxiously. "What happened?"

"I tripped," Nefret said. "She was playing a little game of tag, skipping away from me and laughing, and somehow our feet got tangled up. I am perfectly recovered, and I know,

Professor, you are dying to get back to your statue."

She took his arm and smiled up at him.

I waited until they were out of earshot before I turned to my son.

"Are you all right?"

He started. "I beg your pardon?"

"Did you hurt yourself? You ought not have carried her."

"I did not hurt myself."

"Is your arm painful?"

"Yes. I expect it will be painful for a while. It is functional, however, and that is the main thing. He hasn't turned up yet. Are you certain he is coming?"

I knew to whom Ramses referred. I said calmly, "I don't see how he can fail to respond. I sent similar invitations to a good many other people, but he must know that I had a particular reason for asking him. It is early yet. He will come."

I no longer wonder how the pyramids could have been built with the simplest of tools. The way the men went about raising our statue demonstrated the skill and strength their ancestors must have employed on similar projects. As they continued to deepen the shaft and the statue was gradually freed of the sand that had blanketed it all those years, the danger of its toppling over increased. If it had struck against the stone wall it might have been chipped or even broken.

Emerson was determined that this should not happen. The top half of the statue was now tightly wrapped in rugs and canvas and any other fabric he had been able to find; ropes enclosed the bundle, and several of our strongest workers held other ropes that would, we hoped, prevent it from tipping over.

It was a fascinating process, but I knew I could not allow archaeological fever to distract me from other duties. By early afternoon the crowd of spectators had increased. Some of them had cameras, and they kept on trying to take photographs, despite the fact that — thanks to my efforts — they were too far distant to get anything except a group of Egyptian workmen. I had to bustle busily about, since none of our skilled men could be spared to assist me, and I began to feel like an unhappy teacher trying to control a group of very active, very naughty children. At last I resorted to a clever stratagem. Mounting a fallen block of stone, I gathered most of the tourists to me and delivered a little lecture, stressing the delicacy of the operation and promising them they would get an opportunity to take all the photographs they liked once the statue was out. Strictly speaking, it was not a lie, since I did not specify *what* they could photograph. I try to avoid falsehood unless it is absolutely necessary.

As I spoke — shouted, rather — I scanned

the faces of the spectators. A number of the people I had invited had turned up, as well as a number of those I had not. I thought I caught a glimpse of Percy among the group of military persons who had come from the camp near Mena House, but I could not be certain; the individual in question was surrounded by tall Australians.

I was beginning to be a bit anxious about Russell when finally I beheld him. Like several of the tourists, he was on camelback, but his easy pose and expert handling of the beast did not at all resemble the ineffectual performance of the amateurs. I looked round for Ramses, and found him at my elbow.

"Father thought you might need some assistance in controlling the mob," he explained.

"I certainly do," I replied, taking a firmer grip on my parasol and glaring at a stout American person who was trying to edge past me. He retreated in some alarm before Russell's camel. All camels have evil tempers, and the large stained teeth of this one were bared by curling lips. It knelt, grumbling, and Russell dismounted and removed his hat.

"Everyone in Cairo is talking of your discovery," he said. "I could not resist having a look for myself." He tossed Ramses the reins, as he would have done to a groom.

"Come and have a closer look." I took his arm and led him toward the shaft.

"Not too close. I know the Professor's temper." He lowered his voice. "I presume it was Ramses who prompted your invitation. How can I get a word alone with him?"

"That would be unwise as well as unnecessary," I replied. "I can tell you what needs to be done."

We came to a stop some distance from the ropemen and an even greater distance from the watching tourists. I proceeded to explain the situation to Mr. Russell. He tried once or twice to interrupt me, but I never allow that sort of thing and finally he pursed his lips in a silent whistle.

"What makes him believe Farouk is a spy?"

"Goodness gracious," I said impatiently. "I have already gone over his — our — reasoning on that subject. Let us not waste time, Mr. Russell. I want that man locked up. He has tried once to kill my son; I don't intend to give him another chance. If you won't deal with him, I will do it myself."

"I believe you would at that," Russell muttered. "All right, Mrs. Emerson, your — er — reasoning has convinced me. It can't do any harm and it might lead to something."

"How soon can you act?"

Russell took out his handkerchief and wiped the perspiration from his face. "It will take a while to make the arrangements. To-morrow, perhaps."

"That won't do. It must be sooner."

Russell's erect, military carriage slumped. "Mrs. Emerson, you don't understand the difficulties. I have already been called on the carpet by my chief for failing to inform him of certain of my activities. I am trying to think of a way of doing what you want *without* informing him."

"And thereby, Mr. Philippides."

"Yes, he's the rub, all right." Russell's lips tightened into a firm line. "I've got my eye on him, and someday I'll catch the — er — fellow in flagrante. Until then, the less he knows, the better."

"Is that why you have not kept the shop under surveillance? It would seem to me —"

"And to me, I assure you. It is a matter of manpower, Mrs. Emerson. I don't have enough men I can trust to act on my orders and keep their mouths shut, and I gave Ramses my word I would not involve any of the other services."

"The General knows, does he not?"

"Yes, of course; he had to be informed. It's that motley lot of Clayton's that concerns me; Clayton is a good man, none better, but he's trying to cobble together a working organization out of a scrapbag of his former commands and that collection of intellectuals."

"Surely you don't doubt the loyalty of men like Woolley and Lawrence?" I exclaimed.

"None of them have any practical experience in criminal investigation. That's what is wanted for effective counterintelligence, and the entire table of organization is in such disarray —"

"Well, Mr. Russell, I am sorry about all that, but I really haven't time to listen to your troubles. The raid must be tonight. Delay could be fatal. Come along now. The sooner you get to work on this, the sooner you can act."

Russell allowed himself to be led back toward his camel. He appeared a trifle dazed, but perhaps he was only thinking hard. After a moment he said, "Does the Professor know of this?"

"Not yet. I do not like to distract him when he is engaged in important archaeological activities. But I feel certain he will wish to come with us."

Russell stopped and dug his heels into the sand. "Now just a damned minute, Mrs. Emerson! Confound it, I apologize for my language, but you are really the most —"

"You are not the first person to tell me that," I said with a smile. "Ah, here is your nice camel all ready and waiting."

Russell took the reins from Ramses and, for the first time, looked him squarely in the eyes. Ramses nodded. It was sufficient confirmation of what I had said, and in my opinion Russell ought not have risked further conversation, but he appeared a trifle confused. It might have been the hot sun.

"She intends to be there," he said in an agitated whisper. "Can you —"

"I can try." The corners of Ramses's mouth twitched. "When?"

Russell looked at me and mopped his forehead. "Tonight."

"Excellent," I said audibly. "Now do run along, Mr. Russell; I must get back to work."

He obeyed, of course. Ramses squared his shoulders, cleared his throat, and said, "Mother —"

"I don't intend to argue with you either," I informed him. "We will discuss the logistical details later. I want to see what your father is doing."

We all gathered round to watch. Finally came the moment when the entire statue was exposed except for the base. Emerson, who had kept up a monotonous undercurrent of curses and exhortations, fell silent. Then he drew a deep breath. Turning to Daoud, who held one of the ropes, he gave him a slap on the back.

"You know what to do, Daoud."

The giant gave him a broad smile and a nod. Emerson descended the ladder that leaned against the wall of the shaft. He was followed by Ibrahim, our carpenter. There was only room below for two men to work and I had known Emerson would be one of them.

I had forgotten my duties as guard. I was

vaguely aware that a circle of staring onlookers had gathered, but my full attention was focused on my spouse, who was kneeling and scooping out sand from under the base of the statue. As he removed it Ibrahim shoved the stout plank he had brought into the vacant space. The statue swayed and promptly steadied as Daoud called out directions to the men pulling on the ropes. Finally Emerson straightened and looked up.

"So far so good," he remarked.

The front part of the statue now rested on a solid platform of wood. Emerson and Ibrahim repeated the process at the back of the base. The ropes tightened and loosened as the men followed Daoud's orders. Then more planks, cut to measure, were lowered into the pit and Ibrahim deftly lashed them into place at right angles to the planks on which the statue rested.

Sometimes a heavy weight of that sort could be raised by rocking it back and forth and inserting wedges under the raised side. The space was too narrow for that, however. The statue and its wooden base would have to be pulled up by sheer brute strength, while the ropemen steadied it. Emerson tied cables to the planks with his own hands and tossed the ends up. Twenty men seized each rope and began hauling on it.

Selim, who had been hopping about like a grasshopper with sheer nerves, now stood still, his eyes fixed on his uncle Daoud. Daoud's broad face was set. It was not the heat or the physical effort, but the sense of responsibility that caused the perspiration to pour down his face. My concern was for Emerson, who had sent Ibrahim back up the ladder but had remained below.

"Come up out of there," I shouted, as the massive object began to rise.

"Yes, yes," said Emerson. "I only want to —"

"Emerson!"

It was probably not my exhortation but the knowledge that he could be of more use directing operations from above that finally prompted him to ascend. Cameras clicked as my spouse's disheveled head appeared; the clicking rose to a perfect fusillade as the statue rose slowly and steadily upward. When the base was level with the ground the men inserted long planks under it, bridging the shaft and forming a platform onto which the statue settled as gently as a bird coming to rest on a bough.

Emerson let out a long sigh and wiped the perspiration from his face with his shirtsleeve.

"Well done, Daoud, and the rest of you," he said.

Ramses bent over and examined the base of the statue. "Nefret was right. It's Khafre. 'The Good God, Horus of Gold.' "

Nefret did not say "I told you so," but she looked rather smug. The face and form of the pharaoh did bear a certain resemblance to Ramses, in his stonier moods. He was looking quite affable now; smiles wreathed all our faces as we exchanged mutual congratulations. For once, however, archaeological fever did not entirely overcome my greater concern. Would Russell keep his word? Would the raid on Aslimi's shop succeed? I had determined to do everything in my power to make certain it would.

7

Our return to the house resembled a triumphal procession. Daoud would not hear of using mechanical transport; once the statue platform had been securely fastened to the lengthwise beams, forty men hoisted the entire structure onto their shoulders and set off across the plateau. When they turned onto the Pyramid Road they began to sing one of the traditional work songs, with Daoud shouting out the lines and the men echoing them in a reverberant chorus. Most of the way was downhill, but it was over two miles to the house, and Emerson made them stop frequently to rest and adjust the pads that protected their shoulders. When one man faltered, another sprang to take his place. As I watched, the centuries seemed to shrink, and I felt as if I had been privileged to behold a vision from the past. Just so must the workers of Pharaoh have transported the image of their god king to its original place, chanting as they went.

To be sure, there was no actual depiction of this precise procedure in any of the tomb reliefs. However, it was a thrilling sight, and one I will never forget, nor, I believe, will those who lined the road to watch and cheer as we passed. The tourists got their fill of photographs for once.

By the time we reached the house all the men except Daoud, who had taken his turn as carrier, were on the verge of collapse. Emerson led them through the courtyard to the closest room, which happened to be the parlor. I was too excited to object to this inconvenience, but as it turned out the platform would not go through the doorway, so Emerson directed the bearers to place it in the courtyard, between two pillars. Once the statue had come safely to rest, I had to deal with fifty male persons sprawled in various positions of exhaustion on the tiled floor. Forty-nine, I should say; Daoud, perspiring but undaunted, helped us minister to the fallen, splashing them with water and offering copious quantities of liquid. The sun was setting when we sent them home, with thanks and praise and promises of a fantasia of celebration in the near future.

"I think we should celebrate too," I announced. "Let us dine in Cairo. I told Fatima not to prepare anything for dinner since I was not certain how long the job would take. The triumph is yours, my dear Emerson, therefore I will allow you to choose the restaurant."

As a rule Emerson is pathetically easy to manipulate. He hated dining at the hotels. I knew what establishment he would suggest: a pleasantly unsanitary little place where the menu included his favorite Egyptian delicacies and the owner would have slaughtered an ostrich and cooked it up if Emerson had requested it. Suits and cravats, much less evening clothes, would have been out of place in that ambience — another strong point in its favor, as far as Emerson was concerned.

It was located on the edge of the Khan el Khalili.

Emerson hesitated for only a moment — that brief delay being occasioned by his reluctance to leave his precious statue — before responding precisely as I had planned. I glanced at Ramses, who was looking even blanker than usual. He opened his mouth and closed it without speaking.

Turning to Nefret, I brushed the hair back from her forehead. "Perhaps you ought to stay here and rest," I said. "You have a nasty lump as well as a cut."

"Nonsense, Aunt Amelia. I feel fine and I wouldn't miss dining at Bassam's for all the world."

She tripped away before I could respond. Meeting Ramses's dark gaze, which seemed to me to convey a certain degree of criticism, I gave a little shrug. "Hurry and bathe and change," I ordered. "We must not be late."

Ramses said, "Yes, Mother." Clearly he would have liked to say more, but after a moment's hesitation he started up the stairs.

"All right, Peabody," said my husband. "What are you up to now?"

I had intended to tell him anyhow.

He took the news more quietly than I had expected, though it certainly had the effect of hurrying him up. He was in and out of the bath chamber in a remarkably short period of time.

"Well, well," he remarked, throwing his towel onto the floor, where a puddle began to form around it. "So it occurred to you too that Farouk might have been sent to infiltrate Wardani's organization?"

"Now, Emerson, if you are going to claim you thought of it first —"

"I would not claim to be the first. I did think of it, though."

"You always say that!"

"So do you. I suppose this scheme is practicable, but I wish you had left it to me."

Stung by the criticism, I demanded hotly, "And what would you have done?"

Emerson assumed his trousers. "Stop by Aslimi's and collect the bastard myself. I had scheduled it for tomorrow."

He began to rummage through the drawers in search of a shirt. They are always in the same drawer, but Emerson, who can effortlessly call to mind the most intricate details of stratification and pottery sequences, can never remember which drawer. Watching the pull of muscle across his back and arms, I rather regretted having spoken with Russell. It would have been immensely satisfying to watch Emerson "collect" Farouk; he could have done it without the least effort, and then we (for of course I would have accompanied him) could have searched the shop for incriminating evidence and carried our captive back to the house in order to interrogate him.

However, I had a feeling Ramses would not have liked it. He obviously did not like what I was doing now, but the other would have vexed him even more. Emerson is rather like a bull in a china shop when he is enraged, and this matter was somewhat delicate. I felt obliged to point this out to Emerson.

"We must not be directly involved in an attack on Farouk, or the shop, Emerson; our active participation could increase the enemy's suspicion of Ramses."

"So what is the point of our going there this evening?"

"I only want to be there," I replied, refolding the shirts he had tumbled into a pile. "Or rather, near by. Coincidentally. Casually. Just in case."

I turned and selected a light but becoming cotton frock from the wardrobe. Emerson came up behind me and put his arms round my waist.

"It is important to you, isn't it?"

I dropped the frock onto the floor and

turned into his arms. "Oh, Emerson, if we are right, this could be the end of the whole horrible business! I can't stand much more of this. Every time he goes out I am afraid he will never come back. And David could just . . . disappear. They could throw his body into the river or bury it in the desert, and we would never know what had happened to him."

"Good Gad, my love, that extravagant imagination of yours is getting out of hand! Ramses has been in worse scrapes than this one, and David has generally been in them with him."

I started to deny it but could not. A series of hideous images flashed through my mind: Ramses confronting the Master Criminal and demanding that that formidable gentleman return his treasure; Ramses dragged off to the lair of the vicious Riccetti, whom he had pursued accompanied only by David and the cat Bastet; Ramses strolling into a bandit camp, alone and unarmed . . . I did not doubt there were other incidents of which I had been happily unaware. Oh, yes, he had been in worse scrapes and had got out of them too, but his luck was bound to run out one day.

I was not selfish enough to remind Emerson of that. I would not be one of those whining females who require constant reassurances and petting. Despair drains the strength, not only of the one who expresses it but of the one who is told of it.

"I am sorry, Emerson," I said, stiffening my spine literally as well as figuratively. "I will not give way again. And I have delayed us. We must hurry."

The garment I had intended to wear was now crumpled and covered by large wet footprints. I selected another, while Emerson dried his feet again and, at my request, mopped up the puddle of water on the floor.

"What about Nefret?" he asked.

"I would rather she did not come with us, but there is no way of preventing her. In fact, her presence will make this seem like one of our customary family outings. Behave normally and leave everything to me."

I feared I would have to go through the same thing with Ramses, who was lying in wait for me when I came down the stairs. "There is a button off your coat," I said, hoping to forestall an argument. "I will get my sewing kit and —"

"Stab yourself in the thumb," Ramses said, his formidable frown relaxing into a half-smile. "You hate to sew, Mother, and with all respect, you do it very badly. Anyhow, I've lost the button. What the devil are you —"

"Sssh. Behave normally and follow my lead. Ah, there you are, Nefret, my dear. How pretty you look."

Like the rest of us she was informally dressed, in a neat tweed walking skirt and matching coat. The golden-brown cloth, flecked with green and blue, set off her sun-kissed face and bright hair, which she had twisted into a simple coil at the back of her neck.

"You have a button off your coat," she remarked, inspecting Ramses. "And cat hairs all over the shoulder. Stand still, I'll brush them off."

"You are a fine one to criticize my appearance, with that big purple lump on your forehead," Ramses jeered.

"Damn. I thought I'd arranged my hair to cover it." Her fingers played with the waving locks framing her brow.

"Not quite." He watched her for a moment, and then put out his hand. "Let me."

She stood facing him like an obedient child with her chin lifted and her arms at her sides, while his thin, deft fingers gently loosened the gold-red strands and drew them down over her temple. One long lock curled round his hand and clung. He had to unwind it before he took his hand from her face.

"I've made it worse," he said. "Sorry. Excuse me for a minute."

"Go and tell the Professor we are ready," I said to Nefret, and waited until she had started up the stairs before I went after Ramses, who had disappeared behind the statue. I found him leaning against the wall, staring intently at nothing that I could see.

330

"You are as white as a sheet," I told him. "What is wrong? Sit down. Let me get you —"

"Nothing is wrong. A passing dizzy spell, that's all." His eyes came back into focus and the color began to return to his face. "I'm hungry," he said in surprised indignation.

"Nothing surprising about that," I said, greatly relieved. "You only had a few sandwiches for lunch and it has been a hard day. Here, take my arm."

"I thought you wanted us to behave normally. Mother, why are you . . . I appreciate your concern, but I don't understand what . . ."

I knew what he meant and why he could not say it. Perhaps we were more alike than I had believed. "It has cost me a great deal of mental and physical effort to get you to your present age," I explained. "I would hate to have all that effort go to waste."

"Yes, I see."

A bellow from Emerson ended the discussion. "Peabody! Where have you got to? We are waiting, damn it!"

"Just having a look at the statue," I said, coming forth with Ramses at my heels.

There were three of them waiting — Emerson, Nefret, and the cat. They looked rather comical lined up in a row, with Seshat as expectant as the others. She was sitting bolt upright with her tail curled prettily

331

around her front paws.

"I think she wants to come with us," Nefret said.

Seshat confirmed her assumption by approaching Ramses. Looking up at him, she let out a peremptory mew.

"You will have to wear your collar," he informed her. The response was the equivalent of a feline shrug.

"I'll get it," Nefret offered. "Where is it?"

Ramses looked blank. "I don't know."

"Fatima has it," I said. "I gave it to her to keep, since you were always losing it."

Nefret darted off.

In fact, the collar was seldom used since Seshat was not fond of travel. When she was not hunting hapless rodents in the garden or climbing around the exterior of the house, she spent most of her time in Ramses's room. She seeemed to consider it her duty to watch over his possessions — or else (which is more likely) she considered it *her* room, and Ramses only a congenial and rather incompetent roommate, who required a great deal of looking after. I had never understood what prompted her occasional forays away from the house, and her determination to accompany us that night, of all nights, roused certain forebodings. Did she know something we did not?

Nefret came back with the collar and gave it to Ramses, who knelt to buckle it around

Seshat's neck. Emerson moved to my side. "If you so much as shape the word with your lips, Peabody," he said softly, "I will — er —"

He did not finish the threat, since he could not think of one he would be able to carry out.

"Which word, 'premonition' or 'foreboding'?" I inquired as softly.

"Neither, curse it!"

"You must have felt it too, or you would not —"

"Superstition is not one of my failings. I do wish you would get over your —"

"Now what are you quarreling about?" Nefret asked. "Can we join in?"

"Emerson is just being obstreperous," I explained. "He always behaves this way when he wants his dinner or his tea or his breakfast or —"

"Hmph," said Emerson. He stalked out of the room, leaving me to follow. Ramses lifted the cat onto his right shoulder and offered me his other arm.

"Do you go on, my dear," I said. "Managing that cat is trouble enough. Nefret and I will follow, like obedient females. And try to prevent your father from driving the motorcar!"

"Not much chance of that," said Nefret, as Ramses started for the door with the cat draped over his shoulder. "Aunt Amelia, does it ever occur to you that this family is a trifle eccentric?"

"Because we are taking the cat to dinner with us? I suppose some might consider it eccentric. But we always have done, you know; the cat Bastet went everywhere with Ramses."

"She always rode on his shoulder too," Nefret said reminiscently.

"He needed both shoulders then," I said with a smile.

"Yes. He has changed quite a lot since those days."

"So have you, my dear."

"Yes."

There was a note in her voice that made me stop and look searchingly at her. "Nefret, is something worrying you? Something you might wish to confide to me?"

Nefret looked away. When she spoke, her voice was so soft the words were barely audible. "What about you, Aunt Amelia? I would like to help — to help you — with whatever is worrying you — if you would let me."

I did not at all like the direction the conversation had taken. Evidently my anxiety had not escaped her notice. Was my famed self-control failing? That must not happen!

"How kind of you, my dear," I replied heartily. "If something of the sort does arise, I will certainly request your assistance."

She did not reply, but hastened on. Intervention was called for; I could hear Emerson and Ramses arguing, more or less amiably, about who was to act as chauffeur. Nefret entered into the discussion with all her old zest; her laughter-bright face was so untroubled I wondered if I could have imagined that look of pain and appeal.

Nefret has her own ways of managing Emerson; this time she got round him by declaring that *she* meant to drive the motorcar. Though Emerson is a firm believer in the equality of the female sex, he has some secret reservations, and one of them involves the car. (There is something about these machines that makes men want to pound their chests and roar like gorillas. I speak figuratively, of course.)

In the end it was Emerson who proposed, as a compromise, that Ramses should drive. Nefret agreed with a grumble at Emerson and a look of triumph at her brother. He raised his hand to his brow in a surreptitious salute.

Nothing could have been more normal than that exchange, and it put everyone in a merry mood. Emerson thought he had won, and the rest of us knew we had.

Once we had traversed the Muski and its continuation, the Sikkeh el-Gedideh, our progress slowed, since the thoroughfares (bearing various names with which I will not burden the Reader) were narrower and crowded with people. The sun was setting and I was increasingly anxious to reach our destination but I did not urge Ramses to go faster. We made better progress than some might have done, since people tended to scamper briskly out of the way when they recognized the vehicle. Nodding from side to side, as regally as a monarch on progress, Emerson acknowledged the greetings of passersby. I wondered if there was anyone in Cairo he did not know. Most of them knew him, at any rate.

"Perhaps we ought to have come on foot," I murmured in his ear. "Our presence certainly will be noted."

"It would be noted in any case," said Emerson. "Do you suppose we could go ten yards without being observed? Look at that."

Ramses had slowed almost to a stop in order to give the driver of a particularly stubborn camel time to drag it out of our path. A pack of ragged urchins now hung from both doors, exchanging comments with Ramses and paying compliments to Nefret. The compliments had, I admit, a certain financial element. "O beautiful lady, whose eyes are like the sky, have pity on a poor starving . . ."

Ramses made a remark in Arabic that I pretended not to hear, and the assailants withdrew, grinning appreciatively.

The motorcar had to be left on the Beit el Kadi, since it could not enter the winding ways that surround the picturesque sprawl of the Khan el Khalili. Emerson helped me out and started off without so much as a backward look; he assumed, probably correctly, that none of the local vagabonds would dare touch an object belonging to HIM. Ramses lingered briefly to speak to a man who had come out from under the open veranda on the east side of the square. Something passed from hand to hand, and the fellow nodded, grinning. Goodness, what a nasty suspicious mind the boy has, I thought.

He must have got it from me.

"Wait a moment," I said, tugging at Emerson. "We should all stay together."

"What? Oh, yes, of course." He turned. "Get hold of Nefret, Ramses, and hurry up."

"Yes, sir."

The archway on the east side of the square leads into the narrow lanes of the Hasaneyn quarter and to one of the entrances to the Khan el Khalili. Emerson led the way through this maze without a pause or a false step, despite the increasing darkness. The old houses have enclosed balconies jutting out from the upper stories, almost bridging the narrow street. This made the lanes pleasantly cool during the day and dark as pitch during the night. There are seldom any windows on the lower floors of these houses, and the only illumination came from an occasional lantern hanging over the doorway of a considerate householder.

"Didn't you bring your electric torch?" I

asked, thankful that I was wearing stout shoes instead of low slippers.

"Do you really want to see what you just stepped into?" Emerson inquired. "Hang on to me, my dear, we are almost there."

The restaurant was near the Mosque of Huseyn opposite the eastern entrance to the Khan el Khalili. Mr. Bassam, the proprietor, rushed to embrace us and heap reproaches on our heads. All these weeks we had been in Cairo and we had not visited his place! Every night he had hoped to entertain us, every night he had prepared our favorite dishes! He began to enumerate these.

"It is as God pleases," said Emerson, cutting him off. "We are here now, Bassam, so bring out the food. We are all hungry."

As it turned out, this was the one night Mr. Bassam had not prepared food in advance. He had quite given us up. After all, we had been in Cairo . . .

"Anything you have, then," Emerson said. "The sooner the better."

First a table had to be placed for us at the very front of the restaurant, near the door. This suited me very well. It also suited Mr. Bassam, who wanted such distinguished customers to be seen. He even dusted off the chairs with a towel. I hoped it was not the same one he used to wipe the dishes, but decided I would feel happier if I did not ask.

"And what will she have?" he inquired, as

Ramses put Seshat down on a chair.

"She is omnivorous," Nefret said gravely, in English.

"Ah? Ah! Yes, I will prepare — uh — it at once."

"Don't tease him, Nefret," I scolded. Seshat sat up and inspected the top of the table. Finding nothing of interest there except a few crumbs, she jumped down onto the floor.

"Put her on the lead, Ramses, and tell her she must stay on the chair," I instructed. "I don't want her going out on the street to eat vermin."

"She eats mice all the time," said Emerson, as Ramses returned the cat to her chair and began searching his pockets — a token demonstration, as I well knew, for I had forgotten to mention the lead and he would never have thought of it himself. The collar was primarily for purposes of identification; it bore our name and Seshat's.

"They are *our* vermin," I said.

"Use this." Nefret unwound the scarf from her neck and handed it to her brother.

Seshat accepted the indignity without objection after Ramses had explained the situation to her. The other diners, who were watching us with the admiring interest our presence always provokes, looked on openmouthed.

Mr. Bassam began heaping food, including a dish of spiced chicken, on the table. Seshat was not really omnivorous, but her tastes were more eclectic than those of many cats; she licked the seasoned coating off the chicken before devouring it, with more daintiness than certain of the other patrons displayed, and joined us in our dessert of melon and sherbet.

By the time we finished, darkness was complete. Across the way the gateway of the Khan was hidden in the shadows, but there were lights beyond it, from the innumerable little shops and stalls. The shoppers and sight-seers passing in and out of the entrance included a number of people in European dress and a few in uniform.

"Nothing yet," I whispered to Emerson, while Ramses and Nefret argued amiably over how much melon Seshat should be allowed to eat. "It isn't that far away. We would hear a disturbance, wouldn't we?"

"Probably. Possibly. Cursed if I know." Emerson's curt and contradictory remarks told me he was as uneasy as I had become. Sitting on the sidelines is not something Emerson much enjoys. "Let's go over there."

"Go where?" Nefret asked.

"To the Khan," I replied, with my customary quickness. "I suggested we stroll a bit before returning home. Have we all finished?"

At one time the gates of the Khan were closed before the evening prayer. An increasing number of merchants were now "infidels"

— Greeks or Levantines or Egyptian Christians — and the more mercantile-minded of the Moslem Cairenes had seen the advantage of longer hours, especially when the city was bursting with soldiers who wanted exotic gifts and mementos. (Some of them spent their pay in quite another quarter of the city and took home mementos that were not so harmless. But that is not a subject into which I care to enter.)

The Khan el Khalili is not a single suk, but a sprawling collection of ramshackle shops and ruinous gateways and buildings. The old khans, the storehouses of the merchant princes of medieval Cairo, were architectural treasures, or would have been if they had been properly maintained. A few had been restored; most had not; mercantile establishments occupied the lower floors and huddled close to the flaking walls; but one might catch occasional glimpses of delicately arched windows and tiled doorframes behind the shops.

The smells were no less remarkable. Charcoal fires, donkey and camel dung, unwashed human bodies, spices and perfumes, baking bread and broiling meat blended into an indescribable whole. One may list the individual components, but that gives the reader no sense of the composite aroma. It was much more enjoyable than one might assume, in fact, and no worse than the sort of thing one encounters in many old European towns.

There were times, when the fresh breeze blew across the Kentish meadows carrying the scent of roses and honeysuckle, when I would gladly have exchanged it for a whiff of old Cairo.

As we wandered along the winding lanes, past the tiny cubicles in which silks and slippers, copper vessels and silver ornaments were displayed, I knew that Russell had not yet made his move. The whole place would have been buzzing with gossip had the police descended on a shop anywhere in the Khan. Many of them were closing, the shutters drawn down and the lamps extinguished, for the hour was growing late and the buyers were leaving to return to hotels and barracks. My anxiety could no longer be contained, and I pushed ahead of the others, setting a straight course for Aslimi's establishment. Had Russell been unable to make the necessary arrangements? Had he failed me? Curse it, I thought, I ought not have trusted him. I ought to have handled the matter myself — with a little assistance from Emerson.

Then it occurred to me that Russell might be waiting until the crowds had thinned out. Strategically it was a sensible decision. The fewer people who were about, the less chance that a bystander might be injured or that Aslimi's fellow merchants might be tempted to come to his aid. I hastened on, determined to be in at the kill. Then Emerson caught me up and I moderated my pace. Actually it was Emerson who moderated it for me, grasping my arm and holding it tightly.

"Proceed slowly or you will ruin everything," he hissed like a stage villain.

"Why are you in such a hurry, Aunt Amelia?" Nefret asked.

I turned. We were not far from Aslimi's now; his place was around the next curve of the lane. My ears were pricked. So, I observed, were those of Seshat, perched on Ramses's shoulder. Her eyes reflected the lamplight like great golden topazes. I forced a smile.

"Why, my dear, what makes you suppose I am in a hurry? That is my normal walking pace."

Seshat's tail began to switch and she leaned forward, sniffing the air. Her eyes had lost their luster; the lamp behind me had been extinguished. The shutter of the shop went down with a bang. The steel grille of the establishment next to it slammed into place. All along the lane, lights were going out and doors were closing.

"What is happening?" Nefret demanded. She moved closer to Ramses and took hold of his sleeve. He detached her fingers, gently but quickly, and caught Seshat in time to prevent her from taking a flying leap off his shoulder. Lowering her to the ground, he handed Nefret the scarf. "Hold on to her."

343

"Damnation," said Emerson under his breath. "They know. How do they know?"

It did smack of witchcraft, that unspoken recognition of danger that runs like a lighted fuse through a group of people who live with uncertainty and fear of the law. The mere sight of a uniform, or even a too-familiar face, would be enough of a warning.

"Know?" Nefret repeated. I could barely make out her features, it was so dark. "Know what?"

"That trouble is brewing," Emerson said calmly. A sudden outburst of noise, including a pistol shot, made him add, "Boiled over, rather. Follow me."

A lesser man might have ordered the rest of us to stay where we were. Emerson knew none of us would obey such an order anyhow, and until we had ascertained precisely what the situation was, it was safer to keep together. He switched on his electric torch and led the way along the lane.

The only open door was that of Aslimi's shop. As we hastened toward it, one of the men outside turned with an expletive and a raised weapon. Emerson struck it out of his hand.

"Don't be a fool. What is going on?"

"Is it you, O Father of Curses?" the fellow exclaimed. "We have him cornered — Wardani — or one of his men — there is a fifty-pound reward!"

344

I heard a gasp from Nefret, and then Ramses said, "Where is he?"

"He went into the back room. The door is barred but we will soon have it down!"

It certainly appeared that they would, and that they would smash every object in the shop during the process. Small loss, I thought, as an enthusiastic ax-wielder swept a row of fake pots off a shelf. But . . .

"Hell and damnation!" said Emerson, retreating in such haste that I had to run to keep up with him.

There are no alleyways or conventional back doors in the Khan el Khalili. Most of the shops are mere cubicles, open only at the front. We may have been among the few Europeans who knew that Aslimi's establishment did have another entrance — or, in this case, exit. It opened onto a space between two adjoining structures that was so narrow a casual observer would not have taken it for a passageway, and even knowing its approximate location we would have missed it in the darkness without the aid of Emerson's torch.

"Turn off your torch," Ramses said urgently.

Emerson's only answer was to thrust out his arm in a sweeping arc that flattened Ramses and Nefret against the adjoining wall. Standing square in the opening, he allowed the light to play for a moment on his face before he directed the beam into the passageway. Peering under his arm, I had a fleeting glimpse of a figure that halted for a moment before it disappeared.

"He saw me, I think," Emerson said in a satisfied voice. "After me, Peabody. Bring up the rear, Ramses, if you please."

"Shouldn't we tell the police?" I asked.

"No use now, they'd never track him in this maze."

"But we can!" Nefret exclaimed. She was panting with excitement.

"We may not have to," Emerson said.

Emerson thought he was being enigmatic and mysterious, but of course I knew what he meant. I always know what Emerson means. He had deliberately made a target of himself so the fugitive would see him and, as Emerson hoped, be willing to deal with him. Honesty and integrity, as I have always said, have practical advantages. Every man in Cairo knew that when the Father of Curses gave his word he would keep it.

As it turned out, Emerson's hope was justified. After we had squeezed through the passageway, where Emerson and Ramses had to go sideways, we emerged into a wider way and saw a shadow slip into the darker shadows of what appeared to be a doorway but was, in fact, another narrow street.

The Hoshasheyn district is a survival of medieval Cairo, and indeed most medieval cities must have been like it — dark, odorous, mazelike. Our quarry led us a merry dance, keeping close enough to be seen but not to be apprehended. Our progress was slightly impeded by Seshat, who in her eagerness to follow the fugitive (or possibly a rat) kept winding her lead round our limbs, until Ramses picked her up and returned her to his shoulder, gripping her collar with one hand. Emerson used his torch only when it was absolutely necessary. At last we came out into a small square. A fountain tinkled, like raindrops in the night.

"There," I cried, pointing to a door that stood ajar. Light showed through the opening.

"Hmmm," said Emerson, stroking his chin. "It has the look of a trap."

"It is," Ramses said. "He's there. By the door. He has a gun."

Farouk stepped into view. He did indeed have a gun. "So it is true, as they say of the Brother of Demons, that he can see in the dark. I was waiting for you."

"Why?" inquired Emerson.

"I am willing to come to terms."

"Excellent," I exclaimed. "Come with us, then, and we —"

"No, no, Sitt Hakim, I am not such a fool as that." He switched to English, as if he were demonstrating his intellectual abilities. "Come in. Close the door and bar it."

"What do you think?" Emerson inquired, looking at Ramses.

"In my opinion," I began.

"I did not ask your opinion, Peabody."

Farouk was showing signs of strain. "Stop talking and do as I say! Do you want the information I can give you or not?"

"Yes," Nefret said. Before any of us could stop her she had entered the room. Farouk backed up a few steps. He kept the pistol leveled at her breast.

The rest of us followed, naturally. The room was small and low ceilinged and very dirty. A single lamp cast a smoky light. Emerson closed the door and dropped the bar into place. "Make your proposal," he said softly. "I lose patience very quickly when someone threatens my daughter."

"Do you suppose I don't know that?" The light was dim, but I saw that Farouk's face was shining with perspiration. "I would not be fool enough to harm her, or any of you, unless you force me to, nor am I fool enough to go on with a game that is becoming dangerous to me. Now listen. In exchange for what I can tell you I want two things: immunity and money. You will bring the money with you when we next meet. A thousand English pounds in gold."

"A large sum," Emerson mused.

"You will think it low when you hear what I have to say. She has it. Will you pay it, Nur Misur?"

"Yes," she said quickly.

"Just a minute, Nefret," Emerson said. "Before you agree to a bargain you had better make certain what it is you are paying for. The whereabouts of Kamil el-Wardani are not worth a thousand pounds to us or even to the police."

"I have a bigger fish than that to put on your hook. Wardani is a pike, but I will give you a shark."

"Well-read chap, isn't he?" Emerson inquired of me.

"Do you agree or not?" Farouk demanded. "If you are trying to keep me here until the police come —"

"Furthest thing from my mind," said Emerson.

"We agree," Nefret exclaimed. "Where and when shall we deliver the money?"

"Tomorrow night . . . No. The night after. At an hour before midnight. There is a certain house in Maadi. . . ."

Seshat let out a strangled mew and turned her head to stare accusingly at Ramses. He put her on the floor and straightened to face Farouk. The young villain's lips had parted in a pleased smile. "You know the place," he said.

"I know it," Emerson said.

Farouk's smile broadened. "You will come alone, Father of Curses."

"I think not," Ramses said. "Why should we trust you?"

"What good would it do me to kill him, even if I could? I will have the money, and his promise that he will not tell the police for three days. I will trust his word for that. He is known to be a man of honor."

"Flattering," said Emerson. "Very well, I will be there."

"Good."

Nefret was closer to him than the rest of us. He had only to put out his arm. It wrapped round her and pulled her hard against his body.

I tightened my grip on Emerson, but for once it was Ramses whose temper got the better of his common sense. Quickly as he moved, the other man was ready for him. The barrel of the gun caught him across the side of the head and sent him sprawling.

"Stop it!" Nefret cried. "I'll go with him. Please, Professor! Ramses, are you all right?"

Ramses sat up. A dark trail of blood trickled down his cheek. "No. But I deserved it. Damned fool thing to do. If she comes to harm —"

"If she is injured it will be your fault," Farouk snarled. "I only want her as a hostage, in case I am cornered by the police. You had better pray that I am not."

"If it proves necessary we will head them off," Emerson said. The arm I held felt like stone, but his voice was unnaturally calm. "If she is not back within an hour —"

"I have never known people who talked so much," Farouk cried hysterically. "Stop talking! Go to the west gate of the Khan el Khalili and wait. She will come. In an hour! In the name of God, do not talk any more!"

He backed through the hanging at the other side of the room, pulling her with him.

"Don't even think of following," I said, as Ramses got to his feet.

"No," said Emerson. "He's on the edge of hysteria already. Ramses, that *was* a damned fool thing to do. Not that I blame you. I might have done the same if your mother had not had me in a firm grip."

"No, you wouldn't have," Ramses said. He wiped the blood from his mouth with the back of his hand. I offered him my handkerchief, which he took without acknowledging or even appearing to notice it. "You have better sense."

"Where is Seshat?" I asked, looking round the room.

"Gone after them, do you think?" Emerson asked.

"I don't know," Ramses said. "And at the moment I don't much care. Let's go."

It took us some time to make our way to the western gate of the Khan, which was now closed. The lanes were uncommonly deserted, even for that time of night. Evidently the police had gone in another direction, or had abandoned the hunt. There was a coffee shop under the tiled arch across from the entrance; we sat down on the wooden bench outside, the occupants having politely or prudently departed when they saw us. Emerson asked what I would like.

"Whiskey," I said grimly. "But I will settle for tea."

"She'll be all right," Ramses said. The trail of dried blood looked like a scar. I pried my handkerchief from his fingers and dipped it in the glass of water the waiter had brought.

"He did not strike me as a killer," I said.

"Oh, he's a killer, all right," Ramses said. "But he won't injure someone who has promised to give him a thousand pounds."

Emerson took out his watch. It was the third time he had done so since we sat down, and I informed him I would smash the confounded thing if he did it again. Ramses sat like a block of stone while I cleaned his face. Then he said, "While we are waiting we may as well get our story straight. Do you think she suspects our presence at Aslimi's was no accident?"

"Probably," said Emerson, reaching for his pocket, catching my eye, and extracting his pipe instead of his watch. "She's very quick. But so far as she knows, the police were after Wardani and nothing more. When Farouk offered us a bigger fish . . . Good Gad! You don't suppose that was an indirect attempt at blackmail, do you? It would certainly be worth a thousand pounds to keep him quiet if he knows you are —"

"Don't say it!" I exclaimed.

"I wasn't going to," Emerson said, giving me an injured look.

"I don't see how he could know," Ramses said. The only light came from a lamp that hung beside the grilled arch behind us. I could not make out his features, but I could see his hands. He had taken the handkerchief from me and was methodically tearing it into strips.

"Let us assume the worst," I said. "That he suspects — er — the truth about you and — er — the other one. It cannot be more than a suspicion, and he cannot have passed it on to his — er — employer, or he would not —"

"Curse it, Peabody, don't stutter!" Emerson snarled. "And don't assume the worst! How can you sit there and — and assume things, in that cold-blooded fashion, when she is . . . When she may be . . . What time is it?"

"Father, please don't look at your watch again," Ramses said, in a voice so tightly controlled I expected it to crack. "It's been less than half an hour. I don't believe we need assume anything other than the obvious. The proposition was as direct as he dared make, and Nefret obviously understood his meaning too. She was with you when Russell told you he believed Wardani was collaborating with the enemy. The question of my identity is another matter altogether. There is no reason to believe Farouk knows about that, and Nefret certainly does not."

"I wish we could tell her," I murmured.

"You know why we cannot." His eyes remained fixed on the gateway across the street. "Mother, she walked straight into that filthy den, with a gun pointing at her. She didn't hesitate, she didn't stop to think before she acted. She has always been guided by her heart instead of her head; she always will be. If she lost that fiery temper of hers she might say the wrong thing to the wrong person, and —"

His voice did crack then. I put my hand over his. "There is something more," I said. "Isn't there? Some particular reason why you don't trust her to hold her tongue. You never told us how Percy learned it was you who got him out of the bandit camp. Was it Nefret who gave you away?"

The hand under mine clenched into a fist. "Mother, for God's sake! Not now!"

"Better now than later, or not at all. You said only three people knew — David, Lia, and Nefret. It could not have been David or Lia, they did not arrive in Egypt until after Percy had concocted his dastardly scheme to have you accused of fathering his child. Percy had been pursuing Nefret —"

"She didn't mean to." He spoke in a ragged

whisper, his eyes still on the dark entrance to the Khan. "She couldn't have known what he would do."

"Of course not. My dear boy —"

"It's all right." He had got his breathing under control. "I don't blame her; how could I? It was one of those damnable, unpredictable, uncontrollable sequences of events that no one could have anticipated. All I'm saying is that there's no need for her to know more than she does already. What could she do but worry and want to help? Then I'd have to worry about her."

"You are being unfair," I said. "And perhaps just a little overprotective?"

"If I had been a little more protective or a little quicker, she wouldn't be out there in the dark alleys of Cairo with a man who is approximately as trustworthy as a scorpion." He lit another cigarette.

"You are smoking too much," I said.

"No doubt."

"Give me one. Please."

He raised his eyebrows at me, but complied, and lit it for me. The acrid taste was like a penance. "It was my fault," I said. "Not yours. You didn't want her to come tonight. I thought I was being clever."

"I can't stand this any longer," Emerson muttered. "I am going to look for her."

"It's all right," Ramses said on a long exhalation of breath. "There she is."

355

She came walking out of the dark, her steps dragging a little, her head turning. Emerson's chair went over with a crash. When she saw him running toward her she swayed forward into his outstretched arms, and he caught her to his breast.

"Thank heaven," I whispered.

Ramses said, "And there, by God, is the confounded cat! How the hell did she —"

"Don't swear," I said.

Nefret would not let Emerson carry her and she refused to go home. "Not until after I've had something to drink," she declared, settling into the chair Ramses held for her. "My throat is as dry as dust."

"Nervousness," said her brother, snapping his fingers to summon the waiter.

"Don't be so supercilious. Are you going to claim you weren't nervous about me?"

"I was nervous about what you might do to him," Ramses said.

Nefret glanced pointedly at the litter of cigarette ends on the ground beside him. Her face was smudged with dust and cobwebs, and her loosened hair had been tied back with a crumpled bit of fabric I recognized as the scarf she had lent Seshat for a lead. The cat sat down next to her chair and began grooming herself.

Emerson began, "What did he —"

"Let me tell it," Nefret said. She drank thirstily from the glass of tea the waiter had brought. We were the only customers left; it was long past the time when such places normally close, but no one would have had the audacity to mention this inconvenience to any of us.

"He didn't hurt me," she said, with a reassuring smile at Emerson. "After I had convinced him I wasn't going to run away he only held my arm, to guide me. I tried to question him, but every time I spoke he hissed at me. To keep quiet, I mean. I also tried to keep track of where he was taking me, but it was hopeless; you know how the lanes wind and turn. When he finally stopped I knew we must be outside the danger area, because he seemed calmer. So I asked him who the big fish was —"

"For the love of God, Nefret, you ought not have risked it," Emerson exclaimed. "Er — did he tell you?"

"He laughed and said something rude about women. That they were only good for two things, and that he expected me to supply one of them. He meant money, Professor," she added quickly. Emerson's face had gone purple. "I said I would get it first thing tomorrow and that we would meet him as we had promised. Then he said I was free to go, unless I wanted . . . That was when Seshat bit him."

Ramses reached down and rubbed the cat's head. "She was following you the whole time?"

"She must have been. I heard sounds, but I assumed it was rats. I had intended to ask him where the devil I was, but he left in rather a hurry, and it took me a while to get my bearings. Finally I decided I had better follow Seshat, who kept pushing at me, and she led me here."

Emerson was no longer purple, he was an odd shade of grayish lavender. "He asked you . . . if you wanted . . ."

"Asked," Nefret emphasized. "He was fairly blunt about it, but he didn't insist. Especially after Seshat bit him. Now, Professor, promise you won't lose your temper with him when you go to meet him. It is vitally important that we come to an agreement. Oh, curse it, I oughtn't have told you!"

"Lose my temper?" Emerson repeated. "I never lose my temper."

"You will deliver the money?"

"Certainly."

"And keep your promise to give him time to get away?"

"Of course."

Ramses, who had remained pensively silent, now remarked, "Shall I get the motorcar and bring it round?"

"We may as well all go," Nefret said. "I am perfectly capable of walking that short distance. Professor?"

"Hmph," said Emerson. "What? Oh. Yes."

We paid the sleepy proprietor of the café

358

lavishly and saw the lights go out as we started along the street. Emerson had his arm round Nefret and she leaned against him. Ramses and I followed; he had lifted the cat onto his shoulder. I stroked the animal's sleek flanks and she responded with a soft purr.

"We will have to think of a suitable reward for her," I said.

"Rewarding a cat is a waste of time. They think they deserve the best whatever they do."

"Her behavior was extraordinary, though."

"Not for one of Bastet's descendants. She's an odd one, though, I admit."

We went on a way in silence. Then I said, "Are you going with your father when he delivers the money?"

"I think I had better. You know what he intends to do, don't you?"

"Yes. I am a little surprised that Farouk did not set the meeting for tomorrow night."

"He has another appointment tomorrow night," Ramses said. "The same as mine."

8

After our exertions and our triumph the previous day, even Emerson was in no hurry to return to work. He allowed us to eat breakfast without mentioning more than twice that we were delaying him. Nefret's hair glittered and blew about as it always did after she had washed it. She had spent quite a long time in the bath chamber the night before, removing not only dust and perspiration but a more intangible stain. To a woman of her sensitive temperament the mere touch of such a man would be a contamination, and I had a feeling she had, for obvious reasons, minimized the unpleasantness of the encounter.

She looked none the worse for her most recent adventure, however, and as soon as Fatima left the room she returned to the subject that we had left undecided the previous night.

"I promised Sophia I would spend the afternoon at the clinic. There are several cases requiring surgery. I will stop by the banker's before I go there and —"

"No, you will not," said Emerson, spreading gooseberry jam on a piece of bread. "I will

360

go to the bank this evening."

"But sir —"

"The responsibility is mine," Emerson said.

For once, Nefret did not continue the argument. Cupping her chin in her hands, elbows on the table, she studied Emerson intently. "What precisely are you paying for, then? It is a large sum, as you said."

Emerson was ready for the question and was able to give an honest, if not entirely comprehensive, answer.

"You remember what Russell told us the night we dined with him? It appears that he was right. Wardani is collaborating with the enemy. Said, or whatever his name may be, must be one of Wardani's lieutenants. What I hope to get for my money is the name of the German or Turkish agent with whom they have been dealing."

Nefret nodded. "That's what I thought. He *would* be a big fish, wouldn't he?"

"Or she," said Ramses. "I am surprised, Nefret, to find you so ready to dismiss your own sex from consideration."

Nefret's lip curled. "A woman wouldn't hold such an important position. The Turks and the Germans, and all the rest of the male population of the world, think they're only good for wheedling information out of the men they seduce." After a moment she added, "Present company excepted."

"Hmph," said Emerson. "We've known a few women who were good for more than that. What's the use of speculating? We will know tomorrow. Come and give me a hand, Ramses, I want to have a closer look at the statue before we leave for Giza."

The statue stood where the men had left it, still swathed in its wrappings. After these were removed we all stood in admiring silence for a time. The statue was an idealized image of a man who was also a god, and it radiated dignity. The sure outlines of eyes and mouth, the perfectly proportioned torso and arms were in the best traditions of Old Kingdom sculpture. Some authorities believe that Egyptian art attained its highest perfection in this period. At that moment I would have agreed with them.

"It's beautiful," Nefret murmured. "I suppose it will go to the Museum?"

"Undoubtedly," Ramses replied. "Unless we can come up with something even finer that Quibell might be persuaded to take instead."

"No chance of that," Emerson grunted. "If we had half a dozen of them he might let us have one. We won't find any more, though."

"Don't you want me to take photographs?" Nefret asked.

"Later. Collect your arsenal, Peabody, and let's go."

I had to retrieve my sword parasol from

Jamal, the gardener, who also acted as handyman. He was Selim's second or third cousin once or twice removed, a slender stripling as handsome as Selim but without the latter's ambition and energy. I had explained to him about my parasol release sticking, and he had assured me it would be child's play for a man of his expertise to fix it. I tested it, of course, and was pleased and surprised to find that it was now working properly.

Selim and the rest of the crew were at the site when we arrived. Nefret left us soon after midday, by which time the men had reached bedrock. The cut blocks lining the shaft ended there, but the shaft went on down into the underlying stone of the plateau.

"It cannot be much farther," Selim said hopefully. Like myself, he was getting tired of sifting endless baskets of sand and rubble which contained not so much as a scrap of pottery.

"Bah," said my husband. "It could be another two meters. Or three, or four, or —"

Selim groaned.

"And," said Emerson remorselessly, "you will have to set a guard tonight, and every succeeding night until we have finished with the burial chamber. After the find we made yesterday, every ambitious thief in the area will want to have a go at it."

"But we have found nothing else," Selim said. "Only the statue."

"Yes," said Emerson.

We went on for a few more hours without reaching the bottom of the shaft. Glancing at the sun, from whose position he could tell time almost as accurately as he read a watch, Emerson called a halt to the work. When I expressed my surprise — for surely we now could not be far from the burial chamber — he gave me a sour look.

"We have an errand in the city, in case you have forgotten. I must say it would be a pleasant change to have one season without these confounded distractions."

I ignored this complaint, which I had heard often. "And after we have done our errand?" I inquired, giving *him* a meaningful look.

"I don't know what the devil you mean," said Emerson grumpily.

"I do," said Ramses, who had just joined us. "And the answer is no, Mother. I have already told Fatima I will be dining out this evening. Alone."

"Oh, is that what you meant?" Emerson beetled his brows at me. "The answer is no, Peabody."

Naturally I did not intend to let them bully me. I bided my time, however, until after we had bathed and changed. Nefret had not returned. After the customary squawks and squeals and misconnections I managed to ring through to the hospital. She was still in surgery, where she had been all afternoon. That was what I had hoped to hear. She would return to the house when she was finished and was not likely to go out again. Long sessions of surgery left her wrung-out physically, and sometimes emotionally as well.

When I joined Emerson and Ramses I discovered that they had arrived at a compromise, as Emerson termed it. We would all dine out together and then Ramses would go on to wherever he was going.

"It makes good sense, you see," Emerson explained.

"In what way?"

Pretending he had not heard, Emerson hastily got into the driver's seat. I ordered Ramses to sit in the tonneau next to me and subjected him to a searching inspection. He was looking very nice, I thought, except for a certain lumpiness about the fit of his coat. It could not be bandages; at his emphatic request (and because the healing process was proceeding nicely) I had reduced them in size.

"Are you carrying a firearm?" I inquired.

"Good God, no. The last thing I want to do is shoot someone."

"Take mine, then." I reached into my handbag.

"No, thank you." He caught hold of my wrist. "That little Ladysmith of yours is one of the most ineffective weapons ever invented. I cannot imagine how you ever manage to hit anything with it."

"I usually don't," I admitted. "But if someone has you in a death grip —"

"A knife is more efficient. Anyhow, the trick is to put the other fellow out of commission before he gets hold of you. Mother, what else have you got in that satchel? It is four times the size of your usual evening bag."

Before I could prevent him he had inserted his hand. "As I suspected," he said, pulling out a fold of rusty-black cloth. "You are not going with me tonight, so put the idea out of your head. How would it look for Wardani to bring a woman with him?"

"Tell me where you are going, then, and what you expect will occur."

"Very well."

In my surprise I inhaled a bit of my veiling and had to extract it from my mouth before I spoke. "What, no argument?"

"Since you already know more than you ought," said my son, "it is only sensible to tell you what more you need to know. We three will be seen dining in public and leaving the hotel together; I will slip away and you and Father will go directly home. The rendezvous is the ruined mosque near Burckhardt's grave. Father knows the place. And you needn't come along to protect me. David will be there, in safe concealment. He refused to let me go alone."

"God bless the boy," I murmured.

"Let us hope He will," said Ramses.

We went first to the bank, which was on the Sharia Qasr el-Nil. The transaction did not take long. None of Emerson's transactions take long. When we came out, Emerson was carrying my "satchel," as Ramses had termed it. A thousand pounds in gold weighs considerable.

It was only a short drive from the bank to the Savoy Hotel, where, as Emerson now condescended to inform me, we were dining. I did not ask him why, since he would have told me a pack of lies and I had no doubt his true motive would become apparent in due course. The Savoy was favored by the "Best People" of Cairo officialdom and by British officers.

I believe that none of the persons present will ever forget the sight of Emerson striding into the Savoy carrying a large black satin handbag trimmed with jet beads. Few men but Emerson would have done it. No man but Emerson could have done it with such aplomb. After we had been shown to a table he put the handbag on the floor under the table and planted both feet firmly upon it.

"Are you trying to provoke someone into robbing us?" I inquired. "You might as well have held up a placard announcing we have something of value in that bag."

"Yes," said Emerson, opening his menu.

"Not much likelihood of that," Ramses said. "No robber would rob the Father of Curses."

"Hmph," said Emerson, glowering at him over the menu. "Another of Daoud's sayings? Not one of his best."

He beckoned imperiously to the waiter. After we had got through the business of ordering our meals he planted his elbows on the table and looked curiously round the room.

Not all the tables were occupied. The hour was early for the "Best People." The only ones I recognized were Lord Edward Cecil and several of his set. Catching Lord Edward's eye, I nodded, and the gentleman hastily wiped the grin off his face.

"Who are those people with Cecil?" Emerson inquired.

I told him the names, which would mean no more to my Reader than they did to Emerson. "And that fellow who is smirking at Cecil?" he asked.

"His name is Aubrey Herbert," Ramses said. "One of Woolley's and Lawrence's associates. He was once honorary attaché in Constantinople."

"You know him?" Emerson demanded.

"I have met him." A spark of amusement shone in Ramses's half-veiled eyes. "I've been informed that he considers me frightfully underbred."

"The opinions of such persons should not

concern you," I said indignantly.

"I assure you, Mother, they do not. May I ask, Father, what prompts your interest in him?"

"I am looking for someone," said Emerson.

"Who?"

"That fellow Hamilton. You know him, don't you, Ramses? You can point him out."

"I don't see him," Ramses said. "What made you suppose he would be here?"

"He lives at the Savoy, doesn't he? I know!" Emerson pushed his chair back. "I will send up my card."

And off he went, fumbling in his pockets.

"Why this sudden interest in Major Hamilton?" I asked Ramses, nodding at the waiter to serve the soup. There was no sense in waiting for Emerson, who would return if and when he chose.

"I don't know."

"I do hope he doesn't mean to quarrel with the Major."

"Why should he?"

"The Major was somewhat rude at first, but Nefret said he was charming to her. Oh, dear. You don't think your father intends to warn the Major to stay away from her, or —"

"No, I don't."

"Or perhaps it is the little girl. He might wish —"

"Mother, it is surely a waste of time to speculate. Why don't you eat your soup

369

before it gets cold?"

"Speculation," I retorted, "is never a waste of time. It clears away the deadwood in the thickets of deduction."

Ramses retreated behind his serviette.

"Something caught in your throat?" his father inquired, returning and resuming his seat.

"No, sir. Was the Major in?" Ramses was a trifle flushed. I hoped he was not coming down with a fever.

"That we will discover in due course," said Emerson, beginning on his soup. He eats very neatly but very quickly; he finished before me and then resumed speaking. "I sent up a message saying I was here and wanted to see him."

The response to his message did not take the form he expected. Ramses saw her first; he said something under his breath, and directed my attention toward the door of the dining salon.

"It is only Miss Molly," I said. "Why such bad language?"

"I am beginning to think of her as a Jonah," Ramses said.

"Nonsense," said Emerson, turning to smile at the dainty little figure. She saw us at the same moment and came tripping toward us. I could tell from her affected walk and her pleased face that she thought she looked very grown-up. Her pink satin frock was so fresh she must have just put it on, and the ringlets framing her face were held back with a circlet of artificial rosebuds. Clothing makes the woman, as I always say; in this ensemble, which was more suitable for a jeune fille than a child, she did appear older than her admitted age. It must have been her indulgent uncle who had authorized the purchase.

Miss Nordstrom followed close on the heels of her charge. Her face was even more forbidding than it had been on the occasion of our first meeting, and I thought she looked very tired.

"I hope you are recovered," I said sympathetically.

"Thank you, Mrs. Emerson. It was only a mild — er — indisposition. You must excuse us for interrupting your dinner," she went on. "Come along, Molly, and don't keep the gentlemen standing."

"Can't we sit with you?" Molly asked me.

"As you see, we have almost finished dinner," I said.

"Oh, so have I. Finished dinner, I mean. Nordie said I could come downstairs for a sweet if I drank all my milk. The milk here tastes very horrid." She made a comical face at Emerson, who beamed down at her from his great height.

"Certainly, my dear. And you too, of course, Miss Er-um. Will the Major be joining us?"

The waiter brought two more chairs and we all shifted round, to the great inconvenience of all concerned. Miss Molly settled herself into her chair between me and Ramses with an air of great satisfaction.

"He can't," she said.

"I hope," said Ramses, "he is not suffering from an alimentary indisposition."

Molly giggled. "An upset stomach, you mean? No, that was —"

"The Major was about to leave for a dinner engagement when your message arrived," Miss Nordstrom said, turning pink. "He sends his regrets and hopes to see you another time."

"Ah," said Emerson. If he was disappointed he hid it very well. In fact, if I had not known better, I would have thought he appeared pleased.

Miss Molly took her time about ordering a sweet, asking everyone's opinion in turn. She divided her attention between Emerson and Ramses — getting very little in the way of conversation out of the latter — which left me to entertain Miss Nordstrom. An uphill job it was, too. All she could talk about was how much she disliked Cairo and yearned to return home.

"The food does not agree with me, Mrs. Emerson, and it is impossible to keep to a normal regimen with the child. At home, you know, one has complete control and a proper schedule for school hours, healthful exercise, and visits with parents. The Major's hours are so erratic I never know when he will be here, and then he wants to be with Molly."

"Quite natural," I said.

"Oh, yes, no doubt, but it does not make for proper discipline." She lowered her voice. "I assure you, I would not have allowed her to disturb you if he had not given in to her pleas. I do not hold with such late hours for children, or with such rich food."

The gâteau au rhum which Miss Molly was devouring certainly fell into that category. Her enjoyment was so obvious I could not help smiling.

"A little indulgence now and then does not hurt a child," I said. Miss Molly, talking with her mouth full, did not hear this. Ramses did. He gave me a sidelong look.

As Miss Molly chattered cheerfully on, I began to be a trifle uneasy about the time. Miss Nordstrom had declined a sweet but had accepted coffee. The dining salon was now full, and several acquaintances stopped by to say good evening on their way to or from their tables. One of these was Lord Edward.

The son of Lord Salisbury, he was in birth and lineage the most distinguished of all the young men whom Kitchener had brought into the Egyptian civil service. He had had no training for his position in the Finance Ministry, but by all accounts he had done an excellent job and was high in the confidence of the Government. He also had a certain reputation as the wittiest man in Cairo. Making fun of other people is the easiest way to acquire such a reputation. What he and his set said about us behind our backs I could only imagine. They would never have had the audacity to say it to our faces.

Gravely and deferentially he congratulated Emerson on the discovery of the statue, told me how well I looked, pinched Miss Molly's cheek, and asked after Nefret. Miss Nordstrom got a condescending nod. Last of all he addressed Ramses.

"I thought you might like to know that Simmons has been reprimanded and cautioned to behave himself in future."

"It wasn't entirely his fault," Ramses said.

"No?" Lord Edward raised his eyebrows. "I will tell him you said so. Good evening."

"We must say good evening too," Miss Nordstrom said, after the gentleman had sauntered away. "It is shockingly late."

Miss Molly looked rebellious. "I haven't finished my gâteau."

I said briskly, "You have had quite as much as is good for you. Run along with Miss Nordstrom. Good night to you both."

"And do give our regards to the Major," said Emerson.

"She is becoming something of a nuisance," I remarked, watching the young person being towed away by her governess. "What is the time?"

Ramses took out his watch. "Half past ten."

Emerson hailed the waiter by waving his serviette like a flag of truce.

"Emerson, please don't do that."

"You told me I mustn't shout at the fellow. What else am I supposed to do to get his attention? Finish your coffee and don't lecture."

I took a sip. "I must say the Savoy's cuisine does not live up to that of Shepheard's. The coffee has quite a peculiar taste."

Emerson, occupied with the bill, ignored this complaint, but Ramses said, "Mine was all right. Are you sure you didn't add salt instead of sugar?"

"I don't use sugar, as you ought to know."

"May I?" He took my cup and tasted the coffee. "Not nice at all," he said, wiping his mouth with his serviette. "Would you like another cup?"

"No time," said Emerson, who had finished settling the account.

He bustled us out of the hotel and into the motorcar. As we circled the Ezbekieh Gardens and headed north along the Boulevard Clos Bey, Ramses pulled a bundle from under the seat and began removing his outer garments. No wonder he had looked lumpy;

he was wearing the traditional loose shirt and drawers under his evening clothes.

While he completed the change of clothing I looked back, watching for signs of pursuit. Nothing except another motorcar or a cycle could have kept up with Emerson, and by the time we reached the Suq el-Khashir I felt certain we had not been followed. Turning to Ramses, I beheld a shadowy form swathed in flapping rags. The smell had already caught my attention. Pinching my nose, I said, "Why are your disguises so repulsive?"

"Nefret asked me that once." He adjusted a wig that looked like an untrimmed hedge. It appeared to be gray or white, and it smelled as bad as his clothes. "As I told her, filth keeps fastidious persons at a distance. I expect you and she would rather I rode romantically about in white silk robes, with a gold-braided agab holding my khafiya."

"I cannot see what useful purpose that would serve. The khafiya would become you well, though, with your dark eyes and hawk-like features and —"

"I'm sorry I brought it up," said Ramses, his voice muted by laughter. "Good night, Mother."

He was gone before I could reply, jumping nimbly over the side of the car as it slowed. Emerson immediately picked up speed.

After I had folded Ramses's good evening suit into a neat bundle, I leaned forward to speak to Emerson.

"How far has he to go?"

"A little over three miles. He should be there in plenty of time."

From Manuscript H

The Turk was late. Ramses, lying flat beside one of the monuments, had been there for some time before he heard the creak of wagon wheels. He waited until the slow-moving vehicle had passed before getting to his feet, and he was conscious of a cowardly reluctance to go on as he approached from an oblique angle, stepping carefully over fallen gravestones. Farouk and the others had already arrived, singly or in pairs as he had taught them.

He watched the proceedings for a while through a break in the wall. The Turk was in a hurry, so much so that he actually took a hand in the unloading. He started and swore when Ramses slipped in.

"Don't bother inspecting the merchandise," he growled. "It is all here."

"So you say."

"There is no time." He heaved a canvas-wrapped bundle at Ramses, who caught it and passed it on to Farouk.

"Shall I open it, sir?" Farouk asked.

"No," Ramses said curtly. "Get on with it."

He went to stand beside the Turk. "There

377

has been trouble. Did Farouk tell you?"

"I thought I should leave it to you, sir," said Farouk, in a voice like honey dripping.

Ramses moved back a step. "We cannot use Aslimi's place again. It was raided by the police last night. Every merchant in the Khan el Khalili is talking about it."

The Turk emitted a string of obscenities in a mixture of languages. "Who betrayed us?"

"Who else but Aslimi? He has been on the verge of cracking for weeks. How did you get away from them, Farouk?"

"You were surprised to see me here?"

"No. Every merchant in the Khan knows the police left without a prisoner. Were you warned in advance?"

"No, I was only very clever." He let out a grunt as the Turk passed a heavy box into his arms. "I know the alleys of the Hoshasheyn as a lover knows the body of his mistress. They came nowhere near me."

"They?" Ramses echoed the word.

"The police. Who else would I mean? No one came near me."

That settles that, Ramses thought. If Farouk were loyal to Wardani he would have mentioned his meeting with the Emersons and bragged of his cleverness in duping the formidable Father of Curses out of a thousand pounds in gold. He might be vain enough to think he could get the money without giving anything in return.

"Well done," Ramses murmured. "Aslimi cannot tell the police very much, because we did not tell *him* very much, but we must arrange for another drop. Do you know the Mosque of Qasr el-Ain? It's not much used except on Friday, when the dervishes whirl, and there is a small opening beside one of the marble slabs on the left wall as you go in. It's the one just under the text of the Ayet el-Kursee. You know your Koran, of course?"

"I will find the place. One more delivery. It will be the last."

"Is the time so close, then?"

"Close enough." The wagon was empty. The Turk got onto the seat and gathered the reins. "You will be told when to strike."

This time Ramses did not try to follow him. He stood watching — it would have been below Wardani's dignity to assist with manual labor — while his men covered the loads with bundles of reeds.

Asad edged up to him. "You have recovered, Kamil? You are well?"

"As you see." He put a friendly hand on the slighter man's shoulder, and Asad stiffened with pride.

"When will we see you again?"

"I will find you. Maas salameh."

He waited, with his back against the wall, listening to the creak of the cart wheels. Then he heard another sound, the roll of a pebble

379

under a careless foot. His knife was half out of the sheath before he recognized the dark outline. Too short for Farouk, too thin for any of the others: Asad. He stood uncertainly in the opening, his head moving from side to side, his weak eyes unable to penetrate the darkness.

"Here," Ramses said softly.

"Kamil!" He tripped and staggered forward, his arms flailing. "I had to come back. I had to tell you —"

"Slowly, slowly." Ramses caught his arm and steadied him. What a conspirator, he thought wryly. Clumsy, half-blind, timid — and loyal. "Tell me what?"

"What Mukhtar and Rashad are saying. They would not dare say it to your face. I told them they were fools, but they —"

"What are they saying?"

A great gulp escaped the other man. "That you should give out the guns now, to our people. That it is dangerous to keep them all in one place. That our people should learn how to use them, to practice shooting —"

"Without attracting the attention of the police? It would be even more dangerous, and a waste of ammunition."

Damnation, Ramses thought, even as he calmed his agitated lieutenant. He'd been afraid some bright soul would think of that. He thought he knew who the bright soul was.

"What did Farouk say?" he asked.

"Farouk is loyal! He said you were the leader, that you knew best."

Oh, yes, right, Ramses thought. Aloud, he said, "I am glad you told me. Go now, my friend, and make sure the weapons get to the warehouse. I count on you."

Asad stumbled out. Ramses waited for another five minutes. When he left the mosque it was on hands and knees and in the deepest shadow he could find. The cemetery was not one of the groups of princely medieval tombs mentioned in the guide book; it was still in use, and most of the monuments were small and poor. Crouching behind one of the larger tombs, he exchanged the old fakir's tattered dilk and straggling gray hair for turban and robe, and wrapped the reeking ensemble in several tight layers of cloth that reduced the stench to endurable proportions. He had been tempted to abandon the garment and wig, but it had taken him a long time to get them suitably disgusting.

He slung the bag over his shoulder in order to leave both hands free, buckled the belt that held his knife on over his robe, and started toward the road. Even though he had been half-expecting it, David's appearance made him start back, his hand on the hilt of his knife.

"A bit nervous, are we?" David inquired, his lip curling in the distorted smile of his disguise.

"What happened to the gauzy pantaloons?"

"I couldn't find a pair that was long enough."

They went on in silence for a time, and then Ramses said, "I thought you were going to follow the Turk."

"I concluded it would be a waste of time. We need to know where he's coming from, not where he goes after he has rid himself of his incriminating load. He probably hires a different team and wagon for each delivery, and I doubt he stays in the same place all the time."

"You're protesting too much," Ramses said with a faint smile. "But I don't mind admitting I appreciate your standing guard. Farouk makes me *extremely* nervous."

"He affects me the same way. Especially after what happened at Aslimi's."

"You heard?"

"Yes. The story is all over the bazaars." David's voice was neutral, but Ramses was painfully aware of his friend's disappointment.

"It's not over yet," he said. "We caught up with Farouk and came to an agreement with him. He wants a thousand pounds in gold in exchange for what he called a bigger fish than Wardani. Father is to meet him tomorrow night."

"It could be a ruse." David was trying not

to let his hopes rise.

"It could. But Farouk is an egotistical ass if he thinks he can trick an old hand like Father. He'll keep his word, to hand over the money and give Farouk three days immunity from pursuit — but first the innocent lad will spend a little time in our custody, while we verify the information."

It was typical of David that he should think first of the danger to someone else. "The Professor mustn't go alone. The fellow wouldn't think twice about knifing him in the back, or shooting him. Where are they meeting and when? I'll be there too."

"Not you, no." Ramses went on to explain. "His choice of a rendezvous was no accident. I don't know how much he knows, or how much he has told others, but if something goes wrong tomorrow night you must not be found near that house. I'm going with Father. Between the two of us we should be able to deal with Farouk. The little swine isn't going to shoot anybody until he has made certain we have the money with us."

The area between the edge of the cemetery and the city gate was an open field, used in times of festivals, now deserted. Pale clouds of dust stirred around their feet as they walked under a sickle moon through patches of weeds and bare earth. There was no sign of life but the night was alive with sounds and movements — the sharp baying of pariah dogs, the scuttle of rats. A great winged shape of darkness swept low over their heads and a brief squeak heralded the demise of a mouse or shrew. He had grown up amid these sounds and rich, variegated smells — donkey dung, rotting vegetation — and he had walked paths like this one many times with David. He was reluctant to break the companionable silence, but ahead the glow of those parts of Cairo that never slept — the brothels and houses of pleasure — were growing brighter, and there was more to discuss before they parted.

He gave David a brief account of what had transpired at the rendezvous, and David described his new abode, in the slums of Boulaq. "Biggest cockroaches I've ever seen. I'm thinking of making a collection." Then David said, "What's this I hear about a statue of solid gold?"

Ramses laughed. "You ought to know how the rumor-mongers exaggerate. It is a treasure, though." He described the statue and answered David's questions; but after David's initial excitement had passed, he said, "Strange place to find such a thing."

"I thought that would occur to you."

"But surely it must have occurred to the Professor as well. A royal Fourth Dynasty statue in the shaft of a private tomb? Even the most highly favored official would not possess such a thing; it must have been made to stand in a temple."

"Quite." They passed between the massive towers of the Bab el-Nasr, one of the few remaining gates of the eleventh century fortifications, and were, suddenly, in the city. "It hadn't been thrown in," Ramses went on. "It was upright and undamaged, and not far from the surface. The sand around it was loose, and the purported thieves had left a conspicuous cavity that pinpointed its position."

David pondered for a moment, his head bent. "Are you suggesting it was placed there recently? That the diggers wanted you to find it? Why? It's a unique work of art, worth a great deal of money in the antiquities market. Such benevolence on the part of a thief . . . Oh. Oh, good Lord! You don't think it could have been —"

"I think that's what Father thinks. He sees the dread hand of Sethos everywhere, as Mother puts it, but in this case he could be right. I've been half expecting Sethos would turn up; such men gather like vultures in times of war or civil disorder. He's been acquiring illegal antiquities for years, and according to Mother he keeps the finest for himself."

"But why would he plant one of his treasures in your tomb?" David emitted a gurgle of suppressed laughter. "A present for Aunt Amelia?"

"A distraction, rather," Ramses corrected. "Perhaps he's hoping that a superb find will make her concentrate on the excavation instead of looking for enemy agents."

"Has she been doing that?"

"Well, I think she may be looking for *him*. That is a damned peculiar relationship, David; I don't doubt she is devoted to Father, but she's always had a weakness for the rascal."

"He has rescued her from danger on several occasions," David pointed out.

"Oh, yes, he knows precisely how to manipulate her. If she is telling the truth about their encounters he hasn't made a single false move. She's such a hopeless romantic!"

"He may really care for her."

"You're another damned romantic," Ramses said sourly. "Never mind Sethos's motives; in a way I hope I'm wrong about them, because I'd hate to believe my mind works along the same lines as his."

"He could be one of the busy little spies in our midst, then — perhaps even the man in charge. That isn't a happy prospect." David sounded worried. "He has contacts all over the Middle East, especially in the criminal underground of Cairo, and if he is as expert at disguise as you —"

"He's even better. He could be almost anyone." Ramses added, in a studiously neutral voice, "Except Mrs. Fortescue."

"You're certain?" The undercurrent of laughter was absent from David's voice when he went on. "She could be one of his confederates. He had several women in his organization."

Ramses knew David was thinking of one woman in particular — the diabolical creature who had been responsible for his grandfather's death. She was out of the picture, at any rate, struck down by a dozen vengeful hands.

"Possibly," he said.

"What about that bizarre Frenchman who follows her about? Could he be Sethos?"

Ramses shook his head. "Too obvious. Have you ever seen anyone who looked more like a villain? He'd be more likely to take on the identity of a well-known person — Clayton, or Woolley, or . . . Not Lawrence, he's not tall enough."

They skirted the edge of the Red Blind district. A pair of men in uniform reeled toward them, arms entwined, voices raised in song. It was long past tattoo, and the lads were in for it when they returned to the barracks, but some of them were willing to endure punishment for the pleasures of the brothels and grog shops. Ramses and David stepped out of the way and as the men staggered past they heard a maudlin, off-key reference to someone's dear old mother. David switched to Arabic.

"Why don't you ask the Professor whom he suspects?"

"I could do that," Ramses admitted.

"It is time you began treating your parents like responsible adults," David said severely.

Ramses smiled. "As always, you speak words of wisdom. We must part here, my brother. The bridge is ahead."

"You will let me know —"

"Aywa. Of course. Take care. Maas salameh."

When we reached the house we learned from Fatima, who had waited up for us, that Nefret had returned an hour before. She had refused the food Fatima wanted to serve, saying she was too tired to eat, and had gone straight to her room. My heart went out to the child, for I knew she must be concerned about one of her patients. I stopped outside her door but saw no light through the keyhole and heard no sound, so I went on.

I myself was suffering from a slight alimentary indisposition. I put it down to nerves, and too much rich food, and having rid myself of the latter along the roadside, I accepted a refreshing cup of tea from Fatima before retiring. Needless to say, I did not sleep until I heard a soft tap on the door — the signal Ramses had grudgingly agreed to give on his return. I had promised I would not detain him, so I suppressed my natural impulses and turned onto my side, where I encountered a pair of large, warm hands. Emerson had been wakeful too. In silence he drew me into his embrace and held me until I fell asleep.

Somewhat to my surprise, for she was not usually an early riser, I found Nefret already at the breakfast table when I went down. One look at her face told me my surmise had been correct. Her cheeks lacked their usual pretty color and there were dark shadows under her eyes. I knew better than to offer commiseration or comfort; when I commented on her promptness she informed me somewhat curtly that she was going back to the hospital. One of her patients was in dire straits and she wanted to be there.

Only one thing could have taken my mind off what was to transpire that night, and we did not find it. The burial chamber at the bottom of the deep shaft had been looted in antiquity. All that remained were a few bones and broken scraps of the funerary equipment.

We left Ramses to catalog and collect these disappointing fragments, and climbed the rough ladders back to the surface. I remarked to Emerson, below me, "There is another burial shaft. Perhaps it will lead to something more interesting."

Emerson grunted.

"Are you going to start on it today?"

"No."

I stopped and looked down at him. "I understand, my dear," I said sympathetically. "It is difficult to concentrate on excavation when so much hangs on our midnight rendezvous."

Emerson described the said rendezvous with a series of carefully selected adjectives, adding that only I would stop for a chat while halfway up a ricketty ladder. He gave me a friendly little push.

Once on the surface, Emerson resumed the conversation. "I strongly object to one of the words you used, Peabody."

" 'Midnight' was not entirely accurate," I admitted.

"But it sounds more romantic than eleven P.M., eh?" Emerson's smile metamorphosed into a grimace that showed even more teeth and was not at all friendly. "That was not the word. You said 'our.' I thought I had made it clear to you that the first person plural does not apply. Must I say it again?"

"Here and now, with Selim waiting for instructions?" I indicated our youthful reis, who was squatting on the ground smoking and pretending he was not trying to overhear.

"Oh, curse it," Emerson said.

Daoud got the men started and Selim descended the ladder in order to take Ramses's place in the tomb chamber, assuming, that is, that Ramses would consent to be replaced. After assuring me that David was still safe and unsuspected, and that the delivery of weapons had gone off without incident, and that nobody had tried to murder him, he had rather avoided me. I knew why, of course. Injured and weakened as he had been, he had been forced to rely on me and on his father for help. Now he regretted that weakness of body and will, and wished he had not involved us. In other words, he was thinking like a man. Emerson was just as bad; I always had trouble convincing him that he needed me to protect him. Dealing with not one but two male egos was really going to be a nuisance.

I took Emerson to the rest place, where he immediately began lecturing. I sipped my tea and let him run on until he ran out of breath and patience. "So what have you to say?" he demanded.

"Oh, I am to be allowed to speak? Well, then, I grant you that if he is alone, you and Ramses can probably manage him by yourselves, always assuming he doesn't assassinate one or both of you from ambush as you approach. However —"

"Probably?" Emerson repeated, in a voice like thunder.

"However," I continued, "it is likely that he will be accompanied by a band of ruffians like himself, bent on robbery and murder.

They could not let you live, for they would know you would —"

"Stop that!" Emerson shouted. "Such idle speculation —"

"Clears away the deadwood in the thickets of deduction," said Ramses, appearing out of thin air like the afrit to which he had often been compared. Emerson stared at him in stupefaction, and Ramses went on, "Father, why don't you tell her precisely what we are planning to do? It may relieve her mind."

"What?" said Emerson.

"I said —"

"I heard you. I also heard you utter an aphorism even more preposterous than your mother's efforts along those lines. Don't you start, Ramses. I cannot put up with two of you."

"It was one of Mother's, as a matter of fact," Ramses said, taking a seat on a packing case. "Well, Father?"

"Tell her, then," Emerson said. He added gloomily, "It won't stop her for long, though."

"It will be all right, Mother," Ramses said. He smiled at me; the softening of his features and the familiar reassurance disarmed me — as he had no doubt counted on its doing. "Farouk is not collaborating with the Germans for ideological reasons. He's doing it for the money. We are offering him more than he could hope to get from the other side, so he will come to the rendezvous. He won't want to share it, so he will come alone. He won't shoot Father from behind a wall because he won't know for certain that Father has the money on his person. We will frighten him off if we go in force, so we can't risk it."

I started to speak. Ramses raised his voice and went on. "I will precede Father by two hours and keep watch. If I see anything at all that contradicts my assumptions, or that makes me uneasy, I will head Father off. Is that acceptable to you?"

"It still seems to me —"

"One more thing." Ramses fixed intent black eyes on me. His face was very grave. "We are counting on you to keep Nefret out of this. She will want to go with us, and she mustn't. If she were present, Father would be worrying about her instead of thinking of his own safety."

"And so would you," I said.

Emerson had listened without attempting to interrupt; now he glanced at his son, and said, "Ramses is right. In all fairness I must point out that he acted as impulsively as Nefret, and he was lucky to get away with only a knock on the head."

Ramses's high cheekbones darkened. "All right, it was stupid of me! But if she had let me enter that room first, you can be damned sure Farouk would never have laid a hand on her. I'd probably do something equally stupid if he threatened her again, and so would you, Father. Supposing there is a scrap — wouldn't she wade right in, trying to help us, and wouldn't you fall over your own feet trying to get her out of it?"

"I have heard of such things happening," said Emerson. He looked at me. "No doubt you will accuse us of being patronizing and overly protective —"

"I do. You are. You always have been. But . . ."

Emerson heard the note of hesitation in my voice, and for once he had the good sense to keep quiet. His blue eyes were steady, his lean brown face resolute. I looked from him to Ramses, whose unruly black hair curled over his temples and whose well-cut features were so like his father's. They were very dear to me. Would I put them at even greater risk by insisting on playing my part in the night's adventure?

I was forced to admit that I might. I was also forced to admit that Ramses's analysis of Nefret's character was not entirely inaccurate. Initially it had struck me as being unjust and prejudiced; but I had had time to think about it, and incident after confirmatory incident came back to me. Some of her early escapades might be excused as the result of youthful overconfidence, such as the time she had deliberately allowed herself to be captured by one of our most vindictive opponents, in the hope of rescuing her brother; but maturity had not changed her very much. She had been a full-grown woman when she entered a Luxor bordello and tried to persuade the girls to leave. Then there was the time she had blackmailed Ramses into letting her go with him and David into one of the vilest parts of Cairo in order to retrieve a stolen antiquity — and the time she had single-handedly attacked a thief armed with a knife . . . The list went on and on. Emerson's description of Ramses might equally have been applied to Nefret; she was as brave as a lion and as cunning as a cat, and as stubborn as a camel, and when her passions were aroused she was as quick to strike as a snake. Even her hasty, ill-advised marriage . . .

"Very well," I said. "I still think you are being a trifle unjust to Nefret; she's got you and David out of a few nasty situations, you know."

"I know what I owe her," Ramses said quietly.

"However," I continued, "I agree to your proposal — not because I believe *she* cannot be trusted to behave sensibly but because I know *you* and your father cannot."

Ramses's tight lips relaxed. "Fair enough."

"Hmph," said Emerson.

We scattered to our various tasks.

It was after midday when Nefret turned up. I had been sifting a particularly unproductive lot of rubble for several hours, and was not unwilling to be interrupted. I rose to my feet and stretched. She had changed to her working clothes and I could tell by her brisk stride that she was in a happier state of mind than she had been that morning. She was carrying a covered basket, which she lowered to the ground beside me.

"Not more food?" I exclaimed. "We brought a luncheon basket."

"You know Fatima," Nefret said. "She thinks none of us eat enough. While I was bathing and changing she made kunafeh especially for Ramses; she says he is all bones and skin, and needs to be fattened. Where is he? If he balks, we will stuff it down his throat, the way they do with geese."

"And did even in ancient times," I said, smiling. "Go and call him and Emerson to luncheon, then. They are inside the chapel."

Fatima had also sent a dish of stewed apricots and a sliced watermelon, which had been nicely cooled by evaporation during the trip. We all tucked in with good appetite, including Ramses. The kunafeh was one of his favorite dishes, wheat-flour vermicelli fried in clarified butter and sweetened with honey. Nefret teased him by repeating Fatima's criticism, and he responded with a rather vulgar Arabic quotation about female pulchritude, which clearly did not apply to her, and Emerson smiled fondly at both of them.

"Matters went well today?" he inquired.

Nefret nodded. "I thought last night I would lose her, but she's much better this morning." She spat a watermelon seed neatly into her hand and went on, "You'll never guess who called on me today."

"Since we won't, you may as well tell us," said Ramses.

The next seed just missed his ear. His black eyes narrowed, and he reached for a slice of melon.

"I strictly forbid you to do that, Ramses," I exclaimed. "You and Nefret are too old for those games now."

"Let them enjoy themselves, Peabody," Emerson said indulgently. "So, Nefret, who was your visitor?"

Her answer wiped the amiable smile from Emerson's face. "That degenerate, slimy, contemptible, disgusting, perverted, loath-some —"

"He was very polite," Nefret interrupted. "Or should I have said 'she'?"

"The fact that el-Gharbi prefers to wear women's clothing does not change his sex — uh — gender," Ramses said. He looked as in-scrutable as ever, but I had seen his involun-tary start of surprise. "What was he doing at the hospital?"

"Inquiring after one of 'his' girls." Nefret's voice put quotation marks round the pro-noun. "The same one I operated on last night. He said he had sent her to us, and that the man who hurt her had been . . . dealt with."

Emerson had got his breath back. "That crawling, serpentine trafficker in human flesh, that filthy —"

"Yes, Professor darling, I know the words too. And his taste in jewelry and perfume is quite dreadful!" Observing, from Emerson's apoplectic countenance, that he was in no mood for humor, she threw her arm round his shoulders and kissed him on the cheek. "I love your indignation, Professor dear. But I've seen worse and dealt with worse since I started the clinic. El-Gharbi's good will can help me to help those women. That is the important thing."

"Quite right," I said approvingly.

"Bah," said Emerson.

Ramses said, "Well done, Nefret."

The watermelon seed hit him square on the chin.

My mind was not entirely on my rubbish that afternoon. I was racking my brain trying to think of a way of preventing Nefret from accompanying Emerson and Ramses. A number of schemes ran through my mind, only to be dismissed as impracticable. The inspiration that finally dawned was so remarkable I wondered why it had not occurred to me before.

We dined earlier than was our custom,

since I wanted to make sure Ramses ate a proper meal before leaving. It would take him an hour to reach Maadi by the roundabout routes he had chosen in order to get into position unobserved and unsuspected. When the rest of us retired to the drawing room for after-dinner coffee, he slipped away, but of course Nefret noticed his absence almost immediately and demanded to know where he was.

"He has gone," I replied, for I had determined to tell her the truth instead of inventing a story she would not have believed anyhow.

Nefret jumped up from her chair. "Gone? Already? Hell and damnation! You promised —"

"My dear, you will overturn the coffee tray. Sit down and pour, if you please. Thank you, Fatima, we need nothing more."

Nefret did not sit down, but she waited until Fatima had left the room before she exploded. "How could you, Aunt Amelia? Professor, you let him go alone?"

The bravest of men — I refer, of course, to my spouse — quailed before that furious blue gaze. "Er . . ." he said. "Hmph. Tell her, Amelia."

Nefret pronounced a word of whose meaning I was entirely ignorant, and bolted for the door. I do not know where she thought she was going; perhaps she believed she could intercept Ramses, or (which is more likely) perhaps she was not thinking at all. She did not get far. Emerson moved with the pantherlike speed that had given rise to one of Daoud's more memorable sayings: "The Father of Curses roars like a lion and walks like a cat and strikes like a falcon." He picked Nefret up as if she weighed nothing at all and carried her back to her chair.

"Thank you, Emerson," I said. "Nefret, that will be quite enough. I understand your concern, my dear, but you did not give me a chance to explain. Really, you must conquer this habit of rushing into action without considering the consequences."

I half-expected her to burst into another fiery denunciation. Instead her eyes fell, and the pretty flush of anger faded from her cheeks. "Yes, Aunt Amelia."

"That is better," I said approvingly. "Drink your coffee and I will tell you the plan."

I proceeded to do so. Nefret listened in silence, her eyes downcast, her hands tightly folded in her lap. However, she did not miss Emerson's attempt to tiptoe out of the room. Admittedly, Emerson is not good at tiptoeing.

"Where is he going?" she demanded fiercely.

"To get ready." I was not at all averse to his leaving, since it enabled me to speak more candidly. "For pity's sake, Nefret, don't you suppose that I too yearn to accompany them? I agreed to stay here and keep you with me because I believe it is the best solution."

Her mutinous look assured me she was unconvinced. I had another argument. It was one I was loath to employ, but honesty demanded I should. "There have been times, not many — one or two — in the past, when my presence distracted Emerson from the struggle in which he was engaged, and resulted in considerable danger to him."

"Why, Aunt Amelia! Is it true?"

"Only once or twice."

"I see." Her brow cleared. "Would you care to tell me about them?"

"I see no point in doing so. It was a long time ago. I know better now. And," I continued, before she could pursue a subject that clearly interested her a great deal, and which I was not anxious to recall, "I am giving you the benefit of my experience. Their plan is a good one, Nefret. They swore to me that they would retreat in good order if matters did not work out as they expect."

Her slim shoulders sagged. "How long must we wait?"

I knew then I had won. "They will come straight back, I am sure. Emerson knows if he does not turn up in good time I will go looking for him. He would do anything to avoid that!"

From Letter Collection B

Dearest Lia,

Do you still keep my letters? I suspect you do, though I asked you to destroy them — not only current letters, but the ones I wrote you a few years ago. You said you liked to reread them when we were apart, because it was like hearing my voice. And I said — I'm sorry for what I said, Lia darling! I was horrid to you. I was horrid to everyone! You have my permission — formal, written permission — to keep them if you wish. I would be glad if you did. Someday I may want — I hope I may want — to read them again myself. There was one in particular . . . I think you know which one.

I'm in a fey mood tonight, as you can probably tell. I've put off writing to you because there is so much I want to say that can't be said. The thought that a stranger — or worse, a person I know — might read these letters is constantly in my mind; it's as if someone were lurking behind the door listening to our private thoughts and confidences.

So I will confine myself to facts.

Aunt Amelia and I are alone this evening; the Professor and Ramses have gone out. With the lamps lit and the curtains drawn, this cavernous parlor looks almost cozy, especially with Aunt Amelia darning socks. Yes, you heard me: she is darning socks! She gets these housewifely attacks from time to time, heaven only knows why. Since she darns as thoroughly as she does everything, the stockings end up with huge lumps on toes or heels, and the hapless wearer thereof ends up with huge blisters. I think Ramses quietly and tactfully throws his away, but the Professor, who never pays any attention to what clothing he puts on, goes round limping and swearing.

I take it back. This room is not cozy. It never can be. A fluffy, furry animal might help, but I can't have the puppies here; they chew the legs of the furniture and misbehave on the Oriental rugs. I even miss that wretched beast Horus! I couldn't have brought him, since he refuses to be parted from Sennia, but I wish I had a cat of my own. Seshat spends most of her time in Ramses's room.

Someday, when we are all together again, we will find a better house, or build one. It will be large and sprawling, with courtyards and fountains and gardens, and plenty of room, so we can all be together — but not too close together! If you would rather, we'll get the dear old Amelia out of drydock for you and David and the infant. It will happen someday. It must.

Goodness, I sound like a little old lady, rocking and recalling the memories of her youth. Let me think what news I can write about.

You asked about the hospital. One must be patient; it will take time to convince "respectable" women — and their conservative husbands — that we will not offend their modesty or their religious principles. There has been one very hopeful development. This morning I had a caller — none other than el-Gharbi, the most powerful procurer of el Was'a. They say he controls not only prostitution but every other illegal activity in that district. I had seen him once or twice when I went to the old clinic, and an unforgettable figure he was — squatting on the mastaba bench outside one of his "Houses," robed like a woman and jangling with gold. When he turned up today, borne in a litter and accompanied by an escort — all young and handsome, elegantly robed and heavily armed — our poor old doorkeeper almost fainted. He came rushing to find me. It seems el-Gharbi had asked for me by name. When I went out, there he was, sitting cross-legged in the litter like some grotesque statue of ebony and ivory, veiled and adorned. I could smell the patchouli ten yards away.

When I told the family about it later, I thought the Professor was going to explode. While he sputtered and swore, I repeated that curious conversation. The girl I had operated on the night before was one of his; he had sent her to me. He had come in person because he had heard a great deal about me and he wanted to see for himself what I was like. Odd, wasn't it? I can't imagine why he should be interested.

Did I call him names (I know a lot of good Arabic terms for men like him) and tell him never to darken my door again? No, Lia, I did not. Once I might have done, but I've learned better. It is pointless to complain that the world isn't the way it ought to be. By all accounts he is a kinder master than some. I told him I appreciated his interest and would be happy to treat any of the women who needed my services.

The Professor was not so tolerant. "What damnable effrontery!" was the least inflammatory of the remarks he made. When he wound down, it was Ramses's turn.

Someone who didn't know him well might have thought he was bored by the discussion. He was sitting on the ground with his back against a packing case and his knees raised and his head bent, devouring Fatima's food. Ramses is never a model of sartorial elegance, as you know; he'd been running his fingers through his hair, to push it out of the way, and it was all tangled over his forehead. Perspiration streaked his face and throat and bare forearms, and his shirt was sticking to his shoulders. He raised his head and opened his mouth.

"You need a haircut," I said. "And don't lecture me."

"*I know I do. I wasn't going to lecture you. I was about to say, 'Well done.' *"

Can you imagine that, Lia — Ramses paying me a compliment? You know what a low opinion he has of my good sense and self-control. I wish . . .

I can't write any more. It is very late and and my hand is cramped from holding the pen. Please excuse the atrocious writing. Aunt Amelia is folding up her mending. I love you, Lia, dear.

9

When Nefret asked how long I meant to wait, I did not know the answer. Farouk might be late (although an individual expecting to receive a large sum of money generally is not), and there would certainly be a heated discussion when Emerson insisted upon verification before payment. I did not doubt my formidable husband's ability to overcome an opponent, even one as treacherous as Farouk, but Emerson and Ramses would then have to bind and gag the young villain and transport him across the river to the house. The journey could take anywhere from an hour to two hours, depending on the available transportation, and precipitate action by Nefret and me would only confirm Emerson's unjust (for the most part) opinion of women.

In order to discipline myself, I had turned to a task I particularly dislike — mending. Nefret read for a while, or pretended to; finally she declared her intention of writing to Lia. I ought to have emulated her; my weekly letter to Evelyn was overdue; but it was confounded difficult to write a cheery, chatty letter when I did not feel at all cheery, and it was impossible to chat about the subject uppermost in my mind. We were both masking our true feelings; when Evelyn wrote me she did not mention her worries about her boys in the trenches and her other boy, dear as a son, in exile so far away. I must also prevaricate and equivocate; it would only increase Evelyn's anxiety if she learned that David and Ramses were also risking their lives for the cause. Nor had I forgotten Ramses's warning to Nefret, that the post would almost certainly be read by the military authorities, and his even more pointed remarks about the need for secrecy.

I wondered what the deuce Nefret found to write about. Perhaps her letters to Lia were as stilted as mine to Evelyn.

By half past one o'clock in the morning I had mended eight pairs of stockings. Later I had to discard all but the first pair; I had sewed the toes to the heels and the tops to the soles, passing my needle in and out of the fabric without paying the least attention to what I was doing. After I had run the needle deep into my finger for the tenth time I bit off the thread and pushed the sewing basket aside. Nefret looked up from her letter.

"I've finished," she said. "Is it time?"

"We will wait another half hour."

Nefret bowed her head in silent acquiescence. The lamplight gilded her bright hair and shone on her ringless hands, which rested in her lap. She had removed her wedding ring the day after Geoffrey died. I never asked what she had done with it.

I was trying to think of something comforting to say when Nefret looked up. "They are safe," she said gently. "I'm sure nothing has happened."

"Of course," I said.

Twenty-seven minutes more. I began planning what I would do. At my insistence, Emerson had described the location of the house, which I had never seen. Should we drive the motorcar, disdaining secrecy, or find a boat to take us directly across the river?

Twenty-five minutes. How slowly the time passed! I decided the motorcar would be quicker. I would send Ali after Daoud and Selim . . .

At twenty minutes before two, the shutters rattled. I sprang to my feet. Nefret ran to the window and flung the shutters back. I heard a thump and saw movement, and there was Seshat, sitting on the windowsill.

"Curse it," I exclaimed. "It is only the cat."

"No." Nefret looked out into the dark garden. "They are coming."

Like a butler ushering visitors into a room, Seshat waited for the men to reach the window before she jumped down onto the floor. Emerson was the first to enter. Ramses followed him, and drew the shutters closed.

"Well?" I cried. "Where is he? Where have you put him?"

"He did not come," Emerson said. "We waited for over an hour."

They had had time to accept the failure of our hopes, though I could see it weighed heavily upon them. I turned away for fear Nefret would see what a terrible blow the news had dealt me. Her expressive face had mirrored her own disappointment, but she did not, could not, know how much was at stake.

"So it was a trick after all?" I muttered.

Emerson unfastened the heavy money belt and tossed it onto the table. "I wish I knew. He could have eluded us that night; why would he offer an exchange and then renege? Come and sit down, my dear, I know you have been under quite a strain. Would you like a whiskey and soda?"

"No. Well . . ."

Ramses went to the sideboard. "Would you care for something, Nefret?"

"No, thank you." She sat down and lifted Seshat onto her lap.

"He told Emerson to come alone," I said, taking the glass Ramses handed me. "If he saw you —"

"He did not see me." Ramses does not often venture to interrupt me. I forgave him when I saw his hooded eyes and the lines of strain that bracketed his mouth. He was wearing a suit of dull brown he had recently purchased in Cairo; when I came across it in his wardrobe (in the process of collecting things to be laundered or cleaned), I had wondered why he had selected such an unbecoming shade, almost the same color as his tanned face. I ought to have realized. With the coat buttoned up to his throat he would be virtually invisible at night.

"I beg your pardon," I said. "Please sit down."

"Thank you, I would rather not."

He removed his coat. I let out an involuntary cry of surprise. "You are carrying a gun. I thought you never —"

"Do you suppose I would sacrifice Father's safety to my principles?" He unbuckled the straps that held the holster in place under his left arm and placed the whole contraption carefully down on a table. "I assure you, it was not an idle boast when I said Farouk could not have seen me. Darkness was complete before I reached Maadi, and I spent the next three hours roosting in a tree. There was the usual nocturnal traffic — the occupants of the new villas coming and going in their carriages, the less-distinguished residents on foot. By the time Father got there, no one had come near the house for over an hour. Mahira goes to bed at sundown. I could hear her snoring."

Emerson took up the tale. "Knowing Ramses would have warned me off if Farouk had played us false, I stood under the

411

damned tree, with my back against the wall of the house. Since I could not strike a light to look at my watch, I had no idea how much time had passed; it seemed like a year before Ramses slid down to the ground and spoke to me."

"How did you know the time?" I asked Ramses, who was prowling restlessly round the room.

"Radium paint on the hands and numerals of my watch. It glows faintly in the dark."

Nefret had been stroking the cat, who permitted this familiarity with her usual air of condescension. Now Nefret said, "Perhaps this evening was a test, to make certain you would meet his demands."

"That is possible," Ramses agreed. "In which case he will communicate with us again."

He swayed a little, and caught hold of the back of a chair. Nefret removed the cat from her lap. "I am going to bed. The rest of you had better do the same."

I waited until the door had closed before I went to Ramses. "Now tell me the truth. Were you hurt? Was your father injured?"

"I did tell you the truth," Ramses said, with such an air of righteous indignation that I could not help smiling. "It happened just as we said, Mother. I am only a little tired."

"And disappointed," said Emerson, who had lit his pipe and was puffing away with great satisfaction. "Ah. All those hours without the comforting poison of nicotine added to my misery. Devil take it, Peabody, it was a blow."

"It will be a blow to David too," Ramses said. "I do not look forward to telling — Mother, put that down! There is a shell in the chamber."

"My finger was not on the trigger," I protested.

He took the weapon from my hands, and Emerson, who had leaped to his feet, sat down with a gusty sigh. "Don't even think about 'borrowing' that pistol, Peabody. It is far too heavy for you."

"Quite an ingenious contrivance," I said, examining the holster. "Is this a spring inside? Ouch."

"As you see," said Ramses.

"Your invention?"

"My refinement of someone else's invention."

"Could you —"

"No!" Emerson said loudly.

"How did you know what I was going to ask?"

"I know you only too well, Peabody," said my husband, scowling. "You were about to ask him to fit that little gun of yours with a similar spring. I strictly forbid it. You are already armed and dangerous."

"Speaking of that, Emerson, I am having

problems with my sword parasol. Jamal claimed he had repaired it, but the release keeps sticking."

"I'll have a look at it if you like, Mother," Ramses said. His momentary animation had faded, leaving him looking deathly tired.

"Never mind, my dear, I will let Jamal have another try. Go to bed. As for David, let him hope a little longer. All is not lost; we may yet receive a message."

I spoke confidently and encouragingly, but I was conscious of a growing sense of discouragement that troubled my slumber and shadowed my thoughts all the next day. Blighted hope is harder to bear than no hope at all.

At breakfast next morning Emerson asked Nefret to take photographs of the statue. I stayed to help her with the lighting. We employed the same mirror reflectors we were accustomed to use in the tombs; they gave a subtler and more controlled light than flash powder or magnesium wire. It took us quite some time, since of course long exposures were necessary.

When we had finished and were on our way to join the others at Giza, Nefret remarked, "I am surprised the Professor has not stationed armed guards all round the statue, by night and by day."

"My dear girl, how could a thief make off with something so heavy? It required forty of our sturdiest workmen to lift the thing!"

Nefret chuckled. "It is rather a ludicrous image, I admit: forty thieves, just as in 'Ali Baba,' staggering along the road with the statue on their shoulders, trying to appear inconspicuous."

"Yes," I said, chuckling. It echoed somewhat hollowly. At that time the statue was the least of my concerns.

Before we parted for the night, we had agreed on certain steps to be taken the following day. Ramses, who was still inclined to impart information in dribbles, explained that he and David had arranged several means of communication. He had on one occasion actually passed a message to David when I was present, for one of David's roles was that of a flower vendor, outside Shepheard's hotel. I remembered the occasion well; the flowers had been rather wilted. If we had not heard from Farouk by mid-afternoon we would go to Shepheard's for tea, and after Ramses had seen David, Ramses would try to locate Farouk. He refused to emit even a dribble of information explaining how he meant to go about it, but I assumed that the conspirators had ways of contacting one another in case of an emergency.

None of this information could be imparted to Nefret. If she went with us to Shepheard's I would have to find some means of distracting her while Ramses approached the flower vendor; David's disguise had been good enough to fool me, but her keen eyes might not be so easily deceived.

As it turned out, my scheming was unnecessary. Shortly after midday we received a message that threw all our plans into disarray.

Instead of using basket carriers, as we had done in the past, Emerson had caused to be laid down between the tomb and the dump site a set of tracks along which wheeled carts could run. As I stood watching one of the filled carts being pushed toward the dump, a man on horseback approached. I was about to shout at him to go away when I realized that he was in the uniform of the Cairo Police. I hastened to meet him. At my insistence he handed over the letter he carried, which was in fact directed to Emerson.

This would not have prevented me from opening the envelope had not Emerson himself joined us. He too had recognized the uniform; he too realized that something serious must have occurred. Thomas Russell might as well have sent along a town crier to announce in stentorian tones that the messenger was from him. The uniform was well-known to all Cairenes.

"I was told to wait for an answer, sir," said the man, saluting. "It is urgent."

"Oh? Hmph. Yes."

With maddening deliberation Emerson extracted a sheet of paper from the envelope. I stood on tiptoe to read it over his shoulder.

Professor Emerson:
   I believe you can be of assistance to the police in a case which came to my attention early this morning. The evidence of your son is also required. Please come to my office at the earliest opportunity.

      Sincerely,

      Thomas Russell.

      P.S. Do not bring Miss Forth.

"I will be there in two hours," Emerson said to the officer.

"Oh, no, Emerson, we must go straightaway! How can you bear the suspense? He would not have —"

"Two hours!" Emerson bellowed, drowning me out. The policeman started convulsively, saluted, banged his hand painfully against the stiff brim of his helmet, and galloped off.

"I am sorry, Emerson," I murmured.

"Hmmm, yes. You are sometimes as impulsive as . . . Ah, Nefret. Have you finished the photographing?"

"No, sir, not quite." She was bareheaded, her cheeks rosy with heat, her smile broad and cheerful. "Selim came rushing into the tomb and said there was a policeman here asking for you. Are you under arrest, or is it Aunt Amelia?"

Standing behind her, so close that the hair on the crown of her golden head brushed his chin, Ramses said lightly, "My money is on Mother."

"Damned if I know what he wants," Emerson grumbled. "He might have had the courtesy to say. Assist the police indeed! I suppose we had better go."

"We?" Ramses repeated.

"You and I."

"But this must be about what happened in the Khan the other night," Nefret exclaimed. "I wondered why the police had not got round to questioning us. We must all go. It is our duty as good citizens to assist the police!"

Emerson looked hopefully at his son. Ramses shrugged, shook his head, and inquired, "Precisely what do you think we should tell them?"

"Ah." Nefret stroked her chin in unconscious — or perhaps it was conscious! — imitation of Emerson. "That is a good question, my boy. I am against telling the police about our arrangement with Farouk. They are such blunderers —"

"We do not, at the present time, *have* an arrangement with him," Emerson interrupted. "And this, my dear, is not a symposium. *I* will make the decision after *I* have heard what Russell has to say. Selim! Keep the men at it for another two hours. You know what to watch out for. Stop at once if —"

"My dear, he does know what to watch out for," I said. "Why are you telling him again?"

"Damnation!" Emerson shouted; and off he stalked, bareheaded and coatless, alone and unencumbered. He had gone some little distance before it dawned on me that he was heading for Mena House, where we had left the horses. Nefret let out a mildly profane exclamation and started to run after him.

"Don't forget the cameras," Ramses said.

"You bring them. Curse it, he needn't think he can get away from me!"

Lips compressed, Ramses entered the tomb chamber and began packing the cameras. The ever-present grit and dust was hard on the delicate mechanisms; it would not have done to leave them uncovered any longer than was absolutely necessary. I hesitated for only a moment before following him.

"She cannot come with us," he said, without looking up.

"Mr. Russell specifically mentioned that we were not to bring her; but you and he are both being silly. She is a surgeon. She has seen horrible wounds and performed operations."

"I see we are thinking along the same

419

lines." Ramses drew the straps tight and slung the case over his shoulder.

"It is one possible explanation for his failure to meet you, but it may not be the right one. Let us not look on the dark side!"

"The way our luck has been running, it is difficult not to." The words were flung at me from over his shoulder; he had already started off. I broke into a trot and caught him up. "There is no need to hurry. Your father won't leave without us."

"Sorry." He slowed his steps. After a moment of frowning concentration, he said, "Were you included in the invitation?"

"Not in so many words, but —"

"But you are coming anyhow."

"Naturally."

"Naturally."

We left for Cairo as soon as we had changed. Russell was waiting for us in the reception area of the Administration Building — if a bare, dusty room containing two cracked chairs and a wooden table could be called by that name. His face was set in a look of frozen disapproval, which cracked momentarily when he saw Nefret.

"No!" he exclaimed loudly. "Professor, I told you —"

"He couldn't prevent me from coming," Nefret said. She gave him a bewitching smile and held out a small, daintily gloved hand. "You wouldn't be so rude as to exclude me, would you, sir?"

For once Nefret had met her match. Russell took her hand, held it for no more than two seconds, and stepped back. "I could and I would, Miss Forth. What the Professor chooses to tell you and Mrs. Emerson hereafter is his affair. Police matters are my affair. Take a chair. One of the men will bring you tea. Come to my office, gentlemen."

From Manuscript H

"I asked you here," Russell said, his voice as cold and formal as his manner, "because one of my men informed me you were present night before last when we raided Aslimi's shop. Did you get a look at the fellow we were after?"

"Yes," Emerson said.

"You followed him, didn't you?"

"Yes. Caught him, too," Emerson added.

"Damnation, Professor! You have the infernal gall to stand there and tell me you let the fellow go?"

"I told you when we first discussed the subject that I would not help you capture Wardani, but that I would attempt to speak with him and convince him to turn himself in."

Emerson's voice was as loud as Russell's. Ramses didn't doubt that every police officer in the building was in the corridor, listening.

"It wasn't Wardani!"

"Well, I didn't know that, did I?" Emerson demanded indignantly. "Not until after I had cornered the fellow. As it turned out, he was one of Wardani's lieutenants. We — er — came to an agreement."

"Would you care to tell me what it was?"

"No. I may do after I've spoken with him."

"It's too late for that," Russell said. "Come with me."

They followed him along the corridor and down several flights of stairs. Being underground, the room was a few degrees cooler than the floors above, but not cool enough. The smell hit them even before Russell opened the door. The only furnishings were a few rough wooden tables. All but two were unoccupied. Russell indicated one of the shrouded forms.

"Damned inefficiency," he muttered. "That one should have been buried this morning, he's not keeping well. Here's our lad." He pulled the coarse sheet off the other corpse.

Farouk's face was unmarked except for a line of bruising around his mouth and across his cheeks. If he had died in pain, which he certainly had, there was no sign of it on the features that had settled into the inhuman flatness of death. His naked body showed no signs of injury except for his wrists, which were not a pretty sight. The ropes had dug deep into his flesh and he must have struggled violently to free himself.

Russell gestured, and two of his men turned the body over. From shoulders to waist the skin was black with dried blood over a patchwork of raised welts.

After a moment Emerson said, "The kurbash."

"How can you tell?"

Emerson raised his formidable eyebrows. "You can't? Why, man, it's an old Turkish custom. The marks left by a whip made of hippopotamus hide are quite different from those of a cat-o'-nine-tails or bamboo rod. I've seen it before."

Ramses had seen it too. Once. Like Farouk, the man had been beaten to death. Unlike Farouk, he had not been gagged. He had screamed till his voice gave out and even after he lost consciousness his body convulsed at every stroke of the whip. An old Turkish custom — and one Ramses would have experienced if his father had not burst on the scene before they started on him. The memory still made him break out in a cold sweat of terror, and it was one of the reasons why he had agreed to take Wardani's place. Anything that would help keep the Ottomans out of Egypt.

Fingering his chin, Emerson added, "Government by kurbash. Popular in Egypt, as well."

"We outlawed the kurbash years ago," Russell said stiffly.

Emerson shot out a series of questions. "Any other marks on the body? How long has he been dead? Where was he found?"

"Answer my question first, Professor."

"What question? Oh, that question." Emerson scowled. "If we are going to engage in a prolonged discussion, I would prefer to do it elsewhere."

He led the way back to Russell's office, where he settled himself in the most comfortable chair, which happened to be the one behind Russell's desk. Again Russell left the door ajar. The ensuing dialogue — Ramses could not have got a word in even if he had wanted to — got louder and more acrimonious as it proceeded. Emerson extracted the information he had demanded and gave a grudging, carefully edited account of their activities in the Khan el Khalili on the night in question.

"Why didn't you tell my men about the back entrance?" Russell shouted.

Emerson glared at him. "Why didn't they have the rudimentary intelligence to look for one?"

"Confound it, Professor!" Russell brought his fist down on the desk. "If you had not interfered —"

"If I had not, the fellow would have got clean away. He agreed to meet with me because he trusted my word."

"And because you offered him a bribe."

"Why, yes," Emerson said in mild surprise. "As my dear wife always says, it is easier to catch a fly with honey than with vinegar. Unfortunately it appears the other side got wind of his intentions. Not my fault if he was careless. Well, well, that is everything, I think. Come along, Ramses, we've wasted enough time 'assisting' the police. Trying to do their job for them, rather."

He got up and started for the door.

"Just a damned minute, Professor." Russell jumped up and went after him. "I must warn you —"

"Warn me?" Emerson thundered. He whirled round.

Ramses decided it was time to interfere. His father was enjoying himself immensely, and he was in danger of getting carried away by his role.

"Please, sir," he exclaimed. "Mr. Russell is only doing his duty. I told you we oughtn't get involved."

"I might have expected you would say that," Russell said contemptuously. "Thank you for coming, Professor. You are one of the most infuriating individuals I have ever encountered, but I admire your courage and your patriotism."

"Bah," said Emerson. He gave the door a shove. A dozen pair of boots beat a hasty retreat.

Ramses lingered only long enough to

breathe a few words and see Russell's nod of acknowledgment.

Still in character, Emerson stamped into the waiting room, collected his womenfolk, and swept the entire party out of the Administration Building.

"Well?" Nefret demanded.

"It was he," Emerson replied. "What was left of him. Found early this morning lying in an irrigation ditch near the bridge. Dead approximately twelve hours."

"How did he die?"

Emerson told her. He did not go into detail, but Nefret had an excellent imagination and a good deal of experience. Some of the pretty color left her face. "That's horrible. They must have found out he meant to betray them, but how?"

"The most likely explanation," Ramses said slowly, "is that he told them himself, and demanded more than Father had offered. Oh, yes, I know, it would not have been a sensible move, but Farouk was arrogant enough to think he could bargain with them and get away with it. Being more sensible than he, they simply disposed of an unnecessary and untrustworthy ally, and in a manner that would have a salutary effect on others who might be wavering."

"An old Turkish custom," Emerson repeated. "They have a nasty way with enemies and traitors."

Cursing somewhat mechanically, he dislodged half a dozen ragged urchins from the bonnet of the motorcar and opened the door for Nefret. As Ramses did the same for his mother, he saw that her eyes were fixed on him. She had been unusually silent. She had not needed his father's tactless comment to understand the full implications of Farouk's death. As he met her unblinking gaze he was reminded of one of Nefret's more vivid descriptions. "When she's angry, her eyes look like polished steel balls." That's done it, he thought. She's made up her mind to get David and me out of this if she has to take on every German and Turkish agent in the Middle East.

Hope springs eternal in the human breast, particularly in mine, for I am by nature an optimistic individual. As we drove into Cairo, I told myself that Russell's summons did not inevitably mean the dashing of our hopes; Farouk might have been captured and the end of Ramses's deadly masquerade might be in sight.

I tried to prepare myself for the worst while hoping for the best (not an easy task, even for me.) Yet the hideous truth hit harder than I had anticipated. Equally difficult was concealing the depth of my anger and despair from Nefret. She had only hoped we might do our country a service by destroying a ring of spies; she could not know that we had a personal interest in the matter. I had to bite my lip to control my anger — with Farouk for being stupid enough to get himself killed before we could interrogate him and with the unknown fiends who had murdered him so horribly. How much had he told them before he died?

The worst-possible answer was that Farouk had penetrated Ramses's masquerade and had passed the information on to those who would not hesitate to dispose of Ramses as they had done Farouk. The most hopeful was that he had told them only of our arrangement with him. We could certainly assume that the enemy knew we were on their trail. The conclusion was obvious. We must go on the offensive!

I remained pensively silent, considering various possibilities. They were provocative enough to take my attention off Emerson's driving for once.

"Are we taking tea at Shepheard's?" Nefret asked in surprise. "I thought you would want to return home so we can discuss this unpleasant turn of affairs."

"There is nothing to discuss," said Emerson, coming to a jolting halt in front of the hotel.

"But, Professor —"

"The matter is finished," Emerson declared. "We made the attempt; we failed, through no fault of our own; we can do no more. Curse it, the damned terrace is even more crowded than usual. Don't these idiots have anything better to do than dress in fashionable clothes and drink tea?"

He charged up the stairs, drawing Nefret with him.

We never have any difficulty getting a table at Shepheard's, no matter how busy it is. The arrival of our motorcar had been noted by the headwaiter; by the time we reached the terrace a bewildered party of American tourists had been hustled away from a choice position near the railing, and a waiter was clearing the table.

I leaned back in my chair and glanced casually at the vendors crowded round the stairs. They were not allowed on the terrace or in the hotel — a rule enforced by the giant Montenegrin doormen — but they came as close as they dared, shouting and waving examples of their wares. There were two flower sellers, but neither of them was David.

Poor David. Almost I wished that the failure of our hope could be kept from him. There was no chance of that, though; by now he might have heard of it from other sources. Gossip of that sort spreads quickly; there is nothing so interesting to the world at large as a grisly murder.

One of the disadvantages of appearing in public is that one is forced to be civil to acquaintances. I daresay that Emerson's scowling visage deterred a number of them from approaching us, but Ramses's pacifist views had not made him persona non grata to the younger women of Cairo. As Nefret had once put it (rather rudely, in my opinion), "It's quite like a fox hunt, Aunt Amelia; the marriageable maidens after him like a pack of hounds while their mamas cheer them on." We had not been seated long before a bevy of fluttering maidens descended on us. Some made straight for Ramses, while those who favored more indirect methods greeted Nefret with affected shrieks of pleasure.

"Darling, what have you been doing? We haven't seen you for ages."

"I've been busy," Nefret said. "But I am glad to see you, Sylvia, I intended to pay you a little call. What the devil do you mean, writing those lies to Lia?"

"Well, really!" one of the other young women exclaimed. Sylvia Gorst turned red with embarrassment and then white with terror. The glint in Nefret's blue eyes would have frightened a braver woman than she.

"You know of Lia's situation," Nefret said. "A friend would wish to avoid worrying or frightening her. You've written her a pack of gossip, most of it untrue and all of it malicious. If I hear of your doing it again I'll slap your face in public and — and —"

"Proclaim your perfidy to the world?"

430

Ramses suggested. The corners of his mouth were twitching.

"Not quite how I would have put it, but that's the idea," Nefret said.

Sylvia burst into tears and was removed by her twittering companions.

"Good Gad," Emerson said helplessly. "What was that all about?"

"You were very rude, Nefret," I said, trying to sound severe and not entirely succeeding. "What was it she told Lia?"

"Something about me, I presume," Ramses said. "No doubt you meant well, Nefret, but that temper of yours —"

Nefret shrank as if from a blow, and he stopped in mid-sentence. She pushed her chair back and stood up. "I'm sorry. Excuse me."

"You shouldn't have reproached her, Ramses," I said, watching Nefret hasten toward the door of the hotel, her head bowed. "She had already begun to regret her hasty speech, she always does after she loses her temper."

"I didn't mean what she thought I meant." He looked almost as stricken as Nefret. "Damn it, why do I always say the wrong thing?"

"Because women always take everything the wrong way," Emerson grumbled.

When Nefret came back she was smiling and composed, and accompanied. Lieutenant Pinckney, looking very pleased with himself, was with her. Naturally, with a stranger present, none of us referred to the small unpleasantness. Emerson would not have been deterred by the presence of a stranger, but he still had no idea what the fuss had been about.

After greeting Lieutenant Pinckney I allowed the young people to carry on the conversation. As my eyes wandered over the faces of the other patrons, I was reminded of something Nefret had said: "I feel that everyone I see is wearing a mask, and playing a part." I had the same feeling now. All those vacuous, well-bred (and not so well-bred) faces — could one of them be a mask, concealing the features of a deadly foe?

There was Mrs. Fortescue, clad as usual in black, surrounded as usual by admirers. Many of them were officers; many of them were highly placed. To judge from her encounter with Ramses, the lady (to give her the benefit of the doubt) was no better than she should be. Philippides, the corrupt head of the CID, was also among those present. Was he a traitor as well as a villain? Mrs. Pettigrew was staring at me, and so was her husband; the two round red faces were set in identical expressions of supercilious disapproval. No, surely not the Pettigrews; neither of them had the intelligence to be a spy. The swirl of a black cloak — Count de Sevigny, stalking like a stage villain toward the entrance of the hotel. He did bear a startling resemblance to another villain I had once known, but Kalenischeff was long dead, killed by the man he had attempted to betray.

Ramses excused himself and rose. I watched him descend the stairs and plunge into the maelstrom of howling merchants who immediately surrounded him. Since he was a head taller than most of them, it was not difficult for me to follow his progress. He examined the wares of several flower sellers before approaching another man, bent and tremulous with age. As soon as Ramses had made his purchase, the fellow ducked his head and withdrew.

The pretty little nosegays were rather wilted. Ramses presented one to me and the other to Nefret. She looked up at him with a particularly kindly expression; it was clear that she had taken the flowers as a tacit apology and that all was forgiven. Since she had been deep in conversation with young Mr. Pinckney, I felt sure she had not seen the exchange.

Emerson was fidgeting. He had only agreed to come to Shepheard's to enable Ramses to communicate with David; now that that was done, he allowed his boredom to show.

"Time we went home," he announced, interrupting Pinckney in the middle of a compliment.

I had no objection. I had found the inspiration I sought.

It is impossible to indulge in ratiocination while driving with Emerson. What with bracing oneself against sudden jolts, and warning him about camels and other impediments, and trying to prevent him from insulting operators of other motorcars, one's attention is entirely engaged. I was therefore forced to wait until we reached the house before applying my mind to the idea that had come to me on the terrace of Shepheard's. A long soothing bath provided the proper ambience.

Sethos was in Cairo. I began with that assumption, for I did not doubt it was so. I have no formal training in Egyptology, but I have spent many years in that pursuit, and the peculiar circumstances surrounding the discovery of the statue had not escaped me. I am sure I need not explain my reasoning to the informed Reader (which includes the majority of my readers); she or he must have reached the same conclusion. The statue had been placed in the shaft within the past few days, and there was only one man alive who could have and would have done it.

As for Sethos's motives, they were equally transparent. He was taunting me: announcing his presence, defying me to stop him should he choose to rob the Museum or the storage magazines or the site itself. I had realized early on that the present confusion in the Antiquities Department and in Egypt would be irresistible to a man of Sethos's profession. Some might wonder why he had announced himself by giving up one of his most valuable treasures. I felt confident it was one of Sethos's little jokes. His sense of humor was decidedly peculiar. The joke would be on us if he managed to steal the statue back. What a slap in the face that would be for Emerson!

I leaned back, watching the shimmer of reflected water on the tiled ceiling of the bath chamber. There was no doubt in my mind that Emerson had reached the same conclusion. Very little having to do with Egyptology escapes him. Of course the dear innocent man did not suppose I was clever enough to think of it. He had not told me for the same reason I had kept silent. The subject of Sethos was somewhat delicate. Emerson knew I had never given him cause to be jealous, but jealousy, dear Reader, is not under the control of the intellect. Had I not myself felt its poisonous fangs penetrate my heart?

Yes, I had. As for Sethos, he had made no secret of his feelings. Early in our acquaintance he had tried on several occasions to remove his rival, as he considered Emerson, once before my very eyes. Later he had sworn to me that he would never harm anyone who was dear to me. Obviously that included Emerson, and I sincerely hoped that Sethos agreed. Just to be on the safe side, I decided I had better find him before Emerson did. I had no doubt I could succeed. Emerson had not my intimate knowledge of the man. Emerson would not recognize him in any disguise, as I could do . . . as I had done . . . as I believed I had . . .

I must have a closer and longer look at the man I suspected. The Reader may well ask why, if I believe Sethos to be guilty of nothing worse than stealing antiquities, I should try to find him instead of concentrating on the viler villain, the enemy agent, who might also be a traitor to his country. I will answer that query. In his day, Sethos's web of intrigue had infiltrated every part of the criminal underworld of Egypt. He knew every assassin, every thief, every purveyor of drugs and depravity in Cairo. He could draw upon that knowledge to identify the man I was after — and by heaven, he would, for I would force him to do so! I raised my clenched fist toward the tiled ceiling to reinforce that vow, narrowly missing the nose of Emerson, who had crept up on me unobserved and unheard, owing to the intensity of my concentration.

"Good Gad, Peabody," he remarked, starting back. "If you want privacy you need only say so."

"I beg your pardon, my dear," I replied. "I did not know you were there. What do you want?"

"You, of course. You have been in here for almost an hour. And," Emerson added, studying my toes, "you are as wrinkled as a raisin. What were you brooding about?"

"I was enjoying the cool water and lost track of the time. Would you care to help me out?"

I knew he would, and hoped that the ensuing distraction might prevent him from asking further questions. I was correct.

It was rather late by the time we were dressed and ready to go down. I assumed the others had already done so, but I stopped at Ramses's door to listen. The door opened so suddenly, I was caught with my head tilted and my ear toward the opening.

"Eavesdropping, Mother?" Ramses inquired.

"It is a shameful habit, but cursed useful," I said, quoting something he had once said, and was rewarded by one of his rare and rather engaging smiles. "Are you ready to go down to dinner?"

Ramses nodded. "I was waiting for you. I wanted to have a word with you."

"And I with you," said Emerson. "You had no opportunity to write a note. What did you tell David?"

"To meet me later this evening. We need to discuss this latest development."

"Bring him here," I urged. "I yearn to see him."

"Not a good idea," Emerson said.

"No." Ramses gestured for us to proceed. "There is a coffee shop in Giza Village where I go from time to time. They are accustomed to see me and would not be surprised if I got into conversation with a stranger."

The scheme was certainly the lesser of several evils. Meditating on possible methods of lessening the danger still more, I led the way to the drawing room.

Nefret had been writing letters. "How slow you all are tonight!" she exclaimed, putting down her pen. "Fatima has been in twice to say dinner is ready."

"We had better go straight in, then," I said. "Mahmud always burns the food when we are late."

We got to the table just in time to save the soup. I thought I detected a slight undertaste of scorching, but none of the others appeared to notice.

"Good to have a quiet evening," Emerson declared. "You aren't going to the hospital, Nefret?"

"I rang Sophia earlier, and she said I am not needed at present." Nefret had changed, but not into evening attire; her frock was an old one, of blue muslin sprigged with green and white flowers. It might have been for sentimental reasons that she had kept it; Emerson had once commented on how pretty she looked in it.

"I planned to develop some of the plates this evening," she went on. "I've got rather behind. Will you give me a hand, Ramses?"

"I am going out," Ramses replied rather brusquely.

"For the entire evening?" She raised candid blue eyes, eyes the same shade as her gown.

The innocent question had an odd effect on Ramses. I knew that enigmatic countenance well enough to observe the scarcely perceptible hardening of his mouth. "Just to the village for a bit. I want to hear what the locals have to say about the statue."

"Do you think they are planning to steal it?" Nefret asked, laughing.

"I am sure some of them would like to," Ramses replied. "I won't be late. If you would like to wait a few hours I will be happy to assist."

I offered my services instead and Nefret accepted them. It was an odd conversation altogether; we talked, as we usually did, of our work and our future plans, but I could see that even Emerson had to force himself to take an interest. Not so odd, perhaps, considering that three of the four of us were concealing something from the fourth.

After dinner we went to the parlor for coffee. Several letters had been delivered while we were out; despite the general reliability of the post, many of our acquaintances clung to the old habit of sending messages by hand. There was one for me from Katherine Vandergelt, which I read with a renewed sense of guilt.

"We have seen so little of the Vandergelts," I said. "Katherine writes to remind us of our promise to visit them at Abusir."

Emerson started as if he had been stung. "Damnation!"

"What is it, Emerson?" I cried in alarm. "Something in that letter?"

"No. Er — yes." Emerson crumpled the missive and shoved it in his pocket. "In part. It is from Maxwell, asking me to be present at a meeting tomorrow — another example of the cursed distractions that have plagued this season! I meant to go to Abusir several days ago."

"A war is something of a distraction," Nefret said dryly. "You are probably the only man on that committee who knows what he is talking about, Professor; you are doing Egypt a great service."

Emerson said, "Hmph," and Nefret added, "This can't last forever. Someday . . ."

"Quite right," I said. "You will do your duty, Emerson, and so will we all; and some day. . . ."

Nefret and I spent several hours in the darkroom. When we emerged, both Emerson and Ramses were gone.

From Manuscript H

Ramses could remember a time when carriages and camels and donkeys transported tourists to the pyramids along a dusty road bordered by green fields. Now taxis and private motorcars made pedestrian traffic hazardous and the once isolated village of Giza had been almost swallowed up by new houses and villas. Baedeker, the Bible of the tourist, dismissed it as uninteresting, but every visitor to the pyramids passed through it along the road or the train station, and the inhabitants preyed on them as they had always done, selling fake antiquities and hiring out donkeys. The town relapsed into somnolence after nightfall. Its amenities were somewhat limited: a few shops, a few coffee shops, a few brothels.

The coffee shop Ramses favored was a few hundred yards west of the station. It was not as pretentious as the Cairene equivalents: a beaten earth floor instead of tile or brick, a simple support of wooden beams framing the open front. As he approached Ramses heard a single voice rising and falling in trained cadences, which were broken at intervals by appreciative laughter or exclamations. A reciter, or storyteller, was providing entertainment. He must have been there for some time, for he was deep in the intricacies of an interminable romance entitled "The

Life of Abu-Zayd."

A few lamps, hanging from the wooden beams, showed the Sha'er perched on a stool placed on the mastaba bench in front of the coffee shop. He was a man of middle age with a neatly trimmed black beard; his hands held the single-stringed viol and bow with which he accompanied his narrative. His audience sat round him, on the mastaba or on stools, smoking their pipes as they listened with rapt attention.

The narrative, part in prose, part in verse, described the adventures of Abu-Zayd, more commonly known as Barakat, the son of an emir who cast him off because his dark skin cast certain doubts on the honor of his mother. The emir did his wife an injustice; Barakat's coloring had been bestowed on him by a literal-minded god, in response to the lady's prayer:

"Soon, from the vault of heaven
        descending
A black-plumaged bird of
        enormous weight
Pounced on the other birds and killed
        them all.
To God I cried — O Compassionate!
Give me a son like this noble bird."

Waiting in the shadows, Ramses listened appreciatively to the flexible, melodic voice.

It was quite a story, as picaresque and blood-thirsty as any Western epic, and it was conveniently divided into sections or chapters, each of which ended in a prayer. When the narrator reached the end of the current section Ramses stepped forward and joined the audience in reciting the concluding prayer.

He and his father were among the few Europeans whom Egyptians addressed as they would a fellow Moslem — probably because Emerson's religious views, or lack thereof, made it difficult to classify him. "At least," one philosophical speaker had remarked, "he is not a dog of a Christian."

Emerson had found that highly amusing.

Ramses exchanged greetings with the patrons and politely saluted the reciter, whom he had encountered before. Refreshing himself with the coffee an admirer had presented to him, the Sha'er nodded in acknowledgment.

Ramses edged gradually away from the attentive audience and into the single, dirt-floored room. Only two creatures had resisted the lure of the narrator; one was a dog, sound asleep and twitching, under a bench. The other was stretched out on another bench and he too appeared to be asleep. Ramses shoved his feet rudely off the bench and sat down.

"Have you no poetry in your soul?" he inquired.

"Not at the moment." David pulled himself to a sitting position. "I heard."

"I feared you would." He told David what had happened, or failed to happen, the night before. "How they got wind of his intentions I don't know, unless he tried to blackmail them."

David nodded. "So that's the end of that. What do we do now?"

"Back to the original plan. What else can we do?"

There was no answer from David, who was leaning forward, his head bowed.

"I'm sorry," Ramses said. He decided they could risk speaking English; the narrator's voice was sonorous and no one was paying attention to them.

"Don't be an ass."

"Never mind the compliments. There's one thing we haven't tried."

"Trailing the Turk?"

"Yes. The first time I encountered him I was — er — prevented from doing so. The second time, *you* were prevented by your concern for me. There will be at least one more opportunity, and this time we'll have to do more than follow him. As you cogently pointed out, we need to learn not where he's going but where he came from. He's only a hired driver and he is probably amenable to bribery or persuasion. But that means we'll have to take him alive, which won't be easy."

"The Professor would be delighted to lend a hand," David murmured. "Are you going to let him in on it?"

"Not if I can help it. You and I can manage him."

"One more delivery."

"So I was told. It has to be soon, you know. At least Farouk is out of the picture. If they try to replace him we'll know who the spy is."

"Are you trying to cheer me up?"

"Apparently I'm not succeeding."

"One can't help wondering," David said evenly, "what he told them. The kurbash is a potent inducement to confession."

"What could he tell them, except that the great and powerful Father of Curses had tried to bribe him? He didn't know about you or — or the rest of it."

"He knew about the house in Maadi."

Ramses swore under his breath. It had been a forlorn hope, that David's quick mind would overlook that interesting fact — a fact whose significance had apparently eluded his father. Not that one could ever be sure, with Emerson . . .

"Listen to me," he said urgently. "Father's private arrangement with Farouk was a diversion that had nothing to do with our purpose. We didn't sign on to smash a spy apparatus, we're only trying to prevent an ugly little revolution. If we can do that and come out of it with whole skins, we'll be damned lucky. I refuse to get involved in anything else. They can't expect it of us."

"You had better lower your voice."

Ramses took a long, steadying breath. "And you had better go. I meant what I said, David."

"Of course." David rose and moved noiselessly toward the doorway. Then he pulled back with a muffled exclamation.

Ramses joined him and looked out. There was no mistaking the massive form that occupied a seat of honor in the center of the audience. Emerson was smoking his pipe and listening attentively.

"What's he doing here?" David whispered.

"Playing nursemaid," Ramses muttered. "I wish he wouldn't treat me like —"

"You did the same for him last night."

"Oh."

David let out a soundless breath of laughter. "He's saved me the trouble of following you home. Till tomorrow."

Bowing his head to conceal his height, he began working his way slowly through the men who stood nearby. Ramses moved forward a step and leaned against the wooden frame, as if he had been standing there all along.

He knew his father had seen him. Emerson had probably spotted David too, but he made no move to intercept him. He waited politely until the wail of the viol indicated the end of another chapter, and then rose and went to meet Ramses. They took their leave of the other patrons and started on the homeward path.

"Anything new?" Emerson inquired.

"No. There was no need for you to come after me."

Emerson ignored this churlish remark, but he did change the subject. "I'm worried about your mother."

"Mother? Why? Has something happened?"

"No, no. It's just that I know her well, and I detected an all-too-familiar glint in her eyes this afternoon. She has not my gift of patience," said Emerson regretfully. "What was that? Did you say something?"

"No, sir." Ramses stifled his laughter. "About Mother —"

"Oh, yes. I think she is about to take the bit in her teeth and go on the warpath."

"I had the same impression. Did she tell you what she's got in mind? I hope to God she isn't going to confront General Maxwell and tell him he must call the whole thing off."

"No, I'm going to do that."

"What? You can't!"

"I could, as a matter of fact." Emerson stopped to refill his pipe. "Calm yourself, my boy, you are becoming as hot-tempered as your sister. Sometimes I think I am the only cool-headed individual in this entire family."

He struck a match, and Ramses managed, with some difficulty, to refrain from pointing out that this might not be such a wise move. If anyone had been following them. . . .

Apparently no one had. Emerson puffed happily, and then said, "But I shan't. There is no meeting of the committee tomorrow; that was just my little excuse for calling on him. What the devil, there is too bloody much indirection in this affair. I want to know what Maxwell knows and tell him what I think he ought to hear. Don't worry; I shall be very discreet."

"Yes, sir." Argument would have been a waste of time; one might as well stand in the path of an avalanche and tell the rocks to stop falling.

Emerson chuckled. "You don't believe I can be discreet, do you? Trust me. As for your mother, I think I know what she has in mind. She thinks she has spotted Sethos. I intend to allow her to pursue her innocent investigations, because she is on the wrong track."

"How do you know?"

"Because," said Emerson, "I know . . . Er. Because I know the fellow she suspects is not he."

"Who is it she suspects?"

"The Count." Emerson chuckled.

"Oh. I agree with you. He's too obvious."

"Quite."

They were near the house. "I've got to run into Cairo for a while," Ramses said.

"I will accompany you."

He had expected that and braced himself for another argument. "No. It's not one of my usual trips, Father. There is someone I must see. I won't be long. I'll take one of the horses — not Risha, he's too well known — and be back in an hour or so."

Emerson stopped short, looming like a monolith. "At least tell me where you are going."

Just in case. He didn't have to say it. And he was right.

"El-Gharbi's."

Emerson's breath went out in an outraged explosion, and Ramses hastened to explain. "I know, he's a crawling serpentine trafficker in human flesh and all that; but he's got connections throughout the Cairo underworld. I saw him once before, when I was trying to find out where that poor devil who was killed outside Shepheard's got his grenades. He told me . . . several interesting things. I think he wants to see me again. He didn't stop by the hospital because he was concerned about that girl."

"Not him." Emerson rubbed his chin. "Hmph. You could be right. It's worth the time, I suppose. Are you sure you don't want —"

"I'm sure. It'll be all right."

"You always say that."

"Not always. Anyhow, what would Mother do if she found out you had gone to el Was'a?"

Ramses left the horse, a placid gelding Emerson had hired for the season, at Shepheard's and went on foot from there, squelching through the noisome and nameless muck of the alley to the back entrance he'd been shown. His knock was promptly answered, but el-Gharbi kept him waiting for a good quarter of an hour before admitting him to his presence.

Swathed in his favorite snowy robes, squatting on a pile of brocaded cushions, el-Gharbi was shoving sugared dates into his mouth with one hand and holding out the other to be kissed by the stream of suppliants and admirers who crowded the audience chamber. He gave a theatrical start of surprise when he saw Ramses, who had not bothered to alter his appearance beyond adding a mustache and a pair of glasses. As he had learned, the most effective disguise was a change in one's posture and mannerisms.

Clapping his hands, el-Gharbi dismissed his sycophants and offered Ramses a seat beside him.

"She is a pearl," he announced. "A gem of rare beauty, a gazelle with dove's eyes . . . Now, my dear, don't glower at me. You don't

450

like me to praise your lady's loveliness?"

"No."

"I was curious. So much devotion, from so many admirers! Having seen her, I understand. She has strength and courage as well, that one. Such qualities in a woman —"

"What did you want to see me about?"

"I?" The kohl lining his eyes cracked as he opened them wide. "It is you who have come to me."

When Ramses left the place a quarter of an hour later, he wasn't sure what el-Gharbi had wanted him to know. Fishing for facts in the murky waters of the pimp's innuendoes was a messy job. Once again, Percy had been the main subject — his affairs with various "respectable" women, the secret (except to the all-knowing el-Gharbi) hideaways where he took them, his brutal handling of the girls of the Red Blind District. Ramses thought he would probably never know for certain what Percy had done, or was doing, to annoy el-Gharbi — damaging the merchandise might be a sufficient cause — but one fact was clear. El-Gharbi wanted Percy dead or disgraced, and he wanted Ramses to do the job for him.

10

I had decided to admit Nefret to my confidence — up to a point. We were finishing the last of the photographic plates when I explained my intentions, and for a moment I feared I had spoken too soon. Nefret managed to catch the plate before it broke, however.

"Sethos?" she exclaimed. "The Count? Aunt Amelia!"

"Put that down, my dear. That is right. Come into the other room and I will explain my reasoning."

I was not surprised to find Emerson missing. I had known he would go after Ramses to guard him, since if he had not, I would have done it myself. Nefret did not comment on his absence; she assumed that he had also decided to visit the coffee shop.

I sat Nefret down in a chair and explained my deductions about the statue. I could see that the notion made sense to her; in fact, she tried to tell me she had thought of it herself. Emerson and Ramses do that sort of thing all the time, so I simply raised my voice and proceeded with the next stage of my deductions.

"I was struck, on the few occasions when I

have glimpsed him, by the Count's resemblance to a villain I once knew named Kalenischeff. He was a member of Sethos's gang and a thoroughgoing scoundrel; when he attempted to betray his dread master, Sethos had him killed."

"Yes, Aunt Amelia, I know."

"Oh? I told you about him?"

"You told us about many of your adventures, and Ramses told David and me about others." Her face softened in a reminiscent smile. "We would foregather in Ramses's room or mine, smoking forbidden cigarettes and feeling like little devils, while we discussed your exploits. They were much more exciting than the popular romances."

I was gratified, but I felt obliged to add, "With the additional advantage of being true."

"Oh, yes."

"Sethos has upon occasion mimicked the appearance of a real person," I continued. "I believe he finds it amusing. The fact that the Count has consistently avoided me is also suspicious. Without wishing to boast, I believe I may claim that many newcomers to Cairo try to strike up an acquaintance with me or with Emerson."

"He hasn't avoided me," Nefret murmured.

I gave her a sharp look. She was twisting a lock of hair round her finger; it gleamed like a ring of living gold. "Hmmm. Well, that makes my scheme all the more plausible. I would like you to ask the Count to take you to dine tomorrow night — at one of the hotels, naturally, you must not under any circumstances go off alone with him. You can think of some plausible excuse, such as . . . er . . ."

"I can think of an excuse," Nefret said. "You are serious about this, aren't you?"

"My dear, you can hardly suppose I would ask you to commit such a breach of good manners unless I were. It is not surprising that you should not have suspected the Count; you never met Sethos."

Nefret's lips curved. "I've always wanted to."

That smile aroused certain forebodings, which I felt obliged to express. "You must abandon your girlish, romantic notions about Sethos. Don't try to outwit him. Just get him there — I suggest Shepheard's — so that I can have a good long look at him. Of course I will be disguised."

"Ah," said Nefret. "Disguised. How?"

"Leave that to me. I hear that wretched dog barking. It must be Emerson and Ramses. Are we agreed?"

"I will do anything you ask, Aunt Amelia. Anything. If this will help . . ." She let the sentence trail off into silence.

"I knew I could count on you. Pray do not mention our little scheme."

454

"Aren't you going to tell the Professor, at least?"

"That will depend on . . . Ah, there you are, my dears. Did you enjoy your evening out? We have accomplished a great deal of work while you were amusing yourselves."

By rousting us out at the crack of dawn, Emerson managed to get in several hours at the site before he left to attend his meeting with General Maxwell. He had repeated to me what Ramses had told him about his conversation with David; nothing new had been learned, but at least I had the comfort of knowing that as of ten o'clock last night, David was still alive and well.

It was not comfort enough. Every passing day increased the danger, and I was all the more determined to put an end to the nasty business. Having worked out a course of action which I felt certain would achieve this goal, I was able to concentrate more or less successfully on our archaeological activities. With Emerson gone, I was the person in charge. I explained my intentions to Nefret, Ramses, and Selim. I never had to explain anything to Daoud, since he always did exactly what I told him to do.

"No one admires Emerson's methodology more than I, but in my opinion we have been dawdling over this mastaba longer than we ought. Selim, I want that second chamber completely cleared today."

Ramses said, "Mother —"

Selim said, "But, Sitt Hakim —"

Nefret grinned.

Her grin vanished when I went on, raising my voice loud enough to silence Ramses and Selim. "Nefret and I will both examine the fill. Ramses, you can help Selim label the baskets as they are filled. Make certain you identify the precise square and level from which each is taken. In that way —"

"I believe, Mother, that Selim and I are both familiar with the technique," Ramses said. His eyebrows had taken on a remarkable angle.

Selim's beard parted just a slit. "Yes, Sitt Hakim."

I smiled at Daoud, whose large countenance bore its customary expression of placid affability. "Then let us get at it!"

I daresay my words spurred them all to even greater energy. Daoud kept the Deucaville cars moving. Nefret and I sifted basket after basket, finding very little. Since I wanted to impress Emerson with our efficiency, I kept everyone at it till long past the hour at which we ordinarily stopped for luncheon. Not until Ramses came to join us did a belated realization of other responsibilities strike me.

He had, of course, misplaced his hat. Though he feels the heat less than most, his luxuriant black locks had tightened into curls, and his wet shirt stuck rather too closely to his chest and shoulders. The well-developed muscles it molded were somewhat asymmetrical, despite my effort to reduce the size of the bandages. I could only hope Nefret's eyes were not as keen as mine. She had not commented on Ramses's recent habit of always wearing a shirt on the dig.

"We've come across something rather interesting," he announced. "You will need to get photographs, Nefret."

She jumped up, her face brightening, and Ramses offered me his hand to help me rise. I would have waved it away, but truth compels me to admit I was a trifle stiff. Sitting in the same position for several hours has that effect even on a woman in excellent physical condition.

The chamber had been emptied almost to floor level. There were some fine reliefs and another false door, but that was not what caught my eye. Beyond the south wall the men had exposed the walls of another, smaller chamber, whose existence none of us had suspected. I realized at once that it must be a serdab, a room containing a statue of the deceased. Through a narrow slit in the wall between the serdab and the chapel, the soul of the dead man or woman could communicate with the outer world and partake of offerings.

"How did you find it?" I asked, scrambling along the surface to a point where I could look down into the chamber. Enough of the fill had been removed to define the inner side of the walls. Only one of the original roofing stones remained. A scattering of chips on the surface of the rubble inside the room suggested that the others had fallen and shattered.

"I happened to notice that what had appeared to be only a crack in the wall was suspiciously regular, so I dug outside it and found stonework." Running his fingers through his hair, he went on, "The plan of the mastaba is more complex than we realized; there is an extension of as yet indeterminate size to the south. As for the serdab, you can see why I want photographs before we continue emptying it."

"You think there is a statue down there?"

"One can only hope."

"Yes, yes," I exclaimed. "Hurry, Nefret, get the camera."

We arranged measuring sticks along the walls and against them, and Nefret took several exposures. I was all for continuing, but a general outcry overruled me.

"We ought to wait for Father," Ramses said, and Nefret added, in a fair imitation of Miss Molly's best whine, "I'm hungry!"

An explosive sigh from Selim expressed his opinion, so I gave in. Scarcely had we begun unpacking our picnic baskets when I beheld Emerson approaching.

There was something very strange about his appearance. For one thing, he was still wearing the tweed coat and trousers I had made him put on. To see Emerson in a coat at that time of day, on the dig, indicated a state of mental preoccupation so extreme as to be virtually unprecedented. Further evidence of preoccupation was provided by his blank stare and his frequent stumbles. He looked like a sleepwalker, and it appeared to me that he was in serious danger of falling into a tomb, so I shouted at him.

His eyes came back into focus. "Oh, there you are," he said. "Lunch? Good."

"We have found the serdab, Emerson," I announced.

"The what? Oh." Emerson took a sandwich. "Very good."

Visibly alarmed, Nefret took him by the sleeve and tried to shake him. The monumental form of Emerson was not to be moved thus, but the gesture and her exclamation did succeed in getting his attention.

"Professor, didn't you hear? A serdab! Statues! At least we hope so. Is something wrong? Did the General have bad news?"

"I cannot imagine," said Emerson stiffly, "what makes you suppose I am not listening, or what leads you to surmise that there is bad news. A serdab. Excellent. As for the General, he was no more annoying than usual." He put the rest of his sandwich in his mouth and chewed. I had the impression he was employing mastication to give him time to invent a story. Inspiration came; he swallowed noisily, and went on, "The damned fools are talking about a corvée — forced-labor battalions."

Ramses, who had not taken his eyes off his father, said, "That would be disastrous, especially at the present time."

"And a direct violation of Maxwell's assurance that Great Britain would not demand aid from the Egyptian people in this war," Emerson agreed. "I hope I persuaded them to give up the idea."

"That is all?" Nefret demanded.

"It is enough, isn't it? An entire morning wasted on a piece of bureaucratic bombast." Emerson pulled off his coat, tie, waistcoat, and shirt. I picked them up from the ground and collected several scattered buttons. "Back to work," Emerson went on. "Have you taken photographs? Ramses, let me see your field notes. Peabody, get back to your rubble!"

Emerson's exasperation at discovering he had been in error about the plan of the mastaba was so extreme I was unable to get a private word with him for some time. After further excavation had exposed the head of a statue, and Nefret was taking her photographs, I finally managed to remove Emerson to a little distance.

"What happened, curse it?" I demanded.

"What happened where?" Emerson tried to free himself from my grasp.

"You know where," I hissed — or would have done, had that phrase contained any sibilants. "Something about Ramses? Tell me, Emerson, I can bear anything but ignorance!"

"Oh." Emerson's heavy brows drew apart and his eyes softened. "You are on the wrong track entirely, my dear. The situation is no worse than it was; in fact it has been made safer by the removal of that wretched man. Maxwell assured me that the police will act within a fortnight, as soon as the final shipment of arms is delivered."

"A fortnight! Two more weeks of this?"

"Perhaps we can shorten it."

I waited for him to go on. Instead he put his arm round me and pressed his lips to my temple, the end of my nose, and my mouth.

Yes, Professor, I thought — perhaps we can. And if you think you can distract me you are sadly in error.

However, I am not childish enough to reciprocate in kind when someone tries to deceive me. I bided my time until we stopped work for the day. The serdab contained not one but four statues, all crammed together in that confined space. They were of private individuals — the tomb owner and his family — so they were not of the same superb quality as the statue of Khafre we had found in the shaft, but they had a naive charm of their own, and all were in excellent condition. Leaving them half-buried for their own protection, we started for home, while several of our trustiest men remained on guard. Ramses also remained, ostensibly to discuss security measures with the men. He would go directly from Giza to his assignation.

In point of fact, there was no way on earth I could keep Emerson entirely in the dark concerning my plans for the evening. If he did not observe my absence and Nefret's earlier, he would certainly do so when he discovered he was alone at the dinner table. I therefore determined to give him a (very slightly) modified account of the truth when we were alone. It is always good policy to go on the attack when one's own position is somewhat vulnerable, so I began by asking him what he had meant by suggesting that there might be a method of ending Ramses's masquerade earlier than Maxwell had said.

He was in the bath at the time. Let me add that my choice of location was not an attempt to undermine his confidence. Most individuals become self-conscious and uneasy when they are unclothed. This has never been one of Emerson's weaknesses. One might even claim . . .

But I perceive that I am wandering off the subject. Having assumed undergarments and dressing gown, I went to the bath chamber, which is in the Turkish style. I had caused cushions to be placed round the bath itself, and I settled myself on one of these before addressing my spouse.

The pleased smile with which he had welcomed my appearance vanished. "I might have known you would not let the subject drop," he remarked.

"Yes, you might. Well?"

Emerson reached for the soap. "As you have no doubt realized, locating the supply lines would enable us to intercept and catch the people who are bringing the weapons to Cairo. I am fairly familiar with the Eastern Desert, and I have a theory as to the most likely route. I thought I might ride out that way and have a look round."

It was an idea that had not occurred to me. "When?"

"Tomorrow."

"Yes," I said slowly. "Hmmm. You cannot get all the way to Suez and back in a single day."

"I don't plan to go all the way. It will mean an early start, though, and I may be late returning."

"You won't go alone?"

"Certainly not, my dear. I will take Ramses, if he chooses to come."

"Emerson, are you going to use that entire bar of soap?"

Except for his head, the parts of him above water were white with soap bubbles. Emerson grinned. "Cleanliness is next to godliness, my dear. Here, catch."

The bar of soap slipped through my hands, and by the time I had retrieved it and replaced it in the proper receptacle, Emerson had submerged himself and was rising from the bath.

"Now," he said, reaching for a towel, "I have confided in you. It is your turn. You are up to something, Peabody, I can always tell. What is it?"

I explained my plan. I expected objections. What I got was a whoop of laughter.

"You think the Count is Sethos?"

"I didn't say that. I said —"

"That he was a highly suspicious character. Most people strike you that way, but never mind. Nefret agreed to this preposterous — er — this interesting scheme?"

I did not return his smile. "Her mind is not at ease, Emerson. I know the signs, and I know Nefret. We cannot take her wholly into our confidence, but we can provide her with a safe outlet for that restless energy of hers."

"Well, Peabody, you may be right." Emerson's broad chest expanded as he heaved a mighty sigh. "It is damned unpleasant, keeping things from Nefret. We will tell her the whole story after it's over."

"Of course, my dear. So you agree with my plan?"

"I accept it. I can do no more."

From Manuscript H

When Ramses got back to the house he found his father alone in the drawing room. Emerson looked up from the paper he was holding. "Well?"

Ramses answered with another question. "Where are Mother and Nefret?"

"Out. You can speak freely. How did it go?"

"No one tried to kill me, which I suppose can be taken as a positive sign." Ramses loosened his tie and dropped into a chair. "The lads aren't very happy, though. Asad threw himself into my arms shrieking with relief and the others are demanding action. I had the devil of a time calming them down."

"They had heard about Farouk?"

"Everybody in Cairo has heard about Farouk, and about his encounter with us."

"Ah," said Emerson. "Well, one might have expected that piece of news would get about."

"Especially after your shouting match with Russell." Ramses rubbed his forehead. "One of the actions Rashad suggested was assassinating you. He volunteered."

Emerson chuckled. "I hope you dissuaded him."

"I hope so too. That's the trouble with these young firebrands. When they get excited they want to run about the streets attacking people. I bullied them into taking my orders this time, but I don't know how much longer I can control them."

"And the last delivery?"

"That's another disturbing development. Asad picked up the message yesterday. He didn't know what it said until I deciphered it — the code is pretty primitive, but I'm the only one who has the key. The 'merchandise' won't be delivered directly to us, as before. It will be hidden somewhere and we'll be told when and where to collect it."

"Damnation," Emerson said mildly. "No idea when?"

"No. I had a brief conversation with —" A soft tap at the door warned him to stop speaking. It was Fatima, offering coffee and food. He had to eat a slice of plum cake before she would leave.

"With David?" Emerson asked.

Ramses nodded. "We met on the train platform; he went one way and I the other. There wasn't much to say." He finished the slice of cake.

"Where's Mother got to?"

"Following Nefret," Emerson said. He

chuckled. "In disguise."

"What!?"

"Would you like a whiskey and soda?"

"No, thank you, sir. I've drunk enough over the past few weeks to turn me into a teetotaler, even if most of it did go out the window or into a potted plant."

"Intoxication is a good excuse for many aberrations," Emerson agreed. He sipped his own whiskey appreciatively. "As for your mother, she took it into her head to go spyhunting. She persuaded Nefret to dine with one of her suspects."

"The Count?"

"How did you know?"

"It's like Mother to fix on such a theatrically suspicious-looking character. I don't believe he's an enemy agent, but I wouldn't trust him alone with a woman I cared about."

"They won't be alone," Emerson replied. "You don't suppose your mother will let them out of her sight, do you?"

Ramses's alarm was replaced by a horrible fascination, of the sort his mother's activities often inspired in him. "What's she disguised as?" he asked. A series of bizarre images passed through his mind.

"Well, she borrowed that yellow wig you used to wear, when you weren't so tall and could still pass as a female. And eyeglasses, and a good deal of face paint . . ." Emerson's reminiscent smile broadened into a grin.

"Don't worry, Selim is with her. I must say the tarboosh looked even more absurd on him than it does on most people, but he was tremendously pleased with himself."

"Oh, good Lord. What's he supposed to be, one of those slimy terrassiers who prey on foreign women?"

"There is a question," said Emerson reflectively, "of who preys on whom. The ladies are under no compulsion. Anyhow, they will all enjoy themselves a great deal, and it served to get Nefret out of the way so that we can have a private conversation. Pull up a chair."

He opened the paper he had been looking at, and spread it out on the table. It was a map of the Sinai and the Eastern Desert.

"If you could find out how the weapons are being brought in and catch the people who are bringing them, that would put an end to this business of yours, wouldn't it?"

"Possibly. It would take them a while to find alternate routes, but —"

"They don't have that much time." Emerson took out his pipe. "There will be an attack on the Canal within a few weeks. There are reports of troop movements in Syria, toward Ajua and Kosseima on the Egyptian frontier. Those complacent idiots in Cairo have decided against defending the border; they think the Turks can't cross the Sinai. I think they are wrong. The same complacent idiots have concentrated our forces on the west of the Canal; the few defence posts on the east bank could be taken by a determined goatherd.

"Now, look here." The stem of his pipe stabbed at the long dotted line that marked De Lesseps's great achievement. "Our people have cut the Canal bank and flooded the desert to the north for almost twenty miles. That still leaves over sixty miles to be defended. Boats are patrolling the Bitter Lakes, but the rest of it is guarded by a few trenches and a bunch of Lancashire cotton farmers."

"There's also the Egyptian artillery and two Indian infantry divisions."

"All of whom are Moslems. What if they respond to the call for jihad?"

"They aren't that keen on the Turks."

"Let us hope not. In any case, there aren't enough of them. There are over a hundred thousand of the enemy based near Beersheba."

"I won't ask how you found that out."

"It is common knowledge. Too common. I'd be willing to wager the Turkish High Command knows as much about our defenses as we do. Insofar as your little problem is concerned, transporting arms across the Sinai to the Canal or the Gulf of Suez would not present much difficulty. The question is: how are they getting the arms from there to Cairo? You know the terrain of the Eastern Desert. How well do you know it?"

"Well enough to know that there are only a few practical routes between Cairo and the Canal." Ramses leaned closer to the map. "The northern routes are the ones we use, and there is a good deal of traffic along them, by road and rail. Aside from the problem of crossing the Bitter Lakes with gunboats patrolling them, the terrain south of Ismailia is difficult for camels or carts. It's not a sand desert, it's hilly and rocky, broken by wadis. Some of the mountains are six thousand feet high."

"So?" Emerson inquired, like a patient teacher encouraging a slow child. At least that was how it sounded to his son.

"So the most obvious route is this one." He indicated a dotted line that ran straight from Cairo to Suez. "The old caravan and pilgrim trail to Mecca. It's also the most direct route."

"I agree. Why don't we go out tomorrow and have a look?"

"Are you serious?"

"Certainly." The strong line of Emerson's jaw hardened. "Sooner or later they will have to inform you of the precise date of their attack, so you can time your little revolution to coincide, but if they have the sense I give them credit for, they'll wait until the last possible moment. I want you and David out of this, Ramses. It — er — it worries your mother."

"I'm not especially happy about it either," Ramses said. "Your idea is worth a try, I suppose."

Ramses was even less enthusiastic than he had admitted; it seemed to him extremely unlikely that they would find anything. He understood his father's motive for suggesting the search, though. Wardani's crowd weren't the only ones who were finding it hard to wait.

After they had settled on the details, Emerson picked up a book and Ramses went to the window. The shadowy, starlit garden was a beautiful sight — or would have been to one who did not see prowlers in every shadow and hear surreptitious footsteps in every rustle of the foliage. He wondered morosely whether he would ever be able to enjoy a lovely view without thinking about such things. Knowing his family, the answer was probably no. Even when there wasn't a war, his mother and father attracted enemies the way wasps were drawn to a bowl of sugar water.

There were things he ought to be doing — going over the copies of the tomb inscriptions, checking them with Nefret's photographs. His father ought to be working on his excavation diary. Ramses knew why Emerson was sitting there pretending to read; he hadn't turned a page for five minutes. How much did it cost him to let his wife go off alone, looking for trouble and possibly finding it?

Ramses knew the answer; he felt it too, like a dull headache that covered his entire body.

It was almost midnight before they returned. For once his father's hearing was keener than his; Emerson was out of his chair before Ramses heard the motorcar. They came in together, his mother and Selim, and Ramses sank back into the chair from which he had risen. Outraged laughter struggled with pure outrage. His mother was bad enough, but Selim . . .

"Where did you get that suit of clothes?" he demanded.

Selim whipped off his tarboosh and struck a pose. He had oiled his beard and slicked his hair down; the black coat was too tight across the chest and too long. It had lapels of gold brocade. Ramses turned his stricken gaze to his mother. The eyeglasses rode low on her nose. The flaxen blond wig had slipped down over her forehead, and what in heaven's name had she done to her eyebrows?

Catching his eye, she shoved the wig back onto the top of her head. "Selim was driving quite fast," she explained.

"Sit down and tell us all about it," said Emerson, too relieved to be critical. "You too, Selim. I want to hear your version."

Nothing loath, Selim gallantly held a chair for his lady of the evening (and she looked like one too, Ramses thought).

"It went very well," Selim said with a

broad, pleased smile. "No one knew us, did they, Sitt?"

"Certainly not," said Ramses's mother. "We had a quiet dinner. Nefret was dining with the Count."

"He kissed her hand very often," said Selim.

"What did she do?" Emerson demanded.

"She laughed."

Involuntarily Emerson glanced at the clock, and his wife said, "I did not think it advisable to wait and follow them. They were lingering over coffee when we left, but she should be here before long."

"What if she's not?" Emerson's voice rose.

"Then I will have a few words with her."

"And I," said Emerson, "will have a few words with the Count."

"There will be no need for that. Here she is now."

Nefret came in. Her face was flushed and her eyes sparkled. Ramses found himself in the grip of a severe attack of pure, primitive jealousy. If she had let that monocled swine kiss her . . .

"Did that swine dare to embrace you in the cab?" Emerson demanded furiously.

Nefret burst out laughing. "He tried, but he did not succeed. He's really very entertaining. Aunt Amelia, what do you think?"

"I was mistaken."

This admission stopped Emerson in mid-expletive. He stared open-mouthed at his wife. "What did you say?"

"I said I was mistaken. But it was good of you, Nefret, to make the effort."

It was still dark when they left the house next morning, Ramses on Risha and his father on the big gelding he had hired for the season. They crossed the river on the bridges that spanned the Isle of Roda. The molten rim of the sun had just appeared over the hills when they reached the Abbasia quarter, on the edge of the desert. There wasn't much there except a few hospitals, a lunatic asylum, and the Egyptian Army Military School and barracks. Emerson turned his horse toward the barracks.

"The road's that way," Ramses said, and wished he hadn't, when his father said patiently, "Yes, my boy, I know."

Ramses closed his mouth and after a moment his father condescended to explain. "Maxwell reminded me that the military keep a close eye on people heading into the Eastern Desert. We will report to the officer on duty and comply with the rules."

It was a reasonable explanation, which was why Ramses doubted its truth. His father's usual reaction to rules was to ignore them.

Early as it was, the officers were already at the mess. Emerson sent a servant to announce his presence. The horse was a large animal, and so was Emerson; when several people emerged from the building, he did not dismount but looked down on them from his commanding height with an air of affable condescension. Some of them were known to Ramses, including a tallish man wearing a kilt, who gave Ramses a stiff nod and then introduced himself to Emerson.

"Hamilton!" he barked.

"Emerson!"

"Heard of you."

"And I you."

Hamilton drew himself up, threw his shoulders back, and stroked his luxuriant red mustache. He was at a disadvantage on foot and he was reacting like a rooster meeting a bigger rooster.

"Hadn't expected to see you here."

"No, why should you have done? Following your rules, sir, following your rules. We are on a little archaeological exploration today. There's a ruined structure out there, a few miles southwest of the well of Sitt Miryam. I've been meaning for years to have a closer look."

The Major's narrowed eyes measured Emerson, from his smiling face to his bared forearms, brown as an Arab's and hard with muscle. He seemed to approve of what he saw, for his stern face relaxed. "Probably Roman," he said gruffly.

"Ah." Emerson took out his pipe and began to fill it. "You know the place?"

"I've done a bit of hunting in the area. There are ancient remains all over the place. Way stations and camps, for the most part. Hardly of interest to you."

"For the most part," Emerson agreed. "However, one never knows, does one? Well, gentlemen, we must be off."

"A moment, sir," Hamilton said. "You are armed, aren't you?"

Emerson gave him a blank stare. "Armed? What for?"

"One never knows, does one?" The other man smiled faintly. "Allow me to lend you this — just for the day."

He reached under his coat and pulled out a revolver, which he offered to Emerson. To Ramses's surprise, his father accepted it. "Most kind. I'll try not to damage it."

He tried to put it in his trouser pocket, dropped it, caught it in midair, and finally managed to get it into the pocket of his coat. Watching him, one of the subalterns said doubtfully, "You do know how to use it, sir?"

"You point it and pull the trigger?"

Ramses, who knew that his father was an excellent shot with pistol or rifle, smothered a smile as the young man's face lengthened. "Well, sir, er — more or less."

"Most kind," Emerson repeated. "Good day to you, gentlemen."

After they had gone a little distance Emerson drew the weapon out of his pocket, broke it, and spun the cylinder. "Fully loaded and functional."

"Did you think it wouldn't be?"

"Happened to me once before," Emerson said equably. "A nasty suspicious mind, that's what I've got. Particularly when people with whom I am only slightly acquainted do me favors."

"He seemed cordial enough," Ramses said. "Even to me."

"Highly suspicious," his father said with a chuckle. "Ah, well, perhaps he was won over by my extraordinary charm of manner."

If anyone's charm had influenced the major, Ramses thought, it wasn't yours or mine. He could only hope Nefret had not put ideas into the old fellow's head. He wouldn't be the first to make that mistake.

"Not that a Webley is likely to be of much use," Emerson continued, slipping the gun into his belt. "The cursed things are cursed inaccurate. What sort of weapon have you got?"

No use asking how his father knew. Maybe he'd noticed the bulge under Ramses's arm. The Mauser semiautomatic pistol was big and heavy, but for accuracy and velocity it couldn't be beat. Ramses handed it over, adding, "If one must carry one of the vile things it might as well be the best."

Emerson examined and returned the

weapon. "I presume this is a contribution from the Turks? Hmmm, yes. A nice touch of irony, that."

Once they had reached the top of the plateau, the ground leveled off. The old trail was only slightly harder and better defined than the surrounding desert — not the blowing sand dunes of the Western Desert, but baked earth and barren rock. There were signs of traffic: camel and donkey dung, the whitened bones of animals stripped of flesh by various predators, an occasional cigarette end, the shards of a rough pottery vessel that might have been there for three thousand years or three hours. No sign that the man they were after had passed that way; no sign that he hadn't. As the sun rose higher, the pale-brown of sand and rock turned white with reflected light. At Ramses's suggestion his father put his hat on. By midday they had gone a little over thirty miles, and through the shimmering haze of heat Ramses made out a small clump of trees in the distance.

"About time," said Emerson, who had seen it too. Like Risha his horse was desert-bred and neither had been ridden hard, but they deserved a rest and the water that lay ahead.

They were still several hundred yards away from the miniature oasis when a voice hailed them, and a group of men on camels appeared over a rise north of the track. They rode straight for the Emersons, who stopped to wait for them.

"Bedouin?" inquired Emerson, narrowing his eyes against the glare of sunlight.

"Camel patrol, I think." Whoever the men were, they carried rifles. Ramses added, "I hope."

The uniformed group executed a neat maneuver that barred their path and surrounded them. Their dark, bearded faces would have identified them even without their insignia: Punjabis, belonging to one of the Indian battalions. "Who are you and what are you doing here?" the jemadar demanded. "Show me your papers."

"What papers?" Emerson said. "Curse it, can't you see we are English?"

"Some Germans can speak English. There are spies in this part of the desert. You must come with us."

Ramses removed his pith helmet and addressed one of the troopers, a tall, bearded fellow with shoulders almost as massive as Emerson's. "Do you remember me, Dalip Singh?" he inquired, in his best Hindustani. "We met in Cairo last month."

It wasn't very good Hindustani, but it had the desired effect. The man's narrowed eyes widened, and the impressive beard parted in a smile. "Ah! You are the one they call Brother of Demons. Your pardon. I did not see your face clearly."

Ramses introduced his father, and after an effusive exchange of compliments from everyone except the camels, they rode on toward the oasis, escorted fore and aft by their newfound friends.

A rim of crumbling brickwork surrounded the cistern that was locally known as Sitt Miryam's Well. Almost every stopping place along the desert paths had a biblical name and legend attached to it; according to believers they marked the route of the escape into Egypt, or the wanderings of Joseph, or the Exodus.

There was not much shade, but they took advantage of what little there was. The camels lay down with their usual irritable groans and Ramses watered the horses, filling and refilling his pith helmet from the turgid waters. Emerson and the jemadar sat side by side, talking in a mixture of English and Arabic. Knowing he could leave the questioning to his father, Ramses joined the troopers for a brief language lesson.

At first all of them except Dalip Singh were somewhat formal with him, but his attempts to speak their language and his willingness to accept correction soon put them at ease. He had to have the jokes explained. Some of them were at his expense.

Finally the laughter got too loud, and the jemadar, like any good officer, recalled his men to their duties. They went off in a cloud of sand. Emerson leaned back and took out his pipe.

"When did you learn Hindustani?"

"Last summer. I'm not very fluent."

"Why did that fellow grin at you in such a familiar manner?"

"Well, I suppose we did get a bit familiar. Wrapped in one another's arms, in fact." His father gave him a critical look, and Ramses elaborated. "He boasted that he could put any man in the place on his — er — back, so I took him up on it. He taught me a trick or two, and I taught him one. What did the jemadar say?"

Emerson sucked on the stem of his pipe. "I am beginning to think . . . that we are on . . . the wrong track."

Since he appeared to be oblivious of the pun, Ramses let it go. "Why?"

Emerson finally got his pipe going. "Those chaps and others like them patrol the area between here and the Canal by day and by night. The jemadar insisted nothing as large as a wagon could have got by them on this track. You know how sound carries at night."

"They might have used camels along this stretch."

"Camels make noise too, especially when you hope they won't. Bloody-minded brutes," Emerson added.

"I see what you mean." Ramses lit a cigarette. "It's become altogether too complicated, hasn't it? Land transport from the Syrian border, transfer to boats or rafts, then reloading a second time for the trek across the desert, with the whole area under surveillance."

"There are other routes. Longer but safer."

"From the coast west of the Delta."

"Or from Libya. The Ottomans have been arming and training the Senussi tribesmen for years. The Senussis hate Britain because she supported the Italian conquest of that area. They would be happy to cooperate in passing on arms to Britain's enemies, and they have sympathizers all along the caravan routes, from Siwa westward."

They smoked for a while in companionable silence.

"We may as well start back," Ramses said.

"Since we've come this far," Emerson began.

"Not your damned ruins, Father!"

"The place isn't far. Only a few miles."

"If we aren't back by dark, Mother will come after us."

"She doesn't know where we are," Emerson said with evil satisfaction. "It won't take long. We can water the horses again on our way back."

He knocked his pipe out and rose. Ramses hadn't the courage to argue, though he was not happy about his father's decision. The sun had passed the zenith and had started westward. The air was still blisteringly hot, and the flies seemed to have multiplied a thousandfold.

As he'd feared, Emerson's few miles turned out to be considerably longer. Ahead and to the right, the imposing ramparts of the Araka Mountains stood up against the sky. Another, larger, range was visible to the north of the track. Finally Emerson turned south, skirting the steep slopes of one of the smaller gebels.

"There," he said, pointing.

At first glance the heaps of stones looked like another natural outcropping. Then Ramses saw shapes too regular to be anything but man-made: low walls, a tumbled mass that might once have been a tower or a pylon. There was a long cylindrical shape too, half buried by sand, that could be a fallen column. Emerson's eye couldn't be faulted; this was no way station.

Ramses followed his father, who had urged his reluctant steed into a trot. He was ten feet behind Emerson when he heard the sharp crack of a rifle. Emerson's horse screamed, reared, and toppled over. Ramses pulled Risha up and dismounted. He had not been aware of drawing his pistol until he realized he was holding it; avoiding the thrashing hooves of the wounded animal, he finished the poor creature with a bullet through the head and squeezed off a few random shots in the direction from which the firing had come before he dropped to his knees beside his father.

Emerson had jumped or been thrown off. Probably the former, since he had had time enough and sense enough to roll out of the way of the horse's body. He lay motionless on his side, his arms and legs twisted and his eyes closed. Torn between the need to get him to shelter and the fear of moving him, Ramses carefully straightened his legs, feeling for broken bones. A change in the rhythm of his father's breathing made him look up. Emerson's eyes were open.

"Did you get him?" he inquired.

"I doubt it," Ramses said, drawing a deep breath. "Taught him to keep his head down, I hope. Were you hit?"

"No."

"Anything broken?"

"No. Better get ourselves and Risha behind that wall."

He sat up, turned white, and fell backwards. Ramses caught him before his head, now uncovered, hit the ground. He'd been sick with fear when he feared his father might be dead or gravely injured. Now the lump in his throat broke and burst out of his mouth in a furious cascade of words.

"Goddamn you, Father, will you stop behaving as if you were omnipotent and omniscient? I know we must get under cover! I'll take care of that little matter as soon as I determine how seriously you're injured!"

Emerson gave his son a look of reproach. "You needn't shout, my boy. I put my shoulder out again, that's all."

"That's all, is it?" They both ducked their heads as another shot whistled past. "All right, here we go. Hang on to me."

After an effort that left them both breathless they reached the shelter of the ruined wall, with Risha close on their heels. Ramses eased his father onto the ground and wiped his sweating hands on his trousers.

"Better let him have a few more reminders to keep his head down," Emerson suggested.

"Father," Ramses said, trying not to shout, "if you make one more unnecessary, insulting, unreasonable suggestion —"

"Hmmm, yes, sorry," Emerson said meekly.

"I don't want to waste ammunition. I haven't any extra. It will be dark in a few hours and we're all right here unless he shifts position. If he moves I'll hear him. I'm going to put your shoulder back before I do anything else. Need I continue?"

"Your arm. It isn't . . ." His eyes met those of Ramses. "Hmph. Whatever you say, my boy."

Ramses had heard the story of how his father's shoulder had first been dislocated. His mother's version was very romantic and very inaccurate; according to her, Emerson had been struck by a stone while shielding her from a rockfall. Ramses could believe that all right. What he didn't believe was her claim that she herself had pulled the bone back into its socket. Such an operation required a lot of strength, especially when the victim was as heavily muscled as Emerson. Nefret had once demonstrated the technique, using Ramses as a subject, with such enthusiasm that he could have sworn her foot had left a permanent imprint under his arm.

For a few agonizing moments Ramses didn't think he was going to be able to do it. His right arm was unimpaired, though, and the left was of some little help. A final heave and twist, accompanied by a groan from Emerson — the first that had passed his lips — did the job. Weak-kneed and shaking, Ramses unhooked the canteen from Risha's saddle.

The process had been more agonizing for his father than for him. Emerson had fainted. Ramses trickled water over his face and between his lips, then poured a little into his own hand and wiped his mouth. It was the same temperature as the air, but it helped. His father's face was already dry and warm to the touch. Water evaporated almost instantly in the desert air.

"Father?" he whispered. Now that the immediate emergencies had been attended to, he had leisure to think about what he had said. Had he really sworn at his father and called him . . .

"Well done," said Emerson faintly.

"Done, at any rate. Have a drink. I'm sorry it's not brandy."

Emerson chuckled. "So am I. Your mother will point out, as she has so often, that we ought to emulate her habit of carrying such odds and ends."

He accepted a swallow of water and then pushed the canteen away. "Save it. Mine is on the body of that unfortunate animal, and it's not worth the risk of . . . Er, hmph. May I smoke?"

"You're asking *me?* Uh — I suppose so. Better now than after dark."

"You don't mean to stay here until dark, do you?"

"What else can we do?" Ramses demanded. He took the pipe from his father. After he had filled it he handed it back and struck a match. "Risha can't carry both of us, and it would be insane to expose ourselves to a marksman of that caliber. He dropped your horse with the first shot and the others came unpleasantly close."

The rifle spoke again. Sand spurted up from beside the carcass of the horse. The second bullet struck its body with a meaty thunk.

"He's somewhere on that rocky spur to the southeast," Ramses said. Emerson opened his mouth. Ramses anticipated him. "Forget the binoculars. A flash of reflected sunlight would give him his target. I fired three . . . no, four times. That leaves me with only six shots, and —"

"And a rifle has greater range than a pistol," Emerson said. "You needn't belabor the obvious, my boy. It appears we'll be here awhile."

Ramses looked round. A few yards to his right the ground dropped into a kind of hollow, bordered on two sides by the remains of the wall. He indicated the place to his father, who was graciously pleased to agree that it offered better protection for all concerned. He even accepted the loan of Ramses's arm. Getting Risha into shelter was a more nerve-wracking procedure, but they made it into the hollow without incident.

They celebrated with another swallow of warm water and another smoke. The slanting rays of sunlight beyond their shelter had turned gold.

"Someone will come looking for us in the morning," Ramses said.

"No doubt."

He seemed to have accepted the idea of waiting for rescue. That wasn't like him. Ramses had other ideas, but he did not intend to propose them. Short of knocking his father over the head, there was no way he could keep Emerson from trying to help him, and he didn't want help, not from an injured man who also happened to be someone he . . .

Someone he loved.

Emerson had dropped off to sleep, his head resting on Ramses's folded coat. Ramses watched the shadows darken across his father's still face and wondered why they all found that word so difficult. He loved both his parents, but he'd never told them so; he doubted he ever would. They had never said it to him either.

Was the word so important? He had never seen his mother cry until the other night, and he knew the tears had been for him: tears of worry and relief, and perhaps even a little pride. It had been a greater acknowledgment of her feelings than hugs and kisses and empty words. All the same . . .

Emerson's eyes opened, and Ramses started, as embarrassed as if his father could read his private thoughts. Emerson had not been asleep; he had been thinking. "Were our brilliant deductions about the route wrong after all?"

"I don't think so," Ramses said. "There'd be no point in killing us to prevent us from telling the authorities what we found; we haven't found a damned thing! It's more likely that someone took advantage of our being out here in the middle of nowhere to rid himself of . . . Father, it's me he's after. I'm damned sorry I got you into this."

"Don't be a bloody fool," his father growled.

"No, sir."

Emerson's eyes fell. It took Ramses several long seconds to interpret his expression correctly; he couldn't remember ever seeing his father look . . . guilty? Downcast eyes, tight mouth, bowed head — it was guilt, right enough, and all at once he understood why.

"No," he said again. "*I* didn't get *you* into this, did I? You went out of your way to find Hamilton this morning. You told him we were coming here. You —"

His father coughed apologetically. "Go on," he muttered. "Call me anything that comes to mind. I was the bloody fool; I knew that between the two of us we could deal with a few assassins or an ambush, but I didn't count on falling off the damned horse. If harm comes to you because of my clumsiness and stupidity, I will never forgive myself. Neither will your mother," he added gloomily.

"It's all right, Father." He felt an incongruous rush of pleasure. "Between the two of us . . ." Did his father really think that highly of him? "In fact, there's no one I would rather — er — well, you know what I mean."

Too English, David would have said. Both of them. Emerson raised his head. "Er — yes. I feel the same. Hmph."

Having got this effusive display of emotion

490

out of his system, he accepted a cigarette from the tin Ramses offered and allowed him to light it.

"What made you suspicious of Hamilton?" Ramses asked.

"Hamilton?" Emerson looked surprised. "No, no, my boy, you mistake me. I do not suspect him of anything except being a crashing bore."

"But the other night you implied you had identified Sethos. Don't deny it, Father, you wouldn't have been so certain Mother was on the wrong track if you hadn't suspected someone else. I thought —"

"Well, curse it, Hamilton's avoidance of us was suspicious, wasn't it? I was mistaken. As soon as I set eyes on him I knew he wasn't our man. I mentioned our destination to him as a precaution, so that if we did run into trouble someone would know where we were heading."

"Oh."

"A number of the officers overheard my conversation with Hamilton. One of them might have mentioned our intentions to other people. You see what that means, don't you? We're talking about a limited circle of people — all English, officers and gentlemen. One of them is working for the enemy. He had time to get out here before we arrived."

"Or send someone here to wait for us."

"Or reach someone by wireless." Emerson

shifted uncomfortably. He was obviously in pain, though he would rather have died than admit it.

Ramses unbuckled the holster, took off his shirt, and began tearing it into strips. "Let me strap your shoulder. Nefret showed me how."

"You can't do much worse than your mother," said Emerson with a reminiscent grin. "It was her petticoat she tore up. Women used to wear dozens of them. Useful for bandages, but cursed inconvenient in other ways."

Astonishment made Ramses drop one end of the cloth he was holding. Had that been a mildly risqué double entendre? Nothing double about it, in fact, but to hear his father say such a thing about his mother . . .

Greatly daring, he said, "I expect you managed, though."

Emerson chuckled. "Hmmm, yes. Thank you, my boy. That's much better."

"Why don't you try to get some sleep? We've nothing better to do."

"Wake me in four hours," Emerson muttered. "We'll take it in turn to keep watch."

"Yes, sir."

In four hours it would be dark and the moon would be up. It was a new moon, but there would be light from the brilliant stars. Ramses wasn't sure what he was going to do, but he had to do something. Desert nights were bitterly cold, and they had no blankets and very little water. Emerson had left his coat, canteen, weapon — everything except his precious pipe — on the saddle of the dead horse. Risha stood quietly, his proud head bent. He would have to go hungry and thirsty that night too. Ramses would have given him the last of the water, had he not wanted it for his father. Well, they would survive, all of them, and he'd have been willing to stick it out if the worst they had to fear was discomfort.

Would the assassin give up when darkness fell? Bloody unlikely, Ramses thought. If I'd sent him, I'd want proof that he'd done the job. A grisly picture flashed through his mind: Egyptian soldiers after a battle piling up their trophies of victory. Sometimes they collected the hands of the enemy dead. Sometimes it was other body parts.

Ramses began to unlace his boots.

The sun had just set and a dusky twilight blurred the air when he heard the sound he had been expecting. It was only the faint rattle of a pebble rolling, but in the eerie silence of the desert it was clearly audible. He strained his ears, but heard nothing more. Not an animal, then. Only a man bent on mischief would take pains to move so quietly.

He eased himself upright and moved cautiously along the wall, his bare feet sensitive to the slightest unevenness on the surface of the ground. The bastard knew where they were, of course, but a stumble or a slip would warn him that they were awake and on the alert. Then he heard another sound that literally paralyzed him with surprise.

"Hullo! Is someone there?"

A sudden glare of light framed the speaker — a British officer, in khaki drill jacket and short trousers, cap and puttees. He threw up his arm to shield his eyes.

"I see someone is," he said coolly. "Better switch that off, old boy. The fellow who was firing at you has probably taken to his heels, but one ought not take chances."

Emerson was on his feet. Injured, sick, or half-dead, he could move as silently as a snake, and he had obviously not been asleep.

"Looking for us, were you?" he inquired.

"Yes, sir. You are Professor Emerson? One of the Camel Corps chaps heard gunfire earlier and since you had not turned up, some of us went out looking for you."

"You aren't alone?"

"Three of my lads are waiting for me at the mouth of the wadi, where I left my horse. A spot of scouting seemed to be in order. Is your son with you?"

Pressed against the wall, Ramses held himself still. He could see the man's insignia now — a lieutenant's paired stars and the patch of the Lancashire Forty-second. His hands were empty and the holster at his belt was fastened. The impersonation was almost perfect — but it was damned unlikely that the military would send a patrol at this hour of the night to search for mislaid travelers, and although his accent was irreproachable, the intonations were just a bit off. Ramses had to admire the man's nerve. The ambush had failed and he was hoping to settle the business before daylight brought someone out looking for them.

Emerson was rambling on, asking questions and answering them, like a man whose tongue has been loosened by relief. He kept the torch pointed straight at the newcomer's eyes, though, and he had not answered the question about Ramses's whereabouts.

"Afraid I'll have to ask the loan of one of your horses," he said apologetically. "Banged myself up a bit, you see. If you could give me your arm . . ."

For a second or two Ramses thought it was going to work. The officer nodded affably and took a step forward.

The pistol wasn't in his holster. He had stuck it through his belt, behind his back. Ramses had a quick, unpleasant glimpse of the barrel swinging in his direction, and aimed his own weapon, but before he could fire Emerson dropped the torch and launched himself at the German.

They fell at Ramses's feet. By some miracle

the torch had not gone out; Ramses saw that the slighter man was pinned to the ground by Emerson's weight, but his arms were free and he was trying to use both of them at once. His fist connected with Emerson's jaw as Ramses kicked the gun out of his other hand. Emerson let out a yell of pure outrage and reached one-handed for the German's throat. Ramses swung his foot again and the flailing body went limp.

Emerson sat up, straddling the man's thighs, and rubbed his jaw.

"Sorry for being so slow, sir," Ramses said.

Emerson grinned and looked up. "Two good arms between the two of us. Not so bad, eh?"

"You saved my life. Again."

"I'd say the score was even. I tried to blind him but his night vision must be almost as good as yours. He went for you first because he took me to be unarmed and incapacitated. Now what shall we do with him?"

Ramses lowered himself to a sitting position, wondering if he would ever be able to match his father's coolness. "Tie him up, I suppose. I'll be damned if I know what with, though."

"Yards of good solid cloth in those puttees. Here — I think he's waking up. Stick that pistol of yours in his ear. He's a feisty lad, and I'd rather not have to argue with him again."

It struck Ramses as a good idea, so he complied. Emerson got the torch and positioned it more effectively before he began unwinding the strips of cloth from round the fellow's legs. Ramses studied the man's face curiously. It was a hard face, narrow across the forehead and broadening to a heavy jaw and protruding chin, but the mouth, relaxed in unconsciousness, was almost delicate in outline. He was younger than he had appeared. Hair, mustache, and scanty brows were fair, bleached almost to whiteness by the sun. His lips moved, and his eyes opened. They were blue.

"Sind Sie ruhig," Ramses said. "Rühren Sie sich und ich schiesse. Verstehen Sie?"

"I understand."

"You prefer English?" inquired Emerson, wrapping strips of cloth round the booted ankles. "It's no good, you know. You gave yourself away when you pulled that gun."

"I know."

"Are you alone?"

The pale-blue eyes rolled toward Ramses and then looked down. Emerson had managed to knot the strip of cloth by holding one end between his teeth. With his lips drawn back, he looked like a wolf chewing on a victim's torn garments. The German swallowed.

"What are you going to do with me?"

"Take you back to Cairo," Ramses said, since his father was still tying knots. "First we have a few questions. I strongly advise you to answer truthfully. My father is not a patient man and he is already rather annoyed with you."

"You torture prisoners?" The boy tried to sneer. He can't be much over twenty, Ramses thought. Just the right age for a job like this — all afire to die for the Fatherland or the Motherland or some equally amorphous cause, but not really believing death can touch him. He must have attended school in England.

"Good Gad, no," Emerson said. "But I cannot guarantee what will happen to you in Cairo. You are in enemy uniform, my lad, and you know what that means. Cooperate with us and you may not have to face a firing squad. First I want your name and the name of the man who sent you here."

"My name . . ." He hesitated. "Heinrich Fechter. My father is a banker in Berlin."

"Very good," Emerson said encouragingly. "I sincerely hope you may live to see him again one day. Who sent you?"

"I . . ." He ran his tongue over his lips. "I see I must yield. You have won. I salute you."

He raised his left hand. Ramses saw it coming, but the split second it took him to comprehend the boy's real intent was a split second too long. The muscles of his hand and arm had locked in anticipation of an attempt to seize the gun; before he could turn the weapon away the young German's thumb found Ramses's trigger finger and pressed it. The heavy-caliber bullet blew the top of his head off in a grisly cloud of blood and brains, splintered bone and hair.

"Christ!" Ramses stumbled to his feet and turned away, dropping the pistol. The night air was cold, but not as cold as the icy horror that sent shivers running through his body.

His father put Ramses's coat over his bare shoulders and held it there, his hands firm and steadying. "All right now?"

"Yes, sir. I'm sorry."

"Never apologize for feeling regret and pity. Not to me. Well. Let's get at it, shall we?"

It was a vile, horrible task, but he was up to it now. The search produced a set of skillfully forged documents, including a tattered photograph of a sweet-faced gray haired woman who was probably not the boy's mother. Emerson pocketed them. "Shall we try to find his horse?"

"We can't leave it here to die of thirst."

"No, but to search this terrain in the dark is to risk a broken leg. We will send someone to look for it in the morning, and for his camp."

There was one more thing. Neither of them had to suggest it; they set to work in silent unanimity, deepening the shallow depression in the corner of the wall. Ramses wrapped his coat round the shattered head before they moved the body. A good hard push sent the remains of the wall tumbling down over the grave.

"Do you remember his name?" Emerson asked.

"Yes." It was not likely he would ever forget it, or neglect the request implicit in that single answer to their questions. Someday the banker in Berlin would know that his son had died a hero, for whatever comfort that might give him.

Another death, another dead end, Ramses thought. It appeared there was to be no easy way out.

He got the canteen from the body of Emerson's horse and gave Risha a drink before he addressed his father. "D'you want to go on ahead? You can make better time alone. I'll be all right here."

"Good Gad, no. What if I fell off again? You go. I'll wait here."

He knew exactly what his father had in mind, and now he had no hesitation in saying so. "You want to explore your bloody damned ruins, don't you? If you think I am going to leave you stumbling round in the dark, without food or water or transport, you can think again. We'll go together. You ride Risha, I'll walk."

They had extinguished the torch, to save what was left of the failing batteries. He couldn't make out Emerson's expression, but he heard a soft chuckle. "Stubborn as a camel. Very well, my boy. Give me a hand up, will you? The sooner we get back, the better. God only knows what your mother has been up to."

11

The flat was in the fashionable Ismailiaya district. Waiting in the cab I had hired, I saw him enter the building at a few minutes past three. He had been lunching out.

I do not lie unless it is absolutely necessary. In this case it *had* been absolutely necessary. If Emerson had known what I intended, he would not have let me out of his sight. If I had told Nefret the truth, she would have insisted on accompanying me. Neither would have been acceptable.

I gave my quarry half an hour to settle down, and then inspected myself in the small hand mirror I carried. The disguise was perfect! I had never seen anyone who looked more like a lady bent on an illicit assignation. The only difficulty was my hat, which tended to tip, since the hat pins did not penetrate through the wig into my own hair. I pushed it back into position, adjusted the veil, and crossed the street. The doorkeeper was asleep. (They usually are.) I took the lift to the second floor and rang the bell. A servant answered it; his dark coloring and tarboosh were Egyptian, though he wore the neatly cut suit of a European butler. When he asked my name I put my finger to my lips and smiled meaningfully.

"You need not announce me. I am expected."

Evidently the Count was accustomed to receive female visitors who did not care to give their names. The man bowed without speaking and led me through the foyer. Opening a door, he gestured me to enter.

The room was a parlor or sitting room, quite small but elegantly furnished. A man sat writing at an escritoire near the windows, with his back to me. Apparently he agreed with Emerson that tight-fitting garments interfered with intellectual pursuits. He had removed his coat and waistcoat and rolled his shirtsleeves to the elbow.

I took a firmer grip on my parasol, readjusted my hat, and entered. The servant closed the door behind me — and then I heard a sound that made my breath catch.

I flung myself at the door. Too late! It was locked.

Slowly I turned to face the man who had risen to confront me, his hand resting lightly on the back of his chair. The black hair and mustache and the eyeglass were those of the Count de Sevigny. The lithe grace of his pose, the trim body, and the eyes, of an ambiguous shade between gray and brown, were those of someone else.

"At last!" he exclaimed. "I have waited tea

for you, my dear. Will you be good enough to pour?"

An elegant silver tea service stood on the table he indicated, together with with a dumbwaiter spread with sandwiches and iced cakes.

"Please take a chair so that I may do so," said Sethos politely. "I believe you have a fondness for cucumber sandwiches?"

"Cucumber sandwiches," I said, regaining my self-possession, "do not appeal to me at this moment. Pray let us not stand on ceremony. Sit down and keep your hands where I can see them."

In a single long step he was at my side. "The wig does not become you," he said, deftly whisking off the hat and the wig to which it was (somewhat precariously) attached. "And if you will permit me a word of criticism, that parasol does not match your frock."

The hand that rested on my shoulder fell away as I leaped back. He made no attempt to detain me. Instead he folded his arms and watched with infuriating amusement as I tugged in vain at the handle of the parasol. The release button was still sticking. I would have a few words to say to that lazy rascal Jamal when I returned home!

If I returned home.

"May I be of assistance?" Sethos inquired. He held out his hand.

The mocking smile, the contemptuous gesture gave me the additional strength I required. The button yielded. I whisked the blade out and brandished it.

"Ha!" I cried. "Now we will see who gives the orders here! Sit in that chair."

He appeared quite unperturbed for a man who has a sharp point an inch from his jugular, but he obeyed the order. "An engaging little accoutrement," he remarked. "Put it away, my dear. You won't use it; you are incapable of cutting a man's throat unless your passions are aroused, and I have no intention of arousing yours. Not that sort of passion, at any rate."

His gray — hazel — brown eyes sparkled wickedly. What color were they? I leaned closer. Sethos let out a little yelp. "Please, Amelia," he said plaintively.

A thin trickle of blood ran down his bared throat. "That was an accident," I said in some confusion.

"I know. I forgive you. Do sit down and give me a cup of tea. There is no need for this combative approach, you know. You have won. I yield."

"Have I? You do?"

Sethos leaned back, his hands on the arms of the chair. "I presume you have left the usual message to be opened if you fail to return home, so I can't keep you here indefinitely; your husband and son will not be back for some hours, but there are others who may be moved to come looking for you, including that charming little tigress, your daughter. She isn't really your flesh and blood, though; sometimes, Amelia, I am filled with wonderment at how you can be so clever about so many things and miss others that are right under your nose."

"Confound it!" I cried in considerable confusion. "How do you know . . . What do you mean by . . . You are trying to get me off the subject. We were speaking of —"

"My surrender." Sethos smiled. "I apologize. Conversation with you has such charm, I am always moved to prolong it."

"I accept your surrender. Come with me. I have a cab waiting." I took up a position of attack, feet braced, sword at the ready. Sethos's mouth underwent a series of contortions. Instead of rising, he leaned forward, his hands clasped. They were long-fingered, well-tended hands, and the bared forearms to which they were attached had a symmetry many younger men might have envied.

"You misunderstand me, dear Amelia. You have already captured my heart, and the rest of me is at your disposal, but not if you want to dispose of it into a prison cell. What I meant was that you have destroyed the usefulness of this persona. The Count will never be seen again in Cairo. Now sit down and have your tea, and we will chat like the old friends we are. Who knows, you may be able to trick me into betraying information that will enable you to put an end to me once and for all."

His mouth twitched again. He was laughing at me! All the better, I thought; in his arrogance he believes me incapable of catching him off-guard. We would see about that!

I sat down on the sofa behind the tea table, leaned the parasol, still unsheathed, against one of the cushions, and placed my handbag at my feet. My position was greatly improved thereby, since it left both my hands free. I had been unable to extract the handcuffs or the pistol or the length of rope from my bag while I held the sword. I would defeat him yet! But before I took him prisoner I wanted explanations for several of his enigmatic statements.

"How do you know Ramses and Emerson will not be back for some hours?" I inquired, pouring the tea. "Milk or lemon? Sugar?"

"Lemon, please. No sugar." He leaned forward to take the cup from my hand. His eyes met mine. Surely they were brown?

"And how dare you refer to Nefret so familiarly?" I went on, pouring a cup for myself. Excitement had made me quite thirsty, and I knew the tea could not be drugged since both cups came from the same pot. "And what were you implying when you informed me of a fact I know quite well, namely that she is not —"

"Wait!" Sethos held up his hand. "A little order and method, my dear, if you please. Let me take your questions one by one."

"Pray do."

He indicated the plate of sandwiches. I shook my head. His smile broadened. "They have not been tampered with." He took one, seemingly at random, and bit into it.

"But you expected me. How did you know I would come here today?"

Sethos swallowed. "Another question! These are excellent sandwiches, by the way. Are you sure you won't . . . ? Very well. I expected you today because I knew you had recognized me last night."

"I told you I would know you anywhere, in any disguise."

"Yes. Touching, isn't it? I believed you when you told me that, and I have been careful to stay out of your way, though I was unable to resist presenting you with a token of my affection. Are you going to thank me properly?"

The melting look he gave me would have been more effective if I had not known he was laughing at me. "It was a foolish gesture," I said severely.

"Yes, I suppose it was. A student of psychology like yourself might claim I did it because subconsciously I wanted you to find me. I didn't anticipate you would follow the young lady — is that what you were doing, or

508

was it a joint venture? — but I knew you instantly, in spite of that hideous wig. It works both ways, you know. The eyes of love —"

"Enough of that."

"I beg your pardon. So, knowing your inveterate habit of rushing into action without stopping to consider the possible consequences, I fancied you would drop by today. I was all the more certain after I learned, from sources that shall be nameless, that your husband had gone off into the Eastern Desert looking for ruins. Or so he claimed. What's he after, really?"

I allowed my lips to curve into an ironic smile. "You don't suppose you can trap me into a damaging admission, do you? There is nothing to admit. Emerson is an archaeologist, not some sort of spy."

"And your son?"

The expression in those chameleon eyes made a shiver run through me. I concealed my alarm with a little chuckle. "How absurd. Ramses's views about the war are well-known. They must be known to you as well."

"I know a great deal about that young man. So do others. The individuals in question are in some doubt as to the genuineness of his opinions."

"Individual, you mean," I said. "You are referring to yourself, are you not? A man in your vile profession suspects everyone of double-dealing."

The insult struck home. His face hardened and his form stiffened. "I serve my present employers faithfully. You may not approve my methods, but you are hardly in a position to criticize them."

"What do you mean?" I cried in terror.

"Why . . . only that you would do the same had you my qualifications. Fortunately, you don't; but if you did, you would not hesitate to risk not only life but the appearance of honor."

"I don't understand."

But I did understand, and I felt sick with fear and dismay. He was working for the enemy and he was warning me that his "employers," as he was pleased to call them, were suspicious of Ramses. Those sneering references to the hazarding of life and the appearance of honor described my son's masquerade only too accurately. Sethos had once promised me that none of those I loved would come to harm through him; the oblique warning was his perverse way of keeping that promise.

I reached into the bag at my feet, and saw him stiffen, his eyes following the movement of my hand, his body taut as a coiled spring, and I knew that I had made a fatal error. I had believed that he was guilty of nothing more despicable than dealing in illegal antiquities, and I had counted upon . . . I felt my cheeks grow warm with shame. Yes, I had counted upon that fondness he claimed to feel for me; I had intended to use it in order to induce him to do my bidding. What a fool I had been! He was worse than a thief, he was a spy and a traitor, and I dared not risk his escaping me now, not when my son's life might depend on what he knew. I could not overpower him. I could not bind him or handcuff him unless I rendered him unconscious first, and I doubted he would be obliging enough to turn his back so I could strike him senseless. That left the pistol as my only recourse. But what if I missed, or only wounded him with the first shot? I knew his strength and his quickness; anticipating an attack, as he clearly was, he could be upon me before I extracted the weapon and aimed it. Yes, I had been a fool, but I might yet outwit him.

I picked up the bag and rose to my feet. Sethos's taut muscles relaxed. He smiled amiably at me.

"Leaving so soon? Without getting answers to your other questions?"

"Why, yes." I took hold of the parasol and edged round the table. "We seem to have reached an impasse. I cannot force you to accompany me, and I am willing to accept your word that you will leave Cairo at once. Good-bye, and — er — thank you for the tea."

"Your manners are impeccable!" Sethos

laughed. "But I fear you cannot leave just yet."

He came toward me, with that light, lithe step I knew so well. I backed away. "You said you would not keep me here."

"Not indefinitely, I said. But my dear, you don't suppose I am going to let you go scurrying off to the police? It will take me a few hours to complete the preparations for my departure. Resign yourself to waiting a while. I promise you won't be uncomfortable, and I will take steps to have you released once I am safely on my way."

I raised my parasol. With a sudden sweep of his arm Sethos knocked it out of my hand.

"You drugged the tea," I gasped, as he reached for me.

"No. If your hands were unsteady, it must have been for another reason." He held me in the circle of his arm and pulled me close. The other hand came to rest on my cheek. "Do you remember my telling you once about a certain nerve just behind the ear?"

"Yes. Do it, then! Render me instantly and painlessly unconscious, as you threatened, you — you cad!"

He laughed his soundless laugh. "Oh, my dearest Amelia, I haven't even begun to be a cad. Shall I?"

His long hard fingers slid through my hair and tilted my head back. His face was only a few inches from mine. I peered intently into that enigmatic countenance. His eyes were gray, with just a hint of green. I thought I detected a faint line along the bridge of his nose, where some substance had been added to fill out the shape of that member. His long flexible lips were not quite so thin as they seemed. . . .

They closed in a hard line, and the arm that held me tightened painfully. "For God's sake, Amelia, the least you can do is pay attention when I am trying to decide whether to take advantage of you! After all, why should I not? How many times have you been in my power, and how often have I dared to do so much as kiss your hands? I have never loved another woman but you. These are perilous times; I may never see you again. What is to stop me from doing what I have always yearned to do?"

I couldn't think of anything either.

"Er — your sense of honor?" I suggested.

"According to you, I have none," Sethos said bitterly. "And don't think that tears will deter me from my purpose!"

"I have no intention of weeping."

"No, you wouldn't. That is one of the reasons why I love you so much." His lips came lightly to rest on mine. I felt him tremble; then he clasped me tightly to him and captured my mouth in a hard, passionate kiss.

I struggled, of course. Dignity and my duty to my adored spouse demanded no less. In practical terms it was a wasted effort. Those strong arms held me as easily as if I had been a child. His lips moved to my cheek, and as I gasped for air he whispered, "Don't fight me, Amelia, you will only hurt yourself, and resistance brings out the worst in men of my evil temperament. I refuse to be held wholly accountable for my actions if you continue. There. That is much better. . . ."

Again his mouth covered mine.

I could not have said how long that burning kiss went on. I did not feel the touch that deprived me of consciousness.

When I came to my senses I felt as if I had woken from a restful sleep — pleasantly relaxed and comfortable. Then I remembered. I sat up with a muffled shriek and glared wildly at my surroundings.

I was alone. The room was dark except for the glow of a single lamp. It was a bedchamber. The couch on which I had reposed was soft, piled with cushions and draped with silken hangings of azure and silver. Typical of the Count, and also of Sethos; he had luxurious tastes. On a table beside the bed was a crystal carafe of water, a silver cup, and . . . and . . . a plate of cucumber sandwiches! They were curling at the edges. The manservant might at least have covered them with a damp napkin. But then, I mused, he probably had more urgent duties.

Reflection and investigation (I believe I

514

need not go into detail) persuaded me that Sethos's attentions had not gone beyond those long, ardent kisses. They were quite enough, as Emerson would certainly agree when I told him. . . . If I told him.

My immediate concern was escape. The door was locked, of course. I had expected that. The windows were covered with shutters that had been made fast by some mechanism I could not locate. My watch informed me that several hours had passed since I entered the flat. It was getting on for seven o'clock. Upon investigating my handbag, which had been placed beside me on the couch, I discovered that the handcuffs, the rope, the scissors, and the pistol were missing. The bureau had been swept clean; the drawers had been emptied of their contents (whatever those might have been) and the top was bare of toilet articles. There was nothing in the room that could serve as a weapon or a lockpick.

I removed a hairpin from my untidy coiffure and knelt before the lock.

As I had discovered on an earlier occasion, hairpins are not of much use for picking a lock. However, with my ear close to the door I was able to make out sounds from the room beyond — hurrying footsteps, the movement of a heavy object being dragged across the floor, an occasional brusque order in that familiar, detestable voice. Clearly Sethos was completing his preparations for departure. The final command made this definite. "Bring the carriage round and start carrying the luggage down."

Footsteps approached the door behind which I knelt. Would he open it? Would he wish to bid me another, final farewell — or finish the dastardly deed he had threatened? My heart was pounding as I rose to my feet, prepared to resist to the last of my strength.

All I heard was a long, deep sigh. The footsteps moved away.

I was still standing by the door, my hand pressed to my breast, when a cry from Sethos made me jump. "What the devil —" A door slammed, the servant screamed, and Sethos began to laugh.

"Bit you, did she? Here, let me have her. Now, my dear, there is no need for all this exhausting activity; she is safe and unharmed and if you behave yourself I will allow you to keep one another company while I complete the preparations you so rudely interrupted. If you don't, I will lock you in a dark cupboard with the mops and brooms and black beetles. Good. I see you are susceptible to reason. Hamza, unlock the door. Amelia, stand back; I know you have your ear pressed to the panel, and I am running short of time."

It was as well I obeyed. The door flew open and I saw — as I had known I would — my daughter and my dread adversary. One arm pinned her arms to her sides and held her firmly; the other hand covered her mouth. Her hair was coming down and her eyes shone with fury but she had had the sense to stop struggling.

"It would be a waste of breath to scream or swear, Miss Forth," Sethos said, propelling her into the room. "Do so if it will relieve your feelings, but first give me the knife I feel certain you have concealed about your person. The alternative would be for me to search you, and I will not take that liberty unless you force me to. Amelia would not approve."

He removed his hand from her mouth, leaving the marks of his fingers imprinted on her cheek. She swallowed, and I said quickly, "Give him the knife, Nefret. This is not the time for heroics or temper."

Her eyes moved from me to Sethos, who had backed off a step, and then to the manservant. She was calculating the odds, and admitting they were against us. She reached into a side pocket of her skirt. Set into the seam, it was open at the back, giving her access to the knife strapped to her lower limb. Slowly she withdrew it, hesitated, and then passed it into Sethos's poised, waiting hand.

"How did you know I was here?" I demanded. "And why were you foolish enough to come alone, as I presume you —"

"Forgive me," Sethos interrupted. "You

517

can chat after I have gone. I am in something of a hurry, but so long as I am here . . ."

He took a step toward me, and then stopped and looked quizzically at Nefret. "Turn your back, Miss Forth."

Nefret's eyes widened. "Do it," I said, through clenched teeth. She spun round.

I might have evaded him for a short time; but how undignified, how humiliating would have been that frantic and futile flight, with Sethos close on my heels and his long arms ready to seize me! He would probably be laughing. It would end the same, whatever I did. Better by far to submit and get it over.

So once again I felt his arms close round me and his lips explore mine. For a man who claimed to be in a hurry, he took his time about it. When he let me go I would have fallen — being off balance — had he not lowered me gently onto the foot of the couch.

"Good-bye, Amelia," he said quietly. "And you, my dear Miss Forth . . ."

He took her by the shoulders and turned her to face him. Her face was flushed and her lips were parted. He laughed and kissed her lightly on the forehead.

"Be good, sweet maid, and let who will be clever. Particularly at the present time. Amelia, remember what I told you."

The door slammed and the key turned in the lock.

Nefret groped for a chair and lowered herself into it. "What did he mean?"

"Mean by what? The villain specializes in being enigmatic. My dear, did that man hurt you?"

"No." Nefret rubbed her arm. "He humiliated me, which is even worse. I was waiting on the landing, trying to decide whether to ring or not, when he came out and caught hold of me. Oh, Aunt Amelia, I am sorry, but I didn't know what to do! When I came back from the hospital you were all gone, all three of you, and it got darker and darker, and later and later, and there was no sign of them and no word, and I didn't know where to start looking for them, but I did have a fairly good idea as to where you might have gone, because I suspected you had lied to me about the Count, and I couldn't stand waiting any longer, so . . . I'm sorry!"

"They had not returned by the time you left?"

"No. Something has happened."

"Nonsense," I said firmly. "I can think of a dozen harmless reasons why they might have been delayed. Emerson is easily distracted by ruins. Never mind that now, we cannot do anything about it until we get out of here. Have you any object on your person that we might use to pick the lock or break open a shutter?"

"I had only my knife. You saw what happened to that."

I stood up and began pacing. "Let us consider the situation rationally. We will be freed eventually; I left a message for Emerson, telling him where I had gone, and —"

"So did I. For Ramses. But what if they don't . . ."

"They will. They may have returned by now, and be on their way here. If they are . . . if they are delayed, someone will release us eventually."

I went to the door and put my ear against it. "I don't hear anything. I believe Sethos has gone. He will want several hours in which to make good his escape from Cairo. By midnight —"

"Midnight!" Nefret jumped up. "Good God, Aunt Amelia, we cannot wait so long! What makes you suppose Sethos will take the trouble to inform someone of our whereabouts?"

"He will," I said, with more confidence than I felt. It was necessary to calm the girl; she looked like Medusa, her hair falling loose over her shoulders, her eyes wild. "But I agree we should not wait for rescue. I will get back to work on the lock — I have plenty of hairpins — and you see what you can do with the shutters. First, however . . . Nefret! My dear, this is not the time to succumb to faintness."

She had pressed her hands to her face. I caught hold of her swaying form and lowered her into a chair.

"I'm not going to faint." I had to strain to hear the low voice. Slowly she lowered her hands. "It's all right."

"Have a cucumber sandwich!" I snatched up the plate and offered it to her.

"No, thank you." Her face was glowing with perspiration, but calm. She let out a long breath and smiled. "Cucumber sandwiches, Aunt Amelia?"

"We need to keep up our strength."

"Yes, of course. I am frightfully thirsty too. Can we trust the water, do you think?"

The change in her was astonishing. She had exerted her will, under the dominance of an even stronger will, and was now an ally on whom I could depend.

"I believe we can. As you see, he has left a little note."

It read, "You probably won't believe me, Amelia dear, but the water is not drugged. Neither are the cucumber sandwiches."

I handed it to Nefret, who actually laughed when she read it. "He is an amazing individual. Did he . . . If you don't mind my asking . . ."

"He did not."

"Oh. He did kiss you, though? When he told me to turn my back?"

I did not reply. Nefret took a sandwich. "He kissed *me* on the brow," she muttered. "As if I were a child! He is strong, isn't

521

he? And tall, and —"

"He is a spy and a traitor," I said. "We must stop him before he leaves Cairo. If you have fully recovered, Nefret, let us get to work."

We had a sandwich or two (they were very good, though the bread was beginning to go stale) and a sip of water, before exploring the chamber more intensively than I had done earlier. Nefret tore the place to pieces, in fact, flinging mattress and cushions onto the floor, overturning chairs and, at last, repeatedly dashing a small brass table against the wall until it broke apart. Selecting one of the metal supports, she went to the shutters and began prying at them. Her actions were vigorous but controlled; she appeared to be in a much calmer frame of mind than she had been earlier — calmer than my own. Her statement that Ramses and Emerson had not returned by the time she left had frightened me more than I dared admit even to myself. Emerson was easily distracted by ruins, but Sethos's claim that he had known of their purpose aroused the direst of forebodings.

Nefret's efforts succeeded at last. She let out a cry of triumph. One of the shutters had given way. I hurried to her side as she flung it back and leaned out the window.

It did not open onto the Sharia Suleiman Pasha, but onto a narrower street that had not so much traffic. However, our cries finally attracted attention; a turbaned porter, bent under a load of pots and pans, stopped and looked up. I addressed him in emphatic Arabic. When I told him what I wanted, he demanded money before he would stir a step, and we dickered for a bit before I persuaded him to accept an even larger payment upon the completion of his errand. He was gone some time, and Nefret was knotting the satin sheets into a rope when he finally returned, accompanied by a uniformed constable.

There are advantages to being notorious. As soon as I identified myself to the constable, he was ready to obey my commands. However, by the time our rescuers began banging on the door of the flat I was almost ready to take my chances with Nefret's rope.

My cries of encouragement and impatience directed them to the bedchamber. They got that door open too, and I rushed out, searching the faces of the men who had entered the sitting room. One of them was familiar — but alas, it was not the face I had hoped to see. Mr. Assistant Commissioner Thomas Russell was in evening kit, and this annoyed me to an excessive degree. I seized him by his lapels.

"Enjoying an evening out?" I demanded. "While others risk life and the appearance of . . . Curse it, Russell, while you were lollygagging about, the Master Criminal has escaped! And where is my husband?"

Russell kept his head, which was, I admit, rather commendable of him under the circumstances. He pushed me back into the bedchamber and closed the door.

"For the love of Heaven, Mrs. Emerson, don't tell your business to every police officer in Cairo! What is all this about master criminals?"

"He is the Count de Sevigny. Sethos is the Count. The Master Criminal is Sethos."

"Allow me to get you some brandy, Mrs. Emerson."

"I don't want brandy, I want you to go after Sethos! He is probably in Alexandria or Tripoli by now — or Damascus — or Khartoum — it would not surprise me to learn that he knows how to fly one of those aeroplanes. You must shoot him down before he reaches enemy lines."

Nefret put her arm round me and murmured soothingly, but it was Russell's incredulous question that made me realize I might not have taken the right approach. "Are you telling me, Mrs. Emerson, that you and Miss Forth came alone to the flat of a man you knew to be a spy and — er — Master Criminal?"

"Not together," I said. "When I failed to return home, Miss Forth came to rescue me."

"The devil she did!"

"The devil I didn't," Nefret said with wry

amusement. "Rescue her, that is. I confess neither of us behaved sensibly, Mr. Russell. Don't scold, but get your men after him. Our imprisonment and his flight are, surely, evidence that he is guilty of something."

Russell gave a grudging nod. "Very well. Go home, ladies, and get out of my . . . That is, go home. I will send one of my men with you."

"But what of Emerson?" I demanded. "He and Ramses ought to have been back hours ago."

"Ramses went with him?" Russell's cold eyes grew even frostier. "Where?"

"Into the Eastern Desert. They were looking for —"

Now it was Mr. Russell who was in danger of forgetting himself. I cut short his incoherent anathemas with a useful reminder.

"I will take Miss Forth home, as you advised. You will let us know at once if you — when you hear."

"Yes. And you will send to inform me if — when they return. They had no business . . . Well. Good night, ladies."

As we passed through the sitting room, one of the constables spoke. "Look here, sir. The man *was* a criminal! In his haste he forgot his implements of crime."

They were set out on the tea table: handcuffs, a coil of rope, a little pistol, and a long knife.

"Those are mine," I said, holding out my hand. "Except for the knife. It belongs to Miss Forth."

For some reason this harmless statement brought Russell's temper to the breaking point. He bundled us out the door and directed a constable to put us in a cab.

All along the homeward path I looked for a yellow motorcar being driven at breakneck speed toward the Count's flat. No such vision rewarded my search. When we arrived home we found, not Emerson and Ramses, but Fatima, Selim, Daoud, and Kadija. All of them except the ever-calm Kadija were in a considerable state of agitation. They took turns embracing me and Nefret and peppered us with questions, while Fatima produced platter after platter of food. It took us considerable time to convince them we were unharmed, and then we had to apologize for failing to tell them where we had gone.

"You did not come home for dinner," Fatima said, fixing me with an accusing stare. "Ramses and the Father of Curses did not come back. Then Nur Misur went away. What was I to do? I sent for Daoud, and Selim, and —"

"Yes, I see. I appreciate your concern, but there is nothing to worry about now. It is very late; good night and thanks to you all."

Selim and Daoud exchanged glances. "Yes, Sitt Hakim," the former said.

After they had left the room, Nefret said, "They won't leave, not until Ramses and the Professor are safely back. Go to bed, Aunt Amelia. Yes, I know, you won't sleep a wink, but at least lie down and rest. If they lost their way, they may have decided to wait until daylight before starting back."

Hoping that she at least would rest, I agreed, and we went to our respective rooms. I was removing my crumpled frock when she tapped at my door.

"See who I found, asleep on my bed. I thought you might like her company tonight."

She was carrying Seshat.

It was unusual for the cat to be in my room or Nefret's unless she was in search of something or someone. This did not appear to be the case now; when Nefret put her down on the foot of the bed she curled herself into a neat coil and closed her eyes. Feeling somewhat comforted and more than a little foolish, I stretched out beside the cat, although I knew I would not sleep a wink.

As I neared the top of the cliff I looked up to see a tall, familiar form silhouetted against the pale blue of the early-morning sky. I was in Luxor again, climbing the steep path that led to the top of the plateau behind Deir el Bahri, and Abdullah was waiting. He reached out a hand to help me up the last few feet, and sat down beside me as I sank panting onto a convenient boulder.

He looked as he always did in those dreams — his stalwart form that of a man in the prime of life, his handsome, hawklike features framed by a neatly trimmed black beard and mustache. They remained impassive, but his black eyes shone affectionately.

"Finally!" I exclaimed, when I had got my breath back. "Abdullah, I have wanted so much to see you. It has been too long."

"Long for you, perhaps, Sitt. There is no time here, on the other side of the Portal."

"I haven't the patience for your philosophical vagueness tonight, Abdullah. You claim to know everything that happens to me — you must know how frightened I am, how much in need of comfort."

I held out my hands to him, and he enclosed them in his. "They are well, Sitt Hakim, the two you love best. Soon after you wake you will see them."

I knew I was dreaming, but that reassurance carried as much conviction as the evidence of my own eyes would have done. "Thank you," I said, with a long breath of relief. "It is good news you give me, but it is only part of what I want to hear. How will it end, Abdullah? Will they live and be happy?"

"I cannot tell you endings, Sitt."

"You did before. You said the falcon would fly through the portal of the dawn. Which portal, Abdullah? There are many doorways, and some lead to death."

"And from it. One may pass in or out of a portal, Sitt."

"Abdullah!"

I tried to free my hands. He held them more tightly, and he laughed a little. "I cannot tell you endings because I do not know them all. The future can be changed by your actions, Sitt, and you are not careful. You do foolish things."

"You don't know?" I repeated. "Even about David? He is your grandson — don't you care?"

"I care about all of you. And I would like my grandson to live to see his son." His sober face brightened, and he added smugly, "They will name him after me."

"Oh, it is to be a boy, is it?"

"That is already determined. As for the rest . . ." His eyes dwelt on my face. "I should not tell you even so much as this, but mark my words well. There will come a time when you must trust the word of one you have doubted, and believe a warning that has no more reality than these dreams of yours. When that time comes, act without hesitation or doubt."

He rose to his feet, drawing me to mine, and carried the hands he held to his lips. "You may tell Emerson of this kiss," he said, his eyes twinkling. "But if I were you, Sitt, I would not tell him of those others."

Instead of vanishing into the depths of sleep, as he and his surroundings had done before, he turned and walked away. He did not stop or look back as he followed the long path that led to the Valley where the kings of Egypt had been laid to rest.

When I opened my eyes, the room was filled with the pearly light of early morning. Seshat sat beside me, holding a fat mouse in her mouth. Sluggish with sleep, I was unable to move in time to prevent her from placing it neatly on my chest.

That got me up in a hurry. Seshat retrieved the mouse from the corner where I had flung it, gave me a look of disgust, and went out the window with it. My inadvertent cry — for even a woman of iron nerve may be taken aback by a dead mouse six inches from her nose — brought Nefret bursting into the room. After I had finished explaining and Nefret had finished laughing, she took me by the shoulders.

"You look much better, Aunt Amelia. You did sleep."

"I dreamed."

"Of Abdullah?" Nefret was the only one I had told of those dreams, and of my half-shamed belief in them. "What did he say?"

"Lia's baby is a boy."

Nefret's smile was fond but skeptical. "He has a fifty-percent chance of being right."

"Emerson and Ramses are safe. He said I would see them soon after I woke. And don't tell me the same odds apply to that prediction!"

"No. I am certain he was right about that."

"You needn't humor me, Nefret, I know there is no truth in such visions. But —"

"But they comfort you. I'm glad. I wish I could dream of the dear old fellow too." She gave me a hug. "Fatima is cooking breakfast. They're still here — Daoud and Selim and Kadija — and several of the others turned up."

However, before we reached the breakfast room, our ears were assaulted by one of the most horrible noises I have ever heard. It grew louder and louder. I was about to clap my hands over my ears when it stopped, and in the silence I heard another sound — a sound as sweet as music to my anxious ears — Emerson's voice bellowing my name.

Nefret must have recognized the significance of the racket before I did. She ran to the door. Ali had opened it, and stood staring.

I did not blame Ali for staring. Never had the Father of Curses appeared in such a contrivance. Motorcycles had always reminded me of enlarged mechanical insects. This one, which was bestrode by a pale young man in khaki, had a bulging excrescence on one side. The sidecar, as I believe it is called, was occupied by Emerson. A delighted grin indicated his enjoyment of the experience.

It took three of us, including Ali, to get Emerson out of the contraption. He is so very large that he fitted rather tightly, and — as I soon observed — he had not the use of his left arm. Eventually we extracted him, and I thanked the young man who was still sitting on the vehicle. He turned a glazed stare toward me.

"Are we there?" he asked stupidly.

"You are here," I replied. "Dismount, or get off, as the case may be, and have breakfast with us."

"No, thank you, ma'am, I was told to come straight back." He shook his head. "He kept shouting at me to go faster, ma'am. I never heard such — such . . ."

"Language," I supplied. "I don't doubt it. Are you sure you wouldn't like —"

The motorbicycle roared and rushed off in a cloud of dust.

"Splendid machine," said Emerson, gazing wistfully after it. "I wanted to drive it, but the fellow wouldn't let me. We must have one, Peabody. I will take you for a ride in the sidecar."

"Not while there is breath in my body," I informed him. "Oh, Emerson, curse you, how could you worry me so? What happened?"

Nefret had not spoken. Now a very small

532

voice uttered a single word. "Ramses?"

"Coming," Emerson replied. "He insisted on bringing Risha home himself. The brave creature will want a day or two of pampering; he had a tiring experience."

"So did you, I see," I remarked, inspecting him more closely. He was not wearing a coat. One arm was fastened to his body by strips of cloth. His shirt was torn and dirty, his face bruised, his hands scraped.

"I apologize for my appearance," Emerson said cheerfully. "They offered us baths and bandages and food and so on, but I was determined to relieve your mind as soon as I could."

"Considerate of you," I said. "Come upstairs."

"Upstairs be damned. I haven't eaten a decent meal since yesterday morning. You can clean me up after breakfast. I hope there is a great deal of it."

There was a great deal, and Emerson ate most of it. Nefret hovered over him, trying to examine him, but there was not much she could do when he refused to lie down and stop gesticulating. He was still eating when Ramses arrived. He had borrowed a mount and was leading Risha. He turned the stallion over to Selim, who crooned to the noble beast as he led him to the stable.

"You don't look much better than your father," I said. "What happened to your shirt?

And your nice new tweed coat? That one you are wearing doesn't fit."

"Let him eat first, Aunt Amelia," Nefret said somewhat snappishly.

"Thank you," Ramses said. "I will just put on a clean shirt before I have breakfast; this is Father's coat, and you are quite right; it doesn't fit."

It hid the bandages and the scars of his recent injury, however. I decided I had better go with him and make certain he was not in need of immediate medical attention, for he was not likely to tell me if he was.

He was waylaid in the courtyard by the entire family, including Emerson. After embracing him, Daoud announced, "I will go home. It is well now that you are here."

"Hmph," said Emerson indignantly. "What about me?"

Ramses glanced at his father; his lips parted in a smile so wide I would have called it a grin if I had believed my son's countenance capable of that expression. Then he slipped away and started up the stairs.

I started after him. Emerson caught me by the arm and whispered into my ear, "Don't ask him about his coat."

Emerson's whispers are audible ten feet away. Everyone in the courtyard heard him, including Nefret. "Why not?" she asked.

"He left it, you see," Emerson gabbled. "Forgot it. New coat. Fuss at the boy . . ."

I left him telling lies and went after Ramses.

His door was open. I was somewhat startled to hear him say, "Most kind. However, I am about to eat breakfast. Perhaps we might put it aside for later."

He was standing by the bed holding a dead mouse by the tail.

"So that is what she did with it," I remarked. "I was the first recipient, and I fear I did not accept the gift as graciously as you. I wish you wouldn't talk to the cat as you do to a human being, it is very disconcerting. Take off that coat and let me have a look at you."

Ramses put the mouse on his bureau. Seshat sat down and began washing her face.

"Leave it, Mother." He removed the coat and tossed it onto the bed. Except for the half-healed wounds, his tanned chest and back were unmarked. "I'm as hungry as a pariah dog. Father needs your care more than I. I'm surprised you haven't been at him already."

"He was too hungry." I watched him pull a shirt from the cupboard and slip into it. "He said he'd fallen off his horse when the poor creature stepped into a hole and broke its leg. What happened?"

"He fell, yes. So did the gelding, when it was struck by a bullet." He finished buttoning his shirt. "Can you wait for the rest of it? No, I suppose not. We were ambushed. The

535

fellow had us pinned down, and with Father injured it seemed advisable to stay where we were until dark. The man was a German spy. He came out of hiding, and we had a little skirmish. He killed himself rather than be taken prisoner. We started back. When we got onto the caravan road I fired off a few shots, which eventually attracted the attention of the Camel Corps. They escorted us to the barracks at Abbasia."

The narrative had been as crisp and unemotional as a report. I knew he had not told me everything, and I also knew it was all I was going to get out of him.

Ramses tucked his shirt in. "May we go down now?"

Everyone was having a second breakfast, to Fatima's delight; she liked nothing better than feeding as many people as she could get hold of. As soon as she saw Ramses she concentrated her efforts on him, and for some time he was unable to converse at all as she stuffed him with eggs and porridge and bread and marmalade.

Emerson was telling Selim and Daoud — who had not gone home — about the ruins in the desert. "A temple," he declared dogmatically. "Nineteenth Dynasty. I saw a cartouche of Ramses the Second. We'll spend a few days out there, Selim, after the end of our regular season."

Oh, yes, of course, I thought. A few peaceful days in the desert with German spies skulking about and the Turks attacking the Canal and the Camel Corps shooting at anything that moved. What had they done with the body of the dead spy? That would be a pretty thing to come upon in the course of excavation.

Finally I put an end to the festivities by insisting that Emerson bathe and rest. Selim said they would return to Atiyah and await Emerson's orders. "Tomorrow —" he began.

"Tomorrow?" Emerson exclaimed. "I will join you at Giza in two hours or less, Selim. Good Gad, we've missed half a morning's work as it is."

I took Emerson away. We had a great deal to talk about.

"Two more shirts ruined," I remarked, cutting away the remains of both garments. "I want Nefret to have a look at your shoulder, Emerson. I am sure Ramses did the best he could, but —"

"No one could have done better. Did he tell you what happened?"

"A synopsis only. He was distressed about something, I could tell."

Emerson gave me a somewhat longer synopsis. "The fellow was no older than Ramses, if as old. No one could have stopped him in time, and Ramses's finger was on the trigger when the gun fired."

"No wonder he was upset."

"Upset? You have a gift for understatement, my dear. It was a ghastly sight, and so damnably unnecessary! I hope the bastards who fill the heads of these boys with empty platitudes and then send them out to die burn in the fires of hell for all eternity."

"Amen. But, Emerson —"

A tap on the door interrupted me. "That must be Nefret," I said.

"May as well let her in," Emerson muttered. "She's as bull— as determined as you."

Nefret's examination was brief. "I am glad to see Ramses paid close attention to my lecture. It will be tender for a few days, Professor; I suppose there is no point in my telling you to favor that arm. I will just strap it properly."

"No, you will not," said Emerson. "I want to bathe, so take yourself off, young lady. Why are you still wearing your dressing gown? Put on proper clothing, we will leave for the dig as soon as I am ready."

I encouraged her departure, for I still had a good many questions to put to Emerson. To some of them he could only offer educated guesses, but it was evident that the ambush had been arranged by a man high in military or official circles, and that he was in communication with the enemy by wireless or other means.

"We knew that," I said, pacing up and

down the bath chamber while Emerson splashed in the tub. "And we are no closer to learning his identity. You say a number of officers overheard your conversation?"

"Yes. Maxwell also knew of our intentions. He may have let something slip to a member of his staff."

"Curse it."

"Quite," Emerson agreed. "Too damned many people know too damned much. I don't suppose you have heard from Russell?"

"Er . . ."

Emerson heaved himself up and stood like the Colossus of Rhodes after a rainstorm, water streaming down his bronzed and muscular frame. "Out with it, Peabody. I knew you were guilty of something, you have a certain look."

"I had every intention of telling you all about it, Emerson."

"Ha," said Emerson. "Hand me that towel, and start talking."

Having determined — as I had said — to conceal nothing from my heroic spouse, I told him the whole story, from start to finish. I rather pride myself on my narrative style. Emerson certainly found it absorbing. He listened without interrupting, possibly because he was too stupefied to compose a coherent remark. The only sign of emotion he exhibited was to turn crimson in the face when I described Sethos's advances.

"He kissed you, did he?"

"That was all, Emerson."

"More than once?"

"Er — yes."

"How often?"

"That would depend on how one defines and delimits —"

"And held you in his arms?"

"Quite respectfully, Emerson. Er — on the whole."

"It is impossible," said Emerson, "to hold respectfully in one's arms a woman married to another man."

I began to think I ought to have heeded Abdullah's advice.

"Forget that, Emerson," I said. "It is over and done with. The most important thing is that Sethos has got away. I am afraid — I am almost certain — he knows about Ramses."

"You think so?"

"I told you what he said."

"Hmmm, yes."

I had insisted upon helping him to dress, since it is difficult to pull on trousers and boots with only one fully functional arm. Frowning in a manner that suggested profound introspection rather than temper, he slipped his arm into the shirt I held for him, and made no objection when I began buttoning it.

"What are we going to do?" I demanded.

"About Sethos? Leave it to Russell. Ouch," he added.

"I beg your pardon, my dear. Stand up, please."

He stood staring into space with all the animation of a mummy while I finished tidying him up and wound a few strips of bandage across his shoulder and chest to support his arm. Then I said, "Emerson."

"Hmph? Yes, my dear, what is it?"

"I would like you to hold me, if it won't inconvenience you too much."

Emerson can do more with one arm than most men can do with two. Yielding to his hard embrace, returning his kisses, I hoped I had convinced him that no man would ever take his place in my heart.

There were three statues in the serdab. The most charming depicted the Prince and his wife in a pose that had become familiar to me from many examples, and one which never failed to please me. They stood close to one another, with her arm round his waist, and the two figures were of almost equal height; the lady was a few inches shorter, just as she may have been in life. She wore a simple straight shift and he a kilt pleated on one side. Their faces had the ineffable calm with which these believers faced eternity. Some of the original paint remained: the white of their garments, the black of the wigs, the yellowish skin of the lady and the darker brown of her husband's. Women were always depicted as lighter in color than men, presumably because they spent less time under the sun's rays than their spouses.

There was another, smaller, statue of the Prince, and one of a youth who was identified as his son. By the middle of the afternoon we had them out; not even the largest was anything like the weight of the royal statue.

"Get them back to the house, Selim," Emerson ordered, passing his sleeve over his perspiring brow.

Nefret announced her intention of going to the hospital for a few hours and started toward Mena House, where we had left the horses. As soon as she was out of earshot, Ramses said, "I'm off too."

"Where?" I demanded, trying to catch hold of him.

"I have a few errands. Excuse me, Mother, I must hurry. I will be home in time for dinner."

"Put on your hat!" I called after him. He turned and waved and went on. Without his hat.

When Emerson and I reached Mena House we found Asfur, whom Ramses had ridden that day, still in the stable. "He's taken the train," I said out of the corner of my mouth. "That means —"

"I know what it means. Mount Asfur, Peabody, and I'll lead the other creature. And do keep quiet!"

I realized I ought to have anticipated that Ramses would have to communicate with one or another, or all, of several people. That did not mean I liked it. My nerves had not fully recovered from the anxiety of the previous day and night. Emerson and I jogged on side by side, each occupied with his or her own thoughts; I could tell by his expression that his were no more pleasant than mine. Superstition is not one of my weaknesses, but I was beginning to feel that we labored under a horrible curse of failure. Every thread we had come upon broke when we tried to follow it. Two of the most hopeful had failed within the past twenty-four hours: my unmasking of Sethos, and Emerson's capture of the German spy. Now Sethos was on the loose with his deadly knowledge, and the failure of the ambush would soon be known to the man who had ordered it. What would he do next? What could *we* do next?

Emerson and I discussed the matter as we drank our tea and sorted through the post. I had not done so the day before, so there was quite an accumulation of letters and messages.

"Nothing from Mr. Russell," I reported. "He'd have found some means of informing us if he had caught up with Sethos."

Emerson said, "Hmph," and took the envelopes I handed him.

"There is one for you from Walter."

"So I see." Emerson ripped the envelope to shreds. "They have had another communication from David," he reported, scanning the missive.

"I wish we could say the same. Do you think Ramses will speak with him this afternoon?"

"I don't know." Emerson plucked irritably at the strips of bandage enclosing his arm. "Curse it, how can I open an envelope with one hand?"

"I will open them for you, my dear."

"No, you will not. You always read them first." Emerson tore at another envelope. "Well, well, fancy that. A courteous note from Major Hamilton congratulating me on another narrow escape, as he puts it, and reminding me that he made me the loan of a Webley. I wonder what I did with it."

"Does he mention his niece?"

"No, why should he? What does Evelyn say?"

He had recognized her neat, delicate handwriting. I knew what he wanted most to hear, so I read the passages that reported little Sennia's good health and remarkable evidences of intelligence. "She keeps us all merry and in good spirits. Lately she has taken to dressing Horus up in her dolly's clothing and wheeling him about in a carriage; you would laugh to see those bristling whiskers and snarling jaws framed by a ruffled bonnet. He hates every minute of it but is putty in her little hands. Thank God her youth makes it possible for us to keep from her the horrible things that are happening in the world. Every night she kisses your photographs; they are getting quite worn away, especially Ramses's. Even Emerson would be touched, I think, to see her kneeling beside her little cot asking God to watch over you all. That is also the heartfelt prayer of your loving sister."

"And here," I said, holding out a grubby, much folded bit of paper, "is an enclosure for you from Sennia."

Emerson's eyes were shining suspiciously. After he had read the few printed words that staggered down the page, he folded it again and tucked it carefully into his breast pocket.

There was no message for Ramses that day or the day after, or the day after that. Days stretched into weeks. Ramses went almost every day to Cairo. I never had to ask whether he had found the message he was waiting for. Govern his countenance as he might, his stretched nerves showed in the almost imperceptible marks round his eyes and mouth, and in his increasingly acerbic responses to perfectly civil questions. Some of his visits were to Wardani's lieutenants; like the rest of us, they were becoming restive, and Ramses admitted he was having some difficulty keeping them reined in.

Rumors about the military situation added another dimension of discomfort. In my opinion it would have been wiser for the authorities to publish the facts; they might have been less alarming than the stories that were put about. There were one hundred thousand Turkish troops massed near Beersheba. There were two hundred thousand Turkish troops heading for the border. Turkish forces had already crossed the border and were marching toward the Canal, gathering recruits from among the Bedouin. Jemal Pasha, in command of the Turks, had boasted, "I will not return until I have entered Cairo"; his chief of staff, von Kressenstein, had an entire brigade of German troops with him. Turkish agents had infiltrated the ranks of the Egyptian artillery; when the attack occurred they would turn their weapons on the British.

Some of the stories were true, some were not. The result was to throw Cairo into a state of panic. A great number of people booked passage on departing steamers. The louder patriots discussed strategy in their comfortable clubs, and entered into a perfect orgy of spy hunting. The only useful result of that was the disappearance of Mrs. Fortescue. It was assumed by her acquaintances that she had got cold feet and sailed for home; we were among the few who knew that she had been taken into custody. That gave me another moment of hope, but like all our other leads, this one faded out. She insisted even under interrogation that she did not know the name or identity of the man to whom she had reported.

"She is probably telling the truth," said Emerson, from whom I heard this bit of classified information. "There are a number of ways of passing on and receiving instructions. I understand that chap we saw at the Savoy — one of Clayton's lot — what's his name? — is claiming the credit for unmasking her."

"Herbert," Ramses supplied, with a very slight curl of his lip. "He's also unearthing conspiracies. According to him, he doesn't even have to go looking for them; the malcontents come to him, burning to betray one another for money."

"One of them hasn't," said Emerson. "Damnation! The insufferable complacency of men like Herbert will cost us dearly one day."

I also learned from Emerson that Russell agreed with his and Ramses's deductions about the route the gunrunners had followed. The Camel Corps section of the Coastguards had been alerted, and since their pitiful pay was augmented by rewards for each arrest, one might suppose they were hard at it. However, as Russell admitted, the corruption of a single officer would make it possible for the loads to be landed on the Egyptian coast and carried by camel to some place of concealment near the city, where the Turk eventually picked them up. Thus far Russell had been unable to track them.

It was during the penultimate week of January that Ramses returned one afternoon from Cairo with the news we had so anxiously awaited. One look at him told me all I needed to know. I ran to meet him and threw my arms round him.

Eyebrows rising, he said, "Thank you, Mother, but I haven't come back from the dead, only from Cairo. Yes, Fatima, fresh tea would be very nice."

I waited, twitching with impatience, until after she had brought the tea and another plate of sandwiches. "Talk quickly," I ordered. "Nefret has gone to the hospital, but she will soon be back."

"She didn't go directly to the hospital." Ramses inspected the sandwiches.

"You followed her?" It was a foolish question; obviously he had. I went on, "Where did she go?"

"To the Continental. I presume she was meeting someone, but I couldn't go into the hotel."

"No," Emerson said, giving his son a hard look. "Has she given you any cause to believe she was doing anything she ought not?"

"Good God, Father, of course she has! Over and over! She —" He broke off; his preternaturally acute hearing must have given him warning of someone's approach, for he lowered his voice and spoke quickly. "I need to attend that confounded costume ball tomorrow night."

"What confounded costume ball?" Emerson demanded.

"I told you about it several weeks ago, Emerson," I reminded him. "You didn't say you would not go, so I —"

"Procured some embarrassing, inappropriate rig for me? Curse it, Peabody —"

"You needn't come if you'd rather not, Father," Ramses said somewhat impatiently.

"We'll come, of course," Emerson said. "If you need us. What do you want us to do?"

"Cover my absence while I trot off to collect a few more jolly little guns. I got the message this afternoon." The parlor door opened, and he stood up, smiling. "Ah, Nefret. How many arms and legs did you cut off today? Hullo, Anna, still playing angel of mercy?"

12

Over the years we had become accustomed to take Friday as our day of rest, in order to accommodate our Moslem workmen. The Sabbath was therefore another workday for us, and Emerson, who had no sympathy with religious observances of any kind, refused even to attend church services. He had often informed me that I was welcome to do so if I chose — knowing full well that if I had chosen I would never have felt need of his permission — but it was too much of a nuisance to get dressed and drive into Cairo for what is, after all, only empty ceremony unless one is in the proper state of spiritual devotion. I feel I can put myself into the proper state wherever I happen to be, so I rise early on Sunday morning and read a few chapters from the Good Book and say a few little prayers. I say them aloud, in the hope that Emerson may be edified by my example. Thus far he has displayed no evidence of edification; in fact, he is sometimes moved to make critical remarks.

"I do not claim to be an authority, Peabody, but it seems to me that prayer should take the form of a humble request, not a direct order."

My prayers that Sunday morning may have had a somewhat peremptory tone. Emerson was dressing when I rose from my knees.

"Finished?" he inquired.

"I believe I covered all the necessary points."

"It was a comprehensive lecture," Emerson agreed. He finished lacing his boots and stood up. "I was under the impression that you believed that God helps those who help themselves."

"I am doing all I can."

My voice was somewhat muffled by the folds of my nightdress, which I had started to remove. Emerson put his arms round me and pressed me close. "My darling, I know you are. Don't cry, my love, it will be all right."

"I am not crying, I have several layers of cloth over my nose and mouth."

"Ah. That's easily dealt with."

After a time Emerson said, "Am I hurting you?"

"Yes. I have no objection to what you are doing, but perhaps you could do it a little less vigorously. All those buttons and buckles —"

"They are also easily dealt with."

"I presume you've got some tomfool costume for me to wear this evening," Emerson said. He finished lacing his boots and stood up.

"I have a costume for you, yes, but I shan't

551

show it to you until it is time to put it on. You always complain and protest and bellow and —"

"Not this time. Peabody, is there any way you can conceal my absence as well as that of Ramses? This is the first time they have left the weapons to be picked up later instead of delivering them directly. I want to be there."

"Do you think it's a trick — an ambush?"

"No," Emerson said, a little too quickly. "Only I — er —"

"Want to be there. Are you going to ask Ramses if you may go with him?"

"*Ask* him if I *may* . . ." Emerson's indignation subsided as quickly as it had arisen. "I can't do that. The boy is a trifle touchy about accepting my assistance, though I don't see why he should be."

"Don't you?"

"No! I have the greatest respect for his abilities."

"And you have, of course, told him so."

Emerson looked uncomfortable. "Not in so many words. Oh, curse it, Peabody, don't practice your bloody psychology on me. Make a practical suggestion."

"Very well, my dear. Let me think about it."

I did so, at intervals during the day. We had got the second chapel cleared down to floor level; the walls had all been painted and there was a delightful little false door, with a rock-cut half-length (from the waist up) statue of the owner, looking as if he were emerging from the afterworld with hands extended to seize the foodstuffs placed on the offering table before him. Ramses rambled about the room reading bits and pieces of the inscriptions and commenting on them: " 'An offering which the King gives of bread and beer, oxen and fowl, alabaster and clothing . . . a thousand of every good and pure thing . . .' They had such practical minds, didn't they? An all-inclusive 'every thing,' in case some desirable item had been overlooked. 'One honored before Osiris, Lord of Busiris . . .' Nothing new, just the usual formulas."

"Then stop mumbling over them and help Nefret with the photography," Emerson ordered.

This was a more complex process than it might appear, for photographs were the first step of the method Ramses had devised for copying reliefs and inscriptions. They had to be taken from a carefully measured distance in order to allow for overlap without distortion. A tracing was then made and compared with the wall itself. The final version incorporated not only the reliefs but every scratch and abrasion on the surface. Ramses did not suffer from false modesty regarding his talents as a linguist, but he would have been the first to admit that some future scholar might find something he had missed in those seemingly unreadable scratches. It was an extremely accurate method, but it took a long time.

Ramses began setting up his measuring rods. I went out to watch Emerson, who was directing the men who were clearing the section south of the mastaba. The intervening space between ours and the one next to it had been filled in, by extensions and/or later tombs. There were bits of wall everywhere, looking like an ill-organized maze. Emerson's scowl would have told me, had I not already realized, that he had a hard task ahead trying to sort them out.

"Come here!" he shouted, waving at me.

So I went there, and began taking notes as he crawled about measuring spaces and calling out numbers and brief descriptions.

My mind wandered a bit. I had managed to draw Ramses aside long enough to squeeze a little information out of him. He would not tell me where he had to go that night, but he did give me a rough estimate of how much time he would need. Not less than two hours, probably not more than three.

"Probably," I repeated.

"To be on the safe side, we had better allow for more. What I propose . . ."

What he proposed was that I plead fatigue or indisposition and ask Emerson to take me home during the supper break. Cyrus and Katherine would be happy to look after

Nefret, and when Ramses failed to turn up, the others would assume he had gone with us. Given the crowds and the confusion and a certain amount of alcoholic intake, there was a good chance it would work.

The only remaining difficulty was how to conceal from Ramses the fact that his father meant to follow him that night — for that was what Emerson must do if he wanted to avoid an argument or even a flat refusal from his son. Emerson may sneer at psychology all he likes, but it was not difficult for *me* to understand why Ramses was reluctant to accept his father's help. According to the best authorities, all boys go through such a stage when they approach manhood, and trying to live up to a father like Emerson would put a strain on any individual.

It was difficult to concentrate with Emerson demanding I repeat back the numbers he kept calling out, so I gave it up for the time being. No doubt something will occur to me, I thought; it usually does.

We stopped work a little earlier than usual, since Katherine and Cyrus were dining with us. Something *had* occurred to me. I knew Emerson would not like it at all. I had certain reservations of my own, but I put these aside. Emerson's objections would also have to be put aside, since I did not intend to give him time to argue.

The Vandergelts arrived in time for tea. After they had extricated themselves from the muffling garments motoring requires, we women retired to the roof, leaving Cyrus to admire our latest discoveries, while Emerson told him all about them and Ramses hung about trying to get a word in. Nefret would have liked to stay with them, I think, but Anna did not bother to conceal her disinterest, and my daughter had been too well brought up (by me) to abandon a guest.

Anna was more than happy to talk about her nursing duties. A single courteous question from me produced a spate of information, some of which I could have done without. It was her mother who cut her short.

"Don't talk about wounds and — and infections," Katherine exclaimed. "Especially at teatime."

Anna's lips set. Her physical appearance had improved greatly these past weeks; Nefret had been giving her gentle hints about clothes and hairstyles, but the greatest change was in her expression. Even a plain woman may look attractive when she is happy and proud of herself. Watching the old sullen look dim the girl's face, I thought I just might drop a little hint to Katherine not to be so hard on Anna. Bertie had always been her favorite, and at the present time she was desperately worried about the boy.

I asked whether she had heard from him, and she nodded. "Not much of a letter,

Amelia. It was full of holes, where the censor had cut out various phrases. It is so stupidly unfair! What could he possibly tell me that would give aid and comfort to anyone except me?"

"Some of the censors are overly conscientious, I believe," I agreed. "Evelyn says the same of Johnny's letters. Willy's seem to come through relatively intact, but he has always been more discreet than his brother."

"It is Johnny's sense of humor that leads him into indiscretions," Nefret said with a fond smile. "I can easily imagine him making rude personal remarks about one of his officers, or giving a vulgar description of the food they are served."

"That would be destructive of civilian morale," said Anna, whose sense of humor left a great deal to be desired.

The men finally joined us, followed by Seshat, who, I was pleased to observe, had decided not to contribute to the canapés. She settled down next to Ramses. Cyrus was still talking about the royal statue, which he had the expertise and experience to appreciate fully.

"It just doesn't seem fair," he declared, shaking his head. "Not to take away from you folks, but I sure would like to find some little treasure myself."

"Such as an unrobbed royal tomb or a cache of mummies decked out in jewels?"

Nefret inquired. She and Cyrus were good friends, and he enjoyed her teasing him. His dour face broadened into a grin.

"Something like that. Doesn't it seem to you folks that I'm overdue for a little luck? All those years in Luxor without a single find!"

"Excuse me, sir, but that is a slight exaggeration," Ramses said. "The tomb you found at Dra Abu'l Naga was unique. The plan cast new light on our knowledge of Second Intermediate Period architecture."

"But there wasn't anything in it!" Cyrus protested. "Except a few pots and a broken-up mummy."

"How are you doing at Abusir?" Emerson inquired, taking out his pipe.

"Well, now, there's another thing. I thought sure there'd be private tombs next to that miserable excuse for a pyramid, but what we've come across seems to be a temple."

"What?" Emerson shouted. "The mortuary temple of the unfinished pyramid of Abusir?"

"Goodness gracious, Emerson, you make it sound like the lost city of Atlantis!" I said. "There are a number of unfinished pyramids — too many, in my opinion. This one has not even a substructure."

"And that is the only part of a pyramid that interests you," said Emerson. "Dark, dusty, cramped underground passages! The existence of a mortuary temple suggests that there was a burial after all. What is more important is the temple plan itself. Only a few have been excavated, and —"

"Spare us the lecture, Emerson," I said with a smile. "We all know you prefer temples to pyramids or even tombs."

"I dropped you a hint Christmas Day," Cyrus said. "Been expecting you would drop by to have a look."

"Hmph." Emerson fingered the cleft in his chin. "I have been busy, Vandergelt."

"I reckon you have. What with one thing and another." Cyrus's keen blue eyes moved from Emerson to me. After a moment he went on, with seeming irrelevance, "I called on MacMahon the other day. I'm supposed to be neutral in this war; I've got friends and sons of friends in both armies. But I figure a fellow has to take a stand, and I've made up my mind what side I'm on. Told him I was offering my services, such as they are."

He was offering his services to us as well. He did not have to say so; coming from Cyrus, who knew us so well, the hint was enough. If it had been up to me I would have confided fully in these loyal friends, on whose assistance and advice I had so often depended. I had not the right. I too was under orders.

We had an early dinner and then separated in order to assume our costumes. The

Vandergelts had brought several pieces of luggage, since I had invited them to spend that night and the next with us. Emerson was gracious enough to approve the ensemble I had selected for him — that of a Crusader. I was his lady, in flowing robes and a pointed headdress. Emerson liked his sword and beard very much, but he objected to my pointed hat, on the grounds that it wobbled a bit and would probably poke someone's eye out. Brushing this complaint aside, I took his arm and we proceeded into the drawing room, where we found Katherine and Cyrus waiting, dressed as a lady and gentleman of Louis the Fourteenth's court, complete with powdered wigs.

Before long Ramses joined us. I was relieved to see that he had not assumed one of his more disgusting disguises — a verminous beggar or odorous camel driver. He had better sense than that, of course; it would have been folly to advertise his ability to assume such roles. He hadn't gone to much trouble; a broad-brimmed "ten-gallon hat" borrowed from Cyrus, a neckerchief tied round his bared throat, and a pair of six-shooters strapped around his waist made him into a dashing and fairly unconvincing model of an American cowboy. I doubted very much that American cowboys wore white shirts and riding breeches.

"For pity's sake, Ramses," I exclaimed, as

he swept off his hat and bowed. "Are you carrying those weapons into Shepheards?"

"They are not loaded, Mother."

"What happened to the spurs?" Cyrus inquired, his eyes twinkling.

"I feared they might constitute a hazard on the dance floor."

"You were right about that," I said.

Nefret had taken Anna to her room; they came in together. Anna looked quite nice in a bright-skirted gypsy costume and large gold earrings; but the sight of my daughter, in the full trousers and low-cut shirt of an Egyptian lady, wrung a cry of distress from my lips. The shirt was of very fine fabric and reached only just below the waist.

"Nefret! You are not going to wear that in public, I hope?"

"Why not?" She spun round, so that the legs of her voluminous trousers flared out. At least they were opaque, being made of heavy corded silk. "It covers more of me than an ordinary evening dress."

"But your — er — your shirt is . . . Are you wearing anything under it? My dear girl, when a gentleman's arm encircles your waist in the dance . . ."

"He will enjoy it very much," said Nefret.

"I may have to shoot someone after all," Ramses drawled.

Nefret gave him a bright smile. "The Professor is wearing a sword; he can challenge the offender. That would be much more romantic. Now, Aunt Amelia, don't fuss; this is only the underneath part. I'll wear a yelek and a girdle over it."

Chuckling over the little joke they had played on us, Fatima duly appeared with the garments in question and helped Nefret into them. The yelek was of silk in a delicate shade of pearly white; it was practically transparent, but at least it covered her. Emerson closed his mouth, which had been hanging open since he set astonished eyes on his daughter, breathed a gusty sigh of relief, and offered me his arm to lead me to the motorcar.

I will not describe the ball; it was like others we had attended, except for the uniforms. The patches of khaki were like muddy stains upon the sparkle and brilliance of the costumes. I lost sight of Ramses after he had performed his duty dances with me and Katherine; he might have been avoiding Percy, who made rather a point of putting himself in our way without having the temerity actually to address us. Whenever he was in our vicinity Emerson made grumbling noises and put his hand on the hilt of his sword. I had to remind him that, first, dueling was against the law; second, his weapon was only for show; and third, Percy had done nothing to provoke a challenge.

"Not yet," said Emerson hopefully. "They

are playing a waltz, Peabody. Will you dance?"

"You promised me that if I let you leave off the strapping you would not use that arm."

"Oh, bah," said Emerson, and demonstrated his fitness by sweeping me onto the floor. Emerson's terpsichorean talents are limited to the waltz, which he performs with such enthusiasm that my feet were only on the floor part of the time. After one particularly vigorous spin I looked round and saw that Percy was dancing with Anna. Her cheeks were flushed, and she gazed sentimentally into his smiling face.

"Look there," I said to Emerson, and then wished I had kept silent when Emerson came to a dead stop in the middle of the dance floor. It required some argument to get him started again.

"Doesn't she know about the bastard?" he demanded.

"Perhaps not. Katherine and Cyrus are aware of his Machiavellian machinations with regard to Sennia, but Katherine would not have passed the information on to Anna without my permission. The time for discretion has passed, in my opinion; he cannot be courting her good opinion because he admires her."

"That isn't very kind to the girl," Emerson murmured.

"It is true, however. She is not handsome

enough or rich enough or — er — accommo-dating enough to interest him. He is using her to insinuate a wedge! She must be told of his true nature."

"I will leave that to you," said Emerson. "I can't see that it matters."

"You would not take that attitude if it were Nefret dancing with him instead of Anna."

"Damned right."

When the music ended Percy led Anna off the floor and left her. I lost sight of him after that; sometime later I realized I had also lost sight of Nefret.

I felt obliged to go in search of her. The Moorish Hall was the first place I looked. I disturbed several couples who were enjoying the intimacy of the shadowy alcoves, but Nefret was not among them. After I had fin-ished searching the other public areas I went to the Long Bar. Women were not supposed to be there except at certain times, but Nefret often went where she was not supposed to be. It did not take me long to find her, seated at a table toward the back of the room. When I recognized her companion my heart sank down into my slippers. Kadija had been right after all. How Nefret had managed to elude my supervision I did not know, but it was clear that this was not her first meeting with Percy. Their heads were close together, and she was smiling as she listened.

"Mother?"

I was leaning forward, peering round the doorframe. He startled me so badly I lost my balance and would have stumbled into the room had he not taken my arm.

"What are you doing here?" I demanded.

"The same thing you are doing," said Ramses. "Spying on Nefret. I hope you are enjoying it as much as I am."

His even, controlled voice made a shiver of apprehension run through me. "You are not to go near Percy. Give me your word."

"Do you suppose I'm afraid of him?"

"No, I do not!"

"I am, though."

"You could beat him senseless with one hand."

Ramses let out an odd sound that might have been a muffled laugh. "Your confidence is flattering, Mother, if somewhat exaggerated. I might have to use both hands. That wasn't what I meant, though."

"He can never deceive us again, Ramses. We know his real nature too well. Surely you don't believe Nefret has succumbed to his flattery and his advances?"

"No." The word was too quick and too vehement.

"No," I insisted. "He is everything she loathes and despises. Perhaps . . . Yes, it can only be because she thinks Percy has some new villainy in mind, and that she is helping to protect you."

"That's what I'm afraid of," Ramses said. "Time to retreat, Mother, she's standing up."

We returned to the ballroom. Nefret was not far behind us. Had she seen us? I hoped not; she had some cause for resentment if she believed I had been spying on her.

Emerson had been prowling round the room, looking for me, as he explained accusingly.

"Hand her over, Ramses," he ordered. "The waltzes are all mine, you know."

"Yes, sir."

Emerson took my arm, and I turned to see Nefret beside us. Except for being a trifle flushed, she displayed no evidence of self-consciousness. She put her hand on Ramses's sleeve. "Will you dance with me?"

"Aren't you engaged for this one?"

"I have disengaged myself. Please?"

He could not in courtesy refuse. With a formal bow he offered her his arm.

The music was a waltz, a piece with which I was not familiar, sweet and rather slow. Instead of leading me onto the floor Emerson stood watching our son and daughter.

"This is the first time they have danced together in a long while," he said.

"Yes."

"They look well."

"Yes."

They had always looked well together, but

that night there was a kind of enchantment about the way they waltzed, every movement so perfectly matched, they might have been directed by a single mind. She moved lightly as a bird in flight, their clasped hands barely touching, her other hand brushing his shoulder. They were not looking at one another; Nefret's face was averted and his was the usual impassive mask; but as I gazed, the forms of the other dancers seemed to fade away, leaving the two alone, like figures captured and held forever in a globe of clear glass.

With an effort I shook off this somewhat unnerving fantasy. As I glanced about I realized Emerson and I were not the only ones watching the pair. Percy's eyes followed their every moment. His arms were folded and his face bore a complacent smile.

When the dance ended he turned and withdrew. Nefret had not seen him; her hand still on Ramses's shoulder, she looked up into his face and spoke. Composed and unresponsive, he shook his head. Then another gentleman approached Nefret; she would have refused him, I think, had not Ramses stepped back, bowed, and walked away.

Emerson took hold of me. My eyes on the retreating form of my son, I said absently, "It is not a waltz, Emerson, it is a schottische."

"Oh," said Emerson.

Threading his way through the whirling

forms, Ramses reached the door of the ball-room. Not until that moment, when he stepped aside to allow a party to enter, did I catch a glimpse of his face.

"Excuse me, Emerson," I said.

Ramses was not in the lounge or the Long Bar or the Moorish Hall or on the terrace. Unless he had left the hotel altogether, there was only one other refuge he would have sought. I went round the hotel into the garden. I heard their voices before I saw them. She must have left her partner and followed him, as I had done, but a surer instinct even than mine had led her to the right spot, a little dell where a circle of white rosebushes surrounded a curved stone bench. The flowers glimmered like mother-of-pearl in the moonlight and their scent hung heavy in the still air.

They must have been talking for some little time, for the first words I made out, from Nefret, were obviously a response to something he had said.

"Don't be so damned polite!"

"Would you rather I called you rude names? Or knocked you about? That is, I am told, a demonstration of affection in some circles."

"Yes! Anything but this — this —"

"Keep your voice down," Ramses said.

I moved slowly and carefully along the graveled path until I reached a spot from which I could see them. They stood facing one another; all I could see of Ramses was the white of his shirtfront. Her back was to me; her robe shone with the same pearly luster as the roses that formed a frame round her, and the gems on her wrist twinkled as she raised a gloved hand and placed it on his shoulder. Her touch was not heavy, but he flinched away and Nefret's hand fell to her side.

"I'm sorry!"

"Sorry for what?"

"We were friends once. Before . . ."

"And still are, I hope. Really, Nefret, must you make a scene? I find this very fatiguing."

I did not hear what she said, but it had the effect of finally breaking through his icy and infuriating self-control. He took her by her arm. She twisted neatly away and stood glaring at him, her breast rising and falling.

"You taught me that one," she said.

"So I did. Here is one I did not teach you."

His movement was so quick I saw only the result. One arm held her pressed to his side, her body arched like a bow in his hard grasp. Putting his hand under her chin, he tilted her head back and brought his mouth down on hers.

He went on kissing her for quite a long time. When at last he left off, they were both exceedingly short of breath. Naturally Ramses was the first to recover himself. He released her and stepped back.

"My turn to apologize, I believe, but you really oughn't trust anyone to behave like a gentleman when you are alone with him in the moonlight. No doubt Percy has better manners."

Nefret's hand went to her throat. She started to speak, but he cut her off.

"However, he's not much of a gentleman if he skulks in the shrubbery looking on while a lady is being kissed against her will. He's a little slow, perhaps. Shall we give it another try?"

I could hardly blame her for striking at him. It was not a genteel ladylike slap, but a hard swing with her clenched fist (learned from him, I did not doubt) that would have staggered him if it had landed. It did not. As his hand went up to block the blow she caught herself; and for a long moment they stood like statues, her curled fingers resting in the cradle of his palm. Then she turned and walked away.

Ramses sat down on the bench and covered his face with his hands.

Naturally, if I had happened upon such a scene that involved mere acquaintances I would have discreetly retired without making my presence known. Under these circumstances I did not hesitate to intrude. To be honest, I was not myself in a proper state to think coolly. How could I have missed seeing it — I, who prided myself on my awareness of the human heart?

He must have heard the rustle of my skirts; he had had time to compose himself. When I emerged from the shrubbery he rose and tossed away the cigarette he had been smoking.

"Continue smoking if it will calm your mind," I said, seating myself.

"You too?" Ramses inquired. "I might have known. Perhaps in another ten or twenty years you will consider me mature enough to go about without a chaperone."

"Oh, my dear, don't pretend," I said. My voice was unsteady; the cool, mocking tone jarred on me as never before. "I am so sorry, Ramses. How long have you . . ."

"Since the moment I set eyes on her. Fidelity," Ramses said, in the same cool voice, "seems to be a fatal flaw of our family."

"Oh, come," I said, accepting the cigarette he offered and allowing him to light it for me. "Are you telling me you have never — er . . ."

"No, Mother dear, I am not telling you — er — that. I discovered years ago that lying to you is a waste of breath. How the devil do you do it? Look at you — ruffles trailing, gloves spotless — blowing out smoke like a little lady dragon and prying into the most intimate secrets of a fellow's life. Spare me the lecture, I beg. My moments of aberration — and there were, I confess, a number of them

— were attempts to break the spell. They failed."

"But you were only a child when you saw her for the first time."

"It sounds like one of the wilder romances, doesn't it? Most authors would throw in hints of reincarnation and souls destined for one another down the long centuries. . . . It wasn't so simple as I have made it sound, you know, or as tragic. A weakness for melodrama is another of our family failings."

"Tell me," I urged. "It is unhealthy to keep one's feelings to oneself. How often you must have yearned to confide in a sympathetic listener!"

"Er — quite," said Ramses.

"Does David know?"

"Some of it." Glancing at me, Ramses added, "It wasn't the same, naturally, as confiding in one's mother."

"Naturally."

I said no more. I could feel his need to unburden himself; experienced as I am in such matters, I knew that sympathetic silence was the best means of inducing his confidences. Sure enough, after a few moments, he began.

"It was only a child's infatuation at first; how could it be anything more? But then came that summer I spent with Sheikh Mohammed. I thought that being away from her for months, with the sheikh providing interesting distractions . . ." Catching himself, he added hastily, "Riding and exploring and strenuous physical exercise —"

"Of all varieties," I muttered. "Shameful old man! I ought never have allowed you to go."

"Never mind, Mother. I would apologize for referring, however obliquely, to a subject unsuitable for female contemplation, if I weren't certain that you are thoroughly conversant with it. When David and I came back to Cairo, I thought I'd got over it. But when I saw her on the terrace at Shepheard's that afternoon, and she ran to meet me, laughing, and threw her arms round me . . ." He plucked one of the drooping roses. Twirling the stem between his fingers, he went on, "I knew that day I loved her and always would, but I couldn't tell anyone how I felt; a declaration of undying passion from a sixteen-year-old boy would have provoked laughter or pity, and I couldn't have stood either. So I waited, and worked and hoped, and lost her to a man whose death came close to destroying her. She had begun to forgive me for my part in that, I think —"

"Forgive you!" I exclaimed. "What had *she* to forgive? You were the soul of honor throughout that horrible business. It is for her to ask *your* forgiveness. She ought to have had faith in you."

"And I ought to have gone after her and shaken some sense into her. I realize now that

that was what she wanted me to do — that perhaps she had the right to expect it of me, especially after —"

He checked himself. I said helpfully, "After having been such good friends for so long. That is what your father always did."

"To you? But surely you never gave Father cause to —"

"Shake some sense into me?" My laughter was brief and rueful. "I am ashamed to admit that I did, more than once. There was one occasion — one woman in particular . . . I need not say that my suspicions were completely unfounded, but if love has an adverse effect on common sense, jealousy destroys it completely. Of course the cases are not entirely parallel."

"No." I could tell that he was trying to picture Emerson shaking me as I shouted accusations of infidelity at him. He was obviously having some difficulty doing so. He shook his head. "Unfortunately, I'm not like Father. I have never found it easy to express my feelings. When I'm angry or — or offended — I pull back into my shell. That's my weakness, Mother, just as impulsiveness is Nefret's. I know it's stupid, infuriating, and selfish; one ought at least give the other fellow the satisfaction of losing one's temper."

"I've seen you lose it a few times."

"I've been practicing," Ramses said with a wry smile. "Last year I thought that she was beginning to care a little, but then this other business came up and I didn't dare confide in her. I hoped that one day, when this is over, I could explain and start again; but what I did tonight was the worst mistake I could have made. One doesn't force oneself on a woman like Nefret."

"In my opinion it was a distinctly positive step," I said. "Faint heart never won fair lady, my dear, and, without wishing in any way to condone the employment of physical force, there are times when a woman may secretly wish . . . Hmmm. Let me think how to put this. She may hope that the strength of a gentleman's affection for her will cause him to forget his manners."

Ramses opened his mouth and closed it again. I was pleased to see that my sympathetic conversation had comforted him; he sounded quite his normal self when he finally found his voice. "Mother, you never cease to amaze me. Are you seriously suggesting I should —"

"Why, Ramses, you know I would never venture to urge a course of action on another individual, particularly in affairs of the heart." Ramses had lit another cigarette. He must have inhaled the wrong way, for he began to cough. I patted him on the back. "However, a demonstration of an attachment so powerful it cannot be controlled, particularly by a gentleman who has controlled it only too well, would, I believe, affect most women favorably. I trust you follow me?"

"I think I do," Ramses said in a choked voice.

Rising, he offered me his hand. "Will you come back to the ball now? They will be serving supper soon, and —"

"I know. You can depend on me. But I believe I will sit here a few minutes longer. Do you go on, my dear."

He hesitated for a moment. Then he said softly, "I love you, Mother." He took my hand and kissed it, and folded my fingers round the stem of the rose. He had stripped it of its thorns.

I was too moved to speak. But maternal affection was not the only emotion that prevented utterance; as I watched him walk away, his head high and his step firm, anger boiled within me. I knew I had to conquer it before I saw Nefret again, or I would take her by the shoulders and shake her, and *demand* that she love my son!

That would have been unfair as well as very undignified. I knew it; but I had to force my jaws apart to keep from grinding my teeth with outrage and fury. She ought to love him. He was the only man who was truly her equal, in intelligence and integrity, in loving affection and . . . Still waters run deep, it is said. I, his affectionate mother, ought to have realized that beneath that controlled mask his nature was as deep and passionate as hers.

The heat of anger faded, to be replaced with an icy chill of foreboding. Ramses's feet were set on a path fraught with peril, and a man who fears he has lost the thing he wants most in life takes reckless chances. The young are especially susceptible to this form of romantic pessimism.

Rising, I shook out my skirts and squared my own shoulders. Another challenge! I was up to it! I would see those two wed if I had to lock Nefret up on bread and water until she agreed. But first there was the little matter of making certain Ramses lived long enough to marry her.

The last dance before supper was beginning when I entered the ballroom, to find Emerson lying in wait for me.

"Where have you been?" he demanded. "It is almost time. Has something happened? You are grinding your teeth."

"Am I?" I was. Hastily I got my countenance under control. "Never mind. The crucial hour is upon us! Tell them to bring the motorcar round and I will inform Katherine we are leaving."

I was fortunate enough to find her sitting with the chaperones. I did not give a curse whether those tedious gossips overheard me, but I did not want to have to explain myself to Nefret or face that knowing blue gaze of Cyrus. Katherine responded as I had hoped and expected, even anticipating my request that she look after Nefret and bring her home with them. She did not ask about Ramses.

Oh, yes, I thought, as I hurried to the cloakroom, she and Cyrus suspect something is afoot. After all, this would not be the first time we had been involved in a deadly and secret game. It happened almost every year.

Emerson had already retrieved my evening cloak. He tossed it over my shoulders, grunted, "Take off that damned pointed hat," and led me out the door. The motorcar was waiting, and so was Ramses, hat in hand. He got into the tonneau. I took my place beside Emerson, and watched him closely as he went through the procedures necessary to start the vehicle moving. There was a grinding noise — there always was when Emerson started it — and off we went.

We were several miles south of the city, on the road to Helwan, when Ramses tapped his father on the shoulder. "Stop here."

Emerson complied. Even in the dark, and it was very dark, he knows every foot of the terrain of Egypt. "The quarries at Tura?" he asked.

"Nearby." The door opened and Ramses got out. He was not nearly as odorous as he had been before, but the galabeeyah covered his costume and the turban his hair. "Good night," he said, and disappeared noiselessly into the darkness.

Emerson got out of the vehicle, leaving the engine running. "Now then, Peabody," he said, as he began removing the jangly bits of his armor, "would you care to explain that brilliant scheme you mentioned? Did you arrange for Selim to meet you and drive you home, or do you intend to await me here, or —"

"Not at all." I slid over into the seat he had vacated and took firm hold of the steering wheel. "Show me how to drive this thing."

I was teasing my dear Emerson. I knew how to operate the confounded machine; at my request, Nefret had taken me out once or twice and shown me how to do it. For some reason she had not been able to continue the lessons, but after all, once the fundamentals were explained, the rest was only a matter of practice. I had a little argument with Emerson; it would have been longer if I had not pointed out he must not delay.

"He is already some distance ahead of you, my dear. It is vitally important that you watch over him tonight." I handed him the nice clean striped robe I had brought in my evening bag.

"Why tonight? Curse it, Peabody —"

"Just take my word for it, Emerson. Hurry!"

Torn between his concern for his son and his concern for me (and the motorcar), Emerson made the choice I had hoped he would

579

make. Swearing inventively but softly, he ran off along the path Ramses had taken. Pride swelled my bosom. No husband could have offered a greater testimonial of confidence.

As he told me later, he had concluded that I was bound to run the vehicle into a ditch or a tree before I got a hundred feet. There would not be time for me to get up much speed in that distance, and he would find me waiting, bruised and embarrassed but relatively unscathed, when he returned.

Naturally no such thing happened. I did hit a tree or two, but not very hard. Since I was not entirely confident of my ability to turn the car, I had to go all the way to Helwan before I found a space large enough to drive in a nice circle and head back the way I had come. That was when I hit the second tree. It was only a glancing blow.

The distance from Cairo to Helwan is approximately seventeen miles. It took me almost an hour to reach Helwan; steering the thing was more complicated than I had realized, and the clutch, as I believe it is termed, gave me a little trouble initially. Fortunately there was no traffic on the road at that hour. By the time I started back, I had got the hang of it and was beginning to understand why Emerson had insisted on driving himself. It was just like a man! They always invent feeble excuses to keep women from enjoying themselves. I reached the bridge in a little over a quarter of an hour. There was no time to waste. I had to be home before the others returned from the ball.

I slowed down a bit as I passed the spot where I had left Emerson, but there was no sign of anyone, so I did not stop. The motorcar was as conspicuous as a signpost.

From Manuscript H

From the point where he had left the car, the distance was less than two miles. There were paths, since the quarries were still being worked, and intrepid tourists sometimes visited them, usually by donkey from Helwan. The fine white limestone of Tura had provided the shining exterior coating of the pyramids, and faced temples and mastabas for thousands of years. Some of the ancient workings penetrated deep into the heart of the gebel.

All of which made Ramses wonder why this spot had been chosen as a hiding place. It was the most dangerous one yet, the most likely to be discovered by chance. The change in the arrangements was also disturbing. There had been a long interval between this delivery and the last, and this time the Turk had avoided direct contact. It might have been only a precautionary measure on his part; but the time was drawing near and if the man in charge of the operation doubted Wardani's commitment, this could be a way of testing him — or removing him.

The insects and lizards that infested the cliffs were somnolent now, their body temperature lowered by the cold air. Other animals were on the prowl, hunting and being hunted; he heard the bark of a jackal and a distant rattle of rock under the hooves of an antelope or ibex. Those sounds helped to mask the noises he was making. He had exchanged his boots for sandals, but there was no way of moving in complete silence; bits of bleached bone snapped under his feet and pebbles rolled.

He left the path after a time and made his cautious way down into and up out of a series of small wadis. More pebbles rolled. When he came up out of the last depression he was several hundred feet east of the spot the message had indicated. The brilliant desert stars cast an ethereal ivory light over the white cliffs. Shadows like ink strokes outlined their uneven contours and formed black holes at the entrances of the ancient diggings. He stood still, knowing that immobility served as a kind of camouflage; but his shoulder blades felt naked and exposed and he didn't relax until a man stepped out of one of the openings and raised an arm to wave him on.

"It's all right," David said when Ramses reached him. "Dead quiet. I found the cache."

He'd come by one of the paths that were

used to transport stone down to the river. A small cart and a pair of patient donkeys stood nearby.

"Is it all here?" Ramses asked.

"Don't know. I didn't want to start dragging the boxes out till you got here. Give me a hand."

"Wait a minute." Somewhere to the south a lovesick dog raised its voice in poignant appeal and Ramses raised his, three words uttered before the howl died away. "Father. Come ahead."

David let out a strangled expletive. "You didn't tell me —"

"*He* didn't tell me."

Emerson's large form was hard to make out until he moved; the white-and-black-striped robe faded into the pattern of moonlit rock and dark shadows. He came toward them with the light quick stride unusual in so heavy a man.

"Curse it," he remarked calmly. "I thought I made very little noise."

"It's impossible not to make some noise. I had a feeling you'd follow me. Where did you leave . . . *Please* don't tell me you brought her with you!"

"No, no." Emerson's beard split in a grin. It was an incredible beard, covering half his face and reaching to his collarbone. "Don't worry about your mother. Let's get the job done."

With his help the job was done in half the time Ramses had allowed. His skin prickled when he saw how carelessly the load had been hidden; the artificial nature of the cairn of stones covering the hole was dangerously obvious. Flat on his belly, lifting canvas-wrapped bundles one-handed, Emerson said, "Not a very professional job."

"No." Ramses passed the bundles to David, who placed them in the cart. "Is that all?"

Emerson grunted and reached down. He had to use both hands to lift the rough wooden boxes.

"Grenades and ammunition," Ramses said, tight-lipped. "What's that one?"

It was larger and heavier. Emerson hauled it out. "I think I could hazard a guess, but you'd better have it open."

The lid gave way with a hideous screech. Ramses pried it up just enough to look in.

"Holy God. It's a machine gun. A Maxim, I think."

"And here, I expect, is the mount," said Emerson, removing another box. "That's the last. I wonder how many more there were — and where they are now?"

"So do I," Ramses said grimly. He hoisted the box into his arms and deposited it in the cart. "Someone else has been here."

"It looks that way." His father stood up. "I'll drive the cart. You boys go on your way."

"But, Father —"

584

"If I'm intercepted by a patrol I have a better chance of talking my way out of it than either of you."

Ramses couldn't argue with that. All his father would have to do was identify himself. No one would dare ask what he was doing or what the cart contained.

"I had intended to take them to Fort Tura," Ramses began. Emerson nodded approval.

"The place is in ruins and nobody goes there. After I've unloaded I will proceed placidly back along the main road, a poor hardworking peasant with an empty cart. Where shall I leave your equipage, David?"

"Uh . . ."

Emerson climbed up onto the seat and picked up the reins. He was obviously impatient to be off. "Where did you hire it?"

"I stole it," David admitted in a small voice. "The owner farms a few feddans near Kashlakat. He's a very heavy sleeper."

Emerson chuckled appreciatively. "Then he probably won't notice it's missing until morning. I'll abandon it near the village. He'll find it eventually."

He spoke to the donkeys in Arabic and they groaned into motion. Ramses and David stood watching as the cart jounced along the path.

"He'll be all right, won't he?" David asked anxiously.

"The Father of Curses? He'll be towing those donkeys before he's gone much farther. We might just follow along the same path for a while, though. At a distance."

The creak and rumble of the cart was audible a long way off. It stopped once; David stiffened, and Ramses laughed. "I told you he'd get off and tow the donkeys. There, he's gone on."

There wouldn't be any trouble now. If an attack had been planned it would have already taken place, and he was certain no one had followed Emerson. The release of tension left him limp. He yawned.

"You've got a long walk ahead," David said.

"Not as long as yours."

"I slept most of the day. How was the ball?"

"Jolly."

"I'm sure it was. Here, watch out." He steadied Ramses with a hand on his arm.

"Stubbed my toe," said the later, hopping. "Damn these sandals."

"Let's go back to the road. It's easier walking."

There was no sign of the cart or the motorcar when they reached the road. The dusty surface lay like a pale ribbon in the moonlight.

"How are you and Nefret getting on?" David inquired.

"Why do you ask?"

"Something has happened," David said calmly. "I can always tell."

"Yes, you can, can't you?" He was tired, and the comfort of David's companionship loosened his tongue. "The truth is I . . . It's been more difficult than I expected, staying at a safe distance and trying not to be alone with her. I slipped a few times. And then, tonight, she asked me to dance with her — I couldn't refuse — and I wanted to — God, how I wanted to! I got the hell away as soon as I could, but she followed me into the garden, and I — I couldn't stop myself."

"From doing what?"

"What do you suppose? The options were limited in those surroundings. I kissed her, that's all."

"Finally!" David exclaimed. "Then what happened?"

"Damn it," Ramses said, half laughing and half angry, "you're as bad as Mother. She gave me plenty of advice. I don't need any more from you."

"About Nefret and you?" David asked in surprise. "I thought you didn't want her to know."

"I didn't. I was afraid she'd do precisely what she did tonight, after she saw us together — lecture, sympathize, advise. She was . . . in fact, she was very sweet. And she told me a few things about her and Father that came as a considerable shock!"

"Did you tell her you and Nefret had . . ." David hesitated delicately.

"Tell my *mother* we'd been lovers? Good God, David, are you out of your mind?"

"The Professor doesn't know either, I suppose."

"Not from me," said his son grimly. "He's a Victorian gentleman, and you know how he feels about Nefret. If I'd confided in anyone, it would have been you, but I didn't think I had the right. Lia shouldn't have told you either."

"I'm glad she did. It helped me to understand why Nefret acted as she did."

"You never showed me that letter she wrote Lia."

"Lia never showed it to me — nor should she have done, it was meant for her eyes only. She told me enough, though. Ramses, you damned fool, Nefret was head over heels in love with you, and I believe she still is. Why won't you tell her how you feel? Haven't you forgiven her for doubting you?"

"I forgave her long ago, and I would trust her with my life. But I won't trust her with yours, David. She's been seeing Percy. Secretly."

David sucked in his breath. "Are you sure?"

"Yes, I'm sure. She's met with him several times, and he was hiding in the shrubbery while we — er — talked. I spotted him before I lost complete control of myself, but the only way I could keep matters from proceeding further was to say something utterly unforgivable to Nefret."

"Ah," said David. "So she was not unwilling? Hang it, Ramses, when are you going to stop making a martyr of yourself?"

"As soon as this is over. Once we're in the clear I'll plead with her, humble myself, or drag her off by her hair — whatever it takes. Just now I daren't risk it. Percy's on to me, you know. Oh, not the Wardani business, at least I hope to God not, but he suspects I'm involved in something and he's trying to find out what it is. That's why he's been paying me those extravagant and very public compliments. He probably approached Nefret in the hope that he could learn more. She's the weak link in our circle, or so Percy would assume. He's such a conceited bastard, he thinks no woman can resist him."

"And she, in turn, is hoping to learn something from him? That sounds like Nefret, all right. I don't understand, though. Why should Percy care what you're doing?"

"Doesn't a possible reason occur to you?"

"Aside from the fact that he hates you and would stop at nothing to injure you? There's no chance of that. Even if he found out what you're doing, which God forbid, he couldn't use it against you."

"You don't understand," Ramses said angrily. "Even after all the other things he's done, you don't realize what he's capable of. Why do you suppose I wanted Sennia to stay in England this winter? I knew I'd be preoccupied with this other business and unable to watch over her as closely as I've done before. Percy hates the lot of us, and the sweetest, neatest revenge he could find would be through that child. Can you imagine the effect on Father if anything happened to her?"

"On all of us."

"Yes. She's safe from him, but Nefret is another matter. You may think I'm making a martyr of myself without sufficient cause, but I had to do what I did tonight. Have you forgotten what happened the last time he saw Nefret and me in what he took to be a lover's embrace? His vanity is as swollen and fragile as a balloon. God knows what he might do to her if he thought she was only feigning interest in him in order to trick him. She's too brave and reckless to recognize danger, and too impulsive to guard her tongue when a slip could be disastrous, and he's always wanted her, and he —"

"Stop it." David put an arm round his shoulders. "Don't do this to yourself. Not even Percy would injure Nefret to get back at you."

Ramses felt like Cassandra, howling warnings into deaf ears. He forced himself to speak slowly and calmly.

"He raped a thirteen-year-old girl and left her child — his child! — to be raised as a prostitute. If he didn't kill Rashida with his own hands, he hired someone to kill her. There's nothing he wouldn't do if his safety and reputation were threatened."

"He wouldn't dare harm Nefret," David insisted. "She's not a poor little prostitute, she's a lady, and the beloved daughter of the Father of Curses. Your father would tear Percy to pieces if he laid a hand on her."

Ramses realized he hadn't a chance of making David understand. He was too decent and too honorable to recognize evil. Or — Ramses rubbed his aching forehead — was he the one who refused to recognize reality? Had his loathing of Percy turned into dementia?

They tramped on in silence until they reached the train station at Babylon. Ramses stopped.

"I'm tired," he said dully. "There's a cab. I'm going to hire it, unless you want to."

"You take it; I can sleep as late as I like. Are you angry?"

"No, just a bit on edge. This will boil over within the next few days; the signs are all there. I need to be able to reach you in a hurry if that does happen. Any ideas?"

"I'll be peddling my wilted blossoms outside Shepheard's every day, as we arranged."

"Fine so far as it goes, but I can't always be certain of getting away during the day. Give me an alternative."

David thought for a minute. "There's always the useful coffee shop or café. Do you remember the one that's just off the Sharia Abu'l Ela, near the Presbyterian church? I'll be there every night from now on, between nine and midnight."

"All right."

David's hand rested for a moment on his shoulder. "Get some rest, you need it."

Ramses woke the sleeping driver and got into the cab. He was tired, but his mind wouldn't stop churning. Had his father made it home safely? And what the devil was his mother doing? Emerson had pointedly refused to answer questions about her.

Worst of all was the mounting conviction that had been forced on him by one fact after another. He doubted he could convince anyone else, especially when a crucial clue had been supplied by a transvestite Nubian pimp. He could picture Russell's face when he heard that one!

But he had gone to el-Gharbi to ask where the ineffectual terrorist had procured his grenades, and el-Gharbi had kept dragging Percy into the conversation. El-Gharbi knew everything that went on in the dark world of prostitution, drugs, and crime — and he had kept talking about Percy, hiding his real motive behind a screen of fulsome compliments and pretended sympathy. El Gharbi was approximately as romantic as a cobra; that final sting, about Percy's role in tricking Nefret into marriage, had been designed to give Ramses a single piece of vital information.

Percy's connections with Nefret's husband had been closer than anyone had suspected. Close enough to be a partner in Geoffrey's illegal business activities — drugs and forged antiquities? Percy had spent several months in Alexandria with Russell while Russell was trying to shut down the import of hashish into Cairo from the coast west of the Delta. One way or another, Percy knew the routes and the men who ran the drugs. They were, Ramses believed, the same routes being used now to transport arms.

As Ramses had good cause to know, the grenades had not come from Wardani's people. So whom did that leave? A British officer who had access to a military arsenal? A man who wouldn't scruple to kill an innocent passerby in order to play hero and impress his alienated family?

Most damning of all was the fact that Farouk had known about the house in Maadi. It had been a closely guarded secret between Ramses and David until Ramses took Sennia and her young mother there, to hide them from Kalaan. Ramses had never known how the pimp tracked her down; she might have been the innocent agent of her own betrayal, slipping back to el Was'a to visit friends and boast of the new protector who had, incredibly, offered her safety without asking anything in return. Rashida was dead and Kalaan had not shown his face in Cairo since, and there was only one other person who had been a party to that filthy scheme.

Percy — who was now paying him extravagant, hypocritical compliments and defending his tarnished reputation. If Percy was the traitor and spy Ramses suspected him of being, his interest in his cousin's present activities was prompted by more than idle curiosity.

It made a suggestively symmetrical pattern, but what chance had he of convincing anyone else when even David thought his hatred of Percy had become an irrational idée fixe? Would any of them believe a member of their own superior caste, an officer and a gentleman, would sell out to the enemy?

He knew he couldn't keep the knowledge to himself; he'd have to tell someone. But I'm damned if I'm going after him myself, he thought. Not now. Not until I'm out of this, and I've got David out, and he can go home to Lia, and I can shake some sense into Nefret and keep her safe. I couldn't stand to lose her again.

13

After seeing Nefret and the Vandergelts, and Fatima, who had insisted on waiting up for them, off to bed, I put on a dressing gown and crept downstairs. The windows of the sitting room faced the road, and it was on the cushioned seat under them that I took up my position after easing the shutters back in order to see out. It was very late, or very early, depending on one's point of view; those dead, silent hours when one feels like the only person alive. The moon had set; beyond the limited circles of light shed by the lamps we kept burning at our door, the road lay quiet in the starlight.

I was not aware that Ramses had returned until the sitting room door opened just wide enough to enable a dark figure to slip in. Two dark figures, to be precise; Seshat was close on his heels.

"Do you enjoy climbing that trellis?" I inquired somewhat snappishly. Relief often has such an effect.

He sat down next to me. "I had to report myself to Seshat."

"How did you know I was here?"

"I knew you weren't in your room. I looked

in. I trust you will overlook the impertinence; I was a trifle anxious about Father."

"So you saw him," I murmured.

"Heard him, rather." He gave me a brief account of what had transpired. "I hope you don't think I did wrong in letting him go off alone."

"Good gracious, no. Short of binding him hand and foot, you could not have prevented him."

"How did it go on your end?"

"There was no difficulty. I arrived home well before the others." The area of illumination looked very small against the enveloping darkness. "He has a long way to come," I said uneasily. "Perhaps I ought to take the motorcar out again and go to meet him."

We were sitting side by side, our heads together, so we could converse quietly. I felt his arm and shoulder jerk violently. "Again?" he gasped.

"Didn't your father tell you?"

"No." He seemed to be having trouble catching his breath. "I wondered why he . . . *You* drove the car home? Not all the way from Tura! Where is it?"

"In the stableyard, of course. Take a glass of water, my dear."

"Father would say the situation calls for whiskey," Ramses muttered. "Never mind, just tell me what happened. I don't think I can stand the suspense."

I concluded my narrative by remarking somewhat acerbically, "I do not understand why you and your father should assume I am incapable of such a simple procedure."

"I believe you are capable of anything," said Ramses.

I was pondering this statement when Seshat sailed past me and out the window. A thump and a faint rustle of shrubbery were the only sounds of her passage through the garden.

"Your father!" I exclaimed.

"A mouse," Ramses corrected. "Don't credit her with greater powers than she has."

"Oh. I do hope she will eat it outside and not bring it to you. As for the motorcar —"

"Ssh." He held up his hand.

According to Daoud, Ramses can hear a whisper across the Nile. My hearing was sharpened by affectionate concern, but it was several moments before I made out the sound that had alerted him. It was not the sound of booted feet.

"A camel," I said, unable to conceal my disappointment. "Some early-rising peasant."

The early-rising peasant was in more of a hurry than those individuals usually are. The camel was trotting. As it entered the lamplight, I beheld Emerson, upright and bareheaded, legs crossed on the camel's neck, smoking his pipe.

He yanked on the head rope to slow the beast and whacked it on the side of the neck to turn it toward the front of the house and the window. I winced as my tenderly nurtured roses crunched under four large flat feet. At Emerson's command the camel settled ponderously onto the ground, crushing a few hundred marigolds and petunias, and Emerson dismounted.

"Ah," he said, peering in the window. "There you are, Peabody. Move aside, I am coming in."

I found my voice. "Emerson, get that damned camel out of my garden!"

"The damage is done, I fear," said Ramses. "Father, where did you acquire it?"

"Stole it." Emerson climbed over the sill. "Got the idea from David."

"You can't just leave it there!" I exclaimed. "How are you going to explain its presence? And the owner —"

"Don't concern yourself about the camel, I'll think of something. What did you do to the car?"

"Put it in the stableyard, of course."

"In what condition?"

"Let us not waste time on trivialities, Emerson. The most important thing is that you are here; Ramses is here; I am here. I suggest we all go to bed and —"

"No point in that, it will be light in an hour or two," said my indefatigible spouse. "What about breakfast, eh, Peabody?"

"It would be unkind to rouse Fatima at this hour, when she was so late getting to bed last night."

"Good Gad, no, I wouldn't do that. I will just cook up some eggs and coffee and —"

"No, you will not, you always burn the bottoms off the pans."

"I would offer," said Ramses, "but —"

"But you always burn them too." The idea of breakfast had some merit. I wanted to hear how Emerson had carried out his task, and I knew he would be in a much better humor after he had been fed. The dents in the motorcar were bound to provoke some recriminatory remarks, and the missing lamp . . . "Oh, very well, I will see what's in the larder."

There was quite a lot in the larder, and Emerson tucked into a roast chicken wing with a hearty appetite. Between bites he gave us a description of his adventures.

"It went off without a hitch. What did you expect? After I had stowed the stuff away I drove the cart back to Kashlakat and left it outside the mosque."

"You walked off and left it?"

"The donkeys weren't going anywhere. As for walking, I concluded I would rather not." He stopped chewing and gave me a reproachful look. "I had become very anxious about you, my dear. I expected to find you not far from where I had left you."

"Oh, you did, did you?"

My interest in Emerson's narrative had not prevented me from noticing that Ramses had put very little food on his plate and had eaten very little of that. He finished his cup of coffee and rose.

"No," I said. "Please, Ramses. Don't go out again."

"Mother, I must. I ought to have taken care of it earlier, but I wanted to make certain Father got home all right. I should be back by daylight."

"The others will sleep late," Emerson said. "But — er — don't be any longer than you can help, my boy. Do you know who it was?"

"What —" I began.

Emerson waved me to silence, and Ramses said, "Not for certain, but Rashad is the most likely candidate. If he wakes to see me squatting on the foot of his bed, glowering like a gargoyle, he'll be in a proper state for interrogation."

I said, "What —" and Ramses said, "Tell her, Father. I must hurry."

"You aren't going on foot, I hope," said Emerson.

Ramses's tight lips parted in a smile. "I'll take the camel."

He was gone. I put my elbows on the table and my face in my hands.

"Now, now, Peabody." Emerson patted me on the shoulder.

"How much longer is this going to continue?"

"It can't be much longer. If the last delivery has been made, der Tag must be imminent. Don't you suppose he is as anxious as you are to get this over?"

"I know he is. That is what frightens me. Desperation drives a man to recklessness. I take it Rashad is one of Wardani's lieutenants? Not another of the same ilk as Farouk, I hope."

"Unlikely," said Emerson, with infuriating calm. "Part of the cache was missing. Someone had got there before us. That means there are a hundred rifles and possibly a machine gun or two in unknown hands in an unknown location. Not enough to win a war, but enough to kill quite a number of people. The most likely suspect is this fellow Rashad, who has been exhibiting signs of insubordination, egged on, no doubt, by Farouk. That has been one of Ramses's difficulties all along — keeping that lot of young radicals under control. I know their type — good Gad, I was one of them myself once upon a time! — naive and idealistic and itching to prove their manhood by rioting in the streets. Fists and rocks and clubs can do a limited amount of harm, but a gun is entirely different. It makes a weak man feel like a hero and a strong man feel as if he is immortal, and it removes the last inhibition a killer might feel. You don't have to be close to a man to put a bullet into him. You don't have to see his face."

"Were you a radical, Emerson?"

"I am still, my dear. Ask anyone in Cairo." Emerson's grin faded. "Peabody, Ramses took on this assignment for one reason and one reason only: to keep people from being injured, even those young fools of revolutionaries. He won't rest until he's got those guns back. When he does, he will have accomplished what he set out to do, and this damned business will end, if I have to collect the damned weapons and the damned young fools myself. Are you trying not to cry? Let it out, my darling, let it out, you look dreadful with your face screwed up like that."

"I am trying not to sneeze." I rubbed my nose. "Though your words moved me deeply. Emerson, you have given me new heart. I am ready to act when you are!"

"We'll give Russell time to act first. Not much time, though, curse it. Something is going to happen in the next two or three days. The Turks are within five miles of the Canal in some areas; they've begun digging themselves in east of Kantara and Kubri and el-Ferdan. In the meantime that lot of Clayton's is drawing up maps and 'examining broader questions of strategy,' as they put it! What we need is detailed information: precisely where and when the attack will take place, how many men, what kind of armaments, and so on. Our defenses are dangerously undermanned, but if we knew that, we might be able to hold them."

"Might? Really, Emerson, you are not very encouraging."

"Not to worry, my dear." Emerson's handsome blue eyes took on a faraway look. "If the enemy takes Cairo we will retreat into the wadis and hold out until reinforcements arrive from England. The weapons I concealed at Fort Tura —"

"You'd like that, wouldn't you?"

"I?" Emerson's dreamy smile stiffened into a look of rigid disapproval. "I only want to get on with my excavations, Peabody. What do you take me for?"

I went to him and put my arms round his shoulders. "The bravest man I know. One of them . . . Ow! Emerson, don't you dare kiss me while you are wearing that beard!"

From Manuscript H

Ramses knew where Rashad and the others lived; he kept track of changes of address, which were fairly frequent. This wouldn't be the first time he had dropped in on one of them without warning. He preferred these epiphanies, not only for the sake of safety but because they added to his own mystique. Wardani knows all!

603

Rashad, whose father was a wealthy landowner in Assiut, had a room to himself in a building near el-Azhar, where he was, in theory at least, a student. Whether from inertia or self-confidence or love of comfort, he hadn't shifted quarters lately, and Ramses had decided the best approach was through the window, which gave onto a narrow street leading off the Sharia el-Tableta. The window was on the first floor with a blank wall under it, but the camel would help him with that little difficulty if he could force the balky beast into position.

As he might have expected, the camel walked out from under him as soon as he got hold of the sill, and he had a bit of a scramble to get in. Fortunately, Rashad was a heavy sleeper. He was snoring peacefully when Ramses took up a position at the foot of his bed.

The darkness paled with the approach of dawn, and Ramses decided irritably that he couldn't wait for the lazy lout to have his sleepout. He had to be out of the room before it was light enough for Rashad to get a good look at him. The tweed coat and trousers were the ones he had worn before, and the hat shadowed his face, but he hadn't had time to alter his features with makeup. He lowered his voice to the resonant pitch he had learned from Hakim the Seer of Mysteries (aka Alfred Jenkins), who did a mind-reading stunt at the London music halls.

"Rashad!"

The response would have been entertaining if Ramses had been in a mood for broad humor. Rashad thrashed and squawked and squirmed, fetching up in a sitting position with his back against the wall and his knees drawn up and the sheet clumsily arranged over his naked body.

"Kamil! You! How —"

"Where," Ramses corrected. "Where did you take them?"

There was no argument, but there were plenty of excuses. Ramses interrupted him. "The ruined mosque? You haven't much imagination, have you? They must be moved. I'll see to it myself. I will overlook your insubordination this time, Rashad, but if it happens again. . . ."

He left the threat unspecified, knowing Rashad had enough imagination to picture a variety of ugly possibilities, and went to the door. Rashad had not only barred it but shoved a chair against it. As he removed these pathetic impediments, Rashad continued to squeal apologies. Ramses left without replying. He didn't suppose Rashad would work up nerve enough to follow him, especially since he had taken the precaution of "borrowing" the galabeeyah Rashad had laid out across a chair, ready to put on in the morning.

There was no sign of the camel. He didn't waste time looking for it; it would not be lonely for long, and its original owner would be anonymously and generously reimbursed. In Ramses's opinion he was lucky to be rid of the brute. It had the gait of a three-legged mule and it had tried to bite him on the leg.

He quickened his steps, reaching the mosque as the call to morning prayer ended. After removing his shoes and hat, he went inside, pausing by the fountain to bathe face, hands, and arms. There were few worshipers, since most people preferred to pray at home; and as Ramses went through the prescribed positions, kneeling at last close to the left wall, he hoped what he was doing would not be regarded as profanation. He slipped his hand into the opening in the wall, and paper crackled under his fingers.

The train left him off at Giza Station. Since it was now broad daylight, he was as likely to be seen climbing up the trellis as walking in the front door, so he did the latter. The smell of frying bacon floated toward his appreciative nostrils and he followed it toward the breakfast room.

The Vandergelts weren't down yet, but Nefret had joined his parents at the table. They all turned to stare when he sauntered in.

"Enjoy your walk?" his father inquired,

giving him a cue he didn't need.

Nefret yawned prettily, covering her mouth with her hand. "Such energy! Early to bed and early to rise . . . I hope you are feeling wealthy and wise, because you don't look especially healthy."

"Kind of you to say so."

"You've got those dark smudges under your eyes," Nefret explained. "Very romantic-looking, but indicative, in my experience, of too little sleep. I thought you came home early last night."

"I also woke early. Couldn't get back to sleep, so I went for a long walk." Fatima put a plate of eggs in front of him. He thanked her and told himself to shut up. He was explaining too much.

"You should have hoarded your strength," said his father, with a wolfish smile. "I mean to get in a full day's work, so hurry and finish breakfast."

Ramses nodded obediently. His mother had not spoken, but he hadn't missed the signs of silent relief when he walked into the room. She always carried herself like a soldier, even when she was sitting down; it made him feel like a swine to see those straight shoulders sag and that controlled face lose a little of its color. What he was doing was unfair to David and Nefret, but it was brutal to his parents. Perhaps the news he brought would cheer them up.

He had to wait until they were on their way to Giza before he had a chance to speak with his mother alone. His father had gone on ahead with Nefret, and Ramses held Risha to the plodding pace of his mother's mare.

"I know where he's hidden them," he said without preamble.

"It was the man you suspected?"

"Yes. He was only trying to be helpful! A feeble excuse, but he wasn't in a state to think clearly."

His mother was. She was blind as a mole about some things, but every now and then she hit the nail square on the head. "The Turks are communicating directly with him. They must be, or he wouldn't have known where the cache was located. You didn't tell him, did you?"

"No. You're right, of course. They know where he lives, too. The message was pushed under his door."

"They're having doubts of you — of Wardani."

"They always have had. Now that they've lost their agent, they are trying to undermine my control another way. I doubt it means anything more than that. Time is running out for them. I collected another little missive this morning."

She held out her hand. Ramses couldn't help smiling. "I destroyed it. It said, 'Be ready. Within two days.'"

"Then you can confiscate the weapons and put an end to this. Now, today." She yanked on the reins.

Ramses halted Risha and reached for her hand, loosening her clenched fingers. In her present mood she was quite capable of galloping straight to Russell's office and yelling orders at him across the desk.

"Leave it to me, Mother. Russell is waiting for word; as soon as he gets it, he'll act. It's all been worked out. The worst is over; don't lose your head now."

"I have your promise?"

"Yes."

"Very well." They started forward. After a moment he heard a loud sniff and a muffled, "I apologize."

"It's all right, Mother. Oh, damnation, are you crying? What did I say?"

There were only two tears, after all. She wiped them away with her fingers and squared her shoulders. "Hurry on, your father will be waxing impatient."

Ramses gave his father the same information shortly afterwards, while they were measuring the outer dimensions of the second burial shaft. He didn't get off quite as easily this time. Emerson wanted to know where Rashad had put the guns, and how Ramses meant to inform Russell, and a number of other things that he was probably entitled to know. Just in case.

Having been gracious enough to approve the arrangements, Emerson turned his attention to excavation. Ramses didn't doubt his father fully intended to round up a few revolutionaries himself, and was looking forward to it, but he had a scholar's ability to concentrate on the task at hand.

"We may as well see what's there," he announced, indicating the opening of the shaft. "Get back to work on your walls, my boy, I will start the men here."

"Selim is down there helping Nefret take photographs. They don't need me."

"Oh?" Emerson gave him an odd look. "As you like."

He didn't want to go near Nefret. It would be like showing a hungry child a table loaded with sweets and telling him he must wait until after supper. In a few days, perhaps a few hours, he could confess, beg her forgiveness, and ask her again to marry him. And if she said no he would follow his mother's advice. The idea was so alluring it dizzied him.

They didn't put in a full day's work after all. His mother dragged them back to the house for an early luncheon, pointing out that it would be rude to ignore their guests. Emerson had to agree, though he hated to tear himself away; as the shaft deepened, they began to find scraps of broken pottery and, finally, a collection of small model offering vessels.

The Vandergelts had planned to spend that day and night with them, to enjoy what his mother called "the too-long-delayed pleasures of social intercourse with our dearest friends." She'd enjoy it, at any rate, and Lord knew she deserved a respite. Katherine Vandergelt wasn't looking her usual self either. War was hell, all right, not only for the men who fought but for the women who stayed at home waiting for news.

Ramses knew his father had every intention of working that afternoon, no matter what anyone else did. His description of what they had found that morning made the discovery sound a good deal more interesting than it actually was, and Cyrus declared his intention of joining them.

"I doubt we'll find an untouched burial," Ramses warned him. "Those pottery sherds look like bits of the funerary equipment."

"There may be something interesting left," Cyrus said hopefully. "Katherine?"

"I suppose I may as well come too," said his wife resignedly. "No, Amelia, I know you are aching to see what's down there, and if I stay here you will feel obliged to stay with me. What about you, Anna?"

"I'm going to the hospital." She looked challengingly at Nefret.

"You needn't overdo it, Anna. I rang Sophia earlier; things are quiet just now and she promised to let me know if anything arose that required my presence — or yours."

"You aren't going in today?"

"No. I have other plans. You can spare me for a few hours, can't you, Professor?"

"Where —" Emerson stopped himself and looked at his wife, who said, "Will you be back for dinner?"

"Yes, I think so."

"Enjoy yourself," Anna said. "I shall go to the hospital. There is always something to be done."

Nefret shrugged, excused herself, and left the room. She and Anna must have quarreled; their stiff smiles and sharp voices were the female equivalents of an exchange that would have ended in a brawl if they had been men.

"Be back in time for tea," Katherine ordered.

"I will stay as long as I am needed," Anna snapped. Without excusing herself, she left the table and the room.

"Now what is wrong with her?" Katherine demanded. "She has been in a much better frame of mind lately."

"One must expect occasional relapses when dealing with the young," said Ramses's mother.

It took only half an hour to reach the burial chamber. Ramses was glad of the distraction the work provided; he knew the chance of finding an undisturbed burial was slight, but it always gave him a queer feeling to penetrate a chamber that had not been entered for thousands of years. This one opened off the south side of the shaft and was almost filled by a large stone coffin. It hadn't given its owner the protection he wanted; his bones lay scattered on the floor beside the coffin, whose lid had been shifted just far enough to enable the thieves to drag the body out. They had overlooked only a single piece of jewelry: a small scarab which one of them must have dropped.

"They made a clean sweep, curse them," said Emerson, after he had climbed up out of the shaft. He and Ramses and Selim had been the only ones to go down; Cyrus would have disregarded his wife's objections if there had been anything to see, but he was not inclined to risk the crude wooden ladders for a few dried bones.

"Do you want photographs?" Ramses asked.

"It can wait until tomorrow," his mother said firmly. "No thief is going to bother with those scraps. We have done enough for today. More than enough."

The look she gave Ramses was pointed and somewhat reproachful. If she had had her way, he would have been in Cairo at this moment, making the arrangements he had promised to make. As he had tried to tell her, it wasn't that simple. He had rung Russell before luncheon, only to learn that Russell was out of the office and wasn't expected back until late afternoon. There was a prearranged signal — "inform him that Tewfik Bey has a camel for him." He had left that message, and if Russell received it he would be at the Turf Club that night.

The others went back to the house. Ramses stayed on for a bit to help Selim clean up the site and cover the shaft. When he entered the courtyard Fatima darted out of the sitting room and intercepted him.

"There is someone here, to see you," she whispered.

Wondering why she was behaving like a stage conspirator, he glanced round. "Where?"

"In your room."

"My room?" he echoed in surprise.

Fatima twisted her hands together. "She asked me not to tell anyone else. She said you had invited her. Did I do wrong?"

"No, it's all right." He smiled reassuringly. "Thank you, Fatima."

He took the stairs two at a time, anxious to solve this little mystery. He couldn't imagine who the woman might be. Anna? One of the village women seeking help from an abusive husband or father? It was well known that the Emersons wouldn't tolerate that sort of thing, and some of the younger women were too much in awe of his mother and father to approach them. Obviously they weren't in awe of him.

The smile on his lips faded when he saw the small figure seated on his bed. Reflexively his arm shot out and slammed the door.

"What the — what are you doing here?"

The child's face was limpid with innocence. Streaks had plowed a path through the dust on her cheeks; they might have been caused by perspiration or by tears. She had got herself up in proper visiting attire, but now her pink, low-necked frock was wrinkled, and her hair was loose on her shoulders. With the cool confidence of an invited guest, she had made herself at home; her hat and handbag and a pair of extremely grubby white gloves lay on the bed beside her.

"I wanted to play with the cat," she explained. "But it scratched me and ran away."

A low grumble of confirmation came from Seshat, perched atop the wardrobe, beyond the reach of small hands.

"Don't be childish, Melinda," Ramses said sternly. "Come downstairs with me at once."

Before he could open the door, she had flung herself at him and was hanging on like a frightened kitten. "No! You mustn't tell anyone I'm here, not yet. Promise you'll help me. Promise you won't let him send me away!"

He put his hands over hers, trying to detach them, but they were clenched tight as claws, and he didn't want to hurt her. He lowered his arms to his side and stood quite still. "Your uncle?"

"Yes. He wants to send me back to England. I won't go! I want to stay here!"

"If he has decided you must go, there is nothing I can do to prevent it, even if I would. Melinda, do you realize what an ugly position you've put me in? If your uncle found out you were here with me, alone in my room — if anyone saw us like this — they would blame me, not you. Is that what you want?"

"No . . ."

"Then let go."

Slowly the hard little fingers relaxed. She was watching him closely, and for a moment there was a look of cold, adult calculation in her eyes. It passed so quickly, drowned in twin pools of tears, he thought he must have imagined it.

"*He* hurt me," she said. With a sudden movement she tugged the dress off one shoulder and down her arm almost to the elbow.

Her bones were those of a child, fragile and delicate, but the rounded shoulder and the small half-bared breasts were not. There were red spots on her arm, like the marks of fingers.

"Don't send me away," she whispered. "He beats me. He's cruel to me. I want to be with you. I love you!"

"Oh, Christ," Ramses said under his breath. He couldn't retreat any farther, his back was against the door, and he felt like a bloody fool. Then he heard footsteps. The cavalry had arrived, and in the nick of time, too.

"Pull your dress up," he snapped.

She didn't move. Ramses grasped the handle and opened the door. "Mother? Will you come here, please?"

The girl wasn't crying now. He had never seen so young a face look so implacable. "Hell hath no fury . . . ?" He turned with unconcealed relief to his mother, who stood staring in the doorway.

"We have a runaway on our hands," he said.

"So I see." She crossed the room, heels thudding emphatically, and yanked the girl's dress into place. "What are you running away from, Melinda?"

"My uncle. He beat me. You saw the bruises."

"He took you by the shoulders and shook you, I expect. I cannot say I blame him. Come with me."

She shrank back. "What are you going to do to me?"

"Give you a cup of tea and send you home."

"I don't want tea. I want . . ."

"I know what you want." She directed a quizzical look at Ramses, who felt his cheeks burning. "You cannot have it. Go downstairs to the sitting room. Now."

Ramses had seen that voice galvanize an entire crew of Egyptian workers. It had a similar effect on the child. She snatched up her hat, gloves, and bag, and Ramses stepped hastily out of the way as she ran past him and out the door.

His mother looked him over, from head to foot and back. She shook her head and pursed her lips. "No. There is nothing that can be done about it," she said cryptically. "You had better stay here, I can deal with her more effectively if you are not present."

After he had bathed and put on clean clothes, Ramses skulked in his room for an additional quarter of an hour before he summoned courage enough to go downstairs. Weeping women unnerved him, and this one wasn't even a woman, she was only a little girl. (But remarkably mature for her age, jeered a small nasty voice in the back of his mind. He buried it under a pile of guilt.) What else could he have done, though? "I must be cruel, only to be kind."

What a smug, self-righteous thing to say to someone whose heart you had cleft in twain. Hamlet had always struck him as something of a prig.

I did not have to deal with the young person after all. She had actually ventured to disobey me! When I came down into the court-

618

yard I saw that the front door stood open and that Ali and Katherine were looking out. Katherine turned as I approached.

"What was that all about?" she demanded.

"What was what all about?"

"The frantic flight of little Miss Hamilton. I was crossing the courtyard when she came pelting down the stairs; she almost knocked me over in her wild rush for the door. I didn't know she was here. Should we go after her?"

From where I stood I could see along the road in both directions. There was no sign of a flying pink figure, only the usual pedestrian and vehicular traffic. I considered Katherine's question. The girl had got here by herself. So far as I was concerned, she could get herself away without my assistance. It was not the decision of a kind Christian woman, but at that moment I did not feel very kindly toward Miss Molly.

"I think not," I replied. "She is out of sight now; we have no way of knowing whether she went to the train station, or hired a conveyance."

"She ran out into the road and stopped a carriage, Sitt Hakim," Ali volunteered. "She had money; she showed it to the driver."

That news relieved my conscience, which had been struggling to make itself heard over my justifiable annoyance. I promised myself that I would telephone her uncle later, on some pretext, to make sure she had got home safely.

Katherine was frowning slightly. As we returned to the courtyard she said, "Something must have happened to upset her. What was she doing here?"

The others had come down for tea. I heard voices in the sitting room, and Cyrus's deep chuckle. I saw no need to discuss the affair with the men, so I stopped and gave Katherine an explanation which was the truth, if not the whole truth.

"Her uncle is sending her home. She doesn't want to go. You know how unreasonable children can be; she had some nonsensical notion of staying with us."

"She's old enough to know better," Katherine said.

"But badly spoiled. There is no need to mention this to the others, Katherine."

"As you like, Amelia dear."

Ramses was slow in making an appearance. After a quick involuntary glance at me, to which I responded with a nod and a smile, he avoided my eyes. I trust I may not be accused of maternal prejudice when I say that I did not wonder at the child — or at any of the other women who had made nuisances of themselves about him. He was a fine-looking young man, with his father's handsome features and the easy grace of an athlete, but there was something more: the indefinable glow cast upon a countenance by the beauty of a noble character, of kindness and modesty and courage. . . .

"What are you smiling at, Mother?" He had seen my fond look. It made him extremely nervous. He adjusted his tie and passed his hand over his hair, trying to flatten the clustering curls.

"A pleasant little private thought, my dear," I replied. And private it must remain; he would have been horribly embarrassed if I had voiced my thoughts aloud.

When we parted to dress for dinner, neither of the girls had returned. I was not uneasy about Anna, for I supposed her tardiness was designed solely to annoy her mother, but I had begun to be a bit concerned about Nefret. Fatima had seen her leaving the house dressed in riding kit, so I betook myself to the stables, where I met Ramses coming out.

"She isn't back yet," he said.

"So I gather. Was she alone?"

"Yes. Jamal offered to go with her, but she said she was meeting someone."

"She might have told Jamal that to prevent his accompanying her," I said. "He has developed a boyish attachment to her."

"She might."

"We may as well go and change. She will be along soon, I'm sure."

We returned to the house together. After

Ramses had gone upstairs I stole away into the telephone room and rang through to the Savoy. When I asked for Major Hamilton the servant informed me he was out. Miss Nordstrom was in, however, and in a few moments I was speaking with her.

I am, if I may say so, something of an expert at extracting information while giving away very little. I did not have to be especially clever this time. Poor Miss Nordstrom was in such a state of bustle and exasperation that a single statement set her off.

"I hear that you and your charge will be departing soon for England."

She didn't even ask who had told me. She thanked me effusively for having the courtesy to bid her bon voyage, apologized for the suddenness of their departure, which left her no time to pay the proper farewell calls, lamented over the discomfort of a sea voyage in winter and told me how glad she was to be returning to civilization. Not until the end of the conversation did she mention, as an additional grievance, that Molly had got away from her that afternoon and had not returned until teatime.

"You can imagine my state of nerves, Mrs. Emerson! I was about to send for the police when she came back, as cool and unconcerned as if she hadn't frightened me half to death. She flatly refused to tell me where she had been."

Thank goodness, I thought. I could have invented a story to explain why Molly had come to us — or rather, I could have told that part of the truth that did not involve Ramses — but now I did not have to.

"So," Miss Nordstrom continued, "it is just as well we are sailing tomorrow. She is a very willful young person and I cannot control her properly here. I shudder to think of what could happen to her in this wicked city!"

Not so wicked a city as London. I kept this thought to myself, since I did not wish to prolong the conversation.

My conscience being at ease about the child, I was able to concentrate on my uneasiness about Nefret. It was not unheard of for her to go riding, alone or with a friend, but the fact that she had not mentioned a name roused the direst of suspicions. Instead of going to my room I lingered in the hall, rearranging a vase of flowers, straightening a picture, and listening. I had not realized how worried I was until I heard a prolonged howl from the infernal dog. Relief actually weakened my frame. Nefret was the only one he greeted in that manner.

The door opened and she slipped in. Seeing me, she stopped short. "I thought you'd be changing," she said. It sounded like an accusation.

I could only stare in consternation. Her

loosened hair hung down below her shoulders, and her hands were gloveless. There was something odd about the fit of her tailored coat; it had been buttoned askew. I seized her by the shoulders and drew her into the light.

"Have you been crying?" I demanded. "What happened?"

"Nothing. Aunt Amelia, please don't ask questions, just let me —"

She broke off with a gasp, and I turned to see what she was staring at.

"So you're back," Ramses said. "Is something wrong?"

He hadn't changed, or even brushed his hair, which looked as if he had been tugging at it. As his eyes moved over Nefret's disheveled form and dust-smeared face, a wave of burning red rose from her throat to her hairline.

"I'm late. I'm sorry. I'll hurry." Face averted, she ran for the stairs.

Though I despise social conventions in general, I would be the first to admit that there are sensible reasons behind certain of them. For example, the avoidance of controversial subjects and heated argument at the dinner table promotes digestion. Despite my best efforts I was unable to keep the conversation that night on a light pleasant note. Anna had been so late in arriving that there was not time for her to change before Fatima called us to dinner. I felt certain the girl had done it deliberately to annoy Katherine and perhaps make the rest of us feel like slackers. The dress she wore for her hospital duties was as severe as a proper nurse's uniform.

I caught Katherine's eye before she could speak and shook my head. "We must go in," I said. "Or Mahmud will burn the soup."

Disappointed in her hope of starting a row, Anna continued to be as provoking as possible. Many of the barbs she slipped into the conversation were aimed at Nefret.

In fact, I knew what had set her off. I had, by pure accident, overheard part of a dialogue between the two girls after luncheon. The first complete sentence was Nefret's.

"It's the uniform, don't you see that? You want to be in love with a soldier, any soldier. I don't care how many of them you pursue, but stay away from *him*. He —"

"You're only saying that because you're jealous! I saw you come in from the garden with him. You lured him out there. You want him yourself!"

"Lured?" Nefret gave a strange little laugh. "Perhaps I did. You are mistaken about the rest of it, however. Listen to me, Anna —"

"No! Leave me alone." She went running off.

It had not required much effort to guess whom they were discussing. I had meant to warn Anna about Percy myself, but if she would not heed Nefret, there was little chance she would listen to me, and I did not believe there was any danger of a serious attachment, at least not on Percy's part. Like the generous-hearted man he was, Cyrus had made testamentary provisions for his stepchildren, but Anna was not by any definition a wealthy heiress.

It may have been Anna's sullen mood that infected the rest of us. There was certainly something in the air that night; it would be superstitious to speak of premonitions and forebodings, so I will not. Heaven knows there were sufficient reasons for concern in the events of those times. It was Cyrus who first mentioned the war. I was only surprised we had managed to keep off it so long.

"Heard anything more about an attack on the Canal?"

His question was directed at Emerson, who shook his head and replied somewhat evasively, "One hears a great deal. Rumors, most of them."

Nefret looked up. "People are leaving Cairo. They say the steamers are completely booked."

"The same 'they' who spread such rumors," Emerson grunted. "One never knows who 'they' are."

"But there will be an attack," Anna said suddenly. "Won't there?"

"Don't get your hopes up," Nefret said. "The wounded would be sent to the military hospitals. Anyhow, most of the troops guarding the Canal are Indian — Punjabis and Gurkhas. Not romantic, in your terms."

The venom in her voice was like a slap in the face, and Anna's cheeks reddened as if from an actual blow.

"The Forty-second Lancashire is there," Cyrus said obliviously. "And some Australian and New Zealand troops."

"And the Egyptian artillery," Ramses added. "They are well trained, and the Indian regulars are first-rate fighting men."

He was trying to reassure Katherine — and me? From my conversations with Emerson, I knew the situation was not so comfortable as Ramses implied. The British Army of Occupation had been sent to France, and their replacements were raw and untrained. The safety of the Canal hung on the loyalty of the so-called "native" troops, most of whom were Moslem. Would they be swayed by the Sultan's call for a jihad?

"They certainly are splendid-looking fellows," Nefret said. "I've seen some of them in Cairo, on leave. On the street, that is. They are not allowed in the hotels or the clubs, are they? I don't suppose any of the patriotic ladies of Cairo have gone to the trouble of providing them with a decent place to relax from their duties."

"I don't suppose so either," I said. "There are not enough decent recreational facilities for any of the enlisted men. No wonder the poor lads resort to grog shops and cafés and — er — other even less reputable places of — er — amusement! I will take steps to correct that. I beg your pardon, Ramses, did you speak?"

"No, Mother." He looked down at his plate, but not so quickly that I failed to see the glint of amusement in his black eyes. What he had said, under his breath, was, "Tea and cucumber sandwiches."

So it went, through three additional courses. Cyrus's questioning of Emerson was a transparent request for reassurance; I did not doubt he had seriously considered sending Katherine home — or trying to. Anna and Nefret continued to snipe at one another, and Ramses contributed nothing useful to the converation. After dinner we retired to the parlor, where Katherine sank into a chair.

"If anyone else mentions the war, I will scream," she declared. "Nefret, will you please play for us? Music is said to soothe a savage breast and mine is quite savage just now."

Nefret looked a trifle sheepish. She had certainly done her bit to contribute to the unpleasantness. "Of course. What would you like to hear?

"Something cheerful and comic," Cyrus

suggested. "There are some pretty funny songs in that stack I brought with me."

"Something soft and soothing and sweet," Katherine corrected.

"Something we can all sing," said Emerson hopefully.

Nefret, already seated at the piano, laughed and looked at Ramses. "Have you any requests?"

"So long as it isn't one of those sentimental, saccharine ballads you favor. Or a stirring march."

Her smile faded. "No marches. Not tonight."

She played the old songs that were Emerson's favorites. At her request Ramses stood by to turn the pages for her, and if he found the songs too sentimental for his taste, he did not say so. I managed to prevent Emerson from singing by asking Nefret to do so. Her voice was untrained but very sweet and true, and Emerson loved to hear it.

Katherine put her head back and closed her eyes.

"That was charming, my dear," she said softly. "Go on, if you are not too tired."

Nefret sorted through the sheet music. "Here's one of Cyrus's new songs. Ramses, sing it with me."

He had been watching her, but he must have been thinking of something else, for he started when she addressed him. I knew he was as keenly aware of the time as I was. Within an hour he must leave to meet Thomas Russell.

With a smile and a shrug he held out his hand. "Let me see the music."

"If you are going to be that particular —"

"I only want to look through it first." He had learned to read music, though he did not play. Once I had wondered why he bothered. After a quick perusal, he curled his lip. "It's worse than saccharine, it's precisely the sort of romantic propaganda I was talking about the other day."

"Please, Ramses," Katherine murmured. "This is so pleasant, and I haven't heard you and Nefret sing together for a long time."

Ramses's cynical smile faded. "All right, Mrs. Vandergelt. If it will please you."

It was the first time I had heard the song, which was to become very popular. It did not mention the War; but the wistful reference to "the long, long night of waiting" before the lovers could again walk together into the land of their dreams made its message particularly poignant in those days. Music may be a tool of the warmongers, but it can also bring solace to aching hearts.

They went through it twice, and the second chorus was nearing its final notes when Ramses's smooth voice cracked. "Damn it, Nefret! What did you do that for?"

She was shaking with laughter. "I'm sorry,

I didn't mean to kick you so hard. I just didn't want you to spoil it by breaking into falsetto."

"A scream of pain is preferable?" He rubbed his shin.

"I said I was sorry. Pax?"

She held out her hand. His lips quivered, and then he was laughing too, his hands enclosing hers.

The door opened. Fatima was there. She had neglected to veil her face, and in her hand she held a flimsy bit of folded paper.

"It is from Mr. Walter," she said, holding out the paper as if it were burning her fingers.

How did she know? How did any of us know? Oh, there was a certain logic behind the instinctive expectation of bad news that brought us all to our feet. Telegrams and cables were used primarily for news of great joy or great sorrow, and after only a few months of war, English households had learned to dread the delivery of one of those flimsy bits of paper. But it was more than that, I think.

After a moment Katherine sank back into her chair with a look of unconcealed relief, and shame at that relief. News of her son would not come to her through Walter. Bertie was safe. But some other woman's child was not.

It was my dear Emerson who went to Fatima and took the telegram from her. The lines in his face deepened as he read it.

"Which of them?" I asked evenly.

"Young John." Emerson looked again at the paper. "A sniper. Killed instantly and without pain."

Nefret turned to Ramses and hid her face against his shoulder. He put his arm around her in a gentle but almost perfunctory embrace. His face was as cold and remote as that of Khafre's alabaster statue.

"Evelyn is bearing up well," Emerson said. He kept looking at the telegram, as if he could not remember what it said.

"She would, of course," said Ramses. "That's part of our code, is it not? Part of the game we play, like the marches and the songs and the epigrams. Killed instantly and without pain. Dulce et decorum est pro patria mori." He let the sheet of music fall to the floor. With the same detached gentleness he took Nefret's hands and guided her to a chair. He left the room without speaking again.

From Manuscript H

He saddled Risha himself, waving aside the sleepy stableman's offer of assistance. The great stallion was as sensitive as a human being to his master's moods; as soon as they had left the stableyard Ramses let him out, and he ran like the wind, avoiding the occasional obstacle of donkey or camel without slackening speed. There was more traffic on the bridge and in the city streets, but by that time Ramses had himself under better control. He slowed Risha to a walk.

It was half past eleven when he reached the club. Too early for the rendezvous, but Russell would probably be there. Leaving Risha with one of the admiring doormen, he ran up the stairs and went in. Russell was in the hall. He was alone, reading or pretending to read a newspaper. He was watching the clock, though, and when he saw Ramses he dropped the newspaper and started to rise. Ramses waved him back into his chair and took another next to him.

"What are you doing here?" Russell demanded in a hoarse whisper. "I got the message. Has something gone wrong?"

"Nothing that affects our business. There's been a slight change in plans, though. You can empty the arsenal whenever you like, but it must be done in absolute secrecy, and you mustn't make any arrests. There's another cache hidden in the ruined mosque near Burckhardt's tomb."

Russell's eyes narrowed at the peremptory tone. He was accustomed to give orders, not take them. "Why?"

"Do you want the man who's behind this?"

"You mean . . . Do you know who it is?"

"Yes."

He laid it out with the cold precision of a formula, point by point, ignoring the skepticism that formed a stony mask over Russell's face. Once a slight crack appeared in the mask, but Russell said nothing until he had finished.

"When he was in Alexandria we missed two deliveries. He was at the wrong place."

"Then you believe me. You can convince General Maxwell —"

Slowly Russell shook his head. "It might have been pure incompetence. I thought it was. That's why I relieved him and sent him back to Cairo. He's one of Maxwell's fair-haired boys, and Maxwell would resent my interference."

Ramses knew he was right. Interservice jealousy was a damned nuisance and a fact of life. "Military intelligence hasn't been able to get a line on him," he argued. "At least give me a chance to find the proof."

"How? Whether you're right or wrong, the fellow hasn't made a false move. There's someone running the show here, even Maxwell admits that, but he'll never believe it's one of his pets. We've rounded up a few of the underlings, like that Fortescue woman, but none of them had ever spoken personally with him."

"He must communicate directly with his paymasters, though. Probably by wireless. Obviously he can't keep the equipment in his quarters. That means he's got a private hideaway. I think I know where. He takes women there sometimes."

Russell's lips tightened. "Where did you get that? Your pederast friend?"

"My *friend* is more familiar with his habits than Maxwell or you. Your fine upstanding young officer is well known in el Was'a. Maxwell probably wouldn't believe that either. Allow me to return to the point, please. There's no use raiding the place, he wouldn't keep anything there that would incriminate him. I'll have to catch him in the act. No, don't interrupt me. The uprising is set for tomorrow or the next day. He's too fond of his precious skin to stay in Cairo during a riot, so he'll head for a safe place — possibly the hideaway I mentioned. I'll follow him." He cut off Russell's attempt to speak with a peremptory gesture. "That is why you mustn't do anything to put him on his guard. You can't arrest Wardani's lot without his finding out about it, and then he'll do something — God knows what — I can never predict what the bastard is likely to do. He might decide to sit tight and make no move at all. He might bolt. Or he might take steps to protect himself by removing potential witnesses."

"You really hate his guts, don't you?" Russell said softly.

"My feelings don't come into it. I'm asking a single favor from you, and I believe I have the right."

Russell nodded grudgingly. "You don't

have to do this, you know. You've done your job."

Ramses went on as if he had not spoken. "I'll look for a communication tomorrow morning. If it's there, I'll ring you and leave the message about the camel. If you don't hear from me tomorrow, you'll know it will be the next day." He rose to his feet. "We've talked long enough. Would you care to call me a few names or slap my face? People have been watching us."

A reluctant, hastily hidden grin curved Russell's lips. "I doubt anyone would believe, from our expressions, that this was a friendly conversation. Where is this hideaway?"

Ramses hesitated.

"I won't move in until I hear from you," Russell said. "Or until — I haven't heard from you. In the latter case, I ought to know where to look."

"For the body? You've got a point."

He described the place and its location. Russell nodded. "Do me one favor. No, make that two."

"What?"

"Don't play hero. If he's our man, we'll get him sooner or later."

"And the other favor?"

Russell wet his lips. "Don't tell your mother!"

Ramses backed away, trying to appear angry and insulted. God forgive him, he had almost burst out laughing at the look of abject horror on Russell's face.

After he had mounted, he turned Risha, not toward home, but toward the railroad station and the narrow lanes of Boulaq. There was one more appointment he had to keep. He dreaded it even more than he had the other.

The café was a favorite rendezous for a variety of shady characters, including some of the less reputable antiquities dealers and the thieves from whom they obtained their illegal merchandise. It had been a good choice; even if Ramses was recognized — which was more than likely, considering his wide circle of acquaintances in the antiquities game — the assumption would be that he had come on business.

David was there as promised, wearing a tarboosh and a cheap badly fitting tweed suit and sitting alone at a table. He was unable to conceal a start of surprise when he saw Ramses, and when the latter joined him he said at once, "Mukhtan is here. He's seen you."

"It doesn't matter. You look very neat and respectable," he added. "For a change."

"Tell me," David said quietly.

There was no putting it off; David knew he wouldn't have risked coming there undisguised without a good reason. He got the news out in a single blunt sentence, before

David could imagine even worse.

David sat without moving for a time, his eyes downcast. Johnny had been his foster brother before he became his brother-in-law, but it was of Lia he was thinking now.

"We'll get you on a boat next week," Ramses said, unable to bear the stoic silence any longer. "Somehow. I promise."

David raised his head. His eyes were dry and his face frighteningly composed. "Not until this is over and you're in the clear."

"It's over. I saw Russell before I came here and told him to go ahead. There'll be no uprising."

"What about the Canal?"

"That's not our affair. I'm through. So are you."

"So you're going to let Percy get away with it?"

Ramses had always prided himself on schooling his features so as to give nothing away, but David could read him like a book. He started to speak. David spoke first.

"I've been thinking about what you said last night — and what you didn't say, because I didn't give you the chance. I can put the pieces together too. The house in Maadi, Percy's extraordinary interest in your activities — he's afraid you're after him, isn't he?"

"David —"

"Don't lie to me, Ramses. Not to me. When I think of him smug and safe in Cairo, preening himself on his cleverness, while men like Johnny are dying, I feel sick. You aren't going to let him get away with it. If you don't tell me what you're planning to do, I'll kill the bastard myself."

"Do you suppose Lia would thank you for risking yourself to avenge Johnny? Killing Percy won't bring him back."

"But it would relieve my feelings considerably." David's smile made a chill run through Ramses. He had never seen that gentle face so hard.

"I have a few ideas," Ramses said reluctantly.

"Somehow I thought you would." The smile was just as chilling.

It didn't take long to explain his plan, such as it was. As he listened, David's clenched hands loosened. There were tears in his eyes. He could grieve for Johnny now.

Oddly enough, it wasn't Johnny's face that Ramses kept remembering. It was that of the young German.

From Letter Collection B

Dearest Lia,
At least a week will have passed before you receive this. What good is a letter? It's all I can do. If I were with you I could put my arms round you and cry with you. There's no use saying the pain will lessen and become, in

time, endurable. What comfort is that to someone who is suffering here and now?

You were there to comfort me when I needed you — selfish, ungrateful, undeserving worm that I was — and now I can't be with you when you need me. Believe one thing, Lia — hold on to it and don't lose heart. Someday, someday soon, there will be joyous news. I can't say any more in a letter. I shouldn't be saying this much. Just remember that there is nothing I would not do to bring us all together again.

14

The Vandergelts left us immediately after breakfast next morning. They would have stayed had we asked them to, but I think Katherine understood we wanted to be alone with our grief. The worst of it was that we could do nothing for the loved ones who had suffered most. I had written, and Nefret had done the same; Emerson had cabled, and Ramses had taken the messages to the central post office in Cairo, so that they would arrive as soon as was humanly possible. It was little enough.

Ramses came back in time to bid the Vandergelts farewell. He had left the house before daybreak, and I knew that before posting the letters he had looked for the message that would announce the final end of his mission. Meeting my anxious eyes he shook his head. Not today, then. It would be for tomorrow.

Knowing he had eaten almost nothing before he left, I suggested we return to the breakfast room and give Fatima the pleasure of feeding us again. Her face brightened when I asked her for more toast and coffee.

"Yes, Sitt Hakim, yes! You must keep up

your strength. Will you go to Giza today? I told Selim you might not wish to."

"We could close down for the day," Emerson said heavily. "It would be the proper thing to do."

"I doubt Johnny would care about the proper thing," said Ramses. "But we might plan some sort of ceremony. Daoud and Selim would like it, and the others will want to show their affection and respect."

"Oh, yes, Sitt," Fatima exclaimed. "They will all want to come. Those who did not know him have heard of him, of his laughter and his kindness."

"It is a nice thought," I said, trying to conceal my emotion. "But not today. Perhaps in a day — or two — we will be able to bring stronger hearts to such a ceremony."

I was thinking of David. It would be infinitely comforting to have him with us again. How that part of the business was to be managed Ramses had not said, but if the authorities did not acknowledge his courage and sacrifice immediately, I would just have to have a few words with General Maxwell.

"We may as well go to Giza for a while, then," Emerson said. "Keep ourselves occupied, eh? We will stop at midday. I have other plans for this afternoon."

Ramses's eyebrows shot up. "Father, may I have a word with you?"

"You certainly may," said his father with

considerable emphasis. "Nefret, that frock is very becoming, but hadn't you better change? If you are coming with us, that is."

It was not a frock, but one of her ruffled negligees. I had not reproached her for coming down to breakfast en déshabillé, for she did not look at all well, her eyes shadowed and her cheeks paler than usual. However, she was quick to express her intention of accompanying us, and hurried off to change.

With a wink and a nod, Emerson led us out into the garden.

"I am bloody damned tired of this sneaking and whispering," he grumbled. "What is it now, Ramses? If you tell me the business has been put off I may lose my temper."

"God forbid," Ramses said. "No, sir, it hasn't been put off, but there has been a slight change in plan. Russell wants to wait another day or two before he rounds up the malcontents. If that is what you had in mind for this afternoon, you will have to put it off."

Emerson's heavy brows drew together. "Why?"

"Well, they are harmless enough, aren't they? They are waiting for word, which they won't get because I won't give it, and without weapons there isn't much they can do."

Emerson was obviously not convinced of the logic of this. He was itching to hit someone, or, if possible, a great number of people.

"You weren't thinking of warning certain

of them, were you?" he demanded. "You seem to have a soft spot for that fellow Asad."

"I am thinking," said Ramses, whose narrowed eyes and flushed cheeks indicated that he was close to losing his temper, "that you should leave this in my hands."

To my astonishment Emerson shuffled his feet and looked sheepish. "Er — yes. As you say, my boy."

"There's Nefret. Let's go."

Once we were mounted and on our way, Ramses took the lead, with Nefret not far behind. It was a gray, misty morning, and the gloomy skies reflected my unhappy mood.

"Let them go on ahead," I said to Emerson. "I want to talk to you."

"And I to you. Proceed, my dear; ladies first."

"I was surprised to see you so meek with Ramses. Are you really going to take orders from him?"

"Yes, I am. And so are you. He has earned the right to give them. I have a great deal of — er — respect for the boy."

"Have you told him so? Have you told him you love him and are proud to be his father?"

Emerson looked shocked. "Good Gad, Peabody, men don't say that sort of thing to other men. He knows how I feel. What the devil brought this on?"

"I was thinking of Johnny," I said with a sigh. "When it is too late, one always wishes one had said more, expressed one's feelings more openly."

"Damnation, Peabody, what a morbid thought! You will have ample opportunity to express any feelings you like to Ramses and David. The only thing left for them to do is to pass on the final message to Russell, so that he will know when to act."

"There was no message this morning, so it must be for tomorrow. Will the attack on the Canal occur at the same time?"

"I don't know." Emerson stroked his chin reflectively. "We cannot assume it will coincide with the hour of the uprising. They may want their little insurrection to get underway before they strike at the Canal. If it's bloody enough, it will tie down the troops stationed in Cairo and perhaps necessitate sending reinforcements from the Canal defenses. Oh, the devil with it, Peabody! There won't be an insurrection, and if those idiots on the staff don't know an attack is imminent they haven't been paying attention."

"If you say so, my dear."

"Hmph."

"Your turn now. What was it you wanted to tell me?"

He replied with a question. "When is Lia's child due?"

"March. Unless grief and worry induce premature birth."

"You'd like to be with her, wouldn't you?

645

And with Evelyn."

"Of course."

"They say the steamers are fully booked, but I have some influence. We will sail early next week."

"Emerson! Do you mean —"

"Well, curse it, Peabody, I want to be with them too. I want Ramses out of Egypt for a while. And I want to see the look on Lia's face when David walks in the door."

"You would actually close down the dig?"

"Er, hmph. I thought I might return for a brief season at the end of March. No need for you to come with me if you don't want to."

"Stop for a moment, Emerson."

Embraces between two persons mounted on horseback are not as romantic as they sound. We managed it nicely, though. After Emerson had returned me to my saddle, I said, "You mean David to go with us next week. Can it be done, Emerson?"

"It will be done." Emerson's jaw was set. "Since I am not to be allowed to arrest revolutionaries, I will call on Maxwell this afternoon and order — er — request him to start the legal proceedings. David will need official clearance and papers."

"But in the meantime, is there any reason why he cannot be here with us? Ramses saw him last night and told him about Johnny. He will be in deep distress. We could keep him hidden and feed and comfort him. Fatima wouldn't breathe a word."

"You'd enjoy that, wouldn't you?" Emerson grinned at me. "Let me hear what Maxwell has to say. If he won't cooperate we will do it your way, and smuggle David out of the country in a packing case labeled 'pottery sherds.'"

"Or disguised as Selim, with Selim's papers," I mused. "A packing case would be very uncomfortable. Selim could then go into hiding until —"

"Control your rampageous imagination, Peabody," Emerson said fondly. "For the time being, at any rate. One way or another it will be done."

A ray of sunlight touched his resolute smiling face. The sky was clearing. I hoped that could be regarded as another omen.

Our efforts to distract ourselves with work failed miserably. Not even Emerson could concentrate, and Nefret and Ramses got into a violent argument about one of the photographs she had taken of the false door.

"The lighting's all wrong," Ramses insisted. "What were you thinking of? I need more shadow. The lower part of the left-hand inscription —"

"Do it yourself then!"

"I will!"

"No, you won't. Give me that camera!"

I was about to intervene when Nefret let loose her hold on the camera and passed a trembling hand over her eyes. "I'm sorry," she muttered. "I don't think I am in a fit state to work today."

"It is quite understandable, my dear," I said soothingly. "Perhaps this was not such a good idea after all. I will tell Emerson we had better stop."

Fatima had prepared a large lunch, which no one ate much of. We were still at table when she brought in the post. She handed it to Emerson, who distributed the various messages. As usual, the bulk of them were for Nefret. She sorted rapidly through them, and then excused herself.

Her desire for privacy was suspicious. I followed her.

So had Fatima. As I approached I heard her say, "Do you know now, Nur Misur, whether you will be here for dinner?"

"Yes," Nefret said abstractedly. "Yes, it appears that I will be here after all."

She had opened one of the envelopes and was holding a sheet of paper. She started guiltily when she saw me.

"Did you have an appointment for this evening?" I inquired. "You didn't mention it to me."

Nefret stuffed the paper into the pocket of her skirt. "I'd almost forgot. It was of long standing. I rang earlier to cancel it."

This was not up to Nefret's usual standard of prevarication. The cancellation had not come from her, or by telephone, but from her correspondent. Percy? He was the only one she was likely to lie about. At least I would not have to worry about her being out that evening.

Ramses and Emerson were still at table when I returned. "What was that all about?" the latter inquired. "You went pelting out of here like a hound on the scent."

Nefret had expressed her intention of going to her room for a little rest, so I could speak freely. I told them of my suspicions.

"You are always making mysteries," Emerson grumbled. "Haven't we enough on our minds?"

Ramses's inexpressive countenance had gone even blanker. "Excuse me," he said, and pushed his chair back.

"Where are you going?" I demanded.

"I've finished. Is it necessary for me to wait for your permission before leaving the table? I'll be in my room if you want me for anything."

His brusque tone did not distress me. I gave him a forgiving smile. "Have a nice rest."

I had meant to have one myself, but I could not settle down. A troubled mind is not conducive to slumber. When I was not thinking of Johnny and his bereaved parents I was worrying about Lia and the effect of shock on her unborn child, and about David, grieving alone in some squalid hut, and about the Turks' advancing, and Ramses . . . doing something I would not like. I did not trust him. I never had.

After a while I gave it up and went out to work in the garden. Gardening can minister to a mind diseased, as Shakespeare puts it (referring, in his case, to something else), but when I got a good look at what the camel had done to my flowers I lost the remains of my temper. What the cursed beast had not mashed he had eaten, including several rose-bushes. To a camel, thorns are a piquant seasoning.

I went in search of the gardener, woke him up, and brought him and several gardening implements, with me back to the violated plot. It would all have to be dug up and re-planted. Feeling the need for further relief, I took up a rake and sailed in myself. I was still at it when Nefret came hurrying out. She was wearing street clothes, a hat, and gloves.

"There you are!" she exclaimed. "Good heavens, why are you digging up the garden?"

I plunged my pitchfork into the earth and wiped the perspiration from my brow. "I became bored with nasturtiums. Where are you going? I was under the impression you meant to be here for dinner."

"Sophia rang; they just brought in a woman who may require surgery. I must go at once. I don't know when I will be back."

"Good luck to her, and to you, my dear."

"Thank you. You'll be here this evening? All of you?"

"Why, yes, I believe so."

She looked as if she would have said more, but nodded and hurried off.

I watched her until she was out of sight. Then I left Jamal to his digging and went into the house. When I got through to Sophia, she was obviously bewildered that I had taken the trouble to tell her Nefret was on her way. She thanked me very nicely, though.

At least I knew Nefret had not lied to me this time. Where the devil had she been — and, more important, with whom had she been — the previous afternoon? Whatever she was doing, for whatever reason, I must put a stop to it. My only excuse for having avoided a confrontation was my preoccupation with the other matter, and that was over now. Tonight, I thought. As soon as she comes home.

After my brisk exercise in the garden a nice soak in the tub was now not a luxury but a necessity. I had not seen Emerson all afternoon; he had gone to his study to work or to worry in private. I decided to surprise him by assuming one of the pretty tea gowns Nefret had given me for Christmas. He had expressed his particular approval of a thin yellow silk garment that fastened conveniently down the front. (Convenient to put on, that is.) Sunny yellow is always cheerful. I have never believed in wearing black for mourning; it is a poor testimonial to a faith that promises immortality for the worthy.

When Emerson joined me in the parlor, the brightening of his countenance assured me my selection of attire had been wise. I was about to pour when Ramses came in.

"I won't be here for dinner. I told Fatima."

His face was so guileless I was immediately filled with the direst of forebodings. He was wearing riding breeches and boots, tweed coat and khaki shirt, without a collar or waistcoat — an ensemble that might have been designed for camouflage. I said, "You aren't dressed for dinner."

"My engagement is with one of the Indian N.C.O.'s. They aren't allowed in the hotels, you know; we are meeting at a café in Boulaq."

"What for?" I asked suspiciously.

"A language lesson and perhaps a friendly wrestling match. That is what comes of showing off. He'll probably break both my legs."

"They are allowing men like him to go on leave with the Turks about to attack the Canal?" Emerson demanded. "Folly, absolute folly!"

"Maxwell still doesn't believe an attack is imminent, or that the Turks stand a prayer of getting across. I hope he's right. Don't wait up for me, I may be late." He started for the door.

"Are you going to see David tonight?"

He stopped. "Are you suggesting I ought?"

I recognized his irritating, oblique manner of avoiding a lie, and my temper slipped a little. "I am suggesting that if you do, you bring him home with you. The need for caution is past; if you deem it necessary we can keep him in seclusion for a day or two."

"It shouldn't be necessary." He turned round to face me. "You're right, it's time David came home. Good night."

From Manuscript H

He got to the place at dusk, while it was still light enough to see where he was going yet dark enough to hide his movements. David had objected to his going alone, but he wanted to make a preliminary reconnaissance.

"Percy won't turn up before dark, if he comes at all," he had pointed out. "The show isn't supposed to start until midnight. Everything is set. Russell will raid the warehouse and the mosque at nine, and once he's got the weapons safely tucked away he'll return to his office and wait to hear from me. Do you think I can't handle Percy by myself? Anyhow, I need you to be my lookout. Don't get the wind up now, David. By tomorrow morning it will be over, and we'll be home, and Fatima will be cooking breakfast for you."

And he would be explaining to his irate parents why he hadn't told them the truth. He wasn't looking forward to it. But if they had known tonight was the night they wouldn't have let him out of the house — or else they'd have insisted on accompanying him, which would have been even worse.

In the twilight the old palace looked so forbidding it was no wonder the locals avoided it. It had been built in the late eighteenth century by one of the Mameluke beys whose reputation for cruelty was even greater than those of his peers; it was said that the spirits of his victims roamed the ruins in company with djinn and afreets, moaning and gibbering. There were certainly a great many owls nesting in the broken walls. Avoiding the derelict fountain and fallen columns of the courtyard, pushing through a rampant jungle of weeds and weedy shrubs, he reached a small building that was still in good repair.

Ramses had brought a pocket torch and masked it so that only a narrow slit of light would show. Using it sparingly, he inspected all four sides of the building, which had perhaps been a pleasure kiosk. The arched windows were now closed with crude but heavy wooden shutters, and the door also appeared to be a new addition. There was another entrance, at the bottom of a short flight of stairs, that must lead to rooms underground. Both doors were equipped with new Yale locks. Picking the lock would take time, and might leave traces. It would have to be one of the shutters.

They were locked too, or bolted from the inside. The lever he had brought took care of that. Once inside, he had to use the torch, and as the narrow beam moved round the room his lips pursed in a silent whistle. The room looked like a cross between a bordello and a boudoir, all silk hangings and soft rugs. The bed that occupied most of the space was a bird's nest of tangled linen and scattered cushions.

His search of the room was quick and cursory; even Percy wouldn't be lunatic enough to keep incriminating documents in the room where he entertained his female visitors. The only item of interest he came across was a length of narrow silken ribbon, the kind that might have been threaded through the insertion on a woman's garment. He stood for a moment holding it before he tossed it aside and left the room.

A door across the narrow hallway opened onto a more promising chamber. Percy certainly liked his comforts; Oriental rugs covered the floor and hung from the walls, and the furnishings included several comfortable chairs as well as a well-stocked liquor cabinet, several oil lamps, and a large brass vessel that had served as a brazier. For burning documents? If so, they had been completely consumed.

Nothing in the room betrayed the identity of the man who sometimes occupied it. Acutely aware of the passage of time, Ramses searched the rest of the little building. A door at the end of the hall between bedroom and study opened onto a flight of stairs going down. The cellar was more extensive than the upper floor. There was nothing there now except rats and moldy straw and a few scraps of wood, but he suspected it had once contained the weapons sent on to Wardani — and elsewhere? One section had been subdivided into a series of small, cell-like rooms. All were empty except one. The sturdy wooden door creaked when he pushed it open.

The narrow beam of light showed a floor of beaten earth and walls of mortared stone. The room was about ten feet by fifteen, and it contained two pieces of furniture — a chair and a rough wooden table. A large earthenware jug stood on the table; dead flies floated on the surface of the stagnant water. There was only one other object in the room, aside from several heavy hooks on the wall opposite the door. Coiled and sleek as a snake, it hung on one of the hooks. It had been wiped clean and oiled, but when he looked more closely he saw the dark stains that had soaked into the beaten earth and dried, and he knew, with a sick certainty, that this was where Farouk had died. One of the heavy hooks was about the right height from the floor.

He went back up the stairs, thankful that David wasn't with him. He was sweating and shaking like a timid old woman. Anger, at himself and at the man who had used the kurbash, stiffened him, and he went back to the makeshift office. Damn it, there had to be something, somewhere! Before he began a more intensive search he unbolted the shutters and opened one of them a few inches. It was always a good idea to have another exit handy, and with the window open he would more easily hear an approaching horseman. There was no certainty that Percy would come tonight; but if that letter of Nefret's had been from Percy, he had canceled an engagement that would have kept him in Cairo that evening. Not proof of anything, but suggestive. David was waiting at the crossroads near Mit Ukbeh; Percy would have to pass him whether he came north on the Giza Road or crossed the river at Boulaq, and once Percy had got that far, his destination was certain. Mounted on Asfur, whom Ramses had delivered to David before coming on, David could easily outstrip Percy and arrive in time to give the signal that would warn Ramses his cousin was on the way.

The hiding place wasn't difficult to find after all. Behind one of the hangings was a largish niche, the plaster of its painted walls flaking. The wireless was there, and on a shelf under it a portfolio containing a mass of papers. Ramses picked one at random and examined it by the light of his torch. At first he couldn't believe what he saw. It was a sketch map of the area around the Canal, from Ismailia to the Bitter Lakes. The drawing was crude, but all the landmarks were noted, the roads and the rail lines, and even the larger gebels.

In mounting incredulity he sorted through the other papers. Only Percy would be fool enough to keep such documents: copies of the messages he had sent and received, in clear and in code, memoranda, even a list of names, with notations next to each. None of the names was familiar to Ramses, but he would not have been surprised to learn that certain of the code names referred to individuals he knew or had known. Three of them were crossed out.

What the hell had prompted Percy to keep such incriminating evidence? Couldn't he even remember the names of his own agents? Maybe he was planning to write his memoirs someday when he was old and senile. To do him justice, there wasn't anything in the papers that incriminated *him*. The handwriting was rather clumsily disguised, but it would take more than the conflicting evidence of handwriting experts to convince a military court.

He was about to close the portfolio when belated realization struck him. He extracted one of the papers and read it again. The notes were mere jottings, most of them numbers, without explanation or elaboration, but if that number was a date, and that a time, and the letters indicated the places he thought they stood for . . .

The sound from beyond the hanging made his heart stop. It was the creak of a hinge. The door of the room had opened.

His fingers found the switch of the torch, and blackness engulfed him. There was just time enough for him to damn himself for carelessness and overconfidence before he heard someone speak, and then he realized it wasn't Percy. The voice was deeper and slower, and it had spoken in Turkish.

"No one here. He's late."

The response was in the same language, but Ramses could tell from the accent that it was not the speaker's native tongue. "I do not like this place. He could have met us in Cairo."

"Our heroic leader does not take such risks."

The other man spat. "He is not my leader."

"We have the same masters, you and I and he. He passes the orders on. There will be orders for us tonight. Sit."

As they spoke, Ramses had closed the portfolio and replaced it, and slipped the torch into his pocket. When silence fell, he stood absolutely still, hoping his breathing wasn't as loud as it sounded to him. He hadn't missed David's signal after all. This was a meeting, or perhaps a celebration; so far as the conspirators knew, their job was done. He thought he knew who one of them was. The Turk had been playing a part too. He was no illiterate hired driver, his Turkish was that of the court. Who was the other man? Ought he to risk lifting the rug a fraction of an inch?

The strengthening glow of light round the sides of the hanging told him he ought not. There were only two things he could do: stay in concealment and pray no one would need to use the radio or consult the papers, or make a run for it and pray the element of surprise would give him a chance of getting away. He was not carrying a gun. He doubted he would ever use one again. It wouldn't have done him much good anyhow; he'd got a lot more than he had bargained for that evening, and the odds against him were increasing.

Remaining in hiding was probably the better of the two alternatives, at least for the time being. He adjusted the belt that held his knife so it was more accessible — and then the door opened again.

For a moment no one spoke. Then the newcomer said, in English, "Not here yet, eh? Now, now, my friend, don't point that rifle at me. I am not the one you await, but I am one of you."

"What proof have you?"

"Do you carry papers identifying you as a Turkish agent? The fact that I know of this place should be proof enough. That's the trouble with this profession," he added in tones of mild vexation. "Not enough trust among allies. You two don't indulge in alcohol, I suppose. Hope you don't mind if I do."

Footsteps, slow and deliberate, crossed the room and were followed by the click of glass against glass. Ramses stood motionless. Three of them now — and one, the latest to come, was someone else he knew. The Scots accent had been discarded, but the voice was the same. His father had been on the right track after all. Hamilton might not be Sethos, but he was in the pay of the enemy.

The exchange had given Ramses another useful piece of information: It would not be a good idea to make a break for it while the Turk had a rifle in his hands.

Hamilton had not bothered to close the door. Ramses heard the thump of booted feet. They came to a sudden halt, and Hamilton said coolly, "Finally. What kept you?"

"What the devil are you doing here?" Percy demanded.

"Delivering your new orders from Berlin," was the smooth reply. "You don't suppose the High Command let you in on all their little secrets, do you?"

"But I thought I was —"

"The top man in Cairo? How naive. You've done well so far; von Überwald is pleased with you."

The name meant nothing to Ramses, but Percy obviously recognized it. "You — you report to him?"

"Directly to him. Will you join me in a brandy?"

"Enough of this," the Turk said suddenly. "Let us complete our business."

"There's no hurry," Percy said expansively. "In a few hours the streets of Cairo will be running with blood. Lord, it's close in here. One of you open the shutters."

Ramses knew he was only moments away from discovery. The opened shutter would tell them there had been an intruder, and the niche was the first place they would look. He was already moving when the Turk exclaimed, "They have been opened. Who — there's someone out there!"

He'd meant to head straight for the door, but that exclamation changed his mind. Trapped behind the heavy hanging, Ramses could not have heard David's imitation of an owl's screech, but David must have got there before Percy; he might even have been on the spot in time to see the other three arrive. He would assume Ramses was still inside, possibly a prisoner, and he wouldn't wait long before investigating, not David. . . .

The Turk was at the window, the rifle at his shoulder, his finger on the trigger. There wasn't time to do anything except throw himself, not at the Turk, but at the rifle. His hands were on it when it went off. The explosion almost deafened him and the recoil loosened his clumsy grip. He stumbled forward into a hard object that caught him square across the forehead.

When he came to, he was lying on the floor with his hands tied behind him. They had searched him, removing his coat and his knife. The useful items in the heels of his boots were undisturbed, but he couldn't get to them while he was being watched. There were four feet within the range of his vision; one pair belonged to the Turk, he thought. The second set of feet was encased in elegant leather slippers. Presumably Hamilton and Percy were also among those present, but he couldn't see them without turning his head. There were several excellent reasons for not doing that, including the fact that his head felt as it would explode if he moved it. Someone was talking. Percy.

". . . get the wind up over nothing. Even if they know, they won't have time to bother with us tonight."

"You fool." That was Hamilton, caustic

and curt. "Didn't you recognize the man who got away?"

"He won't get far. He was hit. He could barely hang on."

With an effort, Ramses kept his breathing shallow and slow. Hamilton was quick to reply.

"It was David Todros."

"Who? Impossible. He's in —"

"He's not. I got a good look at him. Now think, if the effort isn't too much for you. If Todros is here it's because the British sent him here. He looks enough like your cousin to pass for him. They've pulled that stunt before. Why would they do it now, and why was it imperative that Todros's presence here shouldn't be known? And what about those rumors about the man in India?"

There was no reply from Percy. "For God's sake," Hamilton said impatiently. "Isn't it obvious? You told that miserable young thug we planted on Wardani to get rid of him. That was not a bad idea; I never trusted Wardani either, and if we had made a martyr of him his people would be raging for revenge against the British."

"That was part of the plan. It would have worked, too, if Farouk hadn't been such a rotten shot. He only wounded the fellow."

"How badly?"

"Well . . . Bad enough, I suppose, to judge from Farouk's lurid description. He wasn't seen for three days."

"Where was he during that time? Where was he the rest of the time? You knew where all the others lived, but you never found Wardani's hideouts, did you? Neither did the police, and God knows they looked hard enough."

"Damn it, don't patronize me!" Percy shouted. "I see what you're getting at, but you're wrong. Yes, I heard the rumors, and yes, I knew there was only one man who could have taken Wardani's place. It wasn't Ramses. I sent Fortescue to Giza to see if he was . . . If he . . . Oh, my God."

"Has the penny dropped at last? I wouldn't count on your little revolution coming off tonight. Ten to one those weapons are already in the hands of the police."

Percy let out a string of obscenities. The toe of his boot caught Ramses in the ribs and rolled him onto his back. "Get him up," Percy snapped. "On his feet."

Two of the hands that hauled him upright belonged to the Turk. The man who gripped his other arm wore the long white woolen haik wound round his body and over his head. The Senussi were religious reformers but not ascetics; this fellow's caftan was of yellow silk trimmed with red braid, and his under-vest glittered with gold. Percy's tone had been that of master to servant, the same tone he used to all non-Europeans, and although the two men had complied with his order, their scowling faces showed their resentment.

Leaning negligently against the back of one of the chairs, a glass in his hand, Hamilton met Ramses's curious gaze with smiling affability. He had abandoned his kilt that evening in favor of ordinary civilian clothes and boots, but that wasn't the only difference in his appearance. The face was that of another man, harder and more alert.

"How much did you hear?" Percy demanded.

"Quite a lot," Ramses said apologetically. "I know eavesdropping is rude, but —"

Percy cut him off with a hard, open-handed slap across the mouth. "Was it you? It wasn't, was it? It couldn't have been!"

He grabbed Ramses by the front of his shirt. Ramses stared back at him. He was not unwilling to prolong the discussion, but he couldn't think of a response. It was such a simple-minded question. What did Percy expect him to say? Why didn't he look for the unmistakable evidence that would verify Hamilton's theory?

Ramses knew the answer. Percy couldn't admit the possibility that he had been outwitted, that all his brilliant plans had collapsed into ruin. He'd deny the truth until someone rubbed his nose in it.

Percy raised his hand for another slap, but

before he could deliver it Hamilton came up behind him and knocked his arm down, and it was Hamilton who opened Ramses's shirt and pulled it off his shoulders.

"Is that proof enough for you?" he asked sardonically.

The Turk let out a muffled exclamation. Ramses wondered idly how detailed Farouk's description had been. Not that it mattered. The scars were there, some of them still healing.

Percy's cheeks turned crimson and his lips puckered into a pout like that of a spoiled child. Because Ramses had half-expected it, he was able to keep from crying out when Percy's fist drove into his shoulder. After the dizziness had passed, he discovered he was still more or less upright. A furious argument was in progress. The Turk was doing most of the shouting.

"Stay, then, fool, and wait for the police. Do you suppose he came here without their knowledge? We have lost this skirmish. It is time to retreat and regroup."

Percy began gabbling. "No. No, you can't go. I need you to help me deal with him."

Ramses raised his head and met the cool, appraising eyes of Hamilton.

"Our Turkish friend has it right," he said. "We mustn't waste any more time. There's no need to question him when the answers are obvious. Tie his feet and arms and let's get out of here."

Percy's jaw dropped. "Leave him alive? Are you mad? He knows who I am!"

"Kill him, then," the Turk said. "Unless the blood tie holds your hand. Shall I cut his throat for you?"

"Don't trouble yourself on my account," Ramses said. He was pleased to find that his voice was steady.

The Turk laughed appreciatively. "It was well played, young one. I regret we will not match wits again."

Keep talking, Ramses thought. Keep them arguing and debating and delaying. It wouldn't delay the Turk for long, he was an old hand at this. There was still a chance, though, so long as David was alive — and he must be — the alternative was unthinkable. Ironically, his only hope of surviving for more than sixty seconds depended on Percy.

"Oh, no," Percy said. "I've looked forward to killing him for years. I'm looking forward to it even more now. Take him downstairs."

"Take him yourself. You don't give orders to me." The Turk released his grip, and Ramses sagged to his knees. Good old Percy, he thought insanely. Always predictable.

"Go then, damn you," Percy shouted. "Both of you. All of you. I can handle him by myself."

"I doubt that," the Turk said with a sneer. "So. Rather than take the chance, I will make certain he is securely bound and helpless before I go. That is how you want him, isn't it?"

The contempt in his voice didn't even touch Percy. "Yes," he said eagerly. "Good. You needn't bother to carry him, just —"

"He will walk to his death," the Turk said flatly. "As a man should. Help him up, Sayyid Ahmad."

Ramses appreciated the implied compliment, but as they pulled him to his feet he wished the Turk's notions of honor were not so painful. Swaying in the grasp of his captors, he said, "I wouldn't at all object to being carried. This sort of thing is somewhat tiring."

The Turk let out a bark of laughter. Percy reddened. "You wouldn't be so cocky if you knew what's in store for you."

"I have a fairly good idea. Whatever would Lord Edward say? 'Torture's caddish, you know.'"

So they had to carry him after all. Percy got in two hard blows across the face before the Turk's blistering comments stopped him. Ramses was only vaguely aware of being lifted by his feet and shoulders and, after a time, of being lowered onto a hard surface. When they cut the ropes that bound his hands he reacted automatically, striking out with feet and knees and the stiffened muscles of his arms. It gained him a few precious seconds, but there were four of them and it didn't take them long to put him out.

There was water dripping off his chin when he came to his senses. He passed his dry tongue over the traces of moisture on his lips and tried to focus his eyes. He was where he had expected to be, in the foul little room in the cellar, stripped to the waist, his hands tied to a hook high on the wall. The lantern was burning brightly. Naturally. Percy would want to see what he was doing.

His cousin put the water jug on the table, caught hold of Ramses's jaw, and twisted his head painfully around so their faces were only inches apart. "How did you find out about this place?" he demanded hoarsely.

"What?"

"Did she tell you? Was that why she . . . Answer me!"

At first he couldn't imagine what Percy meant. "She" couldn't be el-Gharbi; that variety of insult was far too subtle for Percy. Then it came to him, and with it a flood of emotion so strong he almost forgot his aching body. He had told himself she wouldn't be taken in by Percy ever again; he had believed it — but there had always been that ugly doubt, born of jealousy and frustration. The last rotten core was gone now, washed away by the realization of what she had risked for him. He got his feet under him, relieving the strain on his arms and wrists, and met Percy's eyes squarely.

"I don't know what you're talking about. My informant was a man."

"You'd say that, wouldn't you? You'd lie to keep her out of it. Damn the little bitch! I'll get even with her, I'll —"

He went on with a string of vile epithets and promises to which Ramses listened with a detachment that surprised even him. Chivalry demanded that he defend his lady, verbally if not otherwise — and words were about all he was capable of just then — but she was beyond that, beyond praise or blame.

When Percy stopped raving he wasn't literally foaming at the mouth, but he looked as if he were about to. "Well? Say something!"

"I would if I could think of anything pertinent," Ramses said. He hadn't meant to laugh; it was the sort of thing some posturing hero in a melodrama would do, but he couldn't stop himself. "Now's your chance to say something clever," he added helpfully. "He who laughs last laughs best, or fools laugh at men of sense, or what about —"

The side of his head struck the wall as Percy released his grip. He took off his coat and hung it neatly over the back of the chair, removed his cuff links, and rolled his sleeves up. Watching his careful preparations, Ramses was vividly reminded of a scene from their childhood: the bloody, flayed body of the rat Percy had been torturing when Ramses came into the room, too late to prevent it, and Percy's expression, lips wet and slightly parted, eyes shining. His face had the same look now. He'd tried to blame that atrocity on Ramses too. . . .

Once Ramses had believed that he feared the kurbash more than anything in the world, more than death itself. He'd been wrong. He was as frightened as he had ever been in his life — dry-mouthed and sweating, his heart pounding and his stomach churning — but he didn't want to die, and there was still a chance — maybe more than one — if he could hang on long enough. . . .

Percy gripped the handle of the whip, lifted it from the hook and let it uncoil. Ramses turned his face to the wall and closed his eyes.

Emerson and I dined alone and then retired to the parlor. A long evening stretched ahead of us; as a rule Emerson and I had no difficulty finding things to talk about, but I could see he was no more inclined toward conversation than I. The prospect of seeing David, of keeping him safe in my care, was a cheering thought, but the closer the moment came, the more impatient I was to see it. Emerson had sought refuge in the newspaper, so I took up my darning. I had scarcely finished one stocking before Narmer began to howl. The door burst open and Nefret ran in. She flung her cloak aside; it slipped to the floor in a tumble of blue.

"They aren't here," she said, her eyes sweeping the quiet lamplit room. "Where have they gone?"

"Who?" I sucked a drop of blood from my finger.

She struck her hands together. Her eyes were so dilated they looked black, her face was deathly pale. "You know who. Don't lie to me, Aunt Amelia, not now. Something has happened to Ramses, perhaps to David as well."

Emerson put his pipe aside and went to her. "My dear, calm yourself. What makes you suppose they are. . . . confound it! How do you know that David is —"

"Here in Cairo?" She moved away from him and began to walk up and down, her hands clasped and twisting. "I knew the moment I set eyes on him that the man Russell took us to meet wasn't Wardani. I thought it must be Ramses, even though he didn't move quite the same way, and then Ramses produced that convenient alibi, and I saw the whole thing. I don't blame him for not telling me; how could he ever trust me again, after what I did? But you must trust me now, you must! Do you suppose I would do anything to harm him? You must tell me where he went tonight." She dropped to her knees before Emerson and caught hold of his hand. "Please! I beg you."

Emerson's expressive countenance mirrored his distress and pity. He raised her to her feet. "Now, my dear, get hold of yourself and try to tell me what this is all about. What makes you suppose Ramses is in danger?"

She was a little calmer now. Clinging to those strong brown hands, she looked up at him and said simply, "I've always known. Since we were children. A feeling, a fear . . . a nightmare, if I was asleep when it happened."

"Those dreams of yours," I exclaimed. "Were they —"

"Always about him. What do you suppose brought me home that night a few weeks ago? I came straight to his room, I wanted to help and . . ." Her voice broke in a sob. "It was one of the hardest things I've ever done, turning and walking away, pretending to believe he wasn't hurt, that nothing was wrong, but at least I knew you were with him, caring for him." She clasped her hands and gave me a look of poignant appeal. "This is one of the worst feelings I've ever had, even worse than when he was in Riccetti's hands, or the time he . . . I'm not imagining things. I'm not hysterical or superstitious. I *know*."

Abdullah's words came back to me. "There will come a time when you must believe a warning that has no more reality than these dreams of yours."

"Emerson," I cried. "He lied to us, he must have done. It is for tonight. Something has

674

gone wrong. What can we do?"

"Hmph." Emerson fingered the cleft in his chin. "There is only one person who might know their intentions for this evening. I am going to see Russell."

"Ring him," I urged.

"Waste of time. He won't tell me anything unless I confront him and demand the truth. Wait here, my dears. I will let you know the moment I have information."

He hastened from the room. A few minutes later I heard the engine of the motorcar roar. For once I did not worry about Emerson driving himself. If he didn't run into a camel he would reach his destination in record time.

"Wait!" Nefret said bitterly. She jumped up from her chair. I thought she meant to follow Emerson, and was about to remonstrate when she began tugging at her dress. "Help me," she whispered. "Please, Aunt Amelia."

"What are you doing?"

"I'm going to change. So as to be ready."

I did not ask for what, but went to assist her.

My brain still reeled under the impact of the astonishing revelations she had flung at us. Exerting the full strength of my will, I considered the implications of those revelations.

"So all this while you have known the truth about what Ramses and David were doing? And you said nothing?"

"You said nothing to me."

"I could not. I was sworn to secrecy, as was he — under orders, like any soldier."

"That's not the only reason. He was afraid I would betray him again, as I did before. But, dear heaven, surely I've paid for that! Losing him, and our baby, and knowing I had only myself to blame!"

I had believed myself impervious to surprise by now, but this latest revelation made my knees buckle. I collapsed into the nearest chair. "Good Gad! Do you mean when you miscarried, two years ago, it was — it was —"

"His. Ours." The tears on her cheeks sparkled like crystals. "Perhaps now you understand why I went to pieces afterwards. I wanted it, and him, so much, and it was all my fault, from start to finish, every step of the way! If I hadn't lost my temper and betrayed Ramses's secret to Percy — if I hadn't rushed out of the house without even giving him a chance to defend himself — if I hadn't married Geoffrey in a fit of spite — if I had had the wits to realize Geoffrey was lying when he told me he was deathly ill . . . I didn't know I was pregnant, Aunt Amelia. Do you suppose I would have married Geoffrey or stayed with him, under any circumstances, if I had known I was carrying Ramses's child? Do you suppose I wouldn't have used that, without shame or scruple, to get him back?"

I did not ask how she could be certain. Presumably she was in a position to know.

She had mistaken the reason for my silence. Dropping to her knees, she took my hands and looked straight into my eyes. "You mustn't think we were — we were sneaking behind your back, Aunt Amelia. It only happened once. . . ." A faint touch of color warmed her pale face. "One night. We came to you next morning, to tell you and ask your blessing, and that was when . . ."

"You found Kalaan and the child and her mother with us. Good heavens."

"You can't imagine how I felt! I'd been so happy, happier than I could ever have imagined. It was like Lucifer falling from the heights of heaven into the deepest pits of hell in one long descent. Not that there is any excuse for what I did. I ought to have believed in him, trusted him. He will never forgive me for that; how could he?"

I stroked the golden head that now rested on my lap. "He has forgiven you, believe me. But I am in a considerable state of confusion, my dear; I understand some of what you have told me, but what was it you said about betraying Ramses to Percy?"

She raised her head and brushed the tears from her face with the back of her hand. "You are trying to distract me, aren't you? To keep me from losing my head and acting without direction or thought. I've done it before, only too often. It was from me that Percy learned it was Ramses who rescued him from Zaal's camp. David and Lia knew, and they told me, and swore me to secrecy, and I gave my word, and then one day Percy came sneaking round to see me, and he made me so angry, paying me sickening compliments and making insulting remarks about Ramses, and — and —"

I had not tried to stop her; it was only when her breath gave out that I managed to get a word in.

"I understand. My dear, you mustn't blame yourself. How could you have known how Percy would react?"

"Ramses knew. That was why he didn't want Percy to find out. That isn't the point, Aunt Amelia! Don't you see — I lost my temper and betrayed a confidence, and that broken promise was the start of it all. If I can't be trusted to keep my word —"

"Enough of this," I exclaimed, breaking into a tirade of self-reproach. "You meant no harm, and Percy might have used Sennia to injure Ramses anyhow. He has hated Ramses since they were children. Really, Nefret, I thought you had better sense!"

Sympathy would have broken her down. My stern but kindly tone was precisely what was needed. She stiffened her shoulders and gave me a watery smile. "I'll try," she said humbly. "I've been trying to think. There is one place they might have gone, but I don't think Ramses could have known of it, and surely he wouldn't . . ."

She got to her feet and I did the same, taking firm hold of her, for I feared she was on the verge of losing control again. "We cannot act on doubtful grounds, Nefret. If you are mistaken we would lose valuable time and we would not be here when Emerson rings."

"I know. I wasn't suggesting . . ." Then she stiffened and pulled away from me. "Listen."

Her ears were keener than mine; she was halfway to the door before I heard the hoofbeats, and then a shout from Ali the doorman. I followed Nefret through the hall to the front door, in time to see Ali trying to lower a body from the horse that stood sweating and shivering outside. It was that of a man, dead or unconscious. Nefret sprang to Ali's assistance.

"Take his shoulders, Ali," she said crisply. "Get him into the drawing room. Aunt Amelia —"

I helped her to raise the man's feet, and the three of us, staggering under his dead weight, bore him through the hall and into the lighted room, where we lowered him onto the rug.

It was David, deathly pale, insensible, and bleeding, but alive, thank God. There was blood everywhere — on my hands, on those of Nefret, and on her skirts. David's right leg was saturated, from hip to foot. Kneeling beside him, Nefret pulled his knife from the scabbard and began cutting away his trouser leg. She snapped out orders as she worked.

"Ring for Fatima and the others. I want a basin of water, towels, my medical bag, blankets."

Within seconds the entire household was assembled. The shock to poor Fatima on seeing her beloved David, not only here, but desperately injured, was extreme; but she pulled herself together, as I had known she would, and flew into action.

"A bullet wound," Nefret said, tightening the strip of cloth cut from her skirt. "He's lost a great deal of blood. Where the devil is my bag? I need proper bandages. Ali, take Asfur to the stable and have a look at her. The bullet went straight through David's thigh, it may have injured her. Then saddle two of the other horses. Fatima, hold this. Aunt Amelia, ring the hospital. Ask Sophia to come at once."

I did as she asked, telling the doctor to make haste. When I went back to Nefret she was knotting the last of the bandages.

"Twenty minutes," I reported. "Nefret —"

"Don't talk to me now, Aunt Amelia. I've stopped the bleeding; he'll do until she arrives. Fatima, obey Dr. Sophia's orders implicitly. David . . ." She leaned over him and took his face between her small bloody hands. "David. Can you hear me?"

"Nefret, don't. He cannot —"

"He can. He must. David!"

His eyelids lifted. Pain and weakness and the effects of the injection she had given him dulled his eyes — but not for long. His gaze focused on her face. "Nefret. Go after him. They —"

"I know. Where?"

"Palace." His voice was so faint I could scarcely make out the word. "Ruin. On the road to . . ."

"Yes, all right, I've got it. Don't talk anymore."

"Hurry. Took me . . . too long . . ."

"Don't worry, dear. I'll get him back."

He did not hear. His eyes were closed and his head rested heavy in her hands. Nefret kissed his white lips and rose. She looked as if she had been in a slaughterhouse, skirts dripping, hands wet, face streaked with blood — but not with tears. Her eyes were dry, and as hard as turquoise.

"I'm going with you," I said.

She looked me over, coolly appraising, as she would have inspected a weapon to make certain it was functional. "Yes. Change. Riding kit."

Leaving Fatima with David, we hastened up the stairs. "Will he live?" I asked.

"David? I think so." She went into her room.

I exchanged my tea gown for trousers and boots and shirt and buckled on my belt of tools. Nefret seemed to know where we were going. How, I wondered? David had not given us precise directions. I felt torn apart leaving him, even though he was in good hands. How much harder had it been for Nefret, who loved him like a brother and who had the medical skill he needed? There was only one thing on her mind now, however; I did not doubt she would have passed my bleeding form without a second glance if she had to make the choice.

When I hastened to her room I found her lacing her boots. "Not your belt, Aunt Amelia," she said, without looking up. "It makes too much noise."

"Very well," I said meekly, and distributed various useful articles about my person. "Shouldn't we try to reach Emerson?"

"Write him a note. Tell him where we have gone."

"But I don't know —"

"I'll do it." She rose and snatched a sheet of writing paper from the desk. "Send Ali or Yussuf after him. Russell's headquarters first. If he isn't there, they must track him down. I'll make a copy and leave it with Fatima in case the Professor comes back here before they find him."

She had thought of everything. I had seen her in this state before, and knew she would hold up until she had accomplished her aim . . . or had seen it fail. A shiver ran through my frame. What in God's name would become of her if she were unable to save him?

What would become of me, and his father?

We paused in the drawing room long enough to give Fatima her final instructions. David lay where we had left him, covered with blankets and so still my heart skipped a beat. Nefret bent over him and took his pulse.

"Holding steady," she said coolly.

"I have sent for Daoud and Kadija," Fatima whispered. "I hope I did right."

"Exactly right. She has a healer's hands, and Daoud is always a tower of strength. Don't forget, Fatima, if the Professor rings instead of coming, read him that note."

"Yes." She smiled a little. "It was good that I learned to read, Nur Misur."

Nefret hugged her. "Take care of him. Come, Aunt Amelia."

The horses were ready — Nefret's Moonlight, and another of the Arabs. As Nefret swung herself into the saddle I said urgently, "Shan't we take some of the men? Daoud will be here soon, and Ali is —"

"No." She had taken the reins in her hands and was so anxious to be off she was quivering like a hound at the traces; but she spared enough time to explain. "He's not dead — not yet — I would know — but if the place were to be attacked openly, they would kill him at once. We must get into the house without being discovered, and find him before help arrives — if it does."

"And if it does not," I said, "we will do the job ourselves!"

I had heard of the place but I could never have found it without a guide, nor indeed would I have had any reason to seek it out, since it was without archaeological or artistic interest. How Nefret knew its location I had not had time to inquire. That she knew was all that mattered. Once we had passed the crossroads at Mit Ukbeh there were few people on the road and she let Moonlight out. Never once did she stop or slow her pace, even when she turned off the road onto a scarcely discernible track. Before long the cultivation was behind us and the track grew steeper. The waxing moon was high in the sky; its light and that of the stars must have been enough to show her where to go, for there were few landmarks — a huddle of tumbledown houses, a grove of trees. When she pulled Moonlight to a walk, I saw ahead a dark mass that might have been almost anything, so shapeless were its outlines. We drew nearer, and I began to make out details — fallen stones, a clump of low trees — and a light! The regularity of the shape indicated that it issued from a window somewhere beyond the trees.

Nefret stopped and dismounted and gestured me to do the same. When I would have spoken, she put her hand over my mouth.

Then, from her lips, issued the soft but penetrating whistle Ramses used to summon Risha.

It was not long before the stallion's familiar shape emerged from the night. He came toward us, stepping lightly and silently, and Nefret caught hold of his bridle and whispered in his ear.

If the noble beast could only speak! His presence proved that Ramses was here, somewhere in that ruinous blackness.

There was no need for us to confer; the lighted window was our guide and our destination. We left the horses and crept forward. Once, after stubbing my toe on an unseen rock, I tugged at Nefret's sleeve and held out my torch. She shook her head and took my hand.

The window was on the ground floor of a small structure well inside the outer walls. It might once have been a pavilion or kiosk. Crouching, picking our way with painful slowness, we approached; then, cautiously, we raised our heads just enough to look inside.

It was a strange place to find in an abandoned palace of the eighteenth century — a poor imitation of a gentleman's study, with leather chairs and Persian rugs and a few sticks of furniture. In the center of the floor was a large copper brazier or shallow tray; it must have served the former function quite recently, for it was filled with ashes and bits of scorched paper, and the stench of their burning was still strong. Of more immediate interest was the fact that the room was occupied.

Two of the men were unknown to me. One of them was tall and heavily built, gray-bearded and fair-skinned as a European under his tan. The other wore traditional Senussi garb. The third man . . .

The hair of bright auburn, artistically dulled by gray, was a wig, and his face was turned away, but I would have known that straight, lithe form anywhere. I felt a pang — yes, I confess it. Though he had all but openly confessed his treachery, I had cherished a forlorn hope that I might have misunderstood. There could no longer be the slightest doubt. He was guilty, and if Ramses was a prisoner here, Sethos was one of his captors.

"That is the lot, then," Graybeard said, in heavily accented but fluent English. "What sort of incompetent is this man? Keeping the documents was bad enough; leaving us to destroy them while he amuses himself with the prisoner is inexcusable. I am tempted to let the thrice-accursed British catch the thrice-accursed imbecile."

There was not a sound from Nefret, not even a catch of breath. I did not need the painful pressure of her fingers to warn me I must be equally silent.

"One is certainly tempted," the false Scot agreed. I would have ground my teeth had I dared make the slightest sound. I ought to have known that Sethos would have more than one identity; no wonder he had agreed so readily to give up that of the Count! In his other role he had taken even greater pains to avoid me.

Hamilton, as I knew he must be, continued in the same lazy drawl. "We can't risk letting him fall into the hands of the police. He knows too much about us, and they won't have to beat him to get the information out of him; he'll squeal like a pig."

The Senussi's lips curled. "He is a coward and a fool. So we take him with us?"

"By force, if necessary," Sethos said. "And you had better go at once. Leave the back entrance unlocked for me. I'll have a final look round to make certain he hasn't left anything else incriminating."

"What about the prisoner?" Graybeard asked.

"I'll take care of him on my way out — if there's anything left of him."

The gray-bearded man nodded. "Rather you than me."

"Squeamish?" Sethos inquired softly.

"This is war. I kill when I must. But he is a brave man, and he deserves a quick death."

"He will get it." Sethos opened his elegantly tailored coat, and I saw the knife strapped to his belt.

There was no exchange of farewells or instructions. Graybeard and the Senussi simply walked out of the room, leaving Sethos standing by the smoking brazier. After listening for a moment, his head cocked, Sethos turned, knelt, and began sorting through the half burned scraps, tossing them carelessly onto the floor after examining each. Whatever it was he was looking for, he did not find it; a soft but heartfelt "Damn!" was heard, and then he rose to his feet.

Nefret was trembling, but she remained motionless, and her well-nigh superhuman restraint helped me to control my own fury and anxiety. We could not take the slightest chance, not now. I had my pistol and she her knife, but Sethos had other weapons of strength and skill that could overcome us both. We must wait until he left the room and then follow him and catch him off-guard before he could carry out his grisly promise.

Sethos drew back his foot and gave the brazier a hard kick that scattered ashes across the rug. He *was* in a temper! So much the worse for us, or for anyone else who got in his way. He took one of the lamps from the table and strode out of the room, leaving the door swinging on its hinges.

Nefret pulled herself up and over the sill, as quickly and neatly as a lad might have done, and then reached down a hand to assist me. Through the open door I saw what appeared to be a narrow hallway, with another door opposite. I indicated this to Nefret, raising my eyebrows inquiringly. Her lips tightened, and she shook her head.

"This way," she whispered, and led me along the hallway to a flight of narrow stone stairs. The light from the open door of the room we had left and the light of the lantern below enabled us to descend them quickly and noiselessly. There was no sign of Sethos when we reached the bottom of the stairs. He must have entered the room from whose open door the lantern glow came.

Nefret darted forward, with me close on her heels. She did not even pause in the doorway but flew like a stone from a catapult at the man we had followed, pushing him aside with such force that he dropped the knife he held and staggered back. I do not believe she saw him as an individual, only as an obstacle between her and her goal. Standing on tiptoe, she drew her own knife and sawed at the ropes binding Ramses's wrists to a hook on the wall. His bare back was a sickening sight, covered with blood and raised weals, and he appeared to be unconscious; when his hands were free he sank to the floor, clasped tightly in her arms.

I leveled my pistol at the man who stood against the wall. "Don't move! I might have known I would find you here!"

"And I ought to have anticipated you would turn up." He had the effrontry to smile at me. "We always meet under the most extraordinary circumstances. Perhaps someday —"

"Be quiet!" I shifted position slightly, so that I could keep him covered while I shot quick glances at the tableau slightly behind me. Ramses lay sprawled across Nefret's lap, her arms pressing him to her breast and his head resting against her shoulder. His face was bruised and bloodstained and his eyes were closed — but I saw his lips move, in a sigh or a groan, and I knew he lived.

"See if you can rouse him, Nefret," I ordered. "We must make haste, and I doubt we can carry him. You might try . . . Oh."

"He is less of a man than I believe him to be if that doesn't rouse him," Sethos remarked. "I assure you, Amelia, your kisses would bring me back from the dead."

Nefret's bowed head hid Ramses's face, but I saw him raise one arm and place it over her shoulders. The ensuing conversation was extremely incoherent. Most conversations of that nature are. I do not believe Ramses was aware of where he was or why he was there, but I will say for him that he went straight to the point.

"I love you. I was a fool. Forgive me."

"No, it was my fault, all of it! Tell me you love me."

"I did. I do. I —"

Her voice rose. "So you went off, without a word, when you knew you might never come back?"

"That wasn't how . . . I didn't intend . . . Damn it, I left you a letter!"

"Telling me what? That you loved me and were sorry you were dead?"

"Yes, well, what about you? Coming here with that filthy —"

"Stop it at once!" I ordered. "There will be ample time for that sort of thing later. At least I hope there will. Nefret, did you hear me! Oh, curse it! Ramses!"

"Yes, Mother," Ramses murmured. He looked round, blinking. "Good Lord. It *is* Mother. What's going on? Is David —"

"He'll be all right," Nefret said. She kissed him, and for a time I was afraid I would have to shout at them again. However, Ramses seemed to have got a grip on reality at last. Leaning on Nefret, he got slowly to his feet.

"I need you to bind and gag this villain while I hold him at gunpoint," I explained.

Sethos's smile faded. "Amelia, you are on the verge of making a disastrous mistake. I came here to —"

"To murder my son, you villain," I cried. "You have betrayed your country and broken your word to me."

"Wrong as usual, my obstinate darling. But do you think this is an appropriate time for a discussion of my character?"

"Possibly not," I admitted.

"Definitely not," Ramses said. "Though I was not entirely myself at the time, I got the impression that my amiable host was dragged away by two large angry men. However —"

"However," said a voice from the doorway, "he got away from them. You didn't suppose I would allow someone else the pleasure of finishing you off, did you?"

15

His well-bred friends would have had some difficulty in recognizing him. His coat was torn and his shirtfront speckled with small drops of blood; the features I had once thought bore a slight resemblance to my own were dark and distorted with choler and his lips were drawn back over his teeth. "Put your little gun away, Aunt Amelia. Now be honest for once; you never suspected me, did you?"

Rapidly I appraised the situation. It was not promising. Percy's gun was one of those large ugly German weapons and at such close range he could hardly have missed any target he selected. At the moment he appeared to have selected me. If I shot him, Sethos would overpower me before I could fire again, even supposing Percy did not kill me first.

"Not of this," I said. "I had not believed that even you could stoop so low."

Ramses straightened, with what effort I could only imagine. "Give it up, Percy. The game is over. You've lost."

"To you?" His lips writhed. "No. Not to you, damn you! I'll get out of this. No one would believe —"

"Russell knows," Ramses said. "He knows about this place. My failure to report back to him will confirm my accusations."

The words fell as quietly and deadly as stones piled on a grave. Another sort of man might have heeded them, but not Percy. His face was twitching uncontrollably and a look of cunning narrowed his eyes.

"Report back," he repeated. "Not for a while, though, eh? Aunt Amelia and dear little Nefret are all the rescue party? Excellent. There's plenty of time for me to get to the border. I can still be of use to them, and the reward they promised is waiting for me — a handsome villa in Constantinople, with everything I've ever wanted.

"Let me see now," he mused. "How shall I go about this? One bullet for dear Aunt Amelia and one more for the lovers, so closely entwined? Or shall I shoot the gun out of her hand first? It will be extremely painful, though perhaps not as painful as watching me put half a dozen bullets into her son. Then there is Nefret. I hold a grudge against her, for tricking me. A more suitable punishment would be to let her live — with me, in that pleasant villa. Yes, I think I'll take her along when I leave Cairo."

"Over my dead body," I exclaimed.

"Precisely what I had in mind," said Percy.

I grasped at the last frail straw. "Your confederate is unarmed. I will shoot him if you don't drop your gun."

Sethos, who had not moved, now shook his head and sighed. Percy laughed.

"Go ahead. You would probably miss, but our association was about to end anyhow. All right, Ramses, old chap, here's your chance to die like a hero. Shove her out of the way and let me have a clear shot, or I'll put a bullet through the two of you."

The gun turned in their direction. Mine turned back toward Percy. Before I could fire, the weapon was swept from my hand and a hard shove sent me staggering back. Unable to keep my balance, I sat down with such force that I was momentarily paralyzed, and my ears were deafened by a series of explosions so rapid they sounded like those of a machine gun. Too many things were happening at once. My eyes would not focus. Where was Nefret? Where was Sethos? Percy was screaming and pawing at his chest, but he was still upright and the gun was in his hand. Ramses launched himself at Percy and the two fell to the floor. Ramses could not hold him; they rolled over and as his scored back struck the floor Ramses cried out and lay still. Percy crouched by him, groping for the gun he had let fall — and as I half-crawled, half-stumbled toward them, Nefret ran back with her knife in her hand.

The look on her face stopped me like a blow. It was as remote and merciless as that of the goddess whose High Priestess she had once been. Raising the knife in both hands, she brought it down with all her strength, up to the hilt into Percy's back. For a moment she stood unmoving. Then her face crumpled like that of a frightened child, and she turned with a cry into the arms of . . .

Emerson?

Emerson! He was not alone. Men in uniform pushed into the room. There were others in the corridor outside.

Still on hands and knees, I turned my head.

Leaning against the wall, drenched in blood, Sethos tossed my gun away and gave me a twisted smile. "As usual, I have been upstaged. Don't waste a bullet on me, Radcliffe; I haven't much time left."

"You shot Percy," I gasped. "And he shot —"

"I hit him first," said Sethos, with a shadow of his old arrogance. "Twice, and both square on target. I don't mean to sound critical, Amelia dear, but you might consider carrying a larger . . ."

He swayed and would have fallen if I had not hastened to support him. Almost at once my hands were pushed aside and replaced by the strong arm of Emerson. He lowered his old enemy carefully to the floor. "It might be advisable for you to talk fast, Sethos. The Turks are advancing and ten thousand lives depend on you. When will the attack come, and where? Kantara?"

"What in heaven's name are you talking about, Emerson?" I cried. "The man is dying. He gave his life for —"

"You? No doubt, no doubt, but what concerns me at this moment is the fact that he is an agent of British intelligence, and that he was sent here to get that information. Don't stand there gawking at me, Peabody, raise his head. He is choking on his own blood."

Stupefied by disbelief, I sat down and lifted Sethos's head onto my lap. Emerson opened his coat and ripped the bloody shirt away from his body. "Damn," he said. "Nefret, come here. See what you can do."

She came, and Ramses with her; they were interwined like Siamese twins and both looked as dazed as I felt. After she had examined the gruesome wound she shook her head. "It has penetrated his lung. We must get him to hospital immediately, but I don't think . . ."

"Can he talk?" The man who had spoken was a stranger to me, one of General Maxwell's aides, to judge by his uniform. "An ambulance is on the way, but if he can tell us where —"

Sethos opened his eyes. "I don't know. They burned the papers. I couldn't find . . ." Then a spark of the old malicious amusement shone in the gray — brown — green depths. "You might ask . . . my nephew. I rather think he . . . got a look at them."

"Who?" Emerson's strong jaw dropped.

"Who?" I gasped, glaring wildly round the small chamber.

"Me, I think," said Ramses. "By a process of elimination. I had begun to wonder —"

"Don't try to talk, Ramses!" I cried. He was leaning heavily on Nefret, and under the bruises and streaks of blood his face was ashen.

"I think I had better," Ramses said, drawing a long, difficult breath. "Kantara is a feint only. The main attack will come between Toussoum and Serapeum, at half past three. They have steel pontoons to bridge the Canal. Two infantry brigades and six guns are to hold a position two miles northeast of Serapeum —"

"Half past three — today?" The officer broke in. "It is already after midnight. Damn it, man, are you sure? Headquarters expected the attack would be farther north. It will take at least eight hours to get our reserves from Ismailia to Serapeum."

"Then you had better get them started, hadn't you?" said Ramses.

"Damnation," Emerson exclaimed. "The only troops near Toussoum are the Indian infantry, and most of them are Moslems. If they don't hold —"

"They will hold." Ramses looked down at the man whose head rested on my lap. "As I was saying, I began to wonder about Major Hamilton earlier. His suggestion that they leave me alive was a bit too disingenuous. Double agent, I thought — prayed, rather — but it never occurred to me he was . . ." His voice cracked. "*Uncle* Sethos?"

Emerson had gone white. "You were the boy in the snow. My father's . . ."

"Your father's bastard, yes," Sethos whispered. "Did you never suspect why I hated you so? The sight of you that night, the young heir and master, in your handsome coach, while I struggled to help a fainting woman through the drifts . . . She died a week later, in a charity ward in Truro, and was buried in a pauper's grave."

"She loved you," Emerson said, in a voice that cut me to the heart. "You had that, at least. It was more than I had."

"I am mean enough to be glad of that," Sethos said in a stronger voice. "You had everything else. We are more alike than you realize, brother. You turned your talents to scholarship; I turned mine to crime. I became your dark counterpart, your rival . . . I tried to take her from you, Radcliffe, but I failed in that as in all the rest . . ."

"Listen to me." Emerson leaned forward. "I want you to know this. I tried to find you that night. After my mother told me what she had done I went out to look for you. She sent two of the servants to drag me back and lock me in my room. If there is anything I can do to make it up to you —"

"Too late. Just as well; we would all find it a trifle difficult to adjust to these new relationships."

Emerson said gruffly, "Will you give me your hand?"

"In token of forgiveness? It seems I have less to forgive than you." His hand moved feebly. Emerson grasped it. Sethos's eyes moved slowly over the faces of the others, and then returned, as if drawn by a magnet, to mine. "How very sentimental," he murmured. "I never thought to see my affectionate family gathered round me at the end. . . . Fetch the light closer, Radcliffe. My eyes are dimming, and I want to see her face clearly. Amelia, will you grant me my last wish? I would like to die with your kiss on my lips. It is the only reward I am likely to get for helping to save your son's life, not to mention the Suez Canal."

I lifted him in my arms and kissed him. For a moment his lips met mine with desperate intensity; then a shudder ran through him and his head fell back. Gently I lowered him to the ground and folded his bloody hands over his breast.

"Bid the soldiers shoot," I murmured. "And bear him like a soldier to the stage. For he was likely, had he been —"

"Amelia, I beg you will leave off misquoting *Hamlet*," said my husband through his teeth.

I forgave him his harsh tone, for I knew it was his way of concealing his emotions. The scene did rather resemble the last act of the drama, with bodies here and there and soldiers crowding in to assist and to stare.

Sethos and Percy were removed on litters and carried to the ambulance Emerson had commandeered — "just in case," as he explained. Ramses kept insisting he could ride and Nefret kept telling him he could not, which was obviously the case; even Risha's smooth gait would have jolted his back unbearably and the ropes had cut deep into his wrists. He was still on his feet and still arguing when Emerson and I left them, but two of the soldiers were closing in on him, and Nefret assured me they would get him to one of the motor vehicles, with or without her active participation.

Emerson and I took the horses back, leading the one I had ridden. We went slowly, for we had a great deal to talk about. When we arrived at the house we found the others already there. Ramses had insisted on seeing David, who was still deep in a drugged slumber but, Nefret assured us, no longer in danger. After Emerson had left for Cairo, she and I got to work on Ramses, and a nasty job it was. None of his injuries was life-threatening, but there were quite a lot of them, ranging from bruises and cuts to the bloody marks of the whip.

It was not long before Nefret told me to leave the room. She was very nice about it, but I could see she meant it, and the look I got from Ramses indicated he was of the same opinion. So I went to my own room and sat there for a time, feeling very odd. I supposed I would get used to it. There comes a time in every mother's life . . .

Ramses slept most of the day, and I snatched a little nap. It felt strange to lie down with a mind at ease, vexed to be sure by a number of unanswered questions, but free of the anxiety that had tormented every waking and sleeping moment. I do not believe Nefret slept at all. I managed to persuade her to bathe and change her crumpled, filthy, bloodstained garments. I had barely time to adjust the pillows that propped Ramses on his side, and inspect his back (it was, as I had expected, green), and indulge myself in a few small demonstrations of maternal affection (which did not disturb him in the slightest, since his eyes remained closed throughout) before she was back. She had left her hair to hang loose, and she was wearing the pale-blue sprigged muslin frock which, I now realized, someone other than Emerson must have admired.

So I took myself off again, without having to be told, and whenever I chanced to look in

— which I did from time to time — she was sitting in the chair by the bed, her hands folded, her eyes fixed on his sleeping face. Since it was obvious I was not wanted, I went to sit with David, relieving Fatima of that duty. She was not at all keen on being relieved, but when I asked her to prepare a tray for Nefret she bustled off.

David was awake. He gave me a smile and held out his hand. "Thank you for rescuing me, Aunt Amelia. Every time I opened my mouth she tried to shove a spoon into it."

He was full of questions. I answered the most important, knowing that nothing would better assist his recovery than the knowledge that those he loved were safe and the danger over.

"So it was Nefret — and you — who saved the day," he murmured.

I shook my head. "It might be described as a joint enterprise. If you had not made a heroic effort to reach us — if Nefret had not known where to go — if Emerson had not convinced Russell he must not delay . . ."

"And if Sethos had not acted when he did! I don't understand that part, Aunt Amelia. Who —"

"Later, my dear. You must rest now."

It was late when Emerson returned. He refused my offer of dinner with a shake of his head. "I had a bite with Maxwell. Let us see if Ramses is awake and fit for conversation. He and Nefret will want to hear the news too, and there is no sense in repeating myself."

Ramses's door was ajar, as I had left it. I tapped lightly before looking in. He was awake; whether he was fit for conversation was another matter. Nefret knelt by the bed. He held her hands in his, and they were looking into each other's eyes, and I do not suppose they would have cared if the Turks had been shelling the city.

However, I felt certain they would be anxious to hear Emerson's news. I coughed. I had to cough several times before Nefret tore her eyes from his. Until I saw her do it, I had always thought that a somewhat exaggerated figure of speech.

"A touch of catarrh, Mother?" Ramses inquired.

"Very amusing, my dear. I am glad to see you yourself again."

"Near enough. Nefret won't let me get up."

"Certainly not." I settled myself comfortably in the chair Nefret had left, since it did not appear that she intended to return to it.

"I want to see David again," Ramses insisted.

"Perhaps in the morning. What he needs now is rest. So do you, but your father thought you might want to know what has been going on." I added pointedly, "He wouldn't tell *me* anything."

"How inconsiderate," Ramses said. "Please sit down, sir. I presume the Canal is safe, or you would have mentioned it."

"They got across," Emerson said. "At Serapeum and at Toussoum. Our reserves didn't arrive until a few hours ago, but by then a counterattack had cleared most of the enemy off the East Bank. It was the Indian infantry brigades who saved the Canal. You knew they would, didn't you?"

"I thought they would. Well, that is good news. Have they had any luck tracking the Turk and his friend?"

Emerson shook his head. "No, they got clean away. Presumably Percy made such a nuisance of himself that they abandoned him and headed for Libya. They won't want for help along the way. You were right about the chap in the yellow robe; it was the Sherif el Senussi himself."

"I cleverly deduced that after the Turk called him by name," said Ramses gravely.

"They've got a line on the Turk too," Emerson said. "He fits the description of Sahin Bey, who has been missing from his usual haunts recently."

"Good God." Ramses's eyes widened. At least one of them did; the other was half-closed by purpling bruises. "He's become something of a legend in Syria. One of their top men, and high in Enver's favor. I can't believe he'd take a personal hand in our little affair."

"Little?" Emerson's brows drew together and he spoke with considerable vehemence. "The entire Turkish strategy was based on their expectation of an uprising in Cairo. Without it, they hadn't a prayer of crossing the Canal. You and David . . . What are you smiling about?"

"Something Sahin Bey said to me. It doesn't matter. So, are we in line for parades, the cheers of the populace, and the personal thanks of the sovereign? David deserves all of it."

"Ha," said Emerson eloquently. "However, David will be on his way to England, vindicated and pardoned, as soon as he can travel. I was sorely tempted to telegraph Lia this evening, but I didn't want to raise her hopes until . . . The boy will be all right, won't he?"

"The prospect of seeing her and being present at the birth of his son is the best medicine he could have," I said.

No one spoke for a while. Emerson got out his pipe and made a great business of filling it. Nefret had settled down on the floor beside the bed. She was still holding Ramses's hand. He didn't seem to mind.

I suppose we were all reluctant to talk about the rest of it. Great issues of battle and war are remote, almost impersonal, but the other unanswered questions cut too close to the bone.

Nefret was the first to break the silence. "Percy?"

"He died on the way to hospital," Emerson said. "Nefret, it wasn't you who killed him."

"No? I meant to, you know." A shadow of that remote, inhuman look passed over her face. Her blue eyes were clear. Guilt over Percy's death would not come back to haunt her. She had stopped him in the only way she could, and if ever an individual deserved death, it was he.

Women are much more practical about these things than men.

"Oh," Emerson said. "Er. Well, he'd been hit twice in the chest. A heavier-caliber bullet would have killed him outright. One of the twenty-twos must have nicked an artery. He bled to death."

"And Sethos." I sighed. "He redeemed himself in the end, as I had hoped he would. A hero's death —"

"For the second time!" Emerson's well-cut lips curled in a snarl. "It's getting monotonous."

"Why, Emerson," I exclaimed. "It is not like you to play dog in the manger."

"Yes, it is!" Emerson got a grip on himself. "Peabody, please don't provoke me. I want to do him justice. I am trying my damnedest to do him justice. I discovered the truth only three days ago, and it hasn't sunk in yet."

"But you must have known earlier that Sethos was Major Hamilton," Ramses said. I thought I detected a certain note of criticism in his voice. Emerson looked uncomfortable.

"I didn't know for certain, but my suspicions of Hamilton were aroused by the letter he wrote us."

"Curse it," I exclaimed. "Don't tell me you recognized the handwriting. After all these years?"

Emerson grinned. "If it makes you feel happier, Peabody, and I am sure it does, that was a clue you never possessed. I was the only one who saw Sethos's farewell letter to you."

"Yes, you ripped it to shreds after you had read it aloud. I told you at the time you shouldn't have done that."

"It was an extremely annoying epistle," said Emerson. "You were right, though. I couldn't be certain the handwriting was the same, since it had been a long time, but when I remembered how assiduously Hamilton had avoided us, my suspicions increased. Having better sense than some members of this family, I took those suspicions to Maxwell instead of acting on them as I might once have done.

"You can only faintly imagine my astonishment when I learned that Sethos has been, for several years, one of the War Office's most trusted secret agents. He was sent to Cairo by

Kitchener himself. He knew about your little side show, Ramses, but his primary mission was to stop the leaks of information and identify the man responsible for them. It was he who exposed Mrs. Fortescue, whom he had been cultivating in his characteristically flamboyant fashion.

"Maxwell told me all this — he had to, to keep me from going after Sethos myself — but he coolly informed me that Sethos was considerably more valuable than I, and that he would have me put up against a wall and shot if I breathed a word to a living soul. I knew the truth when we stopped by the barracks on our way into the desert. Maxwell had told me Sethos would be there, and ordered me to stay away from him, but — er — well, damn it, I was curious. He's good," Emerson admitted grudgingly. "I'd never have recognized him. Of course I had not the intimate knowledge of the scoundrel that some persons —"

"Nil nisi bonum, Emerson," I murmured.

"Ha!" said Emerson.

"It is a pity," said Ramses, who had been watching his father closely, "that there wasn't time for him to satisfy our curiosity about other things. How did he find out about Percy?"

"He didn't." Emerson's face was transformed by a look of paternal pride. "That discovery was yours, my boy, and yours alone.

Russell wasn't entirely convinced by your reasoning initially, but after he had had time to think about it he concluded that you had made a strong case. He decided he had no right to take the full responsibility, so he went straight to Maxwell. I gather it was not a pleasant interview! Russell stuck to his guns, though, and after storming and swearing, Maxwell agreed to cooperate until the matter could be settled one way or the other. Maxwell informed Sethos, who volunteered to have a look round the place himself."

"Lucky for me he did," Ramses said.

"Yes," Emerson agreed. "I — er — I owe him for that. And for other things."

"If you'd rather not speak of it," Nefret began.

"I would rather not, but I must. I had believed that that part of my life was over, forgotten, obliterated. I was wrong. One never knows when a ghost from the past will come back to haunt one."

He was silent for a time, however, his head bowed and his countenance grave but calm. He had not been so unmoved when he told me part of the story early that morning, as we rode back to the house.

"My mother was the daughter of the Earl of Radcliffe. Why she married my father, who was a simple country gentleman without title or wealth, I never knew. There was . . . one must suppose there was an attraction. It must have ended early in their marriage. My earliest memories are of contemptuous words and bitter reproaches from her to him, for failing to live up to her expectations. As I was to learn, that would have been impossible. Her demands were too great, her ambitions too high. He had, I believe, no desire to improve his position in the world. He was like Walter, gentle and easygoing, but with an inner core of firmness; while he lived, life was not entirely unpleasant. He died when I was fourteen, and then . . .

"She had already decided I was to be the man my father refused to be. When I resisted she tried various means to control me. The worst was what she did to Walter. We had been at the same school until then. You know what they were like, even the best of them; brutal discipline and legalized bullying were thought to make men out of boys. I was big for my age and ready to fight back, but Walter would have had a bad time if I had not been there to take his part.

"She separated us. He was becoming a mollycoddle and a coward, she said, and it was time he stood on his own feet. When I came home for the Christmas holidays the year after my father died, I had not seen Walter for months; he wasn't even allowed to write me. That night it was snowing heavily, and it was in the snow I saw them — a woman and a boy, struggling through the drifts. I caught only a glimpse of his face, so distorted with strain and anger, it was unrecognizable. When I reached the house I told her — my mother — that we must find them and offer them shelter, and that was when I learned the woman had been my father's mistress, that she had come to her former friend asking for help and had been turned away. You heard what happened. She kept me locked in my room till the following day.

"Well, to make a long story short, there was no way I could trace them; I had no money and no power. Matters went from bad to worse after that night. I was about to go up to Oxford when I discovered she was arranging a marriage for me, with the vapid daughter of a local aristocratic imbecile — and then, like an answer to prayer, I inherited a small amount of money from one of my father's cousins. It provided enough income to enable me to pursue my studies and take Walter away from his hellish school. For years he had been torn between his fear and dislike of her and what he considered his filial duty; she made it clear to him that he would have to choose between us, that if he came to me she would never see him or speak to him again. So that settled that.

"Much later I did make an attempt to mend matters." He smiled at me, his blue eyes softening. "It was because of you and Ramses, Peabody; caring as I did for you, I thought perhaps she regretted losing her sons and would be willing to let bygones be bygones. I was wrong. She would not see me. She did not send for me in her last illness, though she knew how to find me. I heard of her death from her lawyers. They told me she tried with her last breath to keep me from inheriting, but she had only the income from her father's money while she lived; in accordance with the patriarchal tradition, the capital went to her eldest son. I haven't touched it. It is yours, Ramses, as is the house that has been in my father's family for two hundred years. So if you are thinking of — er — settling down and — er . . . Well, you are now in a position to support a family."

He looked hopefully from Ramses to Nefret. When the true state of affairs had dawned on my dear Emerson I could not be certain, but he would have to have been blind, deaf, and feeble-witted if he misinterpreted the nature of their affection now. Of course he would claim, as he always did, that he had known all along. There was one aspect of that relationship of which he was certainly unaware. Ramses would never have mentioned it to his father, and Emerson had not been present when Nefret broke down and confessed — finding, I hoped, a greater understanding than she had dared expect.

It was not likely Emerson would be as sympathetic. I decided on the spot that it was none of his business.

Ramses had been as startled as the rest of us by these revelations, but he had sense enough not to refuse the offer. "Thank you, sir. But Uncle Walter's children must have their fair share. And . . . another of my cousins."

There was no need for him to explain. As soon as I knew Sethos and Hamilton were one and the same, I had realized who Molly might be.

"We cannot be certain," I said thoughtfully. "Bertha was Sethos's mistress, but the child she was carrying fourteen years ago might not have been his."

"Fourteen years?" Emerson repeated. "Good Gad, has it been that long? Then it can't be the same child. This girl is — what did you tell me — twelve years of age."

"We had only her word for that. I did think she was remarkably mature for her age."

"What do you mean?" inquired Emerson, staring.

I carefully avoided looking at Ramses, who was carefully not looking at me, and decided to spare him public embarrassment. He had been through quite enough in the past twenty-four hours.

"You were misled by her dreadful clothing on the occasion of our first encounter with her," I explained in a kindly manner. "Even for a child of twelve they were old-fashioned and out of date — but then, so was Miss Nordstrom. I thought nothing of it at the time, but later she was dressed more suitably for her age, and I couldn't help noticing . . . Women do notice such things. So do some men, and I am pleased to find that you are not one of them."

"It's all conjecture," said Emerson stubbornly. "Sethos probably has a dozen . . . Oh, very well, Peabody, I apologize. Whoever her parents were, the child is not our responsibility. He made all the necessary arrangements for her several years ago, when he entered the service, and Maxwell assured me she would be well-provided for."

"You asked about her?" It was Ramses who spoke. His face was even more unreadable than usual because of the bruises.

"Of course," Emerson grumbled. "Well, I had to, didn't I? Couldn't leave the child alone in the world. I admit I was relieved when Maxwell told me Sethos was . . . told me the matter was taken care of. He does not know about the — er — the family relationship, and unless one of you can give me a reason why I should, I do not intend to tell him."

I saw a reason, but I did not speak of it. Perhaps one day, when Emerson was in a softer mood, I could persuade him to bring his courageous and unfortunate brother back to the home of their ancestors, to lie with them in the family plot. In what unknown spot would he now be laid to rest? What would be his monument and what his epitaph? I had already thought of a suitable inscription for the monument I felt certain Emerson would wish to erect someday. It was a quotation from an Egyptian text: "Then Re-Harakhte said, Let Set be given unto me, to dwell with me and be my son. He shall thunder in the sky and be feared." Like his ancient namesake, Sethos had redeemed himself and become one with the Divine Ruler of the cosmos.

This did not seem a propitious time for such a suggestion.

"You could not have prevented it, Emerson," I said.

"Prevented what? Oh!" Emerson gave up the attempt to light his pipe. "No. Russell had his men ready, but I had the devil of a time convincing him we must act without delay. I could hardly tell him, could I, that my urgency was based on — er —"

"Woman's intuition," said Nefret, turning her head to smile at him. "I can imagine how Mr. Russell would have responded to that! Especially when I was the woman in question. How did you persuade him, then?"

"I rang through to the house as I had promised," Emerson explained. "When Fatima told me about David, that settled the matter. I was, to put it mildly, somewhat distressed to hear that you two had gone haring off by yourselves, but there was nothing I could do but wait for Russell to get his caravan together and notify Maxwell of our plans. When we got there, the place was dead quiet, not a sign of life except a lighted window. We found Risha and the other horses, and I didn't know where the devil you were or what you were doing, and I was afraid to risk an open attack. When we heard gunfire we had no choice but to move in, and I fully expected to find you — both of you — all of you — dead or hideously wounded, or —"

"Calm yourself, Emerson," I said soothingly. "It has all come out right in the end."

"No thanks to you," snarled Emerson.

"I beg to differ, Father," Ramses said. "Events got a bit out of hand, but then they always do, don't they, when we're all involved? We may not go about it in the most efficient manner, but we get the job done."

Nefret turned to look at him. "You will keep that in mind, I hope? If you ever do this to me again —"

"Or you to me. What in God's name were you thinking of, letting him take you to that place, letting him —"

"I didn't let him do very much."

"How much?"

Nefret's cheeks were crimson. "Stop talking like some damned ancient Roman! Are you suggesting that my so-called virtue is worth more than your life? I'd have done anything — anything! — to trap him."

"Did you?"

"What would *you* do if I said yes?"

"Ah." Ramses let his breath out. "You didn't. I don't know that I could have accepted that. I'd have had to spend the rest of my life trying to make it up to you. Groveling gets to be hard on the knees after a year or two."

How good it was to hear them arguing again! However, there was a good deal more I wanted to know.

"How did you know it was Percy?"

"It?" Nefret gave me a quizzical look and laughed. "I didn't know *what* he was or what he was trying to do; but when he began praising Ramses to all and sundry I knew he was up to no good, and when he had the infernal gall to come round smirking and fawning at me — as if I would be naive enough ever to trust him again! — I got really angry. And frightened. I was aware that Ramses was playing Wardani and that David was backing him up, that Mr. Russell was party to the scheme and that it was horribly dangerous; but I didn't realize how dangerous until that night after the opera. . . ." She broke off, biting her lip. She was still holding Ramses's hand. He raised the other hand and brushed her cheek lightly with his fingertips. That was all; but it was enough to assure me that they had come to terms with that misunderstanding and others.

"I had to pretend I didn't know how badly he was hurt," she went on unsteadily. "I did, though. I always do. You arranged it very cleverly, all of you, but when the Professor came up with that ingenuous lie about sending Ramses to Zawaiet, I understood what you were doing, and of course I recognized David that evening, even with Aunt Amelia doing her damnedest to distract me by wriggling and squirming. I tried to keep out of the way to make it easier for you."

"My dear girl," I said, much moved as I recalled several small incidents that had meant nothing to me at the time. "Your deliberate and, if I may say so, uncharacteristic obtuseness did make it easier for us, but it must have been horribly difficult for you."

"Yes," Nefret said simply. She gave her lover — for so I must call him — a tender look, and he smiled at her. Even the distortion of his classic features could not spoil the sweetness of that smile. "I didn't understand fully why it was so important that no one else should know," Nefret continued. "But what else could I do but play along, since that was what you wanted?"

"I am filled with admiration for your forbearance and fortitude," I exclaimed.

"It was high time, don't you think? I had to prove to you, and to myself, that I had learned my lesson. Underneath I was wild with worry. I encouraged Percy, since that was the only thing I could think of to do, but it wasn't until after our encounter with Farouk that it dawned on me that Percy might be the traitor Farouk had proposed to betray. From whom else could Farouk have learned about the house in Maadi? I had no proof, though."

"So you set out to get it," I said. "Good gracious, my dear, it was very courageous of you, if somewhat foolhardly."

"Not as foolhardy as you might think," Nefret insisted. "I knew he was completely unscrupulous and vicious, but so long as he believed I was attracted to him, I was in no danger. It didn't take much to make him believe it! My money was the chief attraction, of course, and the only way he could get at that was through marriage, so I didn't think he would —"

"Think," Ramses repeated. His voice was glacial. Nefret looked from him to Emerson, and got no help there; his chin was jutting out and his face was turning red. "You understand, Aunt Amelia," she cried. "You would have done the same."

Emerson could contain himself no longer. "Would? She did do the same! Straight into the lion's den, armed with a parasol and that damnable self-assurance of hers — I suppose *you* thought *he* wouldn't take advantage, Peabody?"

"It wasn't the same at all," I exclaimed.

"No," said Ramses, in an oddly muffled voice. "He didn't want to marry you."

"Are you laughing at your mother, Rams⌒s?" I demanded.

"I'm trying not to. It hurts when I laugh."

He did, though. I gave Emerson an approving nod. His little outburst had cleared the air wonderfully.

"So," I said, after Ramses had stopped laughing, and Nefret had tenderly wiped the blood from his cut lip. "How did you find out about the old palace?"

She sat back on her heels. "From Sylvia Gorst. That, Aunt Amelia, dear, was another of my penances — making it up with Sylvia! You'd have been proud of me if you had seen how I apologized and fawned on her. She's the worst gossip in Cairo, and I felt certain that if she knew anything to Percy's discredit, I could get it out of her.

"He'd never taken her to his little love nest. He only took married women. He assumed they wouldn't talk about it for fear of blemishing their reputations, but of course they did — in strictest confidence to their closest friends. Sylvia pretended to be shocked, but it was such a juicy bit of scandal she couldn't keep it to herself.

"So I confronted Percy with the information. First he denied the whole thing. I'd expected that and was prepared for it; eventually I convinced him that I understood about men having special needs and . . . Ramses, stop gritting your teeth, your lip is bleeding again!"

"Perhaps you had better — er — edit your narrative, Nefret," I suggested. "I understand how you went about persuading him to take you there. That was the afternoon you came home late for dinner? I could see you had had an — er — unpleasant experience."

"I turned bright-red like some silly schoolgirl," Nefret muttered. "I could feel my face burning. It had its unpleasant moments, but I didn't let him —"

"It's all right,' Ramses said softly. "I'm sorry."

Unselfconsciously she bent her bright head and kissed the hand she clasped. "I never was in real danger. I know how to defend myself, and I had my knife. It was a wasted afternoon, though. He never left me alone for a moment. I didn't even see the rest of the house, only the bedroom."

"Nefret," I said quickly, "it is not necessary to say more. Your sacrifice — for it was nothing less, my dear, whatever happened or did not happen — was not in vain. I doubt we could have got directions from poor David, he was in no condition to converse at length. Yes; as Ramses wisely remarked, we work well as a family. Perhaps we have all learned a valuable lesson from this experience."

Emerson's expression indicated that he

doubted such was the case. Before he could mar the felicity of the occasion by expressing that doubt, I went on, "Ramses should rest now. Good night, my dear boy; in case I neglected to mention it earlier, I love you and I am very proud of you." Leaning over him, I found an unmarked spot on his face and kissed him.

"Quite," said Emerson emphatically.

"Thank you," said Ramses, wide-eyed and red-faced.

Nefret rose in a single graceful movement. She came to me and put her hand on my shoulder and kissed me on the cheek. Turning to Emerson, she stood on tiptoe and kissed him too, as she had done when she was a girl. "Good night, Mother," she said softly. "Good night, Father."

My dear Emerson was so overcome I had to lead him from the room. The door closed behind us, and I heard the key turn in the lock.

Emerson must have heard it too, but he was in such a state of emotion we had almost reached our room before he reacted.

"Here!" he exclaimed, coming to a dead stop. "What did she . . . What are they . . ."

"You heard her. I would think you would be pleased."

"Pleased? I have waited half my life to hear her call me Father. I suppose she felt she could not until she had earned the right by . . .

Good Gad, Peabody — she locked the door! He isn't fit —"

"Really, my dear, I don't think you are in a position to determine that." I tugged at him and he let me draw him into our room and push him into a chair. After considering the matter for a moment, I went back to the door and locked it.

"They are going to be married, aren't they?" Emerson inquired anxiously. "When we get back to England?"

"Oh, Emerson, don't be absurd. They will be married as soon as I can make the arrangements. I don't suppose she will want a conventional wedding dress." I began unfastening my gown. "One of those lovely robes of hers, perhaps," I continued thoughtfully. "Fatima will insist on making the cake. Flowers from our garden — if the camel left any — a small reception here afterwards, for our closest friends. We will hold the ceremony in David's room if he is not able to be out of bed. They will both want him to be present. Neither of them cares much about the formalities."

It was clear from Emerson's expression that he cared more than I would have supposed. He started up from his chair. "They aren't married yet," he exclaimed. "Good heavens, Amelia, how can you allow your daughter —"

"Oh, Emerson!" I put my arms round him

and hid my face against his breast. "They love one another so much and they have been so unhappy."

"Hmph," said Emerson. "Well, but if it is only a matter of a few days —"

"Do you remember a night on the dear old *Philae* — the night you asked me to be your wife?"

"Of course I remember. Although," Emerson said musingly, "there is still some doubt in my mind as to who asked whom."

"Am I never to hear the end of that?"

"Probably not," said Emerson, holding me close.

"Do you remember what happened later that night?"

"How could I ever forget? You made me the happiest of men that night, my love. I would not have had the courage to come to you."

"So I came to you. Did you think less of me for that?"

"Are you blushing, Peabody?" He put his hand under my chin and raised my head. "No, of course you aren't. I loved you with all my heart that night, and I have loved you more every day we have been together, and I will go on loving you . . . Er, hmph. Did you lock the door?"

"Yes."

"Good," said Emerson.

Nefret pushed Seshat out onto the balcony. For a breathtaking moment she stood silvered by the moonlight before she closed the shutters and came back to him. "First thing tomorrow morning I am going to speak to Reis Hassan about having the *Amelia* ready for us when we return in April," she announced.

"Is it Mother or Seshat you want to avoid?"

"Both of them. All of them!" She laughed softly and turned her face into his shoulder. "I'm afraid the poor dears were scandalized when I shut them out; people of their generation would never violate the conventions in this way."

His voice muffled by her hair, Ramses murmured ambiguously. He had learned never to make a dogmatic pronouncement about either of his parents.

"I don't care," Nefret whispered. "I don't care about anything except being with you, always, forever. We've lost so much time. If I had only —"

"Nefret, darling." He took her face between his hands. It was too dark to see her features, but he felt the wetness on her cheeks. "Never say that again. Never think it. Perhaps we had to go through the bad times in order to earn —"

"Good Gad, you sound just like Aunt

Amelia!" She kissed him fiercely on the lips. He tasted blood, and so must she have done, for she lifted her head. "I'm sorry! I hurt you."

"Yes, and you're dripping tears all over my face. Stop it at once. Mother would also say that the secret of happiness is to enjoy the present, without regretting the past or worrying about the future."

"I know she would, I've heard her say it at least a dozen times. Does this seem an appropriate time to talk about your mother?"

"You were the one who —"

"I know, and I wish I hadn't. I love her with all my heart, but I won't let her or anyone else come between us now."

"My dearest girl, she'll hustle us into a church as soon as she can make the arrangements — not more than two days, if I know Mother."

"Oh, well, in that case perhaps you would prefer that I leave, and not come back until after —"

"Just try it. I've learned my lesson, too."

"Someday I will, so you can crush me in your arms and overpower me," Nefret said dreamily. "I think I'd like that."

"So would I. Give me a few more days."

She let out a little cry of distress, and pulled away. "I keep forgetting. Your poor face, and your poor back, and your poor hands and —"

"I keep forgetting too. Come here." She

moved lightly into his embrace, and he smoothed the silky hair away from her face and kissed her temples and brows and closed eyes. "Uh — you did lock the door, didn't you?"

"Yes, my love."

"Good," said Ramses.

From Letter Collection B

Dearest Lia,

We will be with you shortly after you receive this. We sail from Alexandria in two days' time. I have so much to tell you I'm fairly bursting with it, but I can't do the subject justice in a letter. So why am I writing? It's because I want you to be the first to whom I sign myself

With fondest love,
Nefret Emerson